T0382017

A Cornish Legacy

Fern Britton is the highly acclaimed author of ten *Sunday Times* bestselling novels. Her books are cherished for their warmth, wit and wisdom, and have won Fern legions of loyal readers. Fern has been a judge for the Costa Book of the Year Award and is a supporter of the Reading Agency, promoting literacy and reading.

A hugely popular household name through iconic shows such as *This Morning* and *Fern Britton Meets* . . . Fern is also a much sought-after presenter and radio host. She has also turned her hand to theatre and toured with Gary Barlow and Tim Firth's *Calendar Girls*.

Fern has twin sons and two daughters and lives in Cornwall in a house full of good food, wine, family, friends and gardening books.

/officialfernbritton
/fernbritton
@Fern_Britton
www.fern-britton.com

By the same author:

Autobiographies
Fern: My Story
The Older I Get

Fiction
New Beginnings
Hidden Treasures
The Holiday Home
A Seaside Affair
A Good Catch
The Postcard
Coming Home
The Newcomer
Daughters of Cornwall
The Good Servant

Short stories
The Stolen Weekend
A Cornish Carol
The Beach Cabin

Published in one collection as
A Cornish Gift

Fern Britton

A Cornish Legacy

HarperCollins*Publishers*

HarperCollins*Publishers* Ltd
1 London Bridge Street
London SE1 9GF

www.harpercollins.co.uk

HarperCollins*Publishers*
Macken House, 39/40 Mayor Street Upper
Dublin 1, D01 C9W8, Ireland

First published by HarperCollins*Publishers* 2025
1

A catalogue record for this book is available from the British Library

ISBN: 978-0-00-846832-3 (HB)

Set in Birka by HarperCollins*Publishers* India

Printed and bound in the UK using 100% Renewable Electricity at CPI Group (UK) Ltd

This book contains FSC™ certified paper and other controlled sources to ensure responsible forest management.

For more information visit: www.harpercollins.co.uk/green

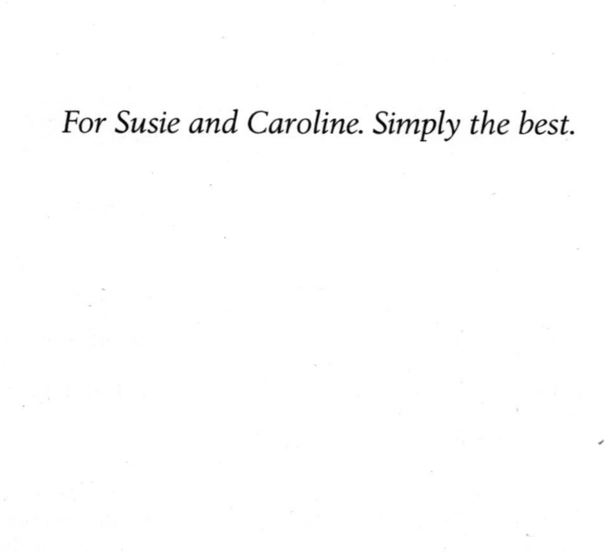

For Susie and Caroline. Simply the best.

Ah. She has returned.

She is on the road, nearing the gate, nearing my crumbling walls. It brings warmth to my old heart and the strength to my foundations once more.

It is a while since I have played host. My great hall has stood for more than one thousand years. Counted and recognized in the Domesday Book, if you do not believe me.

Good Queen Bess, our Virgin Queen and Gloriana, once beheld me with her own eyes and was well pleased.

She came attended by a favourite, Sir Walter Raleigh, on a Royal Progress through Devonshire. The intention was to stay at Buckland Abbey near Tavistock, home of that villainous old privateer Sir Francis Drake. Sir Francis had bought it with the spoils of his circumnavigation of the globe and his looting of enemy Spanish ships.

The poor Queen was forced to endure an entire night in his draughty old barracks. The climate of Dartmoor is ever too cold and damp for any person of note, particularly the rarefied blood of Royalty.

The following morning, Sir Walter easily persuaded her to travel to Cornwall and stay with me.

'Let us to Cornwall,' he preened, 'where the sea air is warm and clean, to a house that surpasses all else on that coast.'

Her Majesty, chilled to the marrow, accepted with alacrity and left poor Drake spitting.

I did not disappoint dear Good Queen Bess. She admired my proportions, my exquisitely carved staircase, my comfortable bedchambers. She favoured my gardens and the vibrancy of the Atlantic Ocean sparkling beyond.

Descending the steps to the gardens, she trod the grass thick with dew, and upon my life, I swear this be the truth, it was here that fawning Raleigh did lay his cloak to save the Royal slipper from any damp.

Ah, but I must return my mind from then to now and to this return of Cordelia.

Mrs Joy did warn me. She heard it might be so.

And here she is.

Welcome, I whisper, welcome.

Part One

CHAPTER ONE

North Cornwall, April, present day

Delia squinted through the windscreen, the sun ahead dazzling her. 'You'll see the turning on the right in a minute,' she said. 'Keep an eye out. I might miss it.'

Sammi tipped the last of the crisps into his mouth and sat up a little straighter. 'My eyes are peeled.' He pulled the sunglasses down from his head. 'Will there be some kind of landmark?'

'There's a big metal sign swinging on a post above the gates. Remember? You said it looked like a gibbet.'

Sammi chuckled. 'The gibbet! Yes, of course! Such a welcome.' He sat up straighter, alert. 'There!'

Delia saw the emerging gap amongst the tangled hedge of rhododendrons, with the rusted sign hanging from the post.

'Is that it?' asked Sammi. 'Can't read the name.'

Delia slowed, changing down through the gears. She wasn't smiling. 'Yep. This is it. Wilder Hoo.' The sight of the tatty sign that she had never wanted or expected to see again forced her stomach into a tight knot. Turning, she slowed the car and braked to a halt. 'I really don't want to be here.'

Sammi reached over for her knee and tapped it briskly. 'You're not on your own. I'm here, and those horrible people are gone. Come on.'

Delia put a hand to her chest and took a deep breath to control the old anxiety welling within. 'It's quite late. Let's go and find somewhere to stay tonight and come back tomorrow.'

'It's only half past four!'

'But it'll be getting dark soon.'

'Darling, it's April, not December.' Sammi's voice became soft and sympathetic. 'I know this is hard. But you *can* do it, and you *will* do it.'

'I don't *want* to do it.'

'The past is past. Dead and buried.'

Sighing heavily, Delia put the car in gear and slowly drove the winding tarmacked drive. 'Dead people can still haunt us.'

Stiff clumps of grass and dandelions had forced themselves between the cracked pitch, and in other places, huge potholes housed red, muddied puddles.

'It'll cost thousands just to repair the drive,' she said. 'Look at it.'

She knew that Sammi saw through different eyes. For him, this was an adventure. When Delia had first told him that the house had been gifted to her, he had been ready to celebrate, despite her horror of the whole thing. He seemed to feel only the thrill of an escapade.

Looking out of his side window at the ancient, rolling parkland with great oaks dotted across the scene he said, 'Delia, this is utterly captivating. Please tell me there's a lake. I'm expecting Colin Firth to stride forth in his wet breeches and shirt.'

Delia was scornful. 'If only. No lake, I'm afraid. Just a beach and all these acres of parkland. Do you know, it takes four men with a tractor each an entire week to cut all that grass? When they get to the end, they have to start again. It's a bloody money pit.' Her eyes flicked to the avenue of ivy-clad beech trees ahead, the bare branches forming a tunnel over sodden leaves. 'That ivy needs cutting back too. Argh. Who can afford all this, I ask you!'

Sammi was not listening. 'How long is this drive again?'

'It's 1.2 miles.'

'Very specific.'

Delia sighed. 'My father-in-law preferred to tell everyone it was two kilometres because that sounded longer.'

'And all this land belongs to the house?'

'Yup.'

Sammi was grinning. 'I'd love to jump on a tractor and spend a whole summer mowing all this.'

'You really wouldn't. Back in the day, there were sheep and deer to crop it.'

'Sheep and deer! Delia.' Sammi laughed. 'And all this is actually yours!'

She shrugged. She was weary and wretched. 'Not for long, I hope.'

They rattled over a cattle grid and onto a sparsely gravelled drive.

'OK. Here we go.' Delia swallowed hard. 'Round this bend, you'll see the house.' She took a nervous breath and added, 'I couldn't do this without you.'

Sammi tutted, 'I wouldn't let you come on your own, would I?'

Delia steered the last curve – and there, suddenly, was Wilder Hoo.

Sammi pressed the palms of his hands on either side of his face. 'OMG!' he managed. 'I mean *wow*.'

She shivered. 'Don't.'

'But look at it!' His eyes shone. 'A. Gorgeous. Old. House. In. Cornwall! And it has a 1.2-mile drive, a VERY big garden and a beach! And—' He made the noise of a three-year-old boy having his first ride on a toddlers' roundabout. 'IT'S YOURS!'

Delia shook her head, refusing to look at the house before her. 'I hate it. I hate the grass. I hate the house. I hate it all.'

'Whaaat.' Sammi was shaking his head. 'You told me it was an unhappy *ruin*, but look! And how can you hate a house with a private beach!'

'I especially hate the beach.'

Sammi pulled at the door handle to get out, while reaching for the old heavy key in the cup holder between them. 'Come on. We're going to take a look.'

Delia didn't move. 'I don't think I can.'

'You're not scared, are you?'

'*Yes*. Oh, this was such a bad idea. Let's find a bed for the night and a couple of estate agents tomorrow. I want to get this problem on the market double quick.'

'No.' Sammi stopped her. 'We're here now.' He smiled to reassure her, but she looked away, fiddling with her watch strap.

'OK,' he said gently. 'We won't go in tonight. But we have to come back tomorrow. We've come all this way. I really want to see if it's as awful as you say it is.'

'It *is*.' Delia turned the ignition key. 'I don't know about you, but I need a drink.'

The nearest village was only a few minutes away, but throughout the short journey, Sammi managed to get on Delia's nerves constantly. She was already on edge – uneasy, restless, fearful. This not helped by Sammi's constant, aggravating commentary on each passing cottage, hedgerow or glimpse of the sun on the shining ocean.

As they neared their destination, Delia prayed that Sammi would not irritate her even more by reading out the village sign.

'*Welcome to Penvare*.' He cheered. 'Well, that's very nice of them, isn't it?'

'Do you have to keep chuntering on? I know where we are. I don't need you to report on *everything* you see.'

Sammi crossed his legs and folded his arms, looking ostentatiously out of his window. 'Pardon me for being interested . . .' A pause, then, 'Oh, look. This looks nice! *The Vare Castle Hotel*.' He read the blackboard on the passing kerb. 'Serving dinner, and they have vacancies. Pull over.'

Delia carried on past.

The Vare Castle Hotel was the last place she wanted to revisit. It had been the scene of countless Sunday lunches, birthdays, anniversaries and Christmases with Johnny and his parents. The last thing she wanted was to be reminded of those times or be recognized by staff who might ask unwanted and difficult questions.

'There's a better pub at the end of the high street,' she mumbled.

'But that looked really nice,' Sammi wailed, watching as the hotel slid behind them.

'It doesn't have rooms.' Delia was curt.

'Yes, it does. It said so. There was a sign.'

'I don't want to go in there, OK?'

Delia drove on passing all the interesting looking shops and cafes until they petered out, giving way to a dingy ribbon of old houses with a bleak looking pub at the end.

'This'll be fine,' she told him, pulling up under a dimly glowing lamp-post.

'*The Tinners Arms*,' Sammi read. 'Well, I can see why you would rather be here than down the road. It reeks of comfort and warmth.'

Two men were playing at the billiards table. Three more were at the bar, and a small group was sitting at a table, watching a football match on television.

As Delia and Sammi stepped through the door, all eyes swivelled towards them and silence fell.

Delia ignored them and strode towards the bar.

The barmaid lifted her chin in the international mime of, *Can I help you?*

'A large gin and tonic and a pint of bitter, please.'

'Will you be wanting any food?' The barmaid nodded towards a slightly greasy laminated menu.

'How delightful.' Sammi grinned. 'My friend and I have just driven down all the way from London for the weekend. Lovely here, isn't it?'

'Better than London,' a man said, licking a cigarette paper.

'Oh, so you know it?' Sammi replied charmingly. 'What was it you didn't like?'

'He ain't been to London.' Another man sniggered. 'He ain't been out of the county.'

'Well, anytime you *do* want to come, I'll show you all the best sights,' Sammi replied. 'And now, my friend and I will dine sumptuously from this extensive menu.' He turned to the barmaid. 'What can you recommend?'

'Cod bites and chips. Sausage and chips – you can add a fried egg if you want, or burger and chips, with or without cheese.'

'Fabulous,' trilled Sammi, stifling a gasp of surprise as Delia kicked his leg.

Once they had ordered, they took their drinks to the table by the unlit fire. Delia sat down heavily. A headache was working its way to the front of her skull.

She wondered why she had made this trip at all. She didn't need to be in Cornwall to sell the house, but it was hard to say no to Sammi. He was her best and oldest friend, and as such, he could really irritate the hell out of her.

She looked across at him. 'Stop sulking,' she said.

'I'm not sulking. Why would I be sulking?'

'Because you'd rather be at The Vare Castle than here.'

'I'd rather be *anywhere* than here.'

'Careful,' said the barmaid, placing two plates down in front of them. 'The chips are just out of the microwave.'

Sammi was about to deliver one of his stingers, but Delia stopped him with a particularly icy glare.

'Any sauces?' the barmaid asked.

'What would you recommend?' Sammi gave her his most winning smile. 'I never know what quite goes best with microwave chips. Such a treat.'

'Most people like red or brown sauce. Some like both.'

'I'll have a bottle of each then.'

Delia kicked him under the table, but he carried on, 'Or maybe a selection of those overly small sachets. Impossible to open but still capable of squirting themselves over everything but the food. I love putting my teeth to the plastic, don't you?'

'I'm sorry about my friend,' Delia said crisply.

'That's all right,' the barmaid replied. 'I'm used to serving tosspots.' She walked away to a ripple of appreciation from her regulars.

Delia laughed properly for the first time that day. 'You deserved that.'

Sammi smiled, then put the chip into his mouth – and immediately spat it out. 'Shit. My tongue is on fire.'

'Don't be so dramatic.' Delia passed him her paper napkin. 'Be nice. We might have to stay here tonight.'

He picked up his beer and clinked it against her gin and tonic. 'Well, a couple more of these, and it'll feel like the Ritz.'

As it happened, there were a pair of vacant rooms, which Delia happily accepted, ignoring Sammi's baleful eyes. Outside their rooms, he hugged her.

'In case I don't survive the night, I want you to know I will not hold my demise against you.'

'Thank you for coming all this way with me.' Delia squashed her face into his neck. 'I couldn't have done it on my own.'

'You're kidding, right? The pleasure is entirely mine. I mean, look at this place! I'm so hoping the candlewick bedspread has an essence of damp. A hint of fungi always sends me off to dream land.' Sammi smiled. 'Sweet dreams.'

The next morning, Delia gasped as she surfaced from the usual nightmare, her heart thumping.

She had to remember that it was over. She was free. For her, the storm had passed. It had wreaked its damage, blown through, leaving her to bear the scars.

She checked her phone. 06.45.

She lay still for a while, thinking about Wilder Hoo and Johnny. Why had he done it? Why give her the house, knowing how much she hated it and what a millstone it was.

She reached for her phone again and began a to-do list:

1. Find a decent estate agent
2. Never come back here again.

CHAPTER TWO

Later that morning, having arranged meetings with three estate agents to come and put a value on the old house, Delia and Sammi were back at Wilder Hoo. Standing outside, they felt the warmth of the sun bouncing off the old brick work. The ticking of the cooling engine was the only thing to disturb the quiet stillness.

Delia offered the old iron key to Sammi. 'You can open up.'

'It's your house.'

'Not for much longer. Go on.'

The key was heavy and almost as long as the palm of his hand. 'Right. Are you ready?'

She shook her head.

'That's the spirit, Delia,' Sammi said.

'Shut up.'

Together, they walked up the portico steps to the double-fronted doors. Wider than they were tall and made of sturdy, silvered oak, they were studded with centuries-old iron nails. The keyhole was big enough for a rat to squeeze through.

Sammi quelled a sudden prickling of his spine and said cheerily, 'Come on, Darling D. We can do this. It's just a house.'

He slid the ancient key into the lock, but it stoutly refused to turn. He had to put his back into it, grunting with extra strength, before it gave way. 'Put WD40 on the shopping list.' He smiled. It was not returned.

'Let's get this over with.' Delia put her hands to the oak and pushed through the memories of the times she had done this in the past. At first, it would not yield, but at last, it swung forward, releasing a gust of air and a scent of damp, mice, and the last vestiges of her ex-mother-in-law's Issey Miyake perfume.

Delia shivered and Sammi went ahead of her, crossing the threshold and unbolting the other half of the door. Sunlight instantly flooded the great hall.

'Bloody hell, Delia. It's *huge*.' He walked to the centre of the room and took it all in. 'Look at all the wood panelling and the carving. And the staircase! Come on in.'

Delia's legs suddenly began to wobble and her head begin to spin. Worried she was about to faint she stayed outside and sat down on the steps.

'Hey.' Sammi was next to her. 'It's OK. I've got you. Deep breaths.'

He sat with her, stroking her back gently as the colour came back to her cheeks. .

'There. How does that feel?'

'Better.'

'Good.'

She smiled thinly. 'Why did I come back?'

'Because I told you to. Because we can't sort out something like this over email. No matter what you think.'

*

The great hall loomed over and around Delia.

With the warm sunlight and open front doors, the fusty air was sweetened and shifted by a gentle breeze. She felt better. 'Those bloody spooky portraits going up the stairs have gone at least.'

'Hmm?' Sammi wasn't listening. He was busy running his hand over the carved oak panelling of the enormous fire surround. He ducked his head inside the hearth and looked up. 'This is huge. I can see the sky.'

'Careful. There can be jackdaws' nests,' Delia warned. 'They'll shit in your eye.'

Sammi ducked smartly out. 'Thank you for that.'

Delia felt the beginnings of confidence. Wilder Hoo really was a beautiful house. Her memories were not happy ones but that was all in the past. She must remember that. Johnny and his parents would never hurt her again.

Then *bang!*

Like a clap of thunder, the front doors slammed themselves shut.

Delia screamed, 'Sammi!' and flung her arms around him, shaking.

'It was the wind.' Sammi prised himself from her and went to reopen the doors.

'What wind? There is no wind.' Her breath caught in her throat. 'Let's go – I can't stay here.'

'No.' He was firm. 'Delia, don't be silly.'

She shook her head. 'I don't like being here. Please, let's go.'

'No.' Sammi checked his phone. 'The first estate agent will be here in under an hour. I need to know where everything is, and you're the only person who can show me.'

Sammi took her elbow and pulled her round to face him. He spoke slowly and calmly. 'You want to sell the house, don't you?'

'Yes.'

'So, you have to show me around. How long will it take? Half an hour?'

'Ten minutes.'

'Don't be silly. Come on. Half an hour, and then you can leave it all up to me and the estate agents.'

Delia looked down. Her new white trainers were already smudged grey with Wilder Hoo dust.

He hugged her tight, and for a few moments, neither of them moved. Then Sammi sprang into action.

'Let's start here.' He turned to the first door on his left, opened it then gasped.

The walls were filled head to toe with empty oak bookshelves, carved with intricate patterns of figures, suggesting the magic of the written word.

Delia came to stand behind him. 'The library.'

'Well yes, obviously.' Sammi said, 'How many books would you need to fill these shelves?'

Delia shrugged. 'A few.'

He turned to her, frowning. 'You are spoilt and wearied by these wonders, milady? Can't you feel the . . . I don't know, the warmth of this place? Can you really not appreciate the beauty of this room? See how the view to the garden is framed exquisitely by the tall window? Being here, it feels like . . . like the room is trying to talk to us.'

Delia sighed. 'Oh wait. Yes I can hear it. It's saying . . . Sell me. Come on – I need to show you the rest, and then I can get outside.'

'Give me another minute.' He walked to the huge sash window. 'These are incredible. Have you read Daphne du Maurier's *Rebecca*?'

Delia was still by the door, desperate to get out of the house. 'Mum's favourite. She read it to me one Christmas.'

'I'm sure there was a scene where some villain climbed in and out of a window like this, not wanting to be seen.'

'I don't remember.'

'Well, we'll have to get this fixed. Imagine climbing straight out onto the terrace for drinks and then down the steps to the garden.'

Delia felt another wave of dizziness. She turned quickly and left the room.

Back in the great hall, Sammi followed her as she crossed the room and headed for another door to the right and opened it. 'Dining room. More big sash windows for you to drool over.'

Sammi literally licked his lips. 'Double aspect dining – sunrise at one window, sunset at the other.'

Delia rubbed her forehead. 'Please stop. We don't have time for you to be thrilled with everything.'

'This is a huge room. How big was the dining table?'

'Stupidly big. They used to push two tables together. It was ridiculous. If you wanted the salt passed, it was quicker to text the person at the other end.'

'Sounds cosy.'

'It wasn't.'

'Not even with a fire in this enormous grate?' Sammi asked.

Delia scoffed. 'That fireplace was blocked up years ago. They had a three-bar electric fire – "like the Queen," my mother-in-law would say. It's a house that doesn't hold heat.'

Sammi was entranced. 'It's gorgeous.'

'See the damp?'

'That can be fixed.'

'Let's hope the new owner is a squillionaire.'

Delia hastened Sammi upstairs, through the dusty and neglected bedrooms and the grimly cobwebbed bathrooms. Some rooms were still half-furnished – a chest of drawers here, a cheval mirror there.

'Those are the stairs to the attics.' She pointed to one end of a long corridor. 'And no, we are not going to see them.'

Back downstairs, and through the great hall, they entered the west wing.

She put her shoulder to the door and pushed hard. 'This has always stuck. The damp again but . . .' She pushed harder, and the door swung open. 'Ta dah.'

The prettiest room was revealed, painted in dove grey with white cornicing and an Art Deco fireplace. A stained carpet of Wedgwood blue lay in the middle, surrounded by dusty oak floorboards.

'The *saloon*, Vivienne always called it. A reception room for evening entertainments. Blah blah.'

'It's so lovely.' Sammi stepped onto the carpet, glancing around. 'The fireplace alone is worth thousands if it's real.'

'Boring.'

'And this room was used for what?'

'Johnny and his father loved games. Monopoly, Charades, Uno . . . all played incredibly aggressively. Neither one of them wanted to lose. Like gladiators, playing to the death.' She paused, stuffing her hands in her jeans pockets. 'Now, that is ironic . . . considering this is where Harvey had his stroke.'

Sammi was at the windows, gazing out at the view beyond. 'This could be a very special place, Dee. It needs saving.'

She walked across to join him and laid her head on his shoulder. 'I can see that. But even if I wanted to save it, how could I afford the work it needs?'

'I think the house wants you to. I think it wants to help you do it.'

Delia lifted her head. 'Don't start all that nonsense.'

'Why not? My ammi would say, *Inshallah*. You know, if God wills.'

Delia frowned and held her hands up, palms facing Sammi. 'Not my scene. Where was God when my mum had her accident? Or throughout the mess of the past few years? I'm not a believer.' She walked to the door. 'I need to get out of here.'

Sammi lingered, giving Delia the space he knew she needed. There really was something about this place, something calling out to him. Was he imagining it? He felt as though the house was trying to communicate with him somehow.

He bowed his head, closed his eyes, and breathed, listening, trying to tune in, asking for whatever was there to trust him. It was something he'd been able to do since he was a child. He never talked about it, but now, yes . . . he was getting an image of this room in a very different time.

A woman wearing what looked like a brown woollen dress with a loose, white cap pulled around her face. She was kneeling at the grate – no longer Art Deco, but larger, deeper, wider, and much older. She was building an intricate cage of wood shavings, kindling, and logs that would surely burn well when lit. The casement windows were no longer clear glass; they were mullioned and open. He could see the autumn russet of trees beyond the terrace.

A man's voice came from outside: gentle, respectful. The servant swiftly stood, shaking fragments of twig from her apron and skirts, then left the room.

A woman's voice was calling his name.

'Sammi! Sammi?' Delia stomped back into the room. 'Come on. We haven't got much time before the first estate agent comes.'

'Sorry.' He smiled at her. 'The stories these old walls could tell, eh?'

As they stepped back into the great hall, a voice said, 'Hello.'

Delia jumped. 'What the . . . '

A woman with a welcoming face was standing by the fireplace. 'Sorry. Did I frighten you? I didn't mean to. I saw the door was open, and I thought I'd locked it last night.' She took a few steps towards Delia, who stiffened in fear.

Sammi stepped ahead of her and introduced himself. 'How do you do? I'm Sammi Hashmi, and this' – he gestured towards Delia – 'is the new owner of Wilder Hoo.'

'Oh, of course. I'm so sorry. I'm Mrs Joy. I'm the housekeeper. Well, I was, but I still like to come in and make sure it's all watertight. I've known the old place for quite a long time now. I still feel it's my duty to keep an eye on it. Silly really, but old habits.'

Sammi shook her hand – it was cool, the skin papery – and she next offered it to Delia.

'I had a feeling you'd come down soon, Mrs Carlisle-Hart.'

Delia took the proffered hand warily. 'No,' she said a little too forcefully. 'That is, I was Mrs Carlisle-Hart, but I have reverted to my maiden name. I'm Delia Jago.'

'Of course. Forgive me, Miss Jago.'

'It's odd we never met before, Mrs Joy. Of course I heard a lot about you.'

Mrs Joy smiled. 'And I you.' She turned to Sammi to explain. 'I always helped Mr and Mrs Carlisle-Hart whenever they prepared to welcome visitors, especially Miss Jago and Mr Johnny. So much to do, and it had to be done just right.'

Delia's head began to swim again. 'Would you excuse me? I need to get some fresh air.'

She headed towards the door, and Sammi stepped after her, concerned, but the housekeeper continued, 'When I heard that Mr Johnny had left Wilder Hoo to you, Miss Jago, I was very surprised but also very pleased.'

Delia was at the open door. She placed her hand on the ancient wood to steady herself and, without turning round, she asked, 'Why?'

'Well you have come back. To see what can be done. It looks worse than it is. A little bit of spit and elbow grease will bring the old place back. All it needs is a young couple ready and willing to breathe fresh life into it. To bring up a family. To make new, happier memories.'

Delia turned and stared at her. 'Sammi and I are not a couple. We're just old friends. And I have three estate agents coming over this afternoon to assess Wilder Hoo's worth.'

'Oh, that's good.' Mrs Joy nodded. 'Very sensible. Get an idea of what needs doing from the experts before you start the repairs.'

'You misunderstand me.' Delia brutally spelt out her intention. 'I want no part of this house or its estate. I am getting rid of it.'

Mrs Joy's pleasant expression fell, and Sammi felt a pang of pity for her. 'Oh.' She fumbled with the cuff of her cardigan and produced a lace edged cotton handkerchief. 'I misunderstood. My apologies.' She wiped her nose. 'Well, if there is anything you need to know about the place . . .' Her fingers fidgeted with the handkerchief. 'Not much I don't know about all its idiosyncrasies.' She smiled again. 'I remember when our old Queen visited, ever such a long time ago. She loved Wilder Hoo.'

Sammi loved anything to do with Royal history and brightened up. 'The Queen came here?'

Delia laughed. 'Of course she didn't. If she had, my in-laws would have told everyone.'

'It was long before they lived here.' Mrs Joy was recalling. 'A very long time ago . . . Let me think.'

Sammi tried to help her. 'Sixties? Seventies? Maybe the Eighties?'

Mrs Joy's brow furrowed as she thought. 'I think it must have been . . . around the Seventies: 1576 or 77, I'd say.'

Sammi smiled. 'You mean 1976 or 77?'

'What did I say?' Mrs Joy asked.

'1577.'

'Did I? Oh dear, when you get old, you get muddled.' The housekeeper wiped her nose again.

Sammi was immediately animated. 'But 1977 would be the time of the Silver Jubilee! My mother slept overnight in the Mall to see the Royal Family wave from the balcony. We had an old biscuit tin with the Queen's face on . . . I wonder what happened to that. It makes sense that the Queen might have visited here. Can you remember if she stayed the night?'

Mrs Joy smiled at the memory. 'Oh yes. Just the one night. So gracious. A real honour for all of us.'

Delia checked her watch impatiently. 'I'm sorry, Mrs Joy, but the first of the estate agents will be here any minute.'

'So soon?' Mrs Joy sighed. 'Oh dear. I'd better be off – don't want to get in the way. Just shout if you need me.'

Delia reached into the back pocket of her jeans and took her phone out. 'Could you give me your phone number?'

Sammi was lost in a daydream. He was visualizing the Duke of Edinburgh striding through the front doors with a broken shotgun over his arm, calling out for his wife, perhaps listening for the patter of Corgi paws.

'Where has she gone?' Delia's voice sounded far away. 'Sammi! Where did Mrs Joy go?'

Sammi looked about him and shrugged his shoulders. 'I don't know. Must've popped off to get something?'

Outside, the sound of a car crunching up the gravel drive caught their attention.

'Estate agent,' Delia said. 'Bang on time. I'm making myself scarce, and you charm the pants off him. Bye!'

CHAPTER THREE

Out in the fresh air Delia immediately felt better again. The warm air slumbered over the parkland, tempting her to walk once more over its emerald grass and rest in the cool of its shadows. She gazed out over swathes of daffodils blooming in the long rides, sharing the ground with the scented bluebells. The jackdaws were busy transporting twigs, readying their nests for the first clutch of eggs.

Beneath her feet, self-seeded poppies and heartsease were growing in between the cracks of the old, flagged path that led from the front of the house round to the rear terrace. Their ability to thrive in the thinnest of earth brought a smile to her face. *New beginnings were possible,* they seemed to say to her. *You can put the past behind you.*

Maybe Sammi was right. There was nothing to fear.

She closed her eyes and listened for the sea, which lay not a quarter of a mile away. If the wind was coming from the west, she would hear it.

She strained to catch the distant rumble. No. She needed to get closer, walk to the end of the path and out onto Wilder Hoo's fabled terrace.

Doubt sprang into her mind. The terrace was the site of many memories, both pleasant and unpleasant.

She steadied herself with a deep breath. 'Come on. That was then, and this is now.' It was just a terrace, after all. '*My* terrace,' she said, and for the first time since that awful night, she stepped quickly around the corner and onto the golden flagstones.

Immediately, she was struck with echoes from the past.

Her father-in-law had started the row

Was it really only almost a year ago that she was last here? It felt like a lifetime ago.

Delia shook herself back into the present.

'I am safe,' she whispered. 'And he is dead.'

The terrace was still beautiful. The wisteria that her mother-in-law was once so proud of was in bud, held to the cream stuccoed walls by rusting wires. The stucco itself was not in bad condition – a little flaked here, a little cracked there, but it still conjured the glamour of a Venetian palazzo under a bright-blue sky.

Out here, the tall casement windows that had seduced Sammi earlier stood brilliant in the sun.

Delia turned from them, refusing their allure, and walked to the stone balustrade. A pair of wide steps swept down either side, landing in the formal garden below.

She began the descent.

According to her former in-laws, this had once been a Tudor knot garden. Delia and Vivienne had spoken of restoring it, but Vivienne had dismissed her plans, and now Delia stood looking at the choked outline of the garden. Maybe whoever bought the old place would give it the love it deserved.

Two seagulls circled overhead, cackling heartily, their wings outstretched on the soft breeze.

The reality of finding herself responsible for this crumbling white elephant by the sea winded her.

She pushed away her memories of Johnny's mother and thought of her own. 'Oh, Mum. What am I going to do? Is selling up the easy way out? What would you do? '

She closed her eyes. A picture began to form in her mind. Her mum was in the kitchen at Jago Fields. She had her sleeves rolled up and a broom in her hands. Her cheeks were glowing from the effort she was putting into her sweeping. But she was smiling.

Delia sighed. 'I'm not as strong as you, Mum. I haven't got it in me to turn this disaster into triumph. I want to be rid of this place, and quickly.'

She left the Tudor knot garden behind her and headed for what had been laughingly known as her father-in-law's 'Good Lawn' – now overgrown and full of weeds.

'Your bloody lawn is nothing now, is it?' she muttered under her breath. 'It's as dead as you are. I remember the croquet matches – nobody allowed to beat you. So you cheated. You thought I didn't see you, but I did.'

A pheasant startled her as it rose noisily from the edge of the woods, less than a hundred yards from where she stood.

Harvey had enjoyed shooting in the woods, always insisting that Johnny joined in. Delia had hated to hear the guns blast and the balls of feathers crashing through the branches.

Entering the woods now, all was quiet and peaceful. Sunrays slanted through the canopy of beech and birch, chestnut and oak. So different from the last time – no sunshine then, just the moon and her breath, panting, terrified, running as far and as fast as she could to get away from Wilder Hoo.

The flashback shook her. Steadying herself on the trunk of a beech tree she took a moment to gather her breathing and slow her pulse. Her therapist had explained that post-traumatic shock could and would assail her at a moment's notice.

She had been given the tools to deal with it and a mantra which she now invoked. 'I am not mad. I am not bad. This, too, will pass.'

She repeated it until the panic drained away and she could connect once again with the earth she was standing on.

Could she confront the past and reset the present? Now? Today? Was she ready?

It would mean walking right through the woods to the cliff path and then down to the beach. If she didn't do it now, would she ever? If Wilder Hoo sold quickly, she might never get another chance. This was the moment.

She strode through the final yards of woodland and, after the cool of the trees, stepped out into the bright sunshine.

She was now on the cliffs. The ocean shining below.

She and Johnny had had the house all to themselves, that first time. His parents were away in Norfolk, he'd explained, for a shooting party. Delia and Johnny barely knew each other, and yet it was as if they had known each other all their lives. He opened his heart to her, and she gave herself to him utterly.

What a fool she had been.

Everything at Wilder Hoo, was a tangible reminder of how Johnny had swept her off her feet, the glittering shell of it all, the empty promises and casual lies. It was a place of ghosts.

She shivered. She had to get back to Sammi and away from this haunted place.

Delia ran through the woods, over the Good Lawn and the knot garden, and then she saw Sammi's face appear over the terrace balustrade above her.

'There you are. The last of the agents has gone. Mission accomplished.'

Relieved, Delia ran up the steps two at a time – but as she neared the top, her foot caught on a loose slab, and her ankle buckled beneath her. She fell awkwardly, gasping at the instant pain.

'Ow.' She instinctively clutched her ankle. 'Sammi! Sammi!'

He reappeared, all concern. 'I'm here. I'm here. What's happened?' He loped down the steps to her. 'Let me look at you. Have you broken anything?'

Delia felt faint at the stabbing pain in her ankle, panic rising in her chest. 'I don't think so. But it hurts.'

'Sorry, did I press too hard?'

'Yes.' Delia felt sick.

He sat back. 'Hmm, well, I'm no paramedic but it's swelling a little too nicely. Can you make it to the car if I help to take the weight?'

She tried to shift some of her weight onto it and winced. 'I . . . think so.'

'Come on then, old girl.'

When Sammi had strapped her safely into the passenger seat, he slid in behind the wheel. 'Right. Where's the nearest hospital? Is there a minor injuries clinic? You need an X-ray, I think.'

She groaned at the thought. 'I'll be fine.'

'I'm not letting you stagger about with an undiagnosed broken ankle. Not when you're in my care.'

His kindness made her want to cry. 'I just want to go back to London. I promise I'll get it checked there tomorrow.'

'Not possible, I'm afraid.'

'Of course it's possible. Just four hours and we'll be back in civilization.'

'I'm not being awkward, but I've laid on a little surprise for you – something to cheer you up after an emotional twenty-four hours.'

She stared at him, waiting for him to continue. 'And?'

'I've booked dinner and rooms for us tonight at The Vare Castle.'

'What? Why?'

'Because it's Saturday night and I don't have to be back in town until Monday. You don't need to be at work at all, and I wanted to treat you to something nice.'

'Sammi, that's lovely, but . . .'

'I know. Too many unhappy memories and someone might recognize you?'

'Exactly. And I haven't packed anything for dinner – the restaurant has a dress code—'

Sammi nodded patiently. 'Which is why I've booked room service.'

Delia opened her mouth to say more, but she couldn't find the words. The pain in her ankle was getting steadily worse. But a night in a comfy hotel room with room service wouldn't do any harm. She'd worry about tomorrow when it came.

The Vare Castle was everything Delia remembered and Sammi approved of: stylish surroundings, welcoming front desk, plus large and comfortable plush bedrooms with en suites you could party in.

'There's a bidet in mine,' Sammi called through the connecting door to his room. 'Fab-u-lous! Oh, and when they brought the bags up, I ordered our room service dinner. A few nibbles to start: olives, padrón peppers, deep-fried halloumi with honey, followed by haddock and pommes frites, avec petit pois de mushy, and a plate of Cornish cheeses with fruit to finish.' He came through the dividing door and struck a pose, drowned by his lush bathrobe. 'Or do we need more?'

Delia lay prone on the glorious bed and laughed weakly. 'Of course we need more. More of more please.'

'I thought so. And for that reason, I have ordered a decent bottle of Malbec and a Margarita each. Just a little something to kick start the evening.'

'That'll make my ankle feel a lot better.'

'That was the plan. And while we wait . . .' He climbed onto the bed beside her. 'What's on the telly?'

Room service arrived with a gentle knock, on a trolley that neatly opened up into a round table with everything they needed. Their fish and chips waited warmly under silvered domes.

The waiter unfurled napkins and talked them through everything on the trolley, and then, pointing out a frozen ice pack, he announced, 'And an ice pack for Mrs Carlisle-Hart's injured ankle. I have an extra napkin for you to use as a wrap.'

Sammi was suddenly brisk and on his feet, ushering the waiter out. 'You are mistaken. There is no Mrs Carlisle-Hart here. Thank you so much. Very kind. Good night.' He closed the door smartly behind him and shook his head. 'Delia, I'm so sorry.'

'What for?'

'You know what for. I made it clear to the receptionist that you were to be addressed as Miss Jago, just in case anyone thought they might be clever. Heads will roll.'

Delia shrugged. 'I suppose the news I'm here will be all over the county by Wednesday.' She smiled. 'That's exactly what my mum would say about any scandal: *all over the county!* Bless her. Pass me my Margarita, please.' She took the glass he handed her and raised it. 'To my mum. The best there ever was.'

'Hear hear,' Sammi solemnly replied. 'And here's to my mum, who gave me these fabulous cheekbones and incredible style.'

Within an hour, the ice, the cocktail, the wine, and a couple of ibuprofen had left Delia virtually pain free. 'I feel better already. I'm sure the swelling is going down. Look.' She gingerly held up her bare foot up for inspection. 'See?'

Sammi frowned. 'It still looks pretty bad to me. There's a big bruise coming. I can always ask the hotel if they have a doctor on call?'

'You are such a drama queen! It's fine.'

'Promise you'll yell for me in the night if anything feels wrong?'

'I promise.'

'OK then.' He yawned. 'What an extraordinary twenty-four hours. Especially the luxury of last night at The Tinners Arms. Please, let's never go there again.' He slipped off the bed and bent to kiss her cheek. 'Night night, old thing. You will be OK, won't you?'

'Definitely. And thank you, Sammi. For everything.'

As soon as he had gone, she got off the bed with care. The Margarita had been potent, and she hobbled over to the bathroom, balancing herself on any helpful piece of furniture on the way.

In the bathroom, Sammi had thoughtfully placed her small overnight bag on a stool. Sitting on the edge of the bath, she managed to remove her socks, but her straight-leg jeans were too narrow to easily release her swollen foot.

Eventually, her clothes were off. She diligently cleaned her teeth and washed, and finally, exhausted, hopped back to her bed.

She pulled back the tightly tucked sheets and positioned a couple of spare pillows upon which to rest her leg.

She switched off the light, then lay back on the cloudy pillows. She thought of Johnny and his parents at Wilder Hoo, of her mum at Jago Fields, and the memories threatened to overwhelm her.

A tear trickled from Delia's eye. She had known that returning to Cornwall would be painful, but she hadn't realized how much.

CHAPTER FOUR

Bozinjal, West Cornwall, thirty years ago

She had tried to stay awake for Father Christmas, but in all her eight years, she had never managed to catch him. How did that happen? Did he wait outside on the roof until she was asleep? Did he cast a spell to send her off?

Next year, she'd remember to send him a proper letter.

Dear Mister Santa Claus,

Please wake me up. I promise I won't tell anyone that I saw you. I really want to meet Rudolph and the other reindeer and stroke them and give them their carrots. Thank you and merry Christmas.

Cordelia Jago xx

She turned her head on the worn cotton pillow and moved her gaze to the bottom of the bed. *Yes!* The old woollen sock she'd left out with her mum the night before was bulging. He'd been!

She could hear her mother and aunt in the kitchen below: the whistle of the kettle on the Aga, the scraping of a potato being peeled, the smell of bacon frying. Christmas Day was here at last. A whole day to be together.

She heard footsteps on the stairs, and then her bedroom door opened slowly. 'Are you awake, Delia?'

She shut her eyes quickly and began to snore loudly.

'Oh dear. Still asleep. Never mind. Your mum and I will just have to open your presents for you.'

'Noooo.' Delia snapped her eyes open and sat up quickly. 'I'm joking, Auntie Rose!'

Her aunt clutched her chest in mock shock. 'You frightened my socks off!'

Delia laughed. 'No, I didn't.'

'Well, you almost did. Now then, put your slippers and dressing gown on, and come downstairs for breakfast.'

Delia swung her legs out of bed and collected up her fat stocking. 'Look, he's been!'

'Oh, that is good news. I haven't checked under the tree yet. Perhaps you could do that?'

'I will! *And* I can smell bacon sandwiches.'

Rose laughed. 'Your mum thought that would wake you up.'

Downstairs, the kitchen was in full sail. The old brown radio provided joyful carols. A chubby turkey, smothered in chunks of butter and bacon, was waiting in a grizzled roasting tin. The peeled potatoes were now in water, ready for parboiling. Sprouts, stuffing, bread sauce, and devils-on-horseback, the prunes glistening inside their bacon stoles, were all lying in varying states of readiness on the scrubbed table.

'Good morning, my darling Cordelia, daughter of the sea.' Her beloved mum, Christine, stood with one hand clutching a bottle of sherry for the trifle, the other outstretched to her daughter. 'Christmas kiss, please.'

'Happy Christmas, Mummy.' Delia clung onto her full stocking as she wrapped her mother's hips in a hug. 'Auntie Rose says I can check under the tree?'

'Good idea. If there are any presents, we'll open them when you are washed and dressed. No poking and prodding beforehand.'

'Not even a little shake?'

'Not even a little shake.'

'OK.'

'Good girl.'

Two minutes later, Delia was back. 'There are tons of presents under the tree. And a huuuuge one' – she stretched her arms wide – 'for me from Father Christmas.'

Christine and Rose shared a warm smile.

'And there are some presents for both of you, too,' Delia added.

'Really?' Christine grinned. 'Well, I'd better get the turkey in and the spuds started, while you and Auntie Rose lay the table for breakfast.'

'Then can I open my stocking?'

'I think so.'

The bacon sandwiches and mugs of tea were quickly dealt with, and it wasn't long before the treasures in the stocking were strewn across the table: a CD of Delia's favourite pop band, some butterfly hairclips, a paperback of Enid Blyton's *Children of Cherry-Tree Farm*, and a pocket-sized teddy bear.

'I shall call him Nicky.'

'You already have a bear called Nicky,' Christine said.

'Yes but, Mummy, that's Big Nicky, so this one is Little Nicky.'

A pack of cards, two satsumas, and a net of chocolate coins.

'Can I eat one now?'

'No, darling – later. Now go and clean your teeth and get dressed. Then we'll go and give the sheep their breakfast and collect the hens' eggs.'

'But what about the presents under the tree?' Delia wailed.

'When we've done the animals. Chop chop.'

Their sloping two-acre small holding, known locally as Jago Fields, earnt its keep with a few sheep, a small flock of free-range hens, and occasional pigs or bullocks – anything that Christine and Rose could collect, fatten up, and sell. It was constant work for them and meant they rarely took more than a night or two away from it – not that holidays were a thing they could easily afford. Everything earnt was ploughed back into the business or spent on Delia's welfare.

Delia was their light and focus of all their love. Her joys were their joys. Her woes were their woes. She had been a gift – a surprise to surpass all others.

The farmers' market at Penzance ran every Saturday, nine to one o'clock, and the Jago Fields stall was respected as the longest running stall there. Their customers were loyal, always looking forward to the seasonal produce the women brought: good eggs, excellent beef, lamb and pork, homemade cakes and, at Christmas, the legendary Jago Fields Christmas cake, mince pies, hand-reared duck and turkey, large bunches of mistletoe and yards of ivy. In spring, they brought daffodils to the stall; in summer, sweet peas, anemones, strawberries, and Rose's homemade clotted cream.

It was tiring work for the two devoted sisters, but Penzance was only a thirty-minute drive in their elderly Land Rover and worth it for the beauty and history of the ancient town.

They liked being out in the fresh air and the catching up with customers old and new. They carried the priceless feeling of knowing that this was where they belonged.

As well as their old Landy, they had recently acquired a quad bike third hand, which took the slog out of the steep walk down to the sheep. The sloping land was often muddy, and more than once, Christine had slid and toppled it onto its side, banging a hip or wrist.

This Christmas morning, however, it was dry and bright. With her breath pluming in the cold air, Delia sat on the back of the quad bike and gripped her mother's waist. They set off past the chicken run, the pig pens, round the duck pond, and down to the three stockades. The first housed six sheep, and the other two were empty, awaiting the next delivery of pigs and calves.

'Happy Christmas, sheepies!' Delia called out as she helped her mother spread two hay bales for their feed.

'Check the water trough, would you?' Christine asked. 'Make sure it's not frozen.'

Delia checked. 'It's cold but not frozen, Mummy.'

In the hen run, the chickens crowded round as Christine filled the feeders and refreshed the water bowls. Delia had already hurried to the hen house and eventually emerged with a bucket full of eggs. 'Auntie Rose will be pleased. Lots of eggs for her market cakes.'

'Hold them tightly then.'

'I promise.'

Back in the kitchen, Rose had drained the potatoes ready to roast and was mixing up some batter for the Yorkshire puddings.

Delia plonked the bucket of eggs next to her. 'Here you are, Auntie Rose. The hens say happy Christmas.'

'Bless those good chicks. Thank you.'

'Now can we open our presents?'

Rose smiled. 'What do you think, Chris? Can we open our presents?'

A fire was already glowing in the grate of the cosy front room when they stepped inside. The Christmas tree stood in the large window, so that anyone who passed on the road beyond could enjoy its twinkling lights.

Delia made a beeline for her gift from Father Christmas. Rose and Christine watched as she tore off the wrapping paper.

'Mummy! Look what Father Christmas brought me!'

'Let me see.'

'How did he know?' Delia was breathless with joy. 'I didn't even put them on my list.' She was holding a huge presentation box full of crayons, paints, felt-tips, and coloured sugar paper. 'I love it.'

Chris and Rose shared a conspiratorial glance over the little girl's head.

'He must know you like painting and drawing.' Christine smiled. 'He is very clever.'

Delia squeezed the gift to her chest. 'I'm so happy!' Then she remembered. 'You haven't opened my present yet, Mummy!' She reached out for a square-shaped box. 'It's this one.'

Chris took it happily. 'I wonder what it is?'

'Open it. Open it!' Delia hopped on the spot with excitement.

'OK.' Chris pulled at the many strips of Sellotape and wrapping paper to reveal a white wooden picture frame. 'Well. This is lovely!'

'I saw one at Debbie's house when I had tea. It's got a picture of her mum and dad on their wedding day. I thought we could put a picture of you and Daddy on your wedding day in it.'

Christine froze for a moment. 'But I don't have a wedding photograph, do I?'

'Not yet, but you will when Daddy comes back, won't you? You'll get married to him, and I shall be a bridesmaid, and Auntie Rose can make a cake, and Debbie can come, too.'

Auntie Rose tried her best. 'What a lovely idea!'

Christine broke in. 'Delia, that's such a lovely thought, and I'm sure that if he could come back, he would, but . . . we'll have to wait and see.'

'It would be sad if he doesn't come back.' Delia was thinking aloud. 'But we can keep this photo frame just in case, so that if I ever get married, we can put my wedding picture in it, can't we? Daddy won't mind.'

Christine felt her heart crack even as she smiled. 'Darling Cordelia – so practical. That is exactly what we shall do.'

'Good. Can I do some drawing now?'

'Of course you can.' Her mother smoothed her hair and dropped a kiss on her crown. 'Happy Christmas, darling.'

'I *love* Christmas,' Delia said as she plonked herself on the rug by the fire. 'Can we play Canasta after lunch?'

'We always do.'

'Good. Now, I'm going to draw a picture of us all with Daddy.' And she turned her full attention to her art box.

In the kitchen, Rose filled the aluminium kettle and put it on the range to boil. Then she asked firmly, 'Will you *ever* tell her the truth?'

Christine began lining the bottom of the trifle bowl with slices of swiss roll. 'No.'

'She should hear it from you,' said Rose, pulling the milk from the fridge, 'rather than anyone else.'

'So you've told me. Many times.'

Rose stood in front of her sister, forcing Chris to listen to her. 'And I shall keep on telling you. Can you imagine how hurt and confused she will be when she finds out that you have lied? That her sainted Daddy doing God knows what on the other side of the world doesn't exist?'

Christine pursed her lips and reached for a tin of mandarins. 'Pass me the tin opener, would you?'

'I know what you're doing – you don't want to talk about it – but she'll be nine next birthday.' Rose handed her the tin opener. 'She's growing up. She needs to know sooner rather than later who her father is.'

Chris angrily tipped the fruit over the jam and sponge. 'He doesn't deserve her.'

'That may be true, but she doesn't deserve to be lied to.'

Christine tipped a shot of sherry on top of the fruit, and Rose rolled her eyes.

'You want to get her drunk now as well, do you?'

Her sister slammed the bottle down. 'Rose. It's Christmas Day, and I am trying to give my daughter some happy memories. I do not need you to tell me how to bring her up or what to tell her about the useless man who lives not half a mile from here in his cosy home with his cosy wife and cosy bloody kids, who happened to give one tiny little bit of genetic material to create her. OK?'

'Chris, I know how badly he hurt you. I will always be here for you. I always have been, but—'

'And you know that he dropped me like a hot brick as soon as he knew I was pregnant. How can he not acknowledge his own bright and beautiful daughter? He had his chance. I hate him, and I will never tell Delia who her father really is.'

The kettle began to whistle, and Rose reached for two mugs.

Christine sat down shakily. 'He doesn't deserve her, Rose.'

'I know, my love.'

'Better for her to have a pretend father who loves her, doing good work on the other side of the world, than to have the real one. How do I tell her that he just doesn't want to know her? I'd rather break her heart by killing the pretend one off than give the real one the privilege.'

'I know, I know. But secrets like this have a habit of coming out.'

Christina shook her head resolutely. 'Not while I'm alive.'

CHAPTER FIVE

North Cornwall, April, present day

Lying in her enormous Vare Castle bed, Delia was sleeping fitfully. Her ankle was very sore, and she needed a pee, but the thought of getting out of bed and negotiating the path to the bathroom did not fill her with joy. She didn't want to risk waking Sammi and causing any commotion. He was the kindest person she had ever known, after her mum and Auntie Rose. She had been almost fourteen when they met, introduced by her friend Harriet, and they had been best friends ever since.

She rolled onto her side gingerly and let her mind wander back to another time.

Bozinjal, West Cornwall, twenty-four years ago

'Mum?' Delia was home from school, clattering into the kitchen with Harriet tagging behind. 'Mum? Where are you?'

Christine had a basket of freshly ironed clothes on her hip. 'Hello. How was school? And who's this?' She put the basket on the kitchen table.

'This is Harriet. She's a new girl.'

Chris nodded to her. 'Hello Harriet.'

'School was fine,' Delia answered, dumping her heavy rucksack on the floor. 'Have you got any cake? Harriet wants to try some because I've told her you make amaaaazing cake.'

'I need to make some tonight for market tomorrow, but Auntie Rose has some fairy cakes, I think.'

'Yum,' said Delia, nudging a grinning Harriet, who added, 'Delia says they are the best, Mrs Jago.'

Christine smiled. 'Flattery will get you everywhere, and please, call me Christine.'

Delia was in the pantry, searching for Auntie Rose's special cake tin. It had a picture of a Jack Russell with a pink bow round her neck, watching over her basket of puppies. Anything in this tin would not go to market and could be eaten at home.

She brought it back to the table with an explanation for Harriet. 'I told you, Mum isn't Mrs Jago. She's Miss Jago, but she doesn't like that because she says it sounds like she's a teacher. One day, when my dad comes back from helping build wells in Africa for people to have fresh water, they'll get married, and she'll be Mrs Jimmy Porter. That's right, isn't it, Mum?'

Christine flushed. 'Delia, you don't have to share all my secrets.'

'Oh, she doesn't mind, do you, Hattie?' Delia said blithely, easing the lid from the tin.

Harriet fixed her eyes on the cakes. 'I think it's very romantic. My mum thought so, too, when I told her. Can I have the big one with the pink icing please?'

'By the way, Mum,' Delia said, 'Debbie's mum is looking for a Saturday girl to help in the salon. And she says I can have a try-out, but I have to ask you first. Harriet's already working there.'

'Is she?' Christine frowned. 'Are you, Harriet?'

'Uh-huh.' Harriet spoke with a mouthful of cake. 'I want Delia to come, too. Debbie's mum is cross because Debbie wants to be a nurse, not a hairdresser, so Debbie's mum needs someone else to take over. Please say yes. It's lots of fun, *and* we get paid. Please, please say yes.'

'You get paid?' Christine asked, impressed.

'Yeah. Last Saturday, I got an extra five pounds in tips.'

'On top of your wages?'

Harriet nodded. 'Yeah.'

'How old are you?'

'Fourteen.'

'Delia won't be fourteen for another two months.'

Harriet was ready with her answer. 'Yes, but you're allowed to do part-time work when you're thirteen. Debbie's mum told me so.'

'You seem to have an answer for everything, Harriet,' Chris replied.

'Thank you. I know.'

'And what time do you start and finish?'

'Open at nine. Close at five. We do the sweeping and I'm learning how to shampoo and give a proper head massage. I get extra tips for that.' Harriet grinned.

Delia was desperate. 'Can I, Mum? Please, please, please, Mum.'

'I'll have to have a think and also talk to Debbie's mum.'

Delia took a crumpled yellow Post-it note from her pocket. 'Here's her number.'

'Why do I think that this is an ambush, hmm?' said Christine. Pocketing the Post-it note, she added, 'I'll give her a ring later.'

When Delia had been sent to bed, Chris asked Rose for her opinion on the job.

Delia had never mentioned any interest in hairdressing before now. Their family of three rarely went to the hairdresser's, and then just for a trim. Chris always wore her hair in a long plait, Rose styled hers in a cottage-loaf bun, and Delia usually had a ponytail – and unbrushed at that.

Neither had Delia ever suggested having any Saturday job other than one she already had: helping her mother and aunt at market. Chris and Rose loved having her with them each Saturday and during the school holidays. She wasn't at all sure she was ready for her little girl to set out on the road to independence.

'Isn't she a bit too young?' she asked Rose.

'She's nearly fourteen, Chris. Why not let her try it? If she hates it, she can leave.'

'I suppose . . .'

'Debbie's a nice girl. Her mum is probably a nice woman. Give her a ring and have a proper chat.' Rose passed Chris the phone.

After a deep breath, she dialled.

Debbie's mum answered on the second ring. 'Hello, Jean speaking.'

'Oh hi, it's Delia Jago's mum – Christine . . .'

Rose waited, holding her breath as she listened.

'And when would you want her to start? This Saturday? Gosh, erm . . .'

Chris looked at Rose again, who had both thumbs up.

'Right, well, yes. That sounds very good. She'll see you on Saturday.'

Rose got out of her armchair. 'I think this calls for a sherry, don't you?'

'Are we doing the right thing? We'll miss her at the market.'

'So will the customers, but a bit of independence is just what she needs. Look at us. Mum and Dad got us involved in the livestock and the market when we were a similar age, and we loved it. Then when Delia was on the way, we didn't panic – we just got on with it. It was the making of us.'

'Without you being so calm, and Mum and Dad so supportive, I don't think I'd have been brave enough to—'

'Don't talk like that. Imagine if we hadn't had Delia. Mum and Dad got over the shock and loved her as much as we do.'

'More, probably.' Christine gave a long sigh. 'I was so stupid to think he loved me at all. How could I have thought he was going to stand by me?'

'Darling,' Rose said gently, 'you're not the first nor the last. Men like that are not worth our tears. Look what he lost and what we gained. It turned out to be the best for all of us. That last time you spoke to him was the start of happiness for the three of us.'

Christine repeated that last conversation stonily: '"If you think I am going to be caught by a little cow like you, you can think again. Read my lips. I am not interested. Never will be. It's not my problem."' She hung her head and pushed her hands through her hair. 'Never have I hated anyone more.'

'Me too, my love. Me too.'

Delia felt she could burst with excitement when she was told the news over breakfast the next morning. 'This Saturday? Oh, Mum! What shall I wear?'

'You can ask Debbie at school today.'

'Oh yes . . . Mum, I can help with the bills now!'

Christine was touched. 'Let's wait and see how much you bring home first.'

Delia couldn't wait. She counted the days, ticking them off in her diary and, with Harriet's help, wrote down a simple budget plan of how much she would give to Auntie Rose and her mum, how much she would save, and how much she would have left to spend.

The night before her first day as a Saturday girl, she barely slept. The plan was to see Mum and Auntie Rose off early for market, then wait at home until Debbie's mum picked her up and drove her to the salon.

During the short car journey, Jean gave Delia her list of 'Golden Rules'.

'A customer is always addressed as "Mrs", "Miss", or "Sir", never by their Christian name, even if you know them well. Never answer the phone unless I ask you to, and always let it ring at least three times before picking it up. This gives the caller a chance to think about what she or he wants to say.

'Answer all calls with: "Just Jean, Delia speaking, how may I help you?" Whatever they ask you, remember it, and then you say, "Would you hold the line please while I find someone who can help you." And be sure to ask which hot drink a customer prefers and whether it's with milk or sugar or both. Make a note of it next to their name in the appointments' book. You won't believe how much people appreciate that, and you might even get an extra tip. Our clients really appreciate being remembered and being greeted with good manners. Understood?'

Delia nodded, her hands tightly clenched. How was she going to remember it all?

'And please call me Mrs Waters when we are in the salon.'

Harriet, sitting next to her on the back seat, squeezed her friend's arm and whispered, 'You'll be fine. Just follow what I do.'

*

The salon was on a small parade of shops known to the locals as Cosy Corner. Its real name was Victory Parade, in recognition of the street that had been obliterated by a German bomber in 1943, dropping its last shells before heading home. No lives had been lost that night, but a more modern shopping experience had risen from the ashes.

Now, apart from Just Jean Hair Salon, there was a minimarket, an off-licence, a newsagent's, an ironmonger's and a café called The Copper Kettle.

The first half an hour went smoothly enough. Delia was shown the location of both the client and staff lavatories and told why they were not to be mixed up. She was shown the cleaning cupboard, which held soft brooms and dustpans on long handles so that you didn't have to bend down to collect the piles of hair, and the staff room, with its small table, two chairs, kettle, fridge, crockery, microwave, and sink.

By the afternoon, Mrs Waters decided that Delia was confident enough to stand near the reception desk, poised and alert for any request.

'Delia?' Mrs Waters was perming an elderly lady's hair. 'Would you get Mrs Jackson a coffee, please? Milky, one sugar.'

Delia sped to the staff room, repeating the order so as not to forget. Milky coffee, one sugar. Kettle on, water boiled, coffee into cup, hot water added, good dollop of milk, one sugar, and she was on her way back, cup and saucer in hand, mission accomplished.

She didn't see the long-handled dustpan that had fallen across the floor until the last second. She managed to hop jerkily over it, slopping most of the coffee into the saucer, and the rest over Mrs Jackson.

Jean's face said it all, but her voice was modulated and low. 'Clean towels. Now.'

As soon as Mrs Jackson was mopped up, Delia had a long weep in the staff toilet.

Harriet talked her down from the opposite side of the door. 'It's all right, Delia. Mrs Jackson is fine, and Mrs W's bark is worse than her bite. I once had a mix up when the vicar asked for his cloak, and I gave him the only cloak I could see – a big red velvet one. I thought vicars wore red cloaks, so I tried to give it to him, but he wouldn't take it, and I said, "It's the only cloak in the cupboard," and he said, "I asked for my coat, not a cloak. Who do you think I am? For your information, I am neither Danny La Rue nor the Pope!"

Delia slid the bolt of the door, then opened it a crack, revealing her anguished, tear-stained cheeks. 'How horrible of him.'

'Yeah. It was awful. Mrs W almost sacked me.'

'Is she going to sack me? I didn't do it on purpose.'

'She knows that. Come on. Wash your face. We've got to go to the newsagent's and get new magazines.'

Mrs Jackson had just paid her bill and was ready to leave when the girls emerged.

Delia gulped. 'I am so sorry, Mrs Jackson.'

'Not to worry, dear,' Mrs Jackson whispered. 'You won't do it a second time.' She pressed a fifty-pence piece into Delia's hand.

'Goodbye, Mrs Jackson.' Jean was all charm, opening the door and allowing Mrs Jackson to locate her husband, who had been waiting in his car, reading his newspaper. 'Goodbye, dear.'

As soon as the door was closed, Jean turned to Delia. 'Don't let that happen again. Do you understand me?'

'Yes, miss.'

Jean clicked her tongue. 'It's Mrs Waters. I'm your employer; you are not at school.'

Harriet scowled. 'Stop being mean to Delia.'

'And you stop your cheek.' Jean opened the till and took out a ten-pound note. 'While you're in the newsagent's, ask Mrs Hashmi if my order for *Hair* magazine has arrived. And if there's any change, you can buy yourselves some crisps or a can of pop.'

In between the salon and the newsagent's was The Copper Kettle. That day, a handful of people were sitting at outdoor tables, drinking coffees.

As the girls walked by, the café door opened and out came a teenage boy, tall and skinny, with a mop of dark hair falling over his eyes. He was holding two lidded polystyrene cups.

'Hattie.' He smiled. 'Mrs Waters's *Hair* magazine is in. I was going to bring it round to you later.'

'We were just coming to get it,' Harriet answered. 'Sammi, meet Delia.'

He smiled. 'Is this your new friend? The one you told me about?'

'Yes. It's her first day today.'

Sammi balanced the two cups one on top of the other and stretched out his hand. 'How do you do? I am Sammi Hashmi.'

Delia shook his hand. She immediately liked the warmth of this smiling boy with old-fashioned manners. 'Hi.'

'Harriet and you are at school together?' he asked.

'Yes.'

'Must be fun to be co-ed.'

'I suppose so.'

'I'm at the grammar school. All boys. Very bad.'

'He's an egghead,' Harriet said.

Sammi laughed. 'I wish. My parents are always telling me to work harder. But I don't want to.'

Harriet sighed. 'Same as my mum.'

'And mine,' agreed Delia.

Sammi shrugged. 'What do parents know?'

They walked the few steps to the newsagent's.

'Welcome to Cosy Corner News. I must apologize for my parents' lack of imagination.' He pushed the door open carefully with his elbow, so as not to spill the coffee. Above the door, a bell tinkled. He lowered his voice. 'Prepare yourself for my mother's interrogation. She's very good!'

'Sammi?' a woman's voice called from the back of the shop. 'You have been so long that the coffee will be cold.'

'Yes, Ammi, it's me. I bumped into Hattie and her friend Delia. They're here to collect Mrs Waters's magazines.'

A graceful woman with dark hair in a neat bun stepped out from a door beyond the counter. She had deep brown eyes perfectly outlined with kohl and was wearing jeans with a hot-pink linen shirt.

'Hello Harriet, and how nice to meet a new friend.' She smiled. 'Delia is a very nice name. Tell me all about yourself. I think my Sammi needs to meet more nice girls.' Mrs Hashmi flashed a teasing glance at her handsome son. 'But how will he find a nice girl when he is so tall and skinny? I call him Mr Skinny Too Tall.' She laughed.

'Hilarious.' Sammi rolled his eyes. 'She really should be on tour.'

'Have some respect for your mother.' She glowered at him mockingly. 'Shall I get out the baby pictures, Sammi?'

'No, thank you.'

She reached round and pinched his cheek with her thumb and forefinger.

'Ow. Stop it, Ammi. You're embarrassing yourself.'

'I don't care.' She let him go, then reached under the counter, bringing up the latest copy of *Hair* magazine. 'Here you are, girls.'

'Thank you.'

'And Jean asked for this month's *Good Housekeeping* and this week's *OK* magazine. Take them off the shelf, please.'

With the small amount of change left, the girls bought a bottle of Coca-Cola to share and a bag of Haribo.

'Come and see me next Saturday,' Mrs Hashmi commanded. 'It is good for Sammi to know some girls.'

Returning to the salon, Hattie and Delia found Jean darting between a customer under the drier and tucking a towel around a gentlemen's neck.

'You took your time,' she said, spotting their reflections in her mirror.

'Sorry, Mrs Waters. You know what Mrs Hashmi is like when she gets talking.' Harriet put the new magazines on the coffee table by the purple velvet sofa.

'I need this floor swept, Delia. And Hattie, make a tea for Mrs Hammond – she's under the drier – and Mr Henderson would like a coffee. Chop chop.'

When she got home that night, Delia had earnt her first pay packet, plus tips of £4.50. But more than that, she had met Sammi.

CHAPTER SIX

North Cornwall, April, present day

'Good morning.' Sammi peeked round the door that joined their rooms. 'Are you decent? I have tea for you.'

Delia pulled herself up the bed and rubbed her eyes. 'I think I may have a slight hangover.'

'Excellent,' Sammi replied, putting the tray down on the ottoman at the bottom of the bed. 'How's the ankle? Did you sleep OK?'

Delia lied with a smile. 'Fine, thank you. How about you?'

'Wonderfully. Here's your tea.'

After she'd taken the cup from him, Sammi settled himself on the empty side of the vast bed. 'I've been thinking.'

'Oh no.'

'Yes. And don't be like that.' He took a sip of his own tea. 'I know you don't want to hear this, but I really liked Wilder Hoo.'

She felt her chest prickle with a panicky rage. 'I don't care what you think. I hate it and I'm going to sell it.'

'Listen, you have here in front of you a proficient expert who makes a living from creating glorious interiors in unpromising homes.'

Delia snapped. 'No, you listen.If I had a huge pile of money, sure, I could turn Wilder Hoo into the house it deserves to be. But I don't. And more than that, I have no desire to.'

Sammi wriggled his eyebrows, which usually made her laugh, and asked, 'Dontcha love a money pit, though?'

'No.'

They drank their tea in silence until Delia said, 'Sorry.'

'You should be.'

She put her cup down. 'I've been thinking. Could we have today out? Go down to Bozinjal maybe, visit some old haunts?'

'Visit Auntie Rose?' Sammi asked carefully.

Delia shrugged. 'I didn't tell her I was coming down. She's probably too busy anyway to fit us in.'

'How is she?'

'Well, the retirement village sounds like heaven, judging from her last card. If she's not playing table tennis or going out for Sunday lunch with the other residents, she's baking cakes for their birthdays. The only thing she misses is the market stall.'

'And you,' Sammi said.

Delia ignored him. 'Can we be very wicked and order room service breakfast?'

'But of course.' Sammi got on the phone and made the order. 'Right, anything else I can do for you?'

'No, thank you.'

'OK. But yell if you need me.' He headed for his room to shower and dress, before their breakfast arrived.

When he was gone, Delia gingerly swung her legs from the mattress to the floor. She needed to test her ankle without

Sammi seeing. It was still very swollen, with a deep purple bruise surrounding it.

'Bugger.'

She stood up, trying not to put too much pressure on the injury. Gritting her teeth, taking slow deep breaths, she limped her way to the bathroom.

It took a little while, but she managed to negotiate the loo and the shower and, sitting on the bathroom stool, to put on some clean underwear.

The pain was not subsiding. She tried to stand up, but it hurt too much.

Sammi was calling. 'Breakfast is here.'

'OK. Erm. I'm just in my underwear. Could you pop my jeans and T-shirt round the bathroom door? They're on the chair.'

'Sure.' She heard footsteps, then the door opened, and Sammi's long slender arm appeared with her clothes. 'Can you reach these or . . . ?'

'I don't think I can . . . Could you . . . ?'

Sammi chuckled. 'Don't tell me you're embarrassed?'

'I am a bit.'

'Would it help if I closed my eyes?' asked Sammi. 'I mean, to be fair I have never knowingly been up close to a semi-naked nearly-forty-year-old woman before.'

Delia giggled. 'OK. Just come in, eyes open. Help me put my jeans on.'

When Sammi saw her ankle, he winced. 'That is not looking good.'

'It's not feeling good, to be honest.'

Kneeling in front of her, he examined the bruising. 'A&E it is.'

'Please put my jeans on first. And can we at least have breakfast?'

*

At the hospital, Delia was quiet.

The young doctor, whose hair was tied into a lank ponytail, had clearly had a long shift, but she was focused as she explained Delia's injury.

'You'll be pleased to hear that there is no fracture, as you can see from the X-ray.'

When Delia remained silent, Sammi spoke for her. 'That is good news. Excellent.' He flashed his most charming smile at the doctor.

'But . . .' The doctor ran a tired hand over the wisps of hair escaping over her forehead, 'You have done some damage to the ligament. It's not torn or ruptured but will need some TLC. I recommend rest, ice, compression, and elevation, or RICE as we say to help you remember. I'll give you some painkillers for the next three days. Take one now.' She handed Delia a small tablet and a paper cup of water. 'They'll make you a bit sleepy, which is probably a good thing. Pain is tiring. Once you've finished the course, use paracetamol as and when. I can refer you to a physio, too. I know you said you weren't local, but I can put the reference through to your local trust. You'll need crutches as well – I'll just fetch some.'

'OK.'

When the doctor left the small room, Sammi turned to Delia. 'Are you OK? You're very quiet.'

'I just want to get out of here.'

The doctor reappeared with the crutches. 'I think these are a matching pair. Do you want to have a little practice on them?'

'I'll be fine—'

Sammi interrupted. 'Yes, she would like to practise.'

Delia obediently took a couple of trial runs up and down the corridor until a nurse signed her off.

'I'll fetch a wheelchair to get you to your car. Any problems, give us a ring.'

Sammi pushed Delia out to the carpark and, with infinite care and gentleness, managed to get her into the car.

'There. Comfortable?'

Delia burst into tears.

Sammi frowned. 'What is it? Have I hurt you?'

'No, no. It's just . . . being in there . . . it all looked the same . . . the last time I was in there, when Mum had her accident.'

CHAPTER SEVEN

Bozinjal, West Cornwall, twenty-one years ago

'Mum? Mum?' Delia clattered excitedly through the back door, bringing with her a blast of cold air and scattering the two stray cats Auntie Rose had invited to stay. She dropped her coat on a kitchen chair and ran to the bottom of the stairs. 'Mum? Are you upstairs?'

A floorboard creaked above her, and Auntie Rose's worried face appeared over the banister. 'Shush. Your mum's resting,' she whispered.

Delia began to climb the stairs, frowning. 'What's the matter with her?'

'She took a bit of a tumble on the quad bike.' Auntie Rose was coming down the stairs, shooing Delia towards the kitchen. 'I'll make you a cup of tea.'

'Is she OK?'

'A bit bruised, but nothing to worry about. She just needs to rest.'

'Have you called the doctor?'

'I might later. How was work?'

Delia couldn't hide her excitement. 'It was *such* a good day. Jean told me I've passed my NVQ Level 2. You're now looking at Delia Jago, junior stylist!'

Rose beamed, overcome with joy. 'Oh my! I'm so happy for you. Wait 'til your mum hears. All the worrying when you and Jean persuaded her you should drop out of sixth form . . .'

'Well, Mum doesn't have to worry about anything anymore. I'll be earning proper money, and I can give you all my hairdressing skills at home for free!' Delia lifted the boiling kettle from the Aga hotplate. 'I'll take Mum up a cuppa and tell her. That will cheer her up.'

The curtains of Chris's room were closed on the darkening February afternoon. Outside, the grey clouds, tinged with yellow, were lowering and threatening snow. A few flakes had already begun to swirl in the dusk.

'Mum?' Delia crept in quietly. 'Mum? Are you asleep?'

Chris was lying motionless on her side, the shape and dip of her shoulders and hips soft under the blankets.

'Hey, Mum. I've brought you a cuppa.'

'Cordelia?' Chris sounded groggy.

'How are you feeling? Auntie Rose has told me what happened.' Delia moved the box of paracetamol and her mum's latest paperback from the small table by the bed, making space for the tea. 'There you are. Would you like me to help you sit up?'

Chris mumbled something.

'Sorry, Mum, what did you say?'

Chris mumbled again and tried to lift herself up. Before Delia could help, a rush of vomit erupted from her mum's mouth, covering her nightdress, the bed clothes, and Delia.

'Oh, Mummy.' Delia felt panic building within her.

Chris was trying to cough – either that or she was choking. Delia tried to lift her to an easier position in case she was sick again, which she was, almost immediately.

'Auntie Rose!' Delia shouted. 'Auntie Rose!' The pitch of her voice grew higher, and her pulse pounded in her ears. 'Auntie Rose, come quick. Mum's been sick.'

The ambulance took longer than expected.

Delia waited, shivering in the cold, her ears straining. The snow was falling thickly now, settling against the lip of the doorstep. Ever darkening clouds blocked any moon or starlight, but the approaching blue lights and siren pierced the gloom.

'Sorry we're a bit later than expected. The lanes are getting icy.' The uniformed woman introduced herself. 'I'm Pamela.'

'I'm Mike,' her colleague said. 'Where's the patient? Lead the way.'

Upstairs, Rose was holding her sister's hand, clearly relieved to see the paramedics. 'Thank you for coming. I've mopped her up a bit, but I couldn't change her nightie without moving her, and I was afraid to.'

'That's all right.' Pamela's voice was professionally reassuring. 'What's the patient's name?'

'Christine. She's my sister.'

Pamela was assessing the scene. 'Hello Christine. Can you hear me? My name's Pamela. I'm with my colleague Mike, and we're paramedics with the ambulance service. I hear you've had a bit of an accident. Is that right?'

Chris mumbled something.

Without taking her eyes off her patient, Pamela asked Rose, 'Can you tell me what happened?'

Rose's voice trembled. 'It was silly, really. She was going down to make sure the water for the heifers wasn't frozen. We'd just heard the forecast, and it was getting so cold. She needed to put the quad away in the barn, so she thought she'd take it down to save time. The field is on a slope, and I told her to be careful – it gets so slippery. I watched her go down from the back door, and she was doing fine at first, but the bloody thing must have hit a stone or something. The back flipped up, and she went over the handlebars.' Rose took a deep breath. 'It's happened before. I thought she'd be OK, but she didn't get up, so I went down there, and she was cross, really swearing. Her leg had got stuck underneath, so together we pushed and pulled and got her out. She told me her leg was sore and that she'd banged her head. Well, I got her indoors and straight up to bed. Two paracetamol and I let her rest.'

Mike passed Pamela an oxygen mask. 'What time was the accident?'

Rose was getting flustered 'About three o'clock, I think.'

'And what happened to make you phone us?'

Delia stood at the end of the bed, not taking her eyes off her mum as Pamela checked her vital signs. 'I came up to give her a cup of tea and tell her that I . . . she was sort of mumbling and then she was sick.'

Delia abruptly felt herself leave her body. She was floating, calm, hyperaware of everything going on in the room. Yet her hearing had become muffled and dreamlike. 'She's tough, though,' she heard herself say. 'She's fallen off the quad before. She'll be OK.'

Pamela and Mike were speaking quickly to each other, using medical terms that meant nothing to Delia.

'Was she wearing a crash helmet?' Pamela asked.

Rose shook her head. 'She can be a bit naughty like that.'

Bumping along the snowy lanes in the old Landy, Delia and Rose followed the ambulance in a state of alert shock.

'Why didn't I tell her to put her helmet on?' Rose said.

'From now on, we'll make bloody sure she wears it.'

'You know what she's like. Bloody stubborn. Thinks she's unbreakable.'

'Yeah.' Delia stared out of the window as the wipers battled the snowflakes. 'We must get hold of my dad somehow. Let him know.'

Rose felt her skin tighten. 'What, dear?'

'Dad. He'll want to know what's happened to Mum. He might have to come back.'

A cold hard lump landed in the pit of Rose's stomach. So here it was. The time had come, without warning or planning. And it was left to her, Rose, to tell Delia the truth? After all the years of begging Chris to come clean?

Fury flashed within her, catching a fuse that could blow them all to smithereens. She quickly squashed it. 'Let's get Mum fixed first.'

Delia shivered. The Landy was cold; the heater had broken long ago. 'I was thinking, maybe next year, when I turn eighteen, Mum could write to him and ask him to come visit? For my birthday.'

'I don't know.'

'The cards he sends are so lovely, and it's nice of him to put money in, but it's not the same as seeing him.'

If Christine had been with them now, rather than in the ambulance ahead, Rose would have strangled her.

'But if Mum really is hurt, maybe he'll . . .'

The ugly hospital building emerged from the snow to the left of them, lights on in every window and ambulances lined up outside the canopy of the Accident and Emergency department.

'We're here now.' Rose pulled up the handbrake and shut down the engine. 'Come on.'

CHAPTER EIGHT

North Cornwall, April, present day

Delia wiped her nose on the sleeve of her jumper.

Sammi passed his handkerchief. 'I should have known this would be the hospital they brought your mum to. They wouldn't take her to the little cottage hospital, would they? That's a really hard memory.'

Delia sniffed. 'It is, but also . . . it's made me feel close to her again, being here. Is that weird?'

'To some people, but not me.' He turned on the ignition. 'Do you still want to go to Bozinjal? It's not too late. Rose doesn't even know we're in Cornwall, so we can just go back and spend another night at The Vare.'

'No. I somehow feel like Mum wants us to see Auntie Rose. I mean, my aunt does love you.'

'Of course she does! Everybody adores me.'

Delia laughed. 'You're insufferable.'

'Thank you. Bozinjal here we come.'

They pulled out of the carpark, heading for the A30 and signs to Penzance. A watery sun couldn't stop a smattering of rain rattling on the windscreen.

'Rainbow.' Sammi nodded his head towards it. 'That's your mum.'

Delia smiled. 'Wishing me luck for what might be an awkward phone call.'

She found Auntie Rose's number on her phone, took a deep breath, and pressed *dial*. After a few rings, the call was answered.

'Hey, Auntie Rose. It's me.'

'You'll have to be more specific,' was Rose's cool reply.

Delia sighed. 'It's Delia, and yes, I know I haven't phoned you for too long, and I'm so sorry.'

'You should be. I do worry, you know.' Rose's voice was tart. 'But let's start again. Hello, my darling. How are you?'

'I'm fine, thank you.'

'No, she's not,' Sammi shouted. 'She's on crutches and painkillers for a torn ankle. We've just left the hospital.'

'Um, I'm with Sammi. You're on speaker phone, so don't say anything too nice about him. His head is already as big as a balloon.'

Auntie Rose's voice softened. 'Hello Sammi, my favourite man. Long time, no see. What are you doing with my niece?'

'Coming to see you!'

Rose's surprise was tangible. 'No? Really? When?'

'Now,' declared Sammi. 'Today.'

'Really? Oh my goodness. I hope you'll have lunch before you get here. I don't have any food in, and I can't get to the shops because we have swimmercise in ten minutes.'

'Ooh. Swimmercise, eh? I bet you look fabulous in your racer-back swimsuit,' Sammi teased.

'We do it naked now. All of us together, men and women.'

'Stop it!'

Delia rolled her eyes; Sammi had always loved bantering with her aunt.

'You brazen woman. Don't start without us – we're just turning into the long drive of your pensioner's enclave, now.'

'You're not?' said Rose, clearly flustered.

Delia took over. 'He's pulling your leg. We're just over an hour away, I'd say. We'll stop for lunch first, so don't worry.'

'Phew,' said Rose. 'We'll have afternoon tea together instead. I have a Victoria sponge here, freshly baked this morning.'

Gradually, the dual carriageways became single carriageways, and the single carriageways narrowed and became lanes. Steep Cornish hedges sprang up, bursting with primroses and bluebells, and when each hedge opened to a farm gate, there were glimpses of little lambs with their mums and fields of yellow rapeseed. And all the time, the sea sparkled beyond.

For the first time since she had heard that Wilder Hoo was hers, Delia's internal agitation subsided. The tension in her shoulders had faded. Even her ankle was hurting less.

'I feel a bit better,' she told Sammi.

He laughed. 'That'll be the drugs.'

'Oh. Yeah.' She glanced out the window. 'Why ever did we leave?'

'One of life's rules: you have to leave to appreciate the return.' Sammi paused. 'You actually have the chance to do that now.'

Delia knew he was referring to Wilder Hoo and she decided to ignore it. 'Fancy a proper trip down memory lane?' she asked.

Sammi raised an eyebrow. 'I know what you're going to say.'

'Go on then, Mr Psychic.'

'You're going to say: "Why don't we have lunch at Cosy Corner?"'

Delia cried, '*YES!* Shall we? I haven't been there in years. I hardly ever went back to visit dear Jean after I left for London.

The odd phone call and Christmas card . . . pretty awful of me. How about you?'

'The last time I was here was . . . three years ago, when Mum and Dad sold the shop and retired to France.'

They passed the village sign for Bozinjal and saw, on their left, standing slightly higher than the main road, the row of shops that everyone called Cosy Corner.

'I used to think this was the centre of the universe,' Delia said. 'I thought it was huge.'

Sammi was driving very slowly, looking for a parking space while also taking in the changes around him. Three of the shops had been knocked together to make a handy Co-op. 'Look what they've done to the old Copper Kettle! The first place I clapped eyes on your ugly mug,' Delia teased.

'Charming.'

'But . . . oh, look, it's doubled in size.'

Sammi swung into a space and looked up at the jaunty green-and-white awnings, the outdoor tables and the word *KETTLES* etched into the windows.

Delia gasped. 'The café has knocked into Jean's! I knew she'd retired. They must have snapped the old salon up.'

'Clever. Shall we try it for lunch? Let me help you out of the car.'

Once Delia had struggled out on her crutches, Sammi supporting her, they turned to gaze up at the shop that had once been his parents' newsagent's.

'Oh, my goodness!' Sammi stood in disbelief. 'It can't be.'

Delia was laughing. 'On the very spot where you obsessed over all classy interior design magazines, building up your mood boards, dreaming of being a famous designer . . . and now the old place is actually a home interiors shop! Don't you think that's weird?'

Sammi was staring through the window. 'I tell you what is weird: this display. I mean, it must appeal to a certain person, but . . .'

'You snob,' Delia replied, still laughing.

'I am *not* a snob.' Sammi straightened his spine. 'I simply have good taste.'

Inside Kettles, they were seated at a table where Delia could take in the surroundings. 'I'm trying to work out where the basins were . . . and the wall of driers. All gone. You know, Jean Waters was a great teacher. Perms, cutting, colouring, and then all the styling and up-dos. She pushed me hard to get all the qualifications possible. If it wasn't for her . . . Well, I hope she knew how much I appreciated her. Loved her by the end. I can't believe I never came back to see her.'

'Once we escaped, it was hard to come back,' Sammi agreed. 'I don't know how my parents endured the racism.'

Delia frowned. 'I never knew about that.'

'Not often very overt but, looking back, there was always a level of anxiety living here: name calling, bullying – you know the sort of stuff. It's why my mum worked so hard to fit in. I couldn't wait to leave.'

Sammi's phone pinged, and he sighed. 'It's Sunday. Don't people rest?' He clicked on the new WhatsApp message. 'Oh, shit.'

'What's happened?'

'That Balham mansion flat I'm designing.'

'What's the problem?'

'My client is having a meltdown because the paint he ordered is the wrong colour, the decorator has scarpered, and the new windows haven't arrived. He wants me to come back tonight.'

Delia felt a flicker of panic. 'You can't leave me here.'

'But you heard what the doctor said,' Sammi replied. 'You need rest and elevations and ice and stuff. You don't need five hours on the motorway.'

'But Auntie Rose is expecting us.'

'She'll understand. I'll take you there, stay for a cuppa, get you settled. Then I really will have to go.'

Delia stared at him. 'What do you mean *get me settled*? She won't be prepared to put me up for the night.'

'Well, I'm not taking you back to London with me. You need rest. Rose is a tough old bird. She'll love the drama.'

'When will you be back?' Delia asked plaintively.

'I'll see how bad it is in Balham and keep you posted. But for now, let's order lunch.'

After a very quick lunch and a trip to M&S to pick up some supplies for Auntie Rose, Sammi and Delia headed for Kernow Autumn Retirement Community.

'Still can't believe she's not at Jago Fields,' said Sammi.

'Me neither.'

'Did she get a lot for it?'

'She went with her heart and sold it to a young couple who are embracing sustainable, green living: growing all they need and selling the surplus; knitting their own sandals and bringing the chickens in to warm their beaks next to the Aga.'

'Better than selling to a developer. You wouldn't want to see the old place bulldozed and twenty houses put up, would you?'

Delia shook her head. 'I suppose not.'

'But then to buy a brand-spanking-new flat in a purpose-built retirement village, cheek by jowl with a bunch of strangers!'

'I know, right! But hey, Auntie Rose spent her entire life at Jago Fields, with its ancient wiring, appalling plumbing, and patchy phone signal. Who can blame her?' Delia pointed ahead to a large sign that read: *Kernow Autumn – Your Future, Now*. 'Here we are.'

'Wow.' Sammi raised an eyebrow as he slowed the car and drove between a pair of wrought-iron gates. He gave a little giggle. 'I love it already.'

Between the fresh hedging, the drive curled its way towards a collection of faux traditional cottages and larger houses, each with a garden, some with an upstairs balcony, and all with parking spaces. In the middle of it all stood a sugar-pink mansion with budding wisteria clambering the walls and a name plate announcing *Kernow Manor*.

'She's at number 3. And that must be her new car,' said Delia, pointing at a sporty, bottle-green two-seater.

Sammi parked and turned the ignition off. 'Ah, you can take the girl out of Jago Fields, and apparently you can also take Jago Fields out of the girl!'

Delia managed to ease herself from the front seat, and Sammi carefully manoeuvred her crutches to a comfortable position. Together, they ventured forward to the imposing front door.

'Even grander than Wilder Hoo,' Sammi joked, turning the huge bronze doorknob, 'and no need for WD40.'

The door opened into a dazzling white hall with a polished marble floor. In its centre was a wrought-iron jardiniere filled with a magnificent display of blue hydrangeas.

'Artificial flowers,' Sammi whispered.

'And your problem is?' Delia whispered back.

'Nothing. It's perfect . . .'

To their left, a door with the number three on it flew open to reveal Auntie Rose. 'Ah, so I wasn't difficult to find after all?' She gave Delia a cool stare. 'I mean, I've only been here almost a year.'

Delia felt her cheeks red hot with shame. 'I'm really sorry, Auntie Rose. It . . . I . . .'

'Oh, come here, you silly maid.' Rose stretched her arms out and held her niece tight. 'You're here now and I've missed you . . .'

'I should have come sooner.' Delia spoke into her aunt's shoulder, breathing in the familiar scent in the wool of her cardigan.

Rose stroked Delia's back, soothing the both of them. 'That's all right. I understand.'

'You haven't changed at all.' Sammi stood back to admire her. 'Have you got a painting in the attic? You look younger every time I see you.'

Auntie Rose tutted. 'You always were a charmer. Now, both of you, come on in and let's get Delia settled. I want to hear about this ankle.'

Sammi hurried back to the car for the shopping and luggage, and by the time he caught up with them, Auntie Rose was in the sitting room, helping Delia into a seat.

Sammi's jaw dropped. He had been expecting to recognize all the furniture he had known since he and Delia were teenagers – perhaps arranged differently, but essentially the same well-loved, old-fashioned, chintzy but comfortable furnishings from Jago Fields.

But the room was dazzling, with sunlight streaming through a pair of glass doors offering a view of the courtyard garden, which was filled with pots of cream daffodils, pink tulips, purple alliums, and a haze of forget-me-nots.

Sammi was impressed. 'The colours of Renoir.' His gaze left the garden and concentrated on the room. 'The sofa! Raspberry velvet. So chic! And it's very roomy for a flat.'

Rose wagged a finger at him. 'Never call it a flat. It's an *apartment*. The sales lady was most insistent about that.'

'And she's quite right,' agreed Sammi.

Auntie Rose smiled. 'What about that painting? Inspired by the sofa and all my own work.'

'You painted that? It's amazing. The colours. So abstract!'

'I did it in Art Club. Are you comfortable, Delia, darling? I'll get you some pillows in a minute to keep your ankle up.'

Delia sighed into the deep cushions. 'You'll never get me out again. It's fabulous.'

Sammi was clocking the rest of the room. 'I looove the armchairs. Ticking stripe is so now!'

Rose beamed. 'Do you recognize them?'

Sammi shook his head – and then recognition dawned. 'Don't tell me they're those old chairs you had either side of the fire at Jago Fields?'

'The very same! Amazing what a bit of upholstery can do.'

He turned a full 360 degrees to take in the room. 'I love it, Rose. Light, bright, airy, and *so* on trend.'

Rose grinned. 'I knew you'd like it. Now, who wants a sandwich and a cuppa?'

Over their afternoon tea, Rose heard all about Delia's accident, and then Sammi broke the news that he needed to return to London.

'When?' Rose asked.

'Now.'

'But you can't take Delia. She must rest her ankle.' They both glanced back to the new sofa, where Delia was half-asleep, her leg propped up.

Sammi nodded. 'I was hoping you might be able to look after her for a couple of days?'

'Well, of course I can. But this client of yours – I don't like the sound of him. Has he been paying you properly?

Sammi twisted his mouth. 'Not yet.'

'Then he can wait. What on earth can you do at midnight on a Sunday? You can bet your arse he'll be tucked up in his bed by the time you get there. Go home to your flat. See to him in the morning.'

'She's right, Sammi,' Delia murmured sleepily from the depths of the sofa.

'And you' – Rose turned to her niece – 'are tired. Where are your painkillers? I always have the spare room made up in case. You're my first overnight visitor.'

'Really?' Delia looked like she might cry. 'That's so lovely.'

Rose smiled, then turned back to Sammi. 'I'll pack you some sandwiches and cake for the drive.'

'Thanks, Auntie Rose. You two look after yourselves while I'm away, and I'll be back for Delia before the week is out.'

Auntie Rose was itching to know why Delia had finally come back to Cornwall. Her niece had told her nothing, in keeping with the pattern of the past few years, but something was going on and she was determined to find out what. Perhaps Delia would finally tell her what exactly ended her marriage to Johnny. All she knew was what Delia had written in her last Christmas card, followed by a rather stilted, unrevealing phone call they'd had a few weeks later. Delia had put her walls up and Rose knew her well enough not to push too hard. Maybe this unexpected visit would be the time she'd finally get the full story.

'Can I get you a glass of wine, darling?' she asked, after Sammi had headed off. 'It'll help you sleep. You look tired.'

'I'm not tired.' Delia yawned. 'But a glass of wine sounds

very nice. Thank you for looking after me. I've missed you. I'm sorry I haven't been down for ages.'

Rose brushed the apology aside. 'Far too emotional for you, what with me leaving Jago Fields. All those memories of growing up. You didn't need that, and I know the past year must have been difficult what with . . . Well, I know you're busy. That's why you fell over and hurt your ankle. Your body is telling you to stop. I saw that article in the paper about you – one of the top ten hair stylists in London. Are you really booked up six months in advance?'

Delia gave a grimace. 'Not exactly,' she muttered.

When bedtime came, she helped Delia undress and get into bed.

'Comfy enough?' Rose asked. 'It's a new bed. Got it in the sale.'

'It's dreamy.' Delia smiled. 'Thank you, Auntie Rose.'

'No need to thank me.' Rose brushed her hand over her niece's, noticing the dark shadows under her eyes and the new lines in her face. 'Night night, darling. Call me if you need me.'

As Rose closed the door softly behind her, a picture of her sister floated into her mind and instantly felled her with grief. Christine should be here, looking after her daughter, listening to all her news. She would be fifty-nine now – in her prime. How proud she would be of Delia's success.

Chris had been only thirty-eight when she died – the age Delia was now. Everything was the wrong way round. How she wished Christine was here.

Rose let the kitchen sink take her weight as she sagged against it with relief. Delia was back in Cornwall at last. Her face, her mannerisms, her voice . . . so like Christine's.

She felt a sob rise in her chest as she finally gave way to the tears she'd kept in for long enough.

CHAPTER NINE

West Cornwall, twenty-one years ago

Delia and her aunt sat in the full, overheated waiting area of the A&E department. Christine was in a side room, but they had not been permitted to see her.

'Delia, darling, when did you last eat?' Auntie Rose asked. 'Shall we find a sandwich?'

'No, thank you.'

'Not a drink?'

'We should stay here in case Mum needs us.'

A wheeled stretcher bumped through the door from the ambulance arrivals bay, bringing in the chill night air.

Delia stared as a child patient was brought in, pale and crying with pain and fear. Her worried mother gripped her hand and hurried along beside her.

'It's all right, darling. We're here now.'

'It's hurting . . . Mummy, it's hurting me.' The little girl's voice was shrill.

She was pushed past the waiting many and sent through a set of double doors. Delia glimpsed a bright corridor with a row of curtained booths on either side. The little girl's crying faded as the doors closed.

A tall slender man in his thirties, wearing scrubs and a stethoscope around his neck, appeared in a doorway.

'Rose Jago?' he called.

'Oh yes.' Rose got up. 'That's us. Come on, Delia.'

They followed him, his trainers squeaking on the polished lino. He ushered them into a windowless room with tufty grey carpet tiles and offered a seat on a row of institutionally beige leatherette armchairs.

Delia began to shake.

'Are you cold?' the doctor asked her. 'Can I get you a hot drink?'

Rose replied, 'She's fine.

'I'm Dr Tyler, and I am one of the team looking after Christine.'

'How is my sister?' Rose asked directly.

Delia's small voice asked, 'Is Mum OK?'

'This is Delia, Christine's daughter,' Rose explained. 'She's just qualified as a junior hairstylist. Her mum doesn't know yet, but we'll have some good news to tell her when we see her, won't we?' Rose reached for Delia's hand and gave it a squeeze.

'Yes.' Delia's eyes felt too wide open, as though she had been staring for a long time. She wondered if she'd ever be able to close them again.

Dr Tyler crossed his long skinny legs and gave them each a tired smile. 'Christine had quite a bump to the head. I'm afraid the MRI shows an intracranial haematoma.'

'What does that mean?' Rose asked.

'It's a bleed in her brain which, as the blood builds up, causes pressure in her skull.'

'Right.' Rose was nodding her head vigorously. Delia noticed that she didn't seem able to shut her eyes either.

'So, to relieve the pressure, we are going to get her into surgery and drain the blood. Do you understand?'

'I think so. How do you do that?'

'We have to make a hole in her skull.'

Delia thought she might be sick. She didn't want to embarrass herself by throwing up in this room, but if she asked for directions to the ladies', she might miss some important information. So she just sat there, eyes wide, immobile.

Dr Tyler was still talking. 'We wouldn't be performing this surgery if your sister' – he looked to Delia – 'your mum, didn't need it. We have an excellent brain surgeon on call, the best, and she is getting Christine ready for surgery now.'

Unconsciously, Auntie Rose began to jiggle her right leg. A sure sign of anxiety. 'Can we see her first? Put her mind at rest. Let her know that we're right here waiting for her when she comes back.'

Dr Tyler rubbed his stubbly chin. 'Regretfully, no. We've had to put Christine into an induced coma, which gives her brain a rest and a chance to heal better.'

Leaning forward, Delia vomited onto the carpet tiles.

She refused to go home to change, in case her mum needed her. Instead, a kind nurse took her to have a shower and provided her with a set of scrubs. 'Not very glamorous, but they'll do you for now.'

When they returned to the room it, too, had been cleaned up, the artificial fragrance of medical soap and sanitizer hanging in the air.

Auntie Rose was trying to remain upbeat. 'Darling, look what they have left us.'

On a melamine tray were two green cups and saucers, a stainless-steel milk jug, a large teapot, some sachets of sugar, and several rounds of buttery white toast.

The horror of Delia's earlier accident and the kindness she had been shown overwhelmed her. 'Can I have a hug, Auntie Rose?'

Enveloped in her aunt's comforting arms, she began to weep. 'I'm so scared.'

Rose rocked her niece and kissed her hair. 'I know, my love. We're all a bit scared. But not Mum. And not the doctors. She's going to be fine.'

Hospitals at night take on a very different atmosphere. The lights are lowered, lending the corridors and rooms a gentle orange glow. Nurses move quietly from their station to their patients. Even the squeaks of their soft soled shoes seem muted. Voices are muffled, uniforms rustle, plastic aprons whisper as they are put on or torn off. Trolleys rattle, patients call out, and the hours crawl by.

When they had nibbled the toast and drunk the tea, an auxiliary nurse provided them with a duvet and pillow each.

'Push two of the chairs together and you can make a little bed,' she told them. 'It's not the Ritz, but if you can get a bit of sleep, it'll do you a lot of good.'

Delia had not expected to sleep at all, but she must have done, because she and Rose were woken by a knock on the door and the appearance of a tired-looking woman in scrubs.

'Sorry to wake you. I'm Carol, Christine's surgeon. Just came to say she's done very well. She's in recovery – not awake yet, but I wanted to tell you that the operation is done.'

Delia and Rose sat up, rubbing the sleep from their eyes.

'Thank goodness,' said Rose. 'Did you stop the bleeding?'

'We think so. We'll know more in the next day or so.'

'Can we see her?' Delia asked.

'Not yet. She's going to be sleeping for some time. If I were you, I'd go home and get some rest. Maybe take it in turns with other family members?'

'We're her only family,' Rose said stoutly. 'Just us. But perhaps we'll nip home and collect some bits she'll need. Wash bag. Clean nightie. Then we'll be back.'

Carol nodded. 'Of course.'

Suddenly, Auntie Rose's tears ran. 'And thank you very much.'

Delia felt her eyes well.

'It's my job.' Carol touched Rose's arm. 'But I will say this: Christine needs you both to be fit and strong in order for her to get fit and strong. No harm in you getting some rest and a good breakfast before you come back.'

Exhausted, Delia and Rose shuffled out to the carpark. The snow was glittering in the lights of the hospital entrance. It was a quarter to five in the morning.

By the time they arrived back at the hospital a few hours later, it was already too late.

Two days after Christine died, Rose came upstairs to find Delia rifling through Christine's desk in the small office.

'We have to find him,' she was saying. 'I can't believe she wouldn't have an address hidden here somewhere. A letter from him? A card? What's the password to her computer?'

'I don't know.' Rose blushed at her lie.

Delia stood in the centre of the room, panting in desperation. Her young, unlined, unblemished face was transfigured by fear, anger, and bald misery. 'We've got to find him, Auntie Rose.' She put her hands on her aunt's shoulders and shook her. 'We've got to. He has to know. He has to come home. We *need* him.'

With her niece so distressed, her voice broken by tears, Rose realized she had to tell her the truth.

All the years that Chris had had a chance to put things right, all the anxiety about how to tell Delia, the long and futile disagreements on how, when, and where they should tell her, had been a long circuitous journey to this moment.

'We can't find him,' Rose said gently.

'Yes, we can!'

'No, we can't, because . . . your mum made him up.' The words were out. They could never be unsaid or unheard.

'What?' It was as if Delia had been slapped. Her agitation halted in an instant.

'We . . . he . . .' Rose's legs gave way, and she collapsed into Chris's old office chair. 'I told her you should know, but . . .' She swallowed hard. 'I'm so sorry. I begged her. But she wouldn't listen, and now it's all too late. I am so, so sorry.'

'What are you saying?' Delia was staring at her. She looked almost as pale as when they'd been told that the surgery hadn't worked after all, that Christine was gone.

'We did it for the best.' Rose's voice cracked. 'We didn't want you to know. We made him up so that you had a father who was clever and brave, saving lives around the world, instead of . . .'

'But he sent me cards and letters.'

Rose nodded miserably. 'It was us. Your mum and I typed them. On the old Olivetti.' She gestured to the dusty relic sitting on the bookshelves.

Delia exploded. 'I don't believe you!' she screamed. 'It can't be true!' She aimed a kick at Rose's legs, then ran to her room, slamming the door behind her.

That evening, Rose was standing at the kitchen sink, washing up from the supper that Delia hadn't come down for. She stared through the window to the dark beyond. She was so angry with her sister. Angry that she hadn't worn her helmet. Angry that she had died. Angry that she had left them. Angry that it had been up to Rose to expose that dirty, ridiculous lie.

She washed the last plate and laid it upside down on the drainer, before tipping the dirty water from the bowl and letting it gurgle its way down the plughole. She pulled off her rubber gloves and draped them over the taps.

She never wanted to leave the house again.

Wrapping her arms around herself, she rocked forwards and backwards, bending her face to the floor to allow the tears to drip on the tiles rather than down her face. No one must see her weakness. She had to be strong now, to help Delia out of this painful mess that she had helped to perpetuate.

Feeling guilty and wretched, Rose opened the fridge and took out the milk. Delia liked hot chocolate, and this might tempt her to at least open her bedroom door. She poured the milk into a pan and put it on the Aga to simmer, then filled the large kettle.

Tea.

What would the British do without it?

She flinched at a sudden sharp knock at the back door.

Who the hell was out there? No one, no friend or neighbour, would be out on a cold February night like this.

A man's voice, loud and dreadfully familiar, was speaking close to the door. 'Rose? Open up. I know you're there. I saw you through the window.'

She froze. She'd wanted curtains at the bloody window above the sink for years, but there was always something else to spend money on. The thought of anyone out there watching her made her shudder. And how had she not heard the latch of the gate?

'Rose!' The voice was aggressive. 'Come on. Open the door.'

How bloody dare he. Especially now, after all the hurt he'd brought to her family. The heartless abandonment when he knew Christine was pregnant.

Fury flushed her veins and gave her the strength of ten men as she unbolted the back door to reveal him.

He looked old. The blue eyes that once sparkled were flat, the cheeky smile gone, his blond curls grey and sparse.

Rose hissed, 'What the hell are you doing here, Gary?'

'Well, that's a nice welcome.'

'Piss off back to St Ives.' She moved to slam the door in his face, but he stuck his boot in the way.

'I don't live in St Ives anymore. Didn't you hear? My old father-in-law died and left the farm to his daughter. Remember? Beauty of a farm. Not ten miles from here. You could say I landed on my bum in butter.' He sniggered. 'A pretty wife, a profitable farm, and two handsome sons any man could be proud of. I reckon I had a lucky escape with your sister.'

Rose felt the rage build inside her. 'No. It was Christine and Cordelia who had the lucky escape.'

'You think so?' He scoffed and tried to shoulder his way in, but she blocked the way. 'Don't be like that, Rose.'

'Get out before I kill you.'

He laughed. 'Not still jealous, are you? Get over yourself.'

She smelt the whisky fumes on his breath, raised her right hand and swung it towards his cheek, wanting to slap the grotesque smirk down his throat, but he caught her wrist and twisted it.

'I'm here to tell you that I'll be coming to Christine's funeral. Pay my respects. Everyone down here will be there. And me, just an old friend of the family. It'll look odd if I'm not there. I'll be with my wife and my boys. I thought I'd better let you know. Out of decency. I don't want any trouble.'

'*Decency?* You don't know the meaning of the word. Let go of me,' she growled.

He laughed again and held her wrist tighter. 'I'm thinking of the girl. Poor cow. She wouldn't want to hear that I could've had the pick of either of you sisters.'

'If you come near Delia, I swear I'll—'

'You'll what? Shoot me? Run me over with the quad bike?' He laughed again. 'I don't suppose it's working too well at the moment after Christine's little crash.'

Rose rolled her tongue around the inside of her mouth, gathered a ball of saliva, and spat.

He was quick, though, turning his face before it landed. 'Calm down, little tiger. I'll keep my mouth shut if you keep yours shut. Unless, of course . . .' He let go of her wrist, grabbed her waist and parted his wet lips.

She gave herself no time to think. The milk had reached boiling point and was spilling over, hissing as it hit the Aga hotplate. She took two steps towards it, picked it up, and swung the red-hot pan and its contents straight at him.

The metal caught his brow. The steaming milk was in his eyes.

'Get OUT. GET OUT!' she bellowed.

Blindly, he stepped back as she swung the pan, ready to hit him again.

'GET OUT!'

'You mad old bitch.' He was turning, trying to get his balance. 'I should never have touched either of you. You and that sister of yours needed locking up years ago.'

Rose pitched the empty pan into the dark after him, satisfied when she heard an angry yell of pain.

Diving back into the kitchen, she reached for the old-fashioned kettle that had begun to sing.

Blinded by the hot milk, he was easy to catch up with. The path was glittering with frost, and he was wildly slipping with every step.

Rose was soon within reach of him. 'Oh yes, I'm mad,' she said, showing him the steaming kettle. 'Mad enough to boil your todger until it looks like a poached cocktail sausage, and there won't be a jury in the land who will convict me.' She raised the kettle with a smile. 'Are you ready?'

He grasped the latch of the gate, scrabbling in his pockets for the keys to his Range Rover.

Rose was less than two metres from him now.

His eyes were streaming, a lump was forming on his brow, and his hands were shaking as he desperately fumbled with the key fob. The moment the locks were open, he wrenched the driver's door open and heaved himself into the seat.

'Are you scared of me?' Rose was now standing in front of the car bonnet. She felt a wild, powerful fury rushing through her. 'When I tell the judge what you did to my sister . . .' She lifted the kettle higher, watching as he covered his face with both arms and ducked behind the steering wheel, whimpering.

Seventeen years of rocket-fuelled rage coursed through Rose now. She flung the hot, heavy kettle at the glass, watching as it bounced off, leaving a small dent and an expensive crack in the windscreen.

'Run, rabbit, run! You spineless piece of human junk!' She was screaming now.

Terrified, he slammed into reverse, and as his car spun away, Rose shouted after him, laughing wildly and waving a double fisted V sign.

As his tail-lights disappeared in the lane, her laughter turned to deep, unstoppable sobs.

'I hate you!' she shouted, and taking a deep breath, she shouted it again. 'I HATE YOU!'

Then, as quickly as the rage had come, it was spent.

She had nothing left but to whisper into the darkness, 'I hate you. I hate you. I hate you.'

'Auntie Rose?'

She looked up to see Delia calling from the back door, peering into the night.

'Auntie Rose? Are you OK?'

Rose picked up the empty kettle from where it lay on the road and walked slowly back to the house, wiping her tears and her nose on her apron.

'What's going on?' Delia asked.

'There was a fox, my love. Just a fox. I scared him off. Your mum would never forgive me if I hadn't.'

She put an arm around her niece's shoulders. 'I made sausage and mash for supper. I put it in the fridge for tomorrow, but I can heat it up if you'd like? And how about a nice mug of hot chocolate?'

CHAPTER TEN

Bozinjal, West Cornwall, twenty-one years ago

When the doorbell rang the week after her mother's funeral, Delia ignored it. She was lying on the sofa, from which she hadn't moved for the last few days, staring sightlessly at the television.

The funeral itself had been bright, cold, and awful, the pews filled with sympathetic faces that Delia hadn't wanted to see. She and Rose had managed little nods and smiles in response to condolences, but all she had been able to think of was the fact that her mum was gone for good.

The bell rang again. She reached for the remote and increased the volume, but the bell kept ringing.

She lifted her head to listen for Auntie Rose coming down the stairs.

There was nothing.

Using a swear word she had recently made a favourite, she threw the duvet from her pyjama-clad legs and shouted, 'I'm coming.'

Sammi was on the doorstep. 'Hey.'

'Oh. It's you.' Delia turned away and returned to the lounge, leaving Sammi to walk in, close the door, and follow her.

He looked shocked by her appearance and the unpleasant body odour that no doubt trailed behind her. Delia didn't care. She was wrapping herself back into her sofa nest, surrounded by half-eaten packets of biscuits and empty bags of crisps.

'What have you been up to?' he asked as he moved a pile of magazines and newspapers from a nearby armchair.

'Having a great time. Partying. Seeing friends. You know.' She gave him a filthy look. 'Durr.'

'Oh, very good. I thought I was King of Sarcasm.'

She rolled her eyes. 'Why are you here, Sammi?'

'Umm. Thought you might like to come for a walk? You know, grab some fresh air.'

'No.'

'OK.'

Delia didn't take her eyes from the television. '*What?*'

'Harriet and I miss you. She would have come, but she's working.'

'Good for her.'

'She's covering for you in the salon.' When Delia didn't respond, he added, 'Jean has had to pass some of your clients to her.'

There was a small pull at the corner of Delia's lips. 'Bully for her.'

'Yeah, my mum said that Jean is going to try to fast track Hattie's Level 2 in case you don't come back. To sort of see if she could ever be as good as you.'

'Yeah?' Delia picked up the remote control and began channel hopping, refusing to rise to the bait. 'Great.'

'Well, you know where I am if you need anything,' said Sammi, getting to his feet.

She looked round. 'Where are you going?'

'To meet Hattie off the bus. We're going out tonight.'

'Where to?'

'Dunno. Grab something to eat. Maybe go bowling or to the cinema.'

'Oh.'

'We thought you might like to come, too.' He paused. 'But I can see you're not up for—'

'Wait.'

Sammi turned. '*Are* you up for it?'

She stared at him. 'I dunno.'

'Hey.' He sat down next to her, careful not to sit on her legs. 'Talk to me.'

'Nothing to say.'

'I'm sure there's lots of things you want to talk about.'

Delia stared at him. 'Like what? Like my mum is dead?'

'That's a good start.'

'Why are you going out with Hattie tonight?'

'She asked me.'

'You're not going to start being boyfriend–girlfriend are you?'

'*Definitely* not. She's not my type. Anything else you want to talk about?'

'Auntie Rose and I aren't really speaking.'

'OK. Let's start there.'

Delia took a deep breath. 'She and Mum lied to me.'

'What about?'

'My dad.' She sniffed and wiped her nose on the sleeve of her sweatshirt.

'Have you heard from him?'

'Well, no, because it's hard to hear from someone who your mum and auntie made up, isn't it?'

Sammi was frowning. 'What?'

'You know I always said my dad was doing important stuff over the other side of the world? Well, it was just a lie.' Swollen tears began to spill from her leaden eyes and past her chin, finally dropping onto her grubby top. 'They made it all up.'

Sammi shook his head in confusion. 'But his Christmas cards? He was in East Africa, wasn't he?'

'Mum and Auntie Rose sent them. I feel so stupid that I never worked it out. All the bloody cards had English stamps on, and Mum said they were posted by friends of his on leave, but if I'd really thought about it – if I'd *wanted* to think about it . . .'

'I'm so sorry,' Sammi said gently. 'But then . . . who is your dad?'

'Auntie Rose won't tell me. I think he might be someone in the village. He came to the house, I think, just before the funeral. I heard Auntie Rose shouting, and I came downstairs to see what was going on. I didn't see his face, but I heard him. He wanted to go to the funeral, and he was saying horrible things. I think Mum and Auntie Rose both kind of . . .' Her whole face squashed into revulsion. 'He was saying stuff like they had both been his girlfriend . . . Auntie Rose was so angry. I think she hit him. She followed him out the gate, and when he was trying to get into his car, she threw the kettle at the windscreen, and I was so scared . . . When she came back, she told me she'd seen a fox. She's good at lying.'

Delia knew her face must be a mess of tears and snot, and sure enough, Sammi handed her his pocket handkerchief.

'Thank you.' She wiped her eyes, then blew her nose. 'I just feel so confused and angry and upset, and I miss Mum so much, and I want to ask her why she made a dad up and never told me about the real one – who by the way I *hate*.'

'Then I hate him, too.'

Delia felt more tears well in her eyes. 'Thank you.'

'But we don't hate your mum?'

'I suppose not,' she murmured.

'Would you like a hug?'

'Yes please.' Delia clung to him tightly. 'I miss Mum so much. Why didn't they tell me the truth?'

'I guess they were scared to,' Sammi said soothingly.

'I've been so horrid to Auntie Rose.'

'She won't mind. She understands.'

'I know.' Delia sniffed. 'But just when she needs me to be kind, I'm . . .' Her voice broke again. 'I've been horrible to her.'

After Chris died, Rose swore that she would never let Delia down, even though the path in the early days of grief was rocky to say the least.

For Rose's part, she wouldn't have minded Delia's destructive moods – a natural reaction to losing her mum and a dad who had never existed. Rose's stomach clenched even now with anger at Christine for having never told Delia the truth. Her sister had left Rose to deal with this fallout and carry the shame of the awful lie.

If only she could get through to Delia, get her to talk, share her feelings. But Rose was exhausted by it all and unable to fight the door-slamming and aggression.

Steeped in her own wretchedness, the simple act of getting up, dressed, running the house, and managing the market stall was enough for Rose. A belief in the power of sheer hard work had seen her and Chris through the shock of Chris's pregnancy and the dark days of losing their parents, but now, on her own, Rose began to dread her market days.

Her old clientele was changing. She had always looked forward to the familiar gossiping, shared aches and pains, and long chats about the weather, family news or the government of the day. But her regular customers were growing older, and their trips to market were less frequent. The Jago Fields' stall still thrived, but now it was attracting young, upwardly mobile families, looking for dairy-free organic butter, sugar-free cakes, organic, artisan moisturizers, and wellness bath oils.

Rose didn't have those, but she did have Jago Fields' free-range eggs, grass-fed meat, homemade pasties, and bunches of seasonal flowers.

Nonetheless, something imperceptible had altered. These newcomers did not have the same sense of shared history that had been tangible amongst the old patrons.

In truth, Rose didn't know what was making her the most unhappy: work or Delia.

After several miserable months, she made an appointment to see her old doctor, Dr Mary, a woman past retirement age but so revered by all in the village that she had accepted she would have to die in harness.

'Good to see you, Rose. Sit down. How are doing without Christine?'

'Fine, really.'

Doctor Mary was not to be fobbed off. 'You look as if you've lost a bit of weight. How are you sleeping?' she asked.

'Oh, you know, some nights better than others.'

'When was the last time you enjoyed yourself? Had a laugh?

'Well, erm . . . there hasn't been too much to laugh about.'

'When was the last time you cried?'

Rose hid the constriction in her throat. 'Erm . . . sorry.' She coughed, but it wasn't helping; her throat was tight, and menacing tears were blurring her vision.

'Ah.' The doctor smiled at Rose and took her hand. 'Tell me all about it.'

Rose's face crumpled. 'Don't be nice to me . . . I'm all right really.'

'You can't kid me, Rose. You're suffering.'

And that did it. The floodgates opened, and Rose poured it all out.

A pile of tissues later, Dr Mary began by suggesting a prescription for something to help her sleep.

Rose bridled. 'I don't want that.'

'It would be just a bridge over troubled water, to get you back into a sleep rhythm, and I think you should have something else to help lift your mood. One a day for a couple of weeks. That's all, and then come back to see me.'

Rose shook her head. 'No. I don't believe in taking pills.'

Dr Mary sat back in her chair and looked steadily at her patient. 'Let me put it this way: if Delia, your niece, came in here telling me that she wasn't sleeping very well or enjoying life the way she should, don't you think it would be a dereliction of my duty not to help her, to give her a little medication to help see the wood for the trees? Hmm?'

'She's different.'

'She really isn't.'

Suddenly, the penny dropped. 'Are you saying Delia is on these pills?'

'Patient confidentiality, I'm afraid,' replied Dr Mary. 'Why don't you have a chat with her tonight . . . ask her the same questions I asked you. I think you may find a way to open her up. Start a conversation.'

It took a couple of weeks for Rose to find the right moment. She wanted to talk, of course, but the thought of opening an emotional can of worms was overwhelming. How would she even start the conversation? Communicating with a girl who had become the spikiest of all cacti was a mountain too high.

Then one day, Rose arrived home, after another shattering

day in Penzance, to hear thumping rock music coming from Delia's bedroom.

She was too tired to deal with her niece, so she emptied the Landy and did all the things that needed doing before mounting the stairs. Hovering on the landing, she reached out for Delia's door handle. The music – if you could call it that – was blessedly coming to its deafening conclusion, and in the silence, she heard the unmistakable sound of Delia crying.

She put her hand on the closed door and began. 'Cordelia?'

'What?'

'Darling, it's me, Auntie Rose.'

'Yes. Obviously. What do you want?'

'I want to talk to you.'

'What about?'

'We both know what about. We can't go on like this, my love.'

There was a faint rustling but no answer.

'I'm not going away until we talk to each other properly.' Rose's patience was worn thin. 'Open this door right now, Cordelia. I'm not taking any more of this self-pity. You think you win the prize for the most miserable person in this house? How do you think I feel? Chris and I put you first in everything we did, but your mum was only human. *I* am only human. We were trying to protect you by inventing a dad you would be proud of. We messed that up. And I can't begin to express how wretched I feel about that. Christine and I argued so many times about when to tell you the truth. But she didn't want you to know that your real dad broke her heart. He didn't want her, and this is so hard to say, but the truth, however painful, has to be faced: he didn't want to be a father to you.' Rose stopped. She was shaking. 'Delia. Please, please, open the door.'

She heard the key turning in the lock. The door opened slowly, until Delia was revealed.

A sob caught in Rose's throat. 'Oh darling.'

'I'm sorry, Auntie Rose.'

'Whatever for?'

'Being horrible.'

Rose opened her arms, and as Delia stepped into the embrace, Rose thought she might never let go.

They stood together, clasped in warmth and love and tears.

'It hurt me so much, Auntie Rose.'

'I know my, love. I know.'

'Are you going to tell me who my real dad is? Was?'

'Do you want to know?'

'No. Yes. I don't know.'

'Shall I tell you what happened, without saying his name?'

'Yes please.'

'OK.' They let go of each other. 'Let's go downstairs and talk over a cup of tea.'

Aunt and niece settled at the old kitchen table surrounded by the pots, pans, kettle, and ornaments that had been so much a part of Christine. It was dusk. A blackbird was calling somewhere from the garden, and the kitchen lamp reflected its yellow light onto the darkening window.

Rose stirred a spoonful of sugar into her tea. 'If I go too far and you want me to stop, just say so.'

Delia nodded. 'OK.'

Rose took a deep breath. 'When I turned twenty-one, I wanted a big party. It was the Eighties, and the music was the best. Still is.'

Delia's lip curled with a wry smile. 'Don't I know it. I was brainwashed by you and Mum singing along to "West End Girls" all the time. You always got the words wrong.'

Auntie Rose managed a small laugh. 'Good memories.'

'Yeah.'

'Well, I did get my party in the end. Mum and Dad, your granny and grandpop, rigged up a small tent down by the pond, with fairy lights strung in the hedges. It was a great party. Dad connected a speaker to the music system so we could play our records. Mum and Christine were in charge of the barbecue. It was such a warm night – the benefits of an August birthday.'

Delia smiled. 'Lucky you.'

'Oh now, don't get all woebegone. March is a lovely month, and I thought you liked your parties walking in the woods and building camps and cooking sausages on the fire?'

'Of course I did.'

'They were the sort of parties that your mum and I had growing up, so it was a bit of a surprise to my parents when I wanted a girly party,' said Auntie Rose. 'Anyway, the party was amazing until a couple of the boys got so drunk they started a fight. Grandpop got a black eye when he tried to break it up. From that moment on, parties at Jago Fields were banned. So, three years later, when your mum turned twenty-one, all ideas of a party were off the table.'

'Poor Mum. What did you do?'

'Your mum and I decided to have a night out at the clubs everyone raved about in St Ives. We didn't tell our parents where we were going, just said we were having dinner with a friend.'

Rose closed her hands around her mug of tea as she remembered.

As they climbed out of the taxi, the muffled beat of music coming from the brightly lit building intoxicated them.

The narrow, cobbled street was filling up with groups of young men laughing and smoking. Hoping to get lucky. And coatless girls giggled as the boys eyed them up.

Two bouncers on the door took their tickets and stamped their hands. 'Don't wash those off. You'll need them to get back in.'

The dancefloor was small and heaving.

'Come on, Rose!' Christine dragged her sister into the melee and began to dance.

It wasn't long before Gary made his move. What he lacked in height, he made up for in muscle and magnetism. His bright-blue eyes and cheeky grin lit up as he jostled Rose out of his way. Her sixth sense warned her that he was trouble, and anxiety roiled in her stomach.

What would her father say if he knew they had lied? Christine might be twenty-one and officially an adult, but their parents still viewed her as the baby of the family. Rose, at twenty-four, was meant to be the responsible one, and she had brought Chris to a club where they knew nobody and nobody knew them.

The DJ didn't call the last dance until 2 a.m., by which time Gary and Chris had been dancing together all night.

'Let's end on an oldie but a goodie: here is 10cc's "I'm Not in Love".'

Rose watched Gary's hands wandering across her sister's body and saw Chris's expression of sheer ecstasy. Feeling sick, Rose nipped to the loo, ready to make a quick escape with Chris when the record finished.

When she came back, the floor was empty, the bright lights were on, and there was no sign of Chris or Gary.

Rose waited outside in the cold. Her watch crawled miserably past five minutes, then ten, then twenty-five until, at last, Christine reappeared, laughing and giggling, entwined in Gary's beefy body.

Rose wanted to hit him. 'Where on earth have you been?'

Rose stopped. She had already said too much. Delia was listening with an increasingly pale face and anxious eyes.

'Where *had* they been?' Delia asked. 'Please tell me, or I'll think the worst.'

Rose rubbed a hand over her forehead, blowing out a long breath. 'It's not great. They'd been down on the beach. Gary called it "their little birthday party for two".'

Rose remembered the way he had said it, how his blue eyes had focused on her. 'If you want, you could join us next time?' The corners of his mouth had twitched into an innocent grin. 'Could be a lot of fun.'

She swallowed the words now. She never wanted Delia to hear them, or how she and Christine had never told their parents about that night, or the many other nights Christine secretly met Gary, using Rose as her reluctant alibi. There were so many other things she knew she couldn't share with Delia, like the night she'd found out that Christine was pregnant, that Gary had abandoned her.

They spent a long tearful night whispering in Chris's bedroom, the furthest room away from their parents, where they were less likely to be overheard. 'Have you taken a test?'

Chris nodded miserably.

'How far along are you?'

'I've missed two periods.'

'Why didn't you tell me sooner? You shouldn't keep this all to yourself.'

'I thought it might be all right . . . I thought he might . . . you know, be pleased, but . . .'

'Oh, Chris, what are you going to do? Do you want to keep it?'

'No. Yes. I don't know. Yes . . . I do.'

'What about Mum and Dad? We'll have to tell them.'

Chris was trembling. 'They're going to be so angry . . . Do you think they'll throw me out? If I can't work on the farm, I'll have to find another job. I could go to Plymouth. There'll be work there.'

'I'll come with you. You won't be able to work once the baby arrives.'

'I'll be OK as long as the baby is OK. Oh, Rose.' Chris put her head in her hands and began to sob again. 'What will I do?'

'You could put it up for adoption?'

'Never. This is *my* baby.'

'And are you sure that Gary . . . won't stand by you? I mean, it's a shock for him. Maybe, once he's got used to the idea . . .'

Chris shook her head. 'He told me that if I said anything to anyone, he'd deny it was his, and then he said . . .' Chris could barely get the words out. '. . . then he said maybe it wasn't his. That he'd always been careful and that I'd been cheating on him . . . but . . .' More wracking sobs. '. . . He knows he's the only man I've been with. I love him, and I thought he loved me . . . but . . . He hasn't spoken to me since. I've been such a fool . . .'

'Oh, Chris.' Rose put her arms around her little sister.

The sound of footsteps on the landing made them freeze. 'Shush . . .'

Chris's eyes frantically scanned Rose's face as they listened. 'It's just Dad having a pee,' Rose whispered.

The girls listened, terrified to move, as they heard the knock of the toilet seat on the china cistern as he lifted the lid, then, a few seconds later, the flush, followed by his footsteps returning to the landing.

Instead of heading to his room, they stopped outside their room. 'Girls? Are you OK?'

The girls watched as the door handle turned and their father tentatively stuck his head round the door. 'Come on, time for lights out . . .' He stopped when he saw the faces of his daughters: Chris pale and tearstained, Rose tense and protective.

The two sisters exchanged glances as they realized they'd have to tell him the truth.

Rose was lost in thought, but Delia was still watching her. 'So, I was conceived on the beach? A one-night stand?'

'Not quite. They went out together for a while, but it turned out he was seeing someone else as well. After Chris told him about you . . . he broke things off.'

'Poor Mum. How did Granny and Grandpop take the news?'

'Oh, they took it all in their stride, loved you from day dot. Like we all did. You made our family perfect.'

'Did he ever come to see me? When I was born?'

Rose had been hoping she wouldn't be asked this question, but here it was. 'No, my love. He didn't. By then, he was engaged to the other girl he'd been seeing. She was pregnant, too.'

Delia's eyes widened. 'I have a half sibling?'

'You have two half-brothers.'

The silence between them reverberated with the horror of Rose's words. She wondered what was going through Delia's mind. The poor girl was only seventeen. She had a future in hairdressing ahead of her if she wanted it, a job she could travel the world with. Christine had wanted Delia to be free to choose her own life; she'd said it often enough to Rose.

'I don't want her ever to feel she's tied to Jago Fields like we are,' Chris had said. 'I want her to be independent – financially and emotionally.'

'Unlike us,' Rose had answered.

'Yes. Unlike us.'

Now, Rose picked up her cold tea mug and took it to the sink. Gary was nothing but a weak bully. One day she would make him pay for his cowardice.

What she would never do was tell Delia that Gary had inherited his father-in-law's farm on the other side of Sennen, not ten miles from Bozinjal. Hundreds of acres of prime farmland had fallen into his lap, just like that. He had money, his wife and two boys, but he wasn't liked very much. He had a reputation, and it wasn't pleasant.

She thought back to the night before the funeral and the fear in his eyes when she'd swung the boiling kettle at him.

'Auntie Rose?' Delia was standing behind her.

'Yes, my darling?'

'Thank you for telling me. I never want to know that man.'

Rose's chin fell to her chest with relief. She turned to face Delia. 'I'm glad.'

'Mum didn't deserve him,' Delia said firmly, 'and he doesn't deserve us.'

CHAPTER ELEVEN

Kernow Autumn, April, present day

Rose stood in her new kitchen, ruminating over Delia's surprise visit. Rose was nobody's fool. She knew there was a reason why her niece had suddenly landed on her doorstep, and it wasn't just because she'd sprained her ankle. For the last few years, Delia had had little time for her aunt, always citing work, or saying she was too tired to make the long journey from London to Cornwall. Either that, or Johnny had made plans for her – plans that wouldn't include Rose. She knew Delia's husband had put a wedge between her and her niece. He had been the one who made sure Rose was kept out of their lives. Since the news late last year that Delia and Johnny were getting divorced, she'd hoped to see more of Delia, but there had only been more silence.

When Delia had phoned out of the blue yesterday to say she was on her way, Rose had been surprised, not to mention miffed. If Sammi hadn't been with her, she'd have given Delia a more frosty reception. But it was hard to be frosty with someone she loved so much.

What had happened to their closeness of old? The Delia with whom she had shared so much?

Rose had been there when Delia was born. When she had taken her first steps, said her first words, first paddled in the sea. Been with her when Chris had died.

Now, having Delia under the same roof again, was everything Rose had been waiting for.

She let Delia sleep in, and when she finally heard sounds of movement from the spare room, she filled the kettle and laid a late breakfast tray to take to Delia in bed. Yes, she probably didn't deserve it, but if Rose was going to get the real reason why Delia was here out of her, it was going to be with sugar, not vinegar.

'You slept all right, did you, darling?' Auntie Rose put the tray on Delia's bedside table.

'Like a log.' Delia stretched herself. 'Do I smell a bacon sandwich?'

'You do. How's your ankle?'

'Feeling better.' She stuck her foot out from under the duvet. 'How does it look?'

'Swelling has gone down quite a bit, but the bruise looks rather dramatic. Oh, and by the way' – Rose reached under the bed – 'I found a couple of chaps who miss you. Here.' She passed Delia a box. 'Open it.'

Delia pulled back the lip to reveal her two old teddy bears. 'Big Nicky and Little Nicky.' She put them to her nose and inhaled. 'They smell just the same. You've kept them all this time?'

'They insisted.'

'Can I take them back to London with me?'

'I think they'd like that. But before that we have a lot of catching up to do, don't we?'

Delia kept her eyes on the teddies. 'Umm, yeah.'

'Let's start with the real reason you're in Cornwall right now. What's going on?'

Delia finally looked up. 'Well, to start with . . . I'm on sick leave.'

Rose's eyes widened in fear. 'Sick leave? What for, my love?'

'No, no, nothing too awful. I'm not going to die or anything. I'm just . . . a bit depressed.'

Rose eyed her niece with pursed lips and a frown. 'I see. How long have you been written off for?'

'Erm, six months.'

Rose felt a stirring of sympathy and worry. 'That's not *a bit* depressed, is it?'

Delia shook her head, unwanted tears building. 'No.'

Rose's intuition was always reliable, and whatever Delia was going to tell her, she was pretty sure Johnny was at the root of it. 'Tell me everything.'

Delia took a deep breath. 'The reason I'm not at work is because I did something awful and I might not be able to go back.'

Rose narrowed her eyes. 'How long ago was this?'

'Three weeks.'

'Three weeks! What happened?'

'Well, I haven't been feeling myself . . . since the separation. I've been so tired all the time. Honestly, Auntie Rose, the salon is so busy. Full on. I love it, of course, but . . .' She took a sip of her tea and sighed. 'Three weeks ago, I had an important client coming in and she was very late, which always has a horrible knock-on effect with the rest of the day's appointments. It made me so cross, because she's *always* late and she never apologizes and then, she was just awful to my junior, who's so sweet, so I whipped the gown off her and shouted at her.

'Everybody heard me, and there she was with her hair dripping wet, shouting back, and I just told her to get out and never come back.'

'Well done,' said Rose, impressed. 'You have nothing to be ashamed of – you were standing up for your junior.'

Delia shook her head. 'I lost my rag. I shouldn't have. But it was like a storm in my head that had been brewing, and it just went off. *Bang.* Someone took hold of me and walked me to the staff room, and I couldn't stop crying. I was sent home.'

Rose folded her hands on her lap, sat back, and said, 'How did you get signed off for six months?'

'My boss, David, insisted I went to his private doctor . . . I was diagnosed with reactive depression.'

'Meaning?'

'It's the sort that happens after things like divorce, bereavement . . .'

'Uh-huh.' Rose nodded, unsurprised. 'And the treatment?'

'Rest, avoid stress, and a prescription for anti-depressants.'

'You're taking them, I hope?'

'Yes.'

'OK. Good. Now, would you please tell me what really brings you back to Cornwall?'

Delia blew out her cheeks. 'How come you always know there's something else?' She glanced at her aunt. 'It's Wilder Hoo.'

Rose frowned in confusion.

'Wilder Hoo,' Delia repeated. 'Johnny's – his parents' place.'

Her aunt's gaze was steady. 'But I thought you and Johnny were over and done with? That's what your Christmas card said.'

Delia sighed. 'A month ago, I got some news. Johnny is . . . he's died. And he's left me the house.'

CHAPTER TWELVE

Bozinjal, West Cornwall, sixteen years ago

Delia had been working at Jean's ever since her mum died. She was a Cornish girl through and through, but against many odds, she proved to possess a rare talent as an apprentice hairdresser. Her scissors were a magic wand, her cutting prefectly tailored to the client's personality.

She had *It*, whatever *It* was.

Two or three times she had turned down offers from rival local salons wanting to poach her. She loved her clients, and she loved living with Auntie Rose at Jago Fields. It was where she felt close to her mum.

Meanwhile, Sammi was building up his interior design business. Second homeowners from up country, with more money than style, were eager to engage him. They all wanted their holiday homes to be kitted out in the beach-chic look they craved. Word of mouth was spreading fast.

Harriet had left Just Jean to take a BSC in Secretarial Administration, a course incorporating IT, accounting, Human Resources, and professional development.

'How *could* you?' Sammi had asked. 'A lifetime in a dull office?'

Harriet had grinned. 'I'm not as creative as you and Delia. Besides, offices usually attract ambitious men who are climbing the greasy pole of success and have lots of money. I may have to test-drive a few before I find Mr Right. But when I do, I'll settle down to life in a beautiful home with a husband who spoils me with extravagant holidays and gifts.'

'And I thought you said you weren't creative?' Delia laughed.

Then, one day, when Delia was taking her lunch break in the staff room, a guilty looking Jean joined her.

'I've done something rather naughty, Delia.'

'You forgot to order the biscuits?'

'Oh bugger, yes, but it's not that.' She hesitated, wanting to say what she had to say as clearly as possible. 'I have got you a four-week try-out with Gilson's of Chelsea.'

Delia's mouth opened in astonishment. 'The David Gilson?'

'Yes. We trained together in Truro but he was always destined for bigger things than me. Anyway, we still keep in touch and he's looking to recruit new young talent and I told him about you.'

'*What?*'

'Don't be cross with me. I know you love being here in Bozinjal, and I love having you, but . . . you deserve to shine in London.'

Delia rubbed her forehead. 'Is this a joke?'

'Listen, Delia. You have the chance to demonstrate how good you are in one of London's best salons.' She sighed and spelt it out. 'David Gilson of Gilson's of Chelsea wants to see you.'

'But I've never been to London.'

'Well, it's about time you went.'

'But Auntie Rose—'

Jean shushed her. 'She knows all about it. I told her a couple of days ago.'

Delia felt strangely angry. Manipulated. ' I don't want to go to London. I'm happy here.'

'It's only four weeks,' said Jean. 'If you don't like London, come home when it's over. But try it – for me. You are so talented. Please don't waste your potential.'

Delia swallowed, thinking hard. It was a lot to take in.

Jean handed her a Post-it note with a phone number on it. 'David's private number. He's waiting for you to call him.'

'But . . . what would I even say?'

Jean clicked her tongue. 'How about, hello, Mr Gilson, it's Delia Jago. He's man of many words and will tell you all you need to know without you asking. You've got twenty minutes before your next client, so do it now.'

In the privacy of the staffroom, Delia took a deep breath and dialled the number.

'Hello, David Gilson speaking.'

'Hello, Mr Gilson, I'm Delia Ja—'

'Oh, hello, darling. Now listen. I want you to come and do four weeks with me next month, and if you're as good as darling Jean tells me, I might offer you a job at the end of it. If not, you can go home, and we won't speak about it again. All right?'

Delia found herself smiling.

One month later, she had accepted a permanent job as a stylist at Gilson's of Chelsea.

*

In that first year, Delia made it home only twice, once for Rose's birthday and then for Christmas. London was getting in her blood, and her reputation was growing.

Within another year, Sammi had moved to London, too, lured by clients who now needed the Sammi Hashmi home styling in their city homes.

Six months after his arrival, Harriet, still single and missing her friends with more money and bigger ideas, begged Sammi and Delia to find her a reason to come to London, too.

Her timing was excellent. There was a position going as receptionist at Gilson's, after the recent incumbent had helped herself to the cash in the till.

Harriet passed the interview easily. David loved her ebullient charm. She hadn't forgotten Jean Waters's golden rules of old, meaning that every client was welcomed with a warm smile, and exactly the right tea or coffee, magazine or newspaper.

Their twenties flew by in a blur of work, fun, and friendship. As Delia's star rose, Harriet took on the task of finding a larger flat for them to share and surpassed herself by acquiring a two-bed ground-floor flat in a Victorian terrace, with access to a small garden, all at an affordable rent.

Delia was amazed. 'I don't know how you did it. It's perfect.'

'Isn't it! And the garden is so pretty. Imagine some lights strung in the tree and a barbecue and handsome boyfriends.'

'Fat chance. When do we have time to find them?'

'You have to make time and be open to the possibility. You don't give yourself a chance. You are either at work, shopping in Tesco, or sleeping.'

Delia sighed. 'Correct. That's been life for a long time now.'

'But we have men coming into the salon all the time . . . don't roll your eyes. I think you should start looking at them properly. Mr Right might be under your nose.'

'I'm not that desperate, Hattie.'

'Hmm, well, I'm going to make it my mission to discreetly check out potential Prince Charmings who need a decent haircut. After all, I did find this flat, didn't I?'

It took nearly a year, but one night, over a Chinese takeaway, a very smug Harriet shared her news.

'I've found him – your perfect man.' She reached across and helped herself to some deep-fried crispy beef.

'Where?'

'I googled him.'

Delia sagged. 'I almost believed you.'

'No. Listen. He's an actor. He needs his hair styled for the film he's making. His make-up artist rang the salon to book him in with you.'

'When?'

'Friday. His name is . . .' She scrabbled for her phone. 'Johnny Carlisle-Hart. Here's his picture.'

Delia saw an open face: nice eyes, big smile, good teeth. 'His hair's all right,' she said, not wanting to admit that he was very good looking.

'Oh, come off it. He's gorgeous.' Hattie shoved the phone back under Delia's nose. 'Look at him. Sort of vulnerable. Little boyish. Looks a bit like Jude Law. I want to squeeze his cheek and snog him all at the same time.'

Delia laughed. 'Ick.'

Johnny Carlisle-Hart arrived while Delia was in the staff room, mixing a tint for a client. Harriet bustled in, firmly closed the door, and leant against it, preventing anyone from entering. 'He's here,' she breathed.

Delia laughed. 'Does he look good in real life?'

'He looks in-cred-ib-le! And smells even better.'

Delia glanced at herself in the small mirror above the sink. She looked the same as she always did: long dark hair, centre-parting, and clear, make-up-free skin.

'You look lovely.' Harriet gave her a wink. 'Off you go.'

'Mr Carlisle-Hart?' Delia arrived behind his chair and smiled at him in the mirror.

'Johnny, please,' he said in a warm, well-modulated voice. 'Thanks for fitting me in. I hear it's not easy to get an appointment with you.'

'Not at all. Your make-up lady left some notes on what she wants for you. Trim the back and sides but keep your curls on top, with the option of gelling them down if a side-parting is needed. Is that right?'

'Yeah, sounds great.'

Conversation was amusing and easy. He told her a little about the filming he'd been doing in Crete – 'Beautiful island. You should go.' – and whenever she looked up at his reflection in the mirror, his Oxford-blue eyes were always on her.

'I haven't taken too much off,' she said, brushing the stray hairs from the collar of his beautiful white shirt.

He moved his head from left to right, checking his reflection. 'That's great, thanks.'

'Any problem, let me know.'

'I'm sure there won't be. I'm not back on set for a couple of days so I'm taking off to Cornwall tonight.'

Delia couldn't hide her smile. 'I grew up in Cornwall!'

'No way? I thought I heard a Cornish lilt. Where?'

'Down west. Near Sennen. Bozinjal?'

'I bet you get spectacular sunsets down there.'

'We do. And the bluefin tuna have come back. I've seen them with my own eyes! Just off Land's End. Leaping they were.'

He gazed at her. 'You should come to Cornwall with me. My parents have a house on the North Coast.'

Delia laughed. 'Don't tempt me.'

'Well, then, why don't you?'

Delia felt a change between him and her. She faltered under the scrutiny of his deep-blue eyes. 'It's impossible, I'm afraid. But thank you.'

'Never mind.'

The moment was gone.

At the reception desk, Harriet was all hair-flicking efficiency. 'Just pop your card in the machine. Shall I make an appointment for next time?'

'I'll call you.'

'OK.' Harriet pulled a smart navy blazer from the coat cupboard. 'Don't forget this.'

'Thanks.' He put his wallet in the back pocket of his jeans and slipped into the perfectly tailored jacket. He turned to Delia. 'Thanks. I'll be back. Bye.'

Harriet sighed as she watched him through the window on his walk towards Sloane Square. 'He must be one of the most beautiful men on the planet.'

Delia's head told her that he was not worth thinking about. But her heart was warm with the connection she had felt run between them.

'You should come to Cornwall with me,' he'd told her. 'I'll be back,' he'd said.

It was almost three months before they met again, by which time Delia's stomach had long since stopped flipping every time the salon phone rang.

It was a Saturday in early September, a beautiful, warm evening. Delia had closed the salon, making sure the till was emptied and the alarm was on before stepping out onto the pavement and double-locking the door behind her. The cafés, pubs, and restaurants around her were busy, their customers spilling out on to the pavement tables and chairs. The yellowing leaves of the plane trees gave the evening a holiday feel. She could have been walking through Paris or Milan.

She didn't have to be back at work until Tuesday and was looking forward to spending her off time wisely. There was a film she wanted to see – but then again, a night in with a book and a glass of wine sounded good, too.

What she *should* do was catch a train to Cornwall to see Auntie Rose. But it was a long journey, and she was tired. She needed sleep. But she hadn't seen her aunt for months. Her last visit, at Easter, hadn't gone very well. The easiness they'd shared when she was young had hardened, become less flexible. Delia was no longer Rose's malleable and devoted niece. She was a successful, financially independent woman in her mid-thirties who Rose couldn't always understand anymore. Phone calls had become short, stilted, and dissatisfying.

Deep in these thoughts, she didn't notice Johnny Carlisle-Hart dashing across the road, dodging the Saturday-night traffic as she headed off towards her bus stop.

It wasn't until she felt a hand on her shoulder and spun round in fright that she saw who her assailant was.

'Bloody hell, you really scared me,' she said crossly.

He held his hands up in supplication. 'I'm so sorry. I saw you and just had to say hello. Hello.'

She just kept staring at him.

'Sorry.' He ran his hand through his hair. 'Um, Johnny Carlisle-Hart. You cut my hair once.'

'Yes, I remember.'

'I was across the road and saw you shutting up shop. Thought I'd just say hi.'

'Well, hi.' She smiled.

'Um . . . I don't suppose you'd care to have a drink, would you? With me, tonight?'

'Tonight?' Delia began walking again, and he fell in step next to her.

'Oh God. I've really made myself look like the worst kind of nutter, haven't I?'

Delia kept walking. 'Yes.'

'Yes, I'm a nutter?'

She couldn't help smiling. 'Yes, I'd like to have a drink with you.'

Seated in a corner of an Italian bar, Delia watched Johnny as he wove his way towards their table to deliver her white wine spritzer and his orange juice.

'Can we start again?' he asked. 'Pretend this is the first time we've met?'

She settled into her seat. 'Sure, why not?'

'Right. My name is Johnny. I'm an actor.'

'How did the filming go?'

'You remember?' He raised his eyebrows in delight. 'Yeah, a good script. Undercover policeman infiltrating the Greek mafia. We had a few weeks on location in Crete, which was fabulous.'

'What part did you play? Undercover cop or Greek mafia?'

'Good question. Neither. I play the boyfriend of a woman who was duped into being a drug mule, so I spend most of the time in the hospital with her because the condom she swallowed burst.'

'A pivotal role?'

'No. But it's work and money, and Crete was nice.'

Delia smiled. 'And your family live in Cornwall, you said?'

'Yes. Only moved there recently. My dad's a property developer – it keeps my mum in gin. They found an incredible house. A wreck. You may have heard of it. Wilder Hoo?'

Delia thought back. 'I think so. Wasn't there a huge campaign to save the place?'

'That's the one.'

'And your parents bought it?' Delia was staggered. 'It must have cost a fortune!'

'Actually, no. The council sold it to Dad for a song, on the proviso that he'll bring it back to its former glory and turn it into a five-star luxury hotel. Restoration of the formal gardens is phase two, then there are all the outbuildings, barns, chapel – perfect for a wedding venue. It's going to be fabulous.'

Delia blinked. 'And your dad has the kind of money to do all that?'

'He will do.' Johnny leant forward and lowered his voice. 'Maybe I could persuade you to come and see it one day?'

She smiled. 'Maybe, but I'm not often in Cornwall.'

They chatted a bit longer and when their drinks were finished, she stood up to leave.

'I'm glad we bumped into each other,' he said.

'Me, too and thank you for the drink.'

He kept his gaze on her. 'Erm, I expect you're very busy, lots to do, but if not, would you perhaps have dinner with me tomorrow night?'

'Oh, erm . . .' She didn't know what to say.

'I'm sorry.' He smiled shyly. 'Your boyfriend probably wouldn't be very happy . . .'

'I don't have a boyfriend actually.'

'You don't? Well that's ridiculous. A beautiful woman like you . . .'

She stared at him. 'Do you have a girlfriend?'

'No, as it happens . . . no.'

'Married? Divorced? Children?'

'Nope. None of the above.'

'In that case . . .' She grinned.

When they stepped outside together, the cool evening air ruffled her hair and made her shiver.

He took off his jacket and held it out to her. 'Just to get you to your bus stop.'

'That's very kind, thank you.'

'Turn round,' he said.

She did as she was told, and he placed his jacket over her shoulders. 'Better?'

She pulled the lapels close and felt the heat from his body caught in the fabric. She could smell the residue of his cologne. 'Much better, thank you.'

'Sure?' He came closer. His eyes, the same blue as his jacket, were soft as they wandered over her face.

'Yes, sure,' she murmured.

'Delia?'

'Yes?'

'May I kiss you?'

Her mouth said nothing while her eyes said everything.

It was a good kiss: soft, warm, gentle. It lasted a few seconds, and she knew she wanted more.

'My car,' he said. 'It's just around the corner if you don't fancy taking the bus this late.'

CHAPTER THIRTEEN

Kernow Autumn, April, present day

After telling Rose the news Johnny was dead, Delia had begun to talk of her former husband as she never had before. Rose was unimpressed by the story of their first date – a hackneyed seduction if ever she'd heard of one. Delia had been as vulnerable to Johnny's attention as Christine had been to Gary's, but she daren't say that while Delia was at last opening up about the relationship.

'It must have been quite a whirlwind for you,' Rose managed.

'Yes. It was dizzying. I felt so happy.'

'And of course he brought you down to show you Wilder Hoo?'

'The very next weekend.'

'What was it like?'

'Breathtaking.' Delia shut her eyes, as though the scene was playing out before her. 'Noble and romantic. It reminded me of that house in that book Mum read us one Christmas. You remember? When the television had broken.'

Rose smiled. '*Rebecca*. The house was Manderley.'

'That's it, yes. Such a good story, and a bit spooky, exactly like Wilder Hoo. But where Manderley was beautiful inside, Wilder Hoo wasn't. It was very rickety – creaky stairs, gaps in the windows so that draughts seemed to be constantly blowing through the whole building. Damp, too. But I could see why Johnny's parents had fallen for it.'

'Sounds very romantic,' said Rose, trying not to sound scornful.

'It really was. Even though there was no hot water or heating, it was fun to explore it all. Johnny showed me the old solid fuel range in the kitchen, which probably hadn't been lit since before the war. I could imagine all those little maids rushing about and the cook shouting at them. Leading off the kitchen are passages to the pantry, still room, laundry, the butler's sitting room, the housekeeper's sitting room. And then there's all the outbuildings and an old farmhouse with barns, you name it. It has its own little beach, too.'

Delia fell silent, as the Wilder Hoo she had seen on Saturday merged with the Wilder Hoo she and Johnny had first visited. She recalled how he had taken a tartan rug from his old rucksack and spread it in the sand dunes, arranging a lump of cheddar, two apples, and a flask on it. They'd lain in each other's arms, eating and drinking, watching the sparkling ocean curl itself up and back, sucking at the sand and shells and seaweed.

After a while, he had pulled a half bottle of Moët from his rucksack and told her he loved her.

Delia was drunk on happiness. In a moment, she felt changed; she had become a desirable, funny, uninhibited, beautiful woman.

That night, he took her to The Vare Castle for the first time, and over cocktails and wine, she told him she loved him, too.

Delia was snapped out of her thoughts by the sound of Auntie Rose's telephone. She still kept a landline, even though she had a mobile, because the signal was negligible at Kernow Autumn. This was thought of as a blessing to the majority of residents, who had enough going on in their social lives without having to take 'duty phone calls' from guilty members of their extended family or former neighbours.

'I'll get it.' Auntie Rose left the comfort of her chair. 'Are you pain-free enough to open a bottle of wine?' she asked on her way to the hall. 'It's almost lunchtime – perfect time for a glass of the decent Chablis I have in the fridge.'

She answered the phone, and Delia couldn't help listening in. 'Hello . . . Oh, Sammi, dear how are you? . . . Yes . . . not until Friday? . . . Of course, we're fine here – do you want to speak to her? . . . She's just getting some wine. She had a good long sleep, and her ankle's moving a lot better, thank you . . . I'll tell her . . . yes . . . OK, Sammi. See you Friday. Bye.'

Delia called from the kitchen. 'What did Sammi want?'

'Mostly to check in on you,' Auntie Rose said, joining her. 'Here, pass me the wine bottle and the glasses.'

Delia hopped her way back to the sofa while Rose poured the wine before getting comfortable in her armchair. 'Sammi isn't coming back until late on Friday, maybe Saturday, so we have all the time in the world for you to tell me the entire story – everything about Johnny and the house. I always felt there was more than the edited version of events that you gave me. Things never really stacked up . . . did they?'

Delia felt ashamed. 'No.'

'Why did you marry him? Love or money?'

'Love, pure and simple.' Delia was certain of that. 'He made me feel like the most precious person in the world. He wanted me with him all the time. He'd pick me up from work when he could, have incredible suppers made ready for me, spoilt me with flowers and foot massages.'

'Was he good in bed?'

'Auntie Rose!'

'I'm only asking.'

Delia was blushing. 'Yes, that side of things was wonderful at first.'

'Good. Some men can be very selfish. They manage to get a Ferrari of a woman into bed with them but can't find the ignition.'

'Auntie Rose!'

'Don't pretend to be shocked. I can't imagine things have changed that much since I was young.'

Delia was curious. 'You've never talked about any boyfriends before.'

'Did you expect me to be a virgin? A few of the men I went out with were very nice. I even had two proposals, but I didn't want to marry any of them. I liked – like – my independence too much. And, don't take this the wrong way, but I couldn't leave your mother on her own.'

Realization dawned for Delia. 'You gave up your own chance of marriage to help Mum with me?'

Auntie Rose tipped her head to one side, mulling over the question. 'On the one hand, yes; on the other, no. I would rather be a happy family with you and Chris than have a thousand miserable husbands.'

'Gosh. I hadn't even thought about any of that. I mean, no offence, but I don't want to think of you or Mum having sex. It's a bit weird.'

She laughed. 'I haven't always been good old Auntie Rose in her retirement village, you know. I have lived a life.'

'Yes, I'm sorry.' Delia leant forward in her seat. 'And now, you don't miss any of that? It must be a long time since—'

'Not *that* long actually.' Auntie Rose laughed at Delia's astonished look. 'Don't be so surprised. I'm still young enough. Sixty-two is nothing nowadays.'

Delia covered her ears. 'Oh my God. Who?'

'That's for me to know and you to wonder, and anyway, he and I went our separate ways. However, there *is* a very nice gentlemen who has recently moved to Kernow Autumn. He might pop in for a drink while you're here.'

'You dark horse!' Delia glanced across at her aunt and laughed. 'I feel really silly now. Look at you. You're in very good shape. You have a lovely face. You're kind, funny, intelligent. Why wouldn't there be men beating their way to your door?'

'That's very kind of you to say. I get choosier the older I get, though. I won't be rushing to Gretna Green anytime soon.' She took a long sip of her wine. 'This is very good, isn't it? Now, get on with the story.'

Delia took a deep breath as her levity slipped away. 'Well, we didn't get back to Wilder Hoo for a month or so, because Johnny had auditions and had started writing a script he'd been thinking about for years.'

'Interesting. Was it any good?'

'I don't know; he didn't let me see it.' Delia rubbed her head. 'So, we went to Wilder Hoo around November. He absolutely adored his mum and was, I think, a little scared of his father, so I was excited to meet them but also nervous. It was late, almost midnight when we got there, but Vivienne and Harvey stayed up to wait for us. Wilder Hoo in November was very different to Wilder Hoo in September.

'When Johnny pushed the ancient doors open, it was so dark and gloomy and incredibly cold. The aged chandelier above the stairs was giving even less light than I remembered from the last time. The house felt so *sad*. Vivienne and Harvey appeared, and they were very glad to see Johnny.'

'Describe them to me,' Rose said. 'I want to be able to picture them.'

'Vivienne had been a model back in the Seventies. She was tall, very thin, long silver hair with a white streak,'

Rose chuckled. 'Cruella de Vil style?'

'That's what Harvey called her sometimes to annoy her. But her face is beautiful: totally symmetrical; classic, almond-shaped, bright-blue eyes below elegant eyebrows; a slender nose with a small tip at the end and proper rosebud lips, full and cushiony.'

'That'll be the filler,' said Rose with a sniff.

'You can be so judgmental, Auntie Rose. I honestly think it was all natural. She has wrinkles, not bad ones, but she has them.'

'Hmm.' Rose didn't believe a word of it. 'She has secrets, and she keeps them.'

'Yes, she did have a secret – one we all knew about but never mentioned. She drinks. A lot. And barely eats.'

This, Rose was satisfied with. 'Ah. That kind of woman. And Harvey?'

'Shorter than his wife. His body was like a square, if you know what I mean. He'd been a boxer in his day. It's how he and Vivienne met, apparently. They were polar opposites: her refined and stylish, him more rough and ready. Liked to think of himself as a man's man.

'On that first night, they shepherded us from the great hall to the saloon, as she called it. I was glad to see that the fire was lit, with two armchairs huddled round it. Johnny and I sat on the rug while his father poured us a whisky each. Vivienne settled back in her chair and began asking me all sorts of questions about my life in London and how I'd met Johnny. It was quite funny at first, because she kept calling me Celia. I felt too awkward to correct her.'

'Didn't Johnny correct her?'

'No. He was talking with his dad about work and stuff. I was tired, and I was relieved when Vivienne announced it was time for bed.'

The next morning, Johnny had made love to her so gently: tender and caring. No other lover compared to him. And because he desired her so passionately and lovingly, she desired him with equal ferocity.

'Cordelia, daughter of the sea,' he whispered as he rolled off her. 'Is that really what your name means? What the hell was your mum thinking?' He lifted his arm. 'Come here.'

Delia snuggled into him, putting her arm across his lightly haired chest. 'Mum and Auntie Rose wanted me to have a Cornish name. I like it.'

'I love it.' He sighed dramatically, then squeezed her. 'I am never going to tire of making love to you. I need you every day and every night.'

Delia tipped her chin up to him and smiled. 'Really?'

'Really.' He returned her smile, his eyes scanning her face with tenderness. 'I even love your monobrow.'

She frowned. 'I don't have a monobrow.'

'Oh, my darling, it's barely noticeable.'

She lifted her hand and felt the skin above her nose. 'I can't feel anything.'

'Don't worry about it. It makes you you.' He hugged her closer. 'I think I might have a snooze,' he whispered and closed his eyes.

When she was certain he was asleep again, she slipped out of bed and went to the cold, outdated bathroom.

In her make-up bag, she had a small double-sided mirror. She flipped it over to its magnifying side. The morning sun was bright, and she positioned herself in front of the large window, through which the cold wind crept. She examined her face. She couldn't see a monobrow, but she would be more vigilant from now on.

'Hey. What are you up to?' Johnny was standing in the doorway.

She instinctively put the hand holding her tweezers behind her back. 'You're awake.'

'I woke up and you weren't there. I miss you. What are you doing? What are you hiding?'

Blushing, she showed him the tweezers. 'Thought I'd better sort the monobrow out.'

He stepped towards her and took her into his arms. 'You didn't believe me, did you? It was a joke. I'm so sorry. Oh, you silly darling. It was just a joke.'

She left the memory behind and spoke aloud again.

'Johnny cooked breakfast for the four of us. Full English for me, him, and his dad. Black coffee and half a corner of toast for Vivienne. All on the wobbly cooker his dad had bought on eBay. Vivienne loathed it but said that it wasn't worth buying a brand-new cooking range because they had so many plans for reviving the house. The kitchen was going to be state of the art, a space to host interiors magazines from across the globe.

'"I like to think out of the box," she told me. "Hollywood loves the quintessential English look. Imagine the movies they could make here. I have already approached Oprah to come over with her book club and, while here, host her own cook school. You see, Celia, when I dream, I dream big."

'To be fair, it is a great space. She was going to commission an enormous kitchen table to seat at least twenty people comfortably, have the flagstone floor scrubbed, regrouted, polished, and brought back to life. And of course, in the deep inglenook where the rusty Victorian range sat, she would install an eight-door Aga in either graphite grey, mocha, buttercup yellow, or lime green.'

'Typical,' sniffed Rose. 'What's wrong with traditional cream?'

Delia laughed. 'If you saw it, you'd agree with her. She showed me her "look book" and "mood boards" for each room, and there are a lot of rooms!'

'Oh, for heaven's sake.' Rose groaned. 'More money than sense.'

Delia shrugged. 'They weren't worried about the cost, and it all sounded very feasible to me. I enjoyed the whole weekend. Vivienne showed me around the gardens, and Harvey drove us around in his ancient Range Rover, pointing out the dilapidated farmhouse and its cottages and barns. He showed us the old chapel and what he called the Good Lawn. He was excited for me to see the Tudor knot garden – totally overgrown, but Vivienne had plans to return it to its Elizabethan glory.'

'Now that sounds interesting,' Rose said.

'Then we drove on through the woods and finally to the cliffs and the beach below. We didn't get right down to the water's edge because it was blowing a cold wind, and when we got out of the car, the sea spray and sand whipped our faces.'

Rose nodded. 'Wild and romantic. It sounds almost too good to be true.'

Delia sighed. 'I fell in love with Wilder Hoo in the same way I fell in love with Johnny. Easily. Trusting the future.' She lifted her gaze and smiled sadly at her aunt. 'I should have known. I should have told you all this from the beginning.'

'Was there any sign of work having started at that time?'

Delia shook her head. 'They were on hold, waiting for the council to agree their plans. It was clear that the entire estate needed a lot of work and a lot of money.'

'What happened then?' Rose asked.

'We went out for lunch to The Vare Castle, their favourite place. The staff fussed around Vivienne and Harvey the moment we arrived, filling wine glasses, taking orders, smiling constantly. Vivienne and Harvey lapped up every drop of all the fawning on offer. As we were shown to "their" table, several diners acknowledged them, and a lot of bonhomie was distributed. Once we'd ordered and Harvey had sniffed and swilled the wine, Vivienne asked me what I did. I had told her the night before, but in retrospect I realize she must have been drunk and forgotten. I think she was impressed when I told her about Gilson's.'

Rose smiled. 'I hope you told her about you winning Hairdresser of the Year.'

'Runner up,' Delia corrected her, 'but that was later. She said, "You young girls all look *très naturelle*. No make-up. No signature style to your hair. You don't worry about your weight. It was so much harder when I was a model, Celia."'

Rose sniffed. 'She was jealous of you, because you look so beautiful and you were going to take Johnny away from her.'

Delia opened her mouth to speak, but Rose cut her off.

'What about Harvey? What did he want to know about you?'

'He was all about money, asking what Gilson's annual turnover was, how high the overheads were, and how much could I earn in tips. As if I were a junior just starting out! I told him that the salon was in the top three in London and that I, after years of experience and hard graft, was the senior stylist and salon manager, which completely bemused him. After that, neither Vivienne nor Harvey spoke to me much. They just wanted to know all about Johnny's movie and the script he was writing.'

'What was this film he was in?' Rose asked. 'The one in Crete, was it?'

'You won't have heard of it. Most of Johnny's scenes didn't make the final cut, and the movie itself went straight to nowhere.'

Rose nodded. 'And were they still calling you Celia?'

'Johnny did try to keep correcting them, but Vivienne could never get it right.'

CHAPTER FOURTEEN

Kernow Autumn, April, present day

When the doorbell rang, Rose jumped up to answer it. 'Goodness, look at the time. That'll be Hugh. It's Bridge Night.'

'Hugh?' Delia asked, but Rose was already out in the corridor.

She returned a moment later with a man at her side. He was tall, handsome, and charming, with longish silver hair brushed back from his forehead and behind his ears, leading to curls at the base of his neck.

'Delia, meet Hugh, my upstairs neighbour.'

'Good to meet you at last,' he said, shaking Delia's hand.

'No time to chat Hugh.' Rose picked up her glasses and phone. 'Delia there's some good cheddar in the fridge if you're hungry. We'll be back in a couple of hours. I want to make sure we get a good table.'

Hugh chuckled. 'Your aunt is very competitive. Hates to play with the beginners.'

'Come along, Hugh. See you later, Delia. Get some rest.'

After they had gone, Delia began to wonder if Rose was relieved to get out and away from listening to her interminable woes. Poor Auntie Rose – no wonder she was so glad to see Hugh, who was, Delia could appreciate, a proper silver fox. A possible lover? A possible husband?

He looked like the kind of man who would propose properly, in a restaurant with a diamond ring at the bottom of a Champagne glass.

Johnny had proposed in the spring at Wilder Hoo.

Delia shut her eyes and sipped her wine, letting the memories flood back.

He'd been running ahead in between the dunes, holding his arms out to brush the seagrass growing either side.

'Come on, Delia.' His words were whipped away by the breeze. 'Let's swim together. Our first!'

By the time she reached him, he had peeled off his T-shirt, which lay inside out at his feet, and was unknotting the cord of his shorts.

'I haven't brought a costume,' Delia said.

He pulled her into his arms and held her. 'You don't need one,' he told her, slipping his hands under her shirt and unhooking her bra. 'You don't need this, and you don't need these.' His hands pulled at the zip of her denim shorts, murmuring, 'Or your naughty little pants.' And with one smooth action, he had pulled both down past her knees.

'*Johnny!*' Delia instinctively covered herself.

'No one will see us.' He pulled his own shorts off and revealed his nakedness with pride. 'Isn't that better?' He grabbed her hand. 'We are going skinny-dipping.'

The chill of the Atlantic waves as they hit her thighs was curiously erotic. Johnny had dived in without a thought. His white bottom, the only part of him untanned, shone clearly beneath the water.

With her elbows gripped to her sides and her hands covering her breasts, she walked slowly forward until she was up to her waist.

Johnny surfaced and swam towards her, his mouth and cheeks below the water, his eyes like a crocodile's above the surface. He got close enough for her to hold her arms out to him, and as she did, so he pulled his face up towards her bare breasts. The warmth of his mouth on one nipple and his fingers on the other was delicious. She cupped his head in her hands, wanting him to kiss her mouth in the same way.

Later, when they lay on their clothes on the sand, Johnny took her hand and said, 'I've never felt this way before.'

She rolled onto her side to look at him. 'What way is that?'

'You are the most incredible woman I have ever met. You are beautiful, funny, kind, talented . . . and very, very sexy.'

She laughed. 'Stop!'

'I'm being serious, Delia. Look at me.'

She shifted slightly to stare into his navy-blue eyes.

'You're so handsome it almost hurts to look at you,' she said softy. She traced his jaw with her finger, enjoying the feel of his unshaven chin, his lips dusted with a trace of sea salt and a half-smile.

'I love you so much, Dee.'

'I love you, too.'

'Enough to marry me?'

'What?'

The wind pushed a strand of hair over her face. Johnny lifted it away. 'I'm asking you to marry me.'

*

'Ma? Pa?' Johnny sprinted over the knot garden towards Wilder Hoo, pulling a laughing Delia with him.

Vivienne's huge black sunglasses peered over the wall as she sat up on her sunbed.

'Where's the fire?' she called. 'Did you have a lovely swim?'

'Oh, we did!' Johnny shouted. 'We have wonderful news, Ma! Is Pa with you?'

'He's mixing a jug of Pimm's,' she said. 'I need a little pick-me-up after last night.'

Johnny and Delia had reached the stone steps and now sprinted up them two at a time.

'Goodness.' Vivienne swatted Johnny away. 'Please don't try to touch me, Johnny – you are all sweaty. Celi— Delia, you are quite scarlet in the face.'

Behind her, Harvey stepped from the library's open sash window out onto the terrace, carrying a tray with a rattling jug of Pimm's. 'Last of the ice, I'm afraid, Vivvi.'

'Good timing, Pa,' Johnny said.

'Oh, Johnny. Do I need to fetch another couple of glasses for you two?' He was clearly hoping they would say no.

'Yes you do because . . .' Johnny threw his arm around Delia's shoulders.

Vivienne readjusted the straps of her swimsuit, gently swung her legs over the side of her sun lounger, and sat up. 'What is it?'

'Delia and I . . . are getting married!' Johnny took Delia's hand and kissed it tenderly. 'Isn't she wonderful?'

Vivienne, rigid, simply stared at them.

Harvey glanced about, looking for somewhere to place the tray.

Vivienne held out her hands. 'Give it to me.'

He did so, then slowly straightened up and, with his hands on his hips, said, 'Now look, old boy, I'm sure you want to do the right thing – a gentleman always will – but you hardly know each other.'

Vivienne quickly poured herself a tall glass of Pimm's, and drained half of it. 'Are you not on the pill?'

Delia unsure if this was a joke or not, smiled uncertainly. 'I'm not pregnant.'

Vivienne waved her hand airily. 'Well, what other reason is there? You've only known Johnny for two minutes and now he's going to marry you?'

Johnny laughed. 'Two things, Mother dear. One, we have been together for nine months, quite long enough, and two, I love Delia. Neither of us are getting any younger, and I've never been more certain of anything.' He rubbed his hands together. 'Come on, Pa – this calls for Champagne!'

'I don't think I have any in.' Harvey shrugged. 'But the Pimm's will do for now, won't it?'

'I suppose we'll have to throw an engagement party,' Vivienne said, without a hint of enthusiasm.

'Here, or in London?' Harvey asked.

'God no, not London,' Vivienne argued. 'How about Spain?'

'Too expensive to fly guests over.'

'You are such a skinflint, Harvey. Perhaps a small dinner at The Vare would be most suitable. You, me, and Johnny, and Delia and her parents – small and discreet.'

Delia shook her head. 'I only have my aunt, Rose. My mum died when I was seventeen.'

'Oh dear,' Harvey said. 'How very sad. What about your father?'

Delia was not going to lie. 'He walked out on my mum before I was born,' she said simply. 'I have no idea who or where he is, and I don't want to know.'

Vivienne finished her Pimm's and held it out for a top up. 'Let's talk about the party another time. I'm rather hungry. Shall we go out for dinner? Try the new Mexican place in Penvare?'

Over dinner, and fuelled by tequila, Harvey dominated the table and especially Delia. 'When I die, Johnny will be a very wealthy man. I bought Wilder Hoo for a song. It's going to be the best thing I ever invested in.' He lifted his hand and began ticking off his plans on his fingers. 'A luxury hotel. Weddings and events. Shooting rights for the woods. A golf course. Equestrian cross-country course. Open up the existing stables to livery. Michelin star restaurant. Kiddies' playground. A beach spa. A cocktail bar . . .' He'd run out of fingers but remembered one last thing: ' And we'll lease the farm land to local farmers for grazing. Oh!' He nudged Johnny, excited. 'We can have open farm days. Get the kids in to pet the lambs or whathaveyou.'

'Sounds amazing,' Delia answered, overwhelmed by the ambition.

Harvey leant forward conspiratorially. 'And has Johnny told you about the Spanish portfolio?'

Delia shook her head.

'I have contracts for building plots, rentals, villas. Very high-end clients waiting for new-build units in Puerto Banús.' He paused, waiting for her admiration.

'Gosh.'

He went on: 'Long before I kick the bucket, I hope to have sold the empire for multi-millions. Vivienne and I will live out our days in our lovely little villa up in the hills that we've had for years. I'll potter about on my boat while Vivienne sits in her favourite bars, chatting shit with The Girls. It's where we go when we can't stick the Cornish winter.'

'Lovely,' Delia said.

'Yes. So, I need to know that whoever Johnny marries understands that my empire must be allowed to flourish, and will therefore, without hesitation, sign away whatever rights they may think are due to them if – and I'm only saying if – the marriage doesn't work out.'

Delia understood the message loud and clear. 'You mean a pre-nup?'

'Good girl.' Harvey patted her hand. 'I knew you'd understand.'

Johnny stepped in. 'Pa, I'm very disappointed in you. Delia is not that sort of girl. She's a successful, independent woman with an incredible career. She's no gold-digger.'

Harvey smiled. 'I can see that, Johnny. I can see that.' His eyes met Delia's, and he winked. 'You're a good girl, Delia. I know you'll keep this little chat in mind.'

Harriet was home in the flat when they got back to London. 'Hey guys! Good weekend?'

Johnny could not keep the grin from his face. 'The best!'

Delia grinned back. 'The absoliute best.'

'Go on then.' Harriet sat down. 'Spill.'

'Delia has agreed to be my wife!'

Harriet leapt to her feet. '*Whaaat!!* I knew you two were made for each other. Group hug!'

They all embraced, but Harriet broke away first. 'Let's see it then.'

'What?' asked Delia.

'The ring.'

'Oh shit!' Johnny laughed. 'I forgot about the bloody ring!'

'We haven't even thought about that, have we?' Delia laughed. 'It was all so spur of the moment.'

Harriet tutted. 'I'll have to go shopping with you, Johnny Boy – just to make sure you choose right.'

'Hang on.' Delia laughed. 'I'm coming too.'

'We'll go as a threesome then,' Harriet said. 'Give the shop assistant something to think about.'

'No, no, wait.' Johnny stopped them. 'Ma always said I could have Grandma's ring. Problem solved!'

Harriet was suspicious. 'Is it a good one? I mean, Delia deserves a whopper. A big fat diamond with lots of big fat diamonds all around it.'

'Of course it's a good one,' Johnny retorted. 'My family don't do tat.'

'Hang on,' Delia said. 'I don't need a *whopper*. Just a small, pretty ring that I can wear for work. After all' – she slipped her hand into Johnny's – 'I already have everything I need in this man.'

CHAPTER FIFTEEN

Kernow Autumn, April, present day

'How was Bridge Night?' Delia was just out of the shower and rubbing her hair dry when Rose arrived home.

'It was OK. Would have won if Hugh hadn't lost concentration. I've sent him back to his flat in disgrace. How's the ankle?'

'Not bad. Having a hot shower helped.'

'Good. I'll go and make a pot of tea while you get yourself sorted.'

When they were both settled back in the sitting room Rose asked, 'Why didn't you tell me about the engagement? A woman I barely knew, down at the market, was the first to tell me. '"I've heard on the grapevine your Cordelia's engaged." She practically shouted it for everyone to hear. I felt like an absolute idiot.'

Delia shook her head in embarrassment. 'I don't know why I didn't. There was just so much going on and Johnny didn't want everyone knowing our business.'

Rose pressed her lips together before saying, 'I'm not everyone. I'm your aunt. It was hard to find out the way I did, especially as I hadn't had a chance to meet him. But I think what hurt me more was not being at the wedding. Why was it all such a secret?'

'Looking back, I wanted to slow things down – to have time to plan the wedding the way I wanted it, before Vivienne and Harvey interfered.'

'*I* wouldn't have interfered,' Rose said. 'I could have helped.'

'I know, I know. I was supposed to be floating around on cloud nine having found the man of my dreams, but I was so overwhelmed. Keeping it a secret while everything was going at a million miles a minute. Trying to make work fit in with it all was impossible. And when Sammi and Johnny met for the first time . . .'

'Ah,' Rose said. 'I have a very soft spot for Sammi. He's a good judge of character. He'd never let you down.'

'I'd wanted to get him and Johnny together for ages, but Johnny's schedule was always changing, until finally we found an evening when we were all free. Harriet was going to cook for us so, after work, she and I swung past the nearest Waitrose to pick up everything she needed, and we bumped into Sammi, who was already there buying a huge bunch of red peonies and a bottle of Champagne for us. You know how generous he is, and it was so good to see him that walking back to the flat we nipped into the pub for a quick drink, just to celebrate being together again. When we got to the flat, Johnny was already in the kitchen. He didn't know we had Sammi with us, and he shouted out, "Table is laid. Hope it's good enough for Kelly Hoppen when he arrives."' Delia winced now at the memory. 'It was so embarrassing, but when Johnny came out of the kitchen, he was unabashed, hand outstretched. Sammi didn't miss a beat. He took Johnny's hand, said, "Lovely of you to think I'm up there with Kelly Hoppen. The Design Queen!"'

Rose smiled. 'Bravo, Sammi.'

Delia nodded. 'Sammi was great that night. Even when Johnny laughed at the red peonies for being common and ugly and the Champagne for not being the right vintage.'

Rose silently fumed. 'Not a great start then?'

'Not stupendous . . . but Johnny got talking about theatre and acting, and Wilder Hoo and discussed interior design, so they found some common ground. It was . . . OK. It meant a lot to me that they had met each other, but it was nerve-racking, and I worried about introducing Johnny to you. I wanted to make sure you were happy for me, that you thought I'd made the right decision, but I didn't know what I'd do if you didn't like him. And when Sammi had gone and we went to bed, Johnny began typing on his phone, and when he finished, he said, "I have a little surprise for you. He'd booked our wedding on line at the local registrars."'

'He didn't ask you first?'

'No, but it was all quite exciting. The romance of a secret wedding and all that. Even though it wasn't going to be the wedding I had imagined planning. Bozinjal Church, a huge dress, you driving me in the Landy, and walking me down the aisle, Harriet as bridesmaid, confetti and a big cake. It was still exciting.' Delia glanced at her aunt, embarrassed. 'I wanted to ring you straight away, but Johnny was adamant it had to be kept secret. He wanted to just go off and do it and tell everyone afterwards. Our day. Simple and pure. One day, he said, we would have the big church wedding, invite all our friends, but he didn't want to wait. So we were getting married at the local registry office on Thursday 15th December, 10.45 a.m.'

'I wish you had told me,' Rose said sadly. 'I would have kept the secret.'

'I know you would, and I found it so hard not to tell you or Sammi or Harriet. And we were buying a flat at the time, too – Johnny said it was a good investment, but it was adding to the stress. He understood, and he kept telling me that having a quiet wedding meant less stress for both of us. For me. He was doing it all for me. I thought my nervousness, wedding jitters, was normal.'

'Planning a wedding should be a happy time,' Rose said, her voice tired.

'I *was* happy!'

'Were you? You and Harriet and I, we should have been choosing a dress together, trawling the shoe shops and florists with a jolly lunch in between.' She stood up suddenly, remorse and anger in her expression. 'How would you feel if I decided to get married and kept it a secret from you?'

'I know,' said Delia, 'but—'

'The flat you bought,' said Rose. 'Was that with your savings – the life insurance money from your mum?'

Delia nodded.

'Why didn't you tell me all this before? I could have helped. Perhaps guided you to make better decisions.'

Delia was instantly on the defensive. 'I'm old enough to make my own mistakes. I'm not a child anymore.'

'Whoa, that's not what I'm saying.'

'Yes, it is,' Delia snapped. 'You have no idea what my life was like then. My work was – I hope will still be – a huge part of my life. Then I met Johnny, and I was so happy to have him. He gave me a life outside of work. I had a reason to go home at night. I felt loved.'

Auntie Rose pursed her lips, her eyes narrowed. 'I remember that time very well. You barely called me from one month to the next. Every time I wanted to come to London to see you,

you would make it impossible. You were tired; you and Johnny already had plans – not to mention the trips to Cornwall to see his parents.' She crossed her arms in front of her. 'You made it very clear that I was no longer important to you.'

'Please, Auntie Rose.' Delia felt wretched, desperate for her aunt to see her point of view. 'Understand what I'm trying to say . . . I should have got in touch more. I love you so much . . .'

'But you didn't love me enough to tell me you were marrying a man I didn't know, that you were buying a flat with your mother's money.'

Delia felt stung. She sat silently as Auntie Rose got up from her chair and said, 'It's late. We're both upset. I have a headache and want to go to bed. Make yourself something to eat if you're hungry. I couldn't eat a thing.'

Once Auntie Rose had left the room, Delia felt tears fill her eyes, spilling down her cheeks. She grabbed a cushion from the sofa and sobbed into it, her whole body shaking. Auntie Rose didn't understand – of course she didn't. How could she, when Delia had shut her out for years?

In that moment, she made a decision: in the morning, she was going to tell her aunt everything, from start to finish. Not the small details of her and Johnny's love story but the harsh, bitter truths of their marriage.

Delia shut her eyes tight and let herself remember.

CHAPTER SIXTEEN

Wilder Hoo, two years ago

The sun was just sinking behind Wilder Hoo, giving its symmetry a sharp outline. Neither Johnny nor Delia had visited since their wedding.

There were no signs of scaffolding or building works, which surprised Delia. 'The builders haven't started yet then?' she asked.

'There's been a building regs delay.'

'When was that?'

'Does it matter?'

'I'm only asking.'

'Well, don't say anything to Pa. He's furious about it all.'

They walked up the steps to the front door, and Johnny tried to open it, but it was either stuck fast or locked.

'Bloody thing.' He pulled his phone out. 'I'll ring them.'

'Hello?' Delia could hear Vivienne's voice coming from the receiver.

'Ma, it's us. Open the bloody door, will you?'

'We're on the terrace! Come round.'

Johnny hung up and sighed. 'Sounds like she's already on the gin. Come on.'

The terrace was suffused in the golden light of the dipping sun. Vivienne was lying on her sun lounger, wearing white palazzo pants, a knee-length, psychedelic kimono, her trademark black sunglasses, and a wide-brimmed straw hat.

Johnny bent to kiss her. 'Hey, Ma.'

'Johnny, my darling boy, here at last.' She reached her arms around his neck and kissed him. 'Your father's gone to get some more ice for Mummy's G&T.' She plucked at his cheek. 'It's so lovely to have my boy here. Just we three. Like the old days.'

Guilt crossed his face. 'Delia's with me.'

Vivienne sat up quickly. 'Where?'

'Hi Vivienne.' Delia, only a metre away, waved at her mother-in-law.

'So you are. I wish I had known. I would have worn something more welcoming.'

Delia smiled diligently. 'You always look incredible. And the terrace in this sun is . . . like a painting or a film set.'

Vivienne wilted back to her previous prone position. 'It is, isn't it?'

Harvey arrived, carrying a tray with bottles of gin and tonic water, a glass of ice, and an empty glass.

'Celia's here.' Vivienne lifted an arm in Delia's direction. 'A surprise for us.'

Delia saw the annoyance that flitted over Harvey's eyes before he quickly adopted an expression of cheerful surprise.

'Johnny, you didn't say you were bringing a guest.'

'Not a guest exactly.' Johnny grinned. 'Delia is officially your daughter-in-law.'

Vivienne's manicured, bony fingers gripped her mouth. 'What?'

'We got married.'

Harvey's jaw literally dropped. Then he began to laugh. 'You can't be married – there hasn't been a wedding!' He looked from Johnny to Delia, to Vivienne and back to Johnny. 'Oh my God, you have, haven't you?' He placed the tray carefully on the rusting wrought-iron garden table. 'Well, well, well! Our little boy, a married man.' He clapped Johnny on the back before taking Delia into a hug. 'You're a lucky man, Johnny. She's absolutely perfect for you. Vivienne and I are delighted to welcome her to the family. Aren't we, Vivvi?'

'Charmed.' Vivienne's smile was flabby. 'Charming Celia,' she drawled. 'That's what I shall call you from now on.'

'Ma, how many times? It's Delia with a D . . . D for Delightful.' Johnny took Delia's hand, 'We have been dying to tell you in person.'

'You must be thrilled to have married so well,' Vivienne said to Delia, before holding her glass for Harvey, who poured at least four fingers of gin into it. 'Just a splash of tonic, darling.'

'I know exactly how you like it, dear.' Harvey turned to the newlyweds. 'How about you two? All out of Champers, I'm afraid. It'll have to be G&T. I'd better get another glass. Johnny, go and get a couple of extra chairs.'

Once they'd gone, Delia and Vivienne were left in an awkward silence. 'When was the happy day?' Vivienne almost whispered.

'Just before Christmas. We had a tiny civil ceremony. Lovely, actually. Two strangers were called down from the office above as witnesses. And afterwards, we had to run for the bus to get home, and Johnny gave me a piggyback. It was so funny. People clapped and wished us luck as we went by.'

She wondered if Vivienne was even listening, but after a difficult pause, her mother-in-law succeeded in finding a word she thought most appropriate. 'Goodness. So that's why Johnny couldn't come down for Christmas. We wondered what was stopping him.'

Harvey and Johnny reappeared, carrying the chairs and cushions and a glass for Delia.

'Here we are. Look at that sunset now.' Harvey settled himself on his sun lounger. 'Are we not the luckiest people in the world to have that view and to be celebrating such happy news?' He raised his glass. 'To Johnny and Delia. May life bring you, health, wealth, and wisdom. Cheers.'

'Cheers,' they all said.

When the sun finally slid below the trees, Vivienne suddenly said, 'Christ, the chicken in the oven will be burnt to a cinder.' She tried to get off the sun lounger, but Delia volunteered.

'Don't move. I'm happy to get it all sorted. The least I can do. Johnny will help me, won't you?'

The kitchen was as cold and barren as Delia remembered.

The only thing to cheer it up was the smell of chicken leaking from the old cooker. By the sink were two saucepans, one filled with peeled potatoes and the other a clump of frozen peas. A pot of Bisto sat next to them, with a handwritten note propped up against it.

> *Chicken needs to rest while potatoes boil. I suggest mashing them. Peas and gravy self-explanatory. I've laid the table for the four of you. Please give my congratulations to Johnny and Delia.*
>
> *Mrs Joy x*

Delia showed it to Johnny.

'That's nice,' he said.

'How did she know I was coming when your parents didn't?' Delia asked.

Johnny frowned, looking for an explanation. 'She must have seen us arrive as she was leaving?'

'How did she know my name?'

'Ma would have said when she told her about the engagement.'

Delia laughed. 'And got my name right for once. Mystery solved.'

Once she'd got the simple supper ready, she decided to prepare the kitchen table. She found the stubs of two pink candles in a drawer and squeezed them into a couple of empty gin bottles from the recycling box. Sitting on the wobbly table, their flickering light shrank the dark space around them, creating a glowing halo in the centre of the room.

Johnny brought his parents down from the terrace.

'Doesn't this look lovely.' Vivienne blinked. 'We can *almost* pretend we're at The Vare Castle.'

'Thank you. Candles make everything look better.' Delia allowed herself to accept this rare compliment at face value.

'Who likes leg and who prefers breast?' Johnny asked as he carved the perfectly cooked chicken.

'You know me, son. I've always liked a bit of both.' Harvey laughed heartily, his horsey teeth gleaming yellow in the candlelight.

Johnny shot him a look. 'I don't think you should be telling sexist jokes like that anymore, Dad.'

'What's sexist about that? We were talking about a bloody chicken, weren't we?' He laughed again.

'Delia and Ma might find it offensive,' Johnny said.

'I'm in my own home. I am not bloody apologizing to my wife . . . or yours. You need to man up, son.'

'It's fine, Johnny,' Delia said quietly. 'Let's just enjoy our dinner.'

'There's a good girl.' Harvey clamped his eyes on Delia's. 'No need to make a fuss, is there?' He turned to his son. 'I must congratulate you, Johnny boy. Smart move, having a secret wedding. You've saved me tens of thousands of pounds. You should have seen what your mother was planning: marquee, band, flowers, five-course meal, disco . . . It would have paupered me.'

Vivienne stared at him through drunken eyes. 'What's that?'

'You don't have to worry about any wedding plans,' Harvey said loudly.

Vivienne threw her arms back expansively. 'It'll be the greatest party Wilder Hoo has ever seen. Nothing too good for our Johnny and' – she placed a palm on her forehead, eyes screwed up – 'Celia,' she announced triumphantly. 'I think I keep getting that wrong. I've called you Delia once or twice, but it's Celia; I've got it now.'

Harvey shook his head. 'Vivvi, they are married. We don't need to do it again. No wedding, no party. All done.'

'No marquee?'

'No.'

'No disco and Chinese lanterns?'

'No.'

Vivienne sank back in her chair. 'Thank fuck for that.'

When Johnny followed Delia up the stairs to bed, she knew she wouldn't be able to hide how much the evening had upset her.

In their room, he closed the door on the rest of the house and took her hands gently. 'I'm sorry about Ma and Pa. One day you will have your big wedding. I promise. If it's that important to you.'

Delia shook her head. 'I don't mind.'

He pulled her close to him, and she leant her head against his shirt. 'The thing is – and please don't tell Ma or Pa I've told you this – the property deal in Spain, the one that will absolutely fund everything we need to do to Wilder Hoo, has hit a delay. Contractors, finance . . . all very complicated and something to do with Brexit. But I promise you this: as soon as the deal is done and the house is up and running, we will reconsecrate the old Wilder Hoo chapel, and you will be the first bride to walk down the aisle for two hundred years. All our friends, your aunt and Sammi will witness how much we love each other. It just might take a while.'

'How long do you think?'

'I wish I could give you an accurate answer, but I'm hoping it won't be more than three to five years.' Johnny's eyes were on her, pleading with her to understand.

Delia blinked, then laughed.

'Why are you laughing?'

'Five years! I'll be over forty! We could have kids by then.'

'Better still!'

Delia wiped her eyes, still smiling. 'I can wait.' She kissed him. 'So, tell me more about your dad and the deal.'

It was Johnny's turn to laugh. 'It's mad.' He pushed his hand through his hair and strode around the room. 'Look, I know my parents can be difficult, but it's a stressful time for them, right now. On paper, Dad's a multimillionaire. In actual cash, he's broke. But as soon as the deal is done, life will be gravy. And, one day, it will all be ours. Just don't tell Dad I told you that.'

Delia's mind was racing as a plan started to form. 'I have an idea,' she said. 'Why don't we help them?'

Johnny frowned. 'What?'

She reached out and squeezed his hand tight. 'I mean it. Let's help your parents put Wilder Hoo to rights.'

CHAPTER SEVENTEEN

As they pulled away in the car, Delia glanced back at her waving in-laws. Wilder Hoo's dilapidation was brutally clear in the unforgiving morning light. She was sensitive to their money concerns and certainly understood how worrying they must be. She'd grown up recognizing how anxieties surrounding a tight budget affected her mum and Auntie Rose.

Delia might not like Vivienne and Harvey very much, but she adored their son. She glanced over at Johnny, who was driving with one hand on the wheel, humming along to the radio. She would do anything to make him happy. His own worries about lack of auditions and income rendered him sometimes tense or moody, but she understood and always worked hard to bring him back to the Johnny who adored her, who made her feel loved and alive. The love she felt between them gave her wings to fly over any problems and wrap him safely in her care. If he was happy, she was happy.

She determined to be the best wife, best daughter-in-law, and best colleague she could. Which would mean telling her boss, David Gilson, that she had to find a better work–life balance.

As soon as she was back in London, she popped her head around the door of his tiny office.

'David? Can you spare a few minutes?'

'Well, darling, how can I help you?' he asked, once she was settled in an old velvet armchair. 'Please don't tell me you're pregnant; I can't do without you at the moment.'

'I am not pregnant.' Delia could say this with absolute certainty. She and Johnny had decided to hold fire on that one for now.

'Oh, thank God.'

She took a deep breath. 'I need to change my working pattern and take one long weekend off every four weeks – which would mean leaving on a Thursday after work and not returning until Tuesday morning.'

David leant back in his chair, mouth wide open in horror. 'You're killing me! What for?'

'It's Wilder Hoo – my in-laws' place. There are things that need doing to it before the big plan comes online, and I need to support Johnny in helping with it. It's a wreck: only intermittent hot water, no central heating, cold air coming in through all the loose windows, rain coming through the roof . . . There's not a lot I can do about the structural damage, because we need permissions from the council – they're in a muddle because they thought it was Grade I listed, which it's not, but it should be.' She sighed. 'But we *can* get some cosmetic work done: coat of paint, get the boiler fixed, make it look more like a home than a squat. And that's why I need the time off.'

David put his heavy-framed, square glasses on top of his balding head and rubbed his eyes. 'If you really must, I can't deny you. You've put in enough long years here, *but*—' He held up his index finger. 'I want a similar deal. I shall take a long weekend once a month, too, in between yours, and you'll cover for me. And why? Well, my own national treasure, my dear old mum, gets a bit lonely at home while I'm at work. It's about time I looked after her better. Fair is fair. Is it a deal?'

Delia grinned. 'Deal.'

The first Cornwall long weekend was in early May. Delia and Johnny headed down on the Thursday evening, having fish and chips on the way down so as not to put Vivienne to any trouble. Johnny was in an ebullient mood on the drive, making Delia laugh until she cried with a story of the latest audition he'd gone to.

'Just another day in the life of a jobbing actor.' His smile slipped, and he rubbed his temples. 'I'm sorry, darling. You didn't sign up to have a husband who is a total failure. No work. No money.'

She took her hand from the steering wheel and held his. 'But you have all my love and total confidence. Your time will come. It's just around the corner.'

He held her hand to his lips and kissed it. 'I have opened my heart so wide to you, Cordelia. You hold it in your hand. You could crush it at any moment, and I would die.'

By the time they arrived at Wilder Hoo, the night air was cold and the house stood in darkness. After creeping quietly up the shadowy stairs, they fumbled their way down the gloomy corridor to their room and, with relief, climbed into the icy bed with all their clothes on, hugging each other for warmth.

Delia woke first and checked the time on her phone: twenty past eight. Good. She had made a plan and was determined to execute it. Slipping out of bed, she peeked through the old curtains, trying to ignore the shower of dust drifting down from the pelmets.

It was a beautiful day. A primrose-yellow sun rose above the drive, pushing long shadows of the ancient oaks across the dewy parkland.

'Close the curtains,' Johnny groaned from the bed. 'It's too bright.'

'It's lovely out there.'

'Come back to bed.'

'I was thinking of making a cup of tea.'

'Come back to bed, and I'll make you one after.'

She smiled. 'After?'

He held the bedclothes open, inviting her in. 'You must be cold standing there. Let me warm you up,' he whispered.

Afterwards, he did bring her a cup of tea and got back into bed, where she happily nestled into him.

'Are your parents up yet?' she asked.

'What do you think?' Johnny raised his eyebrows. 'They'll sleep in 'til noon if we let them. They have retreated to their adolescence.'

'I need to talk to Vivienne. I do worry about your mum and dad living here. One dropped cigarette and the whole place goes up in smoke.'

'I thought you just wanted to paint a couple of rooms?' Johnny yawned. 'It's not that bad.'

'Are you kidding? We need roofers, electricians, plumbers, plasterers.' She ticked them off on her fingers. 'Wilder Hoo needs life support or your dad may not have a house or business left.'

'A bit dramatic. And maybe the worse it gets, the more grants Dad will get to restore it.'

'What? That's mad thinking.'

'I'm *joking*.' He stretched his arms above his head. 'There's not enough money in the Wilder Hoo pot for a new kettle, let alone a new boiler and a mended roof.'

'I can help with stuff like that. I have some savings and I'm family now. I know your parents don't think I'm good enough for you.'

'Oh, Delia—'

'But it's true, isn't it?' She sat up straighter. 'I'll prove to them that I am. Let me show my allegiance to your parents' dream.'

Delia was sitting at the kitchen table, making a shopping list for her trip to the local hardware store, when Vivienne's arrival made her jump.

'Celia, dear, you're up with the bloody lark. I thought we had burglars with all the noise you were making.'

'Good morning,' Delia replied, knowing full well it was well after midday.

Vivienne tottered to the sink to fill the kettle. 'I need coffee. Would you like one? I'll make it while you scramble some eggs for us all.' She waved an arm towards the larder. 'It should all be in there. Mrs Joy is an angel. Where's Johnny?'

'I'm here.' Johnny stood in the doorway. 'If you're making coffee, Ma, I'll have one. Any bacon going?'

The ring of leather-soled brogues coming down the passage to the kitchen announced the arrival of Harvey. 'Cooked breakfast, eh? Wouldn't say no to a sausage.'

An hour later, the three Carlisle-Harts disappeared into the garden, discussing whether to pay a local farmer to cut the fields or buy a second-hand tractor to do it themselves. Delia watched them through the window over a pile of dirty plates and pans, waiting for the kettle to produce some hot water to wash them with. There was still no working hot water supply to the kitchen.

Harvey was pointing at a well-spaced group of poplar trees, waving towards the branches. Whatever he was discussing, Vivienne clearly didn't agree: she was shaking her head and flicking him a V-sign behind his back

Delia watched the curious family of which she was now a part, seemingly fond of each other and yet also so easily irritated and judgmental. She found Harvey particularly hard to figure out.

How did fathers fit into families? She often wondered how different her life would have been if her own father had stayed. Would he have read bedtime stories as well as her mum did, doing all the voices? Would he have carried her on his shoulders, kissed a banged knee better, always provided a lap to clamber on?

Would she have had siblings? Real siblings who she had grown up with, not half-siblings she would never know?

Would Auntie Rose have moved out, moved on, made her own home with a husband and children?

Would her own mum still be alive? How different her life would have been with a husband who had cared for her, helping her to farm Jago Fields, getting out of their warm bed in the early hours and all weathers, leaving his wife to slumber peacefully. A man who would never have allowed his wife to die on a second-hand quad bike.

If only.

Two of the most dangerous words in the English language.

She reminded herself that the man Auntie Rose had told her about would never have been a father or a husband like that.

She dried up the dishes and plates and returned them all to their rightful places.

She glanced out of the window again, looking for Johnny, who she hoped would come to the hardware store with her, but there was no sign of him or Vivienne or Harvey.

They hadn't come inside; she would have heard them come through the back door.

She went out to the garden and walked the path surrounding Wilder Hoo, calling their names, shielding her eyes from the bright sun.

It wasn't until she walked round to the front of the house that she saw Harvey's car was gone. They had gone out without her.

What was she supposed to do? Stay and wait for them to come back, like a family dog?

She went to the kitchen and made herself a cup of tea. She opened a new pack of biscuits and deliberately left it open, with crumbs around it.

Let them clear it up.

But a few minutes later, she recognized this small rebellion as childish and closed the packet, sweeping the crumbs into her hand and thence to the bin.

She sighed. 'Right, Cordelia Jago, stop feeling abandoned and get on with what you came here to do.'

She picked up her bag, her list, her car keys, and headed for her car. She sang a little song to herself, 'Hey diddly dee, it's B&Q for me,' which cheered her up a bit.

It was almost 4 p.m. when she returned with cleaning products, bucket, mop, dusters, small stepladders, tester pots of paint, a decent vacuum cleaner, and a microwave. She had also picked up at the checkout several business cards for local plumbers and electricians.

After installing the microwave in the kitchen and plugging it in to the one remaining, least dangerous socket, she lugged everything else up to Vivienne and Harvey's living quarters: a set of rooms she had never been invited to see, but had walked past countless times. They were situated in prime position, directly opposite the stairs. She knocked at the door, just in case, for some odd reason, all three of the Carlisle-Harts were playing a bizarre game of hide and seek with her and, on hearing nothing, she turned the handle and entered.

Ahead of her, three great windows overlooked the terrace, the gardens, the woods, all the way down to the sea.

Delia stood, imagining how it must have looked when first built. How the oak panelled walls must have shone with flickering candlelight. What magnificent drapes must have hung at the windows.

Once restored, it would surely be the jewel of the house.

But what a lot it needed. Lumps of plaster drooped from the ceiling, leaving glimpses of the black space above. Damp was spreading along the oak skirting boards. The red Turkish carpet might have been an original from the early Victorian period, but it smelt of mushrooms and had all the signs of mice activity.

It was, however, a room that deserved respect: a good vacuum and a dust.

Delia searched for a usable socket, but the ones she did find were dangling from the walls on bare wires.

Eventually, she found a four-socket extension cable next to her in-laws unmade, king-size divan bed, made to look miniature by the enormous room, and plugged the vacuum into the one available place.

Out of the corner of her eye, she saw a small brown mouse running for cover and hesitated. If she turned the vacuum on, would the noise bring out more?

She closed her eyes and told herself that a mouse had never killed anyone, then switched the machine on. There were no more mice, but she disturbed a couple of very large spiders and a few woodlice. She kept going until things looked brighter and more respectable. Next, she made the bed, dusted the meagre bits of furniture and hung up the many clothes that were scattered around.

How did her in-laws live like this? Maybe all owners of great crumbling houses did the same? Keeping up appearances while sharing life with mice, damp, and cold.

She thought of Auntie Rose and her mum. They had always kept a clean and tidy house. They would be astonished, if not horrified, to see how Vivienne and Harvey lived.

Next stop was the bathroom, through a door to the right, which was small and very damp. Someone had put a bucket under the sky-high cistern to catch a drip that was rotting the floorboards. The iron bath was enormous, deep, and stained, the taps old and bulbous.

'Blimey, it must take hours to fill you up,' she told it. 'When was the last time you were used? And look at the sink! Big enough for a baby to swim in.'

She got to work. After an hour, with the window open, bringing in fresh air, the room looked a little more cheery – cold, but cheery. The place had scrubbed up reasonably well.

From downstairs, she heard voices, Johnny calling, 'Delia!'

She went out onto the landing and saw Johnny's face looking up at her from the hall. 'There you are,' he said.

'Where have you been?' she asked, careful to modulate her voice so that she didn't sound cross.

'We went to the farm sale. We did tell you.'

'It's just that you didn't say goodbye—'

'We got a tractor for a song. Needs some work. It'll be a nice little project for me and Dad. Right, Ma's got tea and cake in the saloon. We had a bite to eat in the café in Penvare. Really good. We should go sometime. Brought home your favourite: coffee sponge.'

Delia didn't tell him that her favourite was actually Victoria sponge.

A fire was lit in the saloon, but it hadn't had time to heat the room yet. Vivienne, still in her coat, had pulled her armchair as close to the flames as she could. Harvey and Johnny were congratulating themselves on their new purchase.

Delia wrapped her hands around the warm mug of tea and tried to take an interest. 'What make is the tractor? My grandfather swore by his old Massey Ferguson.'

Harvey disregarded her comment. 'Lovely old John Deere. Better than anything else. Thirty-two horsepower. Plenty for us. Rear drawbar included. Diesel. Great buy. We did well there, my son.'

'I couldn't believe it when the hammer fell in our favour.' Johnny smiled at Delia. 'I mean, always sad when a farm goes under, and they have to sell it off, but for us . . .' Johnny rubbed his hands. 'It's brilliant.'

Harvey heartily agreed. 'Good business today, lad. Good business was done.'

Delia wanted to hear more. 'How much was it?'

'Starting price was 3k. We got it at five and a half.'

Delia was surprised. If they had that kind of money, fixing the plumbing seemed more of a priority. 'That does sound good. Does the engine run OK?'

Harvey barked a laugh. 'We've got the logbook. Services all recorded. We just need to tinker with it. It's got years left in it.'

Vivienne, who had declined a cup of tea but accepted a large G&T, drained the glass and stood up. 'All that excitement and fresh air has made me utterly exhausted. I'm going upstairs to have a little nap.'

Delia smiled. 'I hope you don't mind, but I gave your room a little dust and polish.'

'Why?' Vivienne asked. 'Mrs Joy did it last week.'

'Oh.' Delia was embarrassed. 'Sorry, I didn't realize.'

Vivienne waved her apology away. 'I suppose you were being kind . . .' She walked, slightly unevenly, to the door, then turned. 'I don't suppose, now you're in domestic mode, you'd like to make dinner tonight, would you, Celia dear? That would be such a weight off my mind.'

Dinner in the old-fashioned, rustic kitchen was easier than Delia had expected. On the table, there was a note from Mrs Joy.

I have popped in and put a beef casserole and a sherry trifle in the fridge. There are some green beans and peeled potatoes ready to boil, by the sink. Until next week.
Mrs Joy x

Delia would have kissed her if she ever got a chance to meet her. The woman was a fairy godmother.

Sitting round the dinner table that evening, the conversation turned to the screenplay Johnny had started to write.

'How is it going, darling?' Vivienne took her hand and tenderly cupped one side of Johnny's face. 'You're such a clever boy.'

'Thanks, Ma. It's coming on, but' – he turned and took Delia's hand – 'I had a phone call while we were out.' His eyes were on her, his face lit by that boyish grin she loved.

Delia put her hand to her lips, her eyes sparkling. 'Is it what I think it is? Was it them?'

He winked. 'It was.'

Vivienne opened her eyes wide and adoringly. 'Well, what is it?'

'I've got a role in a drama for telly. A spy thriller.'

Delia was shaking with anticipation. 'Well done, my love. Well done!'

'God, I love those thrillers,' Vivienne slurred. 'The plots are all so complicated. I often don't understand what's happening, but maybe that's the point?'

Harvey pushed his chair back noisily and reached for the bottle of wine behind him. 'The only reason you don't understand them, Vivvi, is because you are too pissed and fall asleep in the middle.'

'If I fall asleep, it's because you're such a crashing bore, Harvey. Now, let Johnny tell us more.'

'Well, it's a spy drama all shot on location around London, so I'll be home.' He squeezed Delia's hand. 'The part is good. Not the first lead or even second, but a really nice pivotal role as the genius computer analyst who the rest of the team rely on. He's quite funny, too.'

'Brilliant.' Vivienne lurched back in her chair. 'I'll be at the premiere.'

CHAPTER EIGHTEEN

Returning to London, and desperate to be in peak physical condition for his new job. Johnny threw himself into a committed relationship with the local gym.

Delia became accustomed to the 5.00 a.m. alarm for his morning run, the constant stubbing of her toes on heavy dumb bells he'd leave anywhere and a washing basket full of sweaty shorts and running vests.

By the end of the summer, the major topic of any conversation with him was now about his abs, glutes, delts, quads, and his daily runs through the park with his new personal trainer.

She missed living with Harriet, of course, but she loved the home she and Johnny were building together. They still saw a lot of Hattie, having her round regularly for dinner or drinks, but Johnny and Sammi hadn't quite hit it off, so Delia saw him less often.

Johnny had been right that it was nice to own a place of their own. She had never lived with any man before him, and it was a learning curve, but Delia was sure that was what marriage was all about: give and take, adapting to each other's routines and needs.

Johnny was happy, and that always made Delia happy. She enjoyed hearing about his latest running route and congratulating him on his first 10K run. He even started running around the grounds of Wilder Hoo when they were there for their long weekends. While Delia scrubbed and tidied, painted and repaired, Johnny would be outside, training hard.

By late autumn, Delia was feeling the strain. Her work at Gilson's was enough but the long hours of graft at Wilder Hoo, with little obvious appreciation from Vivienne or Harvey, were wearing her down.

Arriving tired for work one morning, she was alarmed to find the whole team gathered in the salon and looking mystified. She found Harriet. 'What's going on?'

Hattie shrugged. 'David says he has an announcement to make. I thought you'd know.'

Delia shook her head as David appeared.

'Morning everyone.' David waited for quiet to settle. 'As you know, we are heading into our manic Christmas season. I expect you to work all the hours so that we can give our clients the very best experience – better even than they expect. But for the first time since I can remember, after we shut on Chrsitmas Eve, I will not be reopening the salon.'

The team stood in stunned silence.

Delia was furious. Why hadn't he discussed this with her, his second in command, before now? She was about to remonstrate with him when he broke into a smile. 'I am closing the salon for a major refit, ready to open again mid-January, and I'm giving you all paid leave while we're shut.'

A whole two weeks off! Delia couldn't remember the last time she'd had such a long break from work. In the staff room, she went to phone Johnny and tell him the good news, then remembered he was filming today. Instead, she found her finger hovering over Auntie Rose's name in her contacts.

She hadn't seen her in months, and their phone calls had grown short and tense lately. She knew her aunt was hurt that she'd been excluded from the wedding, but that was nearly a year ago now. She wished Auntie Rose could understand and just be happy for her. Perhaps now with the salon closing, there was the opportunity to build some bridges. Johnny and she would spend Christmas at Jago Fields.

She dialled Auntie Rose's number before she could change her mind.

'Oh, darling, that's wonderful,' said Auntie Rose, once she'd told her the good news. 'It will be lovely to have you both for Christmas. Perfect timing, too. It'll be our last at Jago Fields.'

Delia's heart dropped. Rose had mentioned the possibility of selling Jago Fields earlier in the year, but she hadn't realized things were at this stage. 'You've had an offer?'

'Yes, from a lovely young couple.'

'Gosh. Our last Christmas at home then.' Delia said sadly.

'We'll make sure it's wonderful. Just as our darling Chris would want. It might be a bit hard for us, saying goodbye to the old place and . . .' Delia heard her aunt swallow the lump. '. . . all its memories.'

Delia wiped her eyes. 'Mum would be happy for you, though.'

'She would. Happy for us both.'

A few hours later, Delia pushed open the flat's front door with a smile on her face. 'Johnny, I've got some good news.'

But when she explained about the time off and her call with Auntie Rose, Johnny's brow furrowed. 'Not possible, I'm afraid.'

'What do you mean?'

'I've told Ma and Pa that we're spending Christmas with them at Wilder Hoo.'

Delia smiled, masking her anxiety, hoping to avoid a row. 'I'm sure we can work something out. Why not share it? Christmas Day with Auntie Rose and Boxing Day at Wilder Hoo?'

Johnny rubbed his forehead, speaking slowly and clearly as if to a child. 'No. I'm back filming second week of January and I want to spend from Christmas Eve until then with my parents. The Vare Castle has a very decent gym and pool, so I can keep up my regime. You know how important that is right now.'

Delia frowned. 'I know, but Auntie Rose is selling Jago Fields. This is the last Christmas I'd get to spend there. Why don't we drive down to Auntie Rose first, on Christmas Eve, have Christmas lunch there and then drive up to Wilder Hoo for Christmas night and the rest of our time off?'

'We can't.' Johnny spoke firmly. 'I've told you before it's our tradition to have Christmas Eve dinner at The Vare Castle. It's all booked. I'm not upsetting my parents' plans just to appease your aunt.'

Delia blinked, feeling tears sting her eyes. How could he not see what this meant to her? 'Johnny, we see your parents every month—'

'I said no. End of discussion.'

Something in Delia snapped. 'Well, you and your parents can have Christmas Day together, but I'll be at Jago Fields.'

Johnny stared at her, clearly surprised at her response, but then his face hardened, 'Your decision.'

'Johnny.' She put her hand on his arm but he shrugged it off. 'Johnny, don't be like that.'

'After all I do for you, and you can't spend Christmas with my family?'

'That's not what I said.'

'Yes it is. You've made yourself very clear. Now, if you'll excuse me, I'm going for a run. I need to clear my head.'

And so began an episode of The Silent Treatment.

Not for the first time.

A few days later, Delia decided to confide in Harriet. They went out for a drink after work, and over a glass of wine, Delia talked through the whole sorry story.

'I know his focus is all on the TV series right now. It's an important breakthrough for him. I get that. But a last Christmas at Jago Fields is important to me, too. Last night, I told him that not speaking to me was silly and we had to sort things out, and he said he hadn't decided when he was going to speak to me about it, and that was that. I really want him to come to Bozinjal and spend Christmas with me and Auntie Rose – just one day, but he won't budge. It's like he doesn't care at all.'

'Oh, Delia, he *does*.' Harriet leant forward in her seat. 'He rang me last night and told me all about it.'

Delia frowned. 'Johnny rang you?'

'He was so upset, and I think he just wanted a friend to talk things through with. We had a long chat, and he explained how he was feeling. He knows that this might be your last Christmas at Jago Fields, and he wants you to have the best memories of it, but he feels he'd be the spectre at the feast. Out of his depth. You and Rose have all those memories, and he would never be able to share them.'

Delia felt a bit dizzy. 'He said that?'

'Yes.' Harriet filled Delia's glass of wine. 'I thought it was rather sweet of him not to want to get in the way.'

'But—'

'He said something else really kind, too,' Harriet went on. 'He was worrying about his parents being cross with you, because they've already paid for Christmas Eve dinner and Christmas lunch for four people at The Vare Castle. Anyway, you know I was going to spend Christmas on my own after me and Max split up, so Johnny said why didn't I come to Wilder Hoo?'

Delia blinked, puzzled. 'He said what?'

'Well, it makes sense, really,' said Harriet. 'That way his parents won't be angry at you about the booking. And you two go on so much about Wilder Hoo, I'm dying to see it.'

'So . . . you're going to go?'

'Yes. I'm happy to.'

Delia felt a spark of anger. Did Johnny expect her to suddenly drop Auntie Rose and spend Christmas at Wilder Hoo out of . . . jealousy? Was that what this was about?

Or maybe he was just trying to be a good friend to Harriet and to keep his parents happy.

She ran her hand through her hair and tried to make her voice light. 'Well, if you're going to Wilder Hoo, you'd better pack your winceyette nightie and thermal undies. It's a *very* cold house. And Vivienne can be a bit tricky.'

'You don't mind, do you?' Harriet asked. 'I mean, it is only me. And Johnny doesn't mind that you're taking Sammi to Jago Fields.'

'I haven't asked Sammi.' Delia was beginning to feel a bit queasy.

'Haven't you?' Harriet frowned. 'Johnny thinks you have.'

'No, we haven't spoken about anything like that. To be honest, I just really want to see Auntie Rose and have her to myself.' A wicked thought popped into her head. 'Although . . . you could always come to Bozinjal with me?'

Before Harriet could answer, Delia's phone rang, and she checked the caller ID. 'It's Sammi.' She pressed *answer*. 'Hi! I'm with Harriet. How are you?'

Harriet grabbed the phone. 'Sammi, what are you doing for Christmas? . . . why don't you go to Jago Fields with Delia to spend Christmas with Auntie Rose?'

Delia snatched the phone back. 'Ignore her, Sammi . . . What? . . . You can? . . . Yeah, I'm thinking of driving down on Christmas Eve after work . . . Four o'clock . . . Auntie Rose loves you, too. Aw, Sammi, this is great . . . You've made my day. Bye.' Delia grinned as she put her phone back in her pocket.

'See?' Harriet was smiling. 'Perfect, right?'

She held up her glass as though in a toast, and Delia felt her worries slip away. Harriet and Johnny were just friends, like she and Sammi were just friends. She really mustn't let herself get caught up in silly suspicions.

She clinked her wine glass against Harriet's.

Back in the flat that night, Johnny, sprawled on the sofa, simply sighed when Delia asked him about his invitation to Harriet. 'She's a mate. Ma and Pa will love her, and we can have some fun while you're down in Bozinjal.'

Delia felt the sting but smiled as if she was thrilled. 'Sammi's going to come to Bozinjal with me, too.'

'Is he?' Johnny's laugh was laced with sarcasm. 'At least you'll be safe with him, won't you?'

Delia did not rise to the provocation. 'Exactly.'

'Come here.' Johnny patted the sofa and put an arm around her shoulder when she sat down. 'Are we speaking again?'

Her voice was quiet but firm. 'I wasn't the one who stopped speaking.'

'Don't start that again.' He nuzzled into her neck. 'I've missed you.' He ran his hands over her abdomen. 'Fancy an early night? I had a fantasy the other day – I tied you up with silk, and you were all mine . . .'

He clearly didn't see the small frown that creased her brow. 'That's not my thing.'

He continued to nuzzle. 'Don't knock it until you've tried it.'

'I don't want to try it.'

He stopped nuzzling. 'Oh, for goodness' sake. Loosen up. Just a joke. For Christ's sake.' He sat up. 'How to ruin the mood in one easy step.'

He strutted off to the kitchen and began noisily opening and shutting drawers and cupboards.

She followed him, and asked hesitantly, 'Are you hungry? I've got fish fingers in the freezer—'

He turned back towards her. 'I miss you. We haven't made love all week.'

She sighed. 'Can we try again?'

'Now?'

'Yes.'

'Where?'

'Here?'

'In the kitchen? Oh, you naughty girl.'

He stepped towards her and slipped his hands under her blouse and inside her bra, freeing a nipple.

'Take your jeans off,' he whispered. 'Take everything off.'

He hastily undid his trousers and stepped out of his underpants, leaving his shirt on. He watched her disrobe intently.

When Delia was fully naked, he put his hands on her waist and lifted her onto the small kitchen table. It was cold on her back as she lay down, and she shivered.

Johnny began kissing her from her shoulders to her inner thighs. Then, with his newly muscled arms, he flipped her onto her stomach and moved his hand to part her buttocks.

'No, Johnny. Not that.'

'I think you should be a little more open-minded.' His hand found its way between her buttocks again, probing. 'You might like it.'

She tensed up and said more firmly, 'No. I don't want it like that.'

'How do you know until you've tried?' His other arm was underneath her, pulling tighter around her stomach now. Insistent. Pulling her towards him. Pressing himself against her.

'No, Johnny. No.'

'Go on. Just this once.' His grip was strong, and he pushed inside her.

The pain was immediate. She tried to wriggle away from him. 'I said no. It hurts. Please stop.'

But her words seemed only to excite him further.

When he'd finished, he loosened his hold and kissed her neck and shoulders again. 'There.' He nuzzled into her ear. 'That wasn't so bad, was it?'

Delia could not move, let alone speak.

He let go of her and began searching for his underwear. 'Fancy a Chinese?'

CHAPTER NINETEEN

London, eighteen months ago

The run up to Christmas at Gilson's was frenetic, with long days filled with Christmas party blow-dries, special occasion styling, and the usual high-profile clientele, and Delia had to block the reality of what Johnny had done, simply to keep going. When it was less vivid, less upsetting, and less likely to cause a row, she'd discuss it with him.

But at the moment, he seemed happier and more loving than ever. Their separate plans for Christmas not mentioned. It was easier to continue as they were, rather than create a mountain out of a mole hill. A blip. Everyone had them. Least said, soonest mended.

Anyway, she had enough to occupy her mind with back-to-back appointments for faithful clients shoehorned into diary slots that barely existed.

She couldn't wait to be back at Jago Fields, and was counting down the days to Christmas Eve. She felt confident that the awkwardness between her and Auntie Rose would be fixed as soon as they saw each other, especially in the absence of Johnny. Rose had been rather relieved that Sammi had been substituted but had been nonplussed about Harriet's invitation to Wilder Hoo. Delia had done her best to explain: 'His parents had everything booked, and poor Harriet had nowhere else to go. So it makes sense. And you, me, and Sammi will have a great time. Johnny and I have our whole lives to spend Christmas together.'

Gilson's closed at 4 p.m. on Christmas Eve, but Johnny arrived an hour early to collect Harriet for the trip to Cornwall. 'Hello darling.' He strode over to where Delia was cutting the hair of an elderly male client. 'I don't mean you, sir.' He patted the man's caped shoulder. 'Do you mind if I give my wife here a Christmas kiss?'

'No at all, young man,' replied the client.

'You're early, Johnny.' Delia couldn't keep the coolness from her voice.

'Snow coming.' Johnny stuck his hands in his pockets. 'Don't want to get stuck on the motorway.'

'Is there?' She glanced out of the windows and saw a flurry of light snowflakes falling gently onto the King's Road. 'Oh yes. How lovely. But, Johnny, Harriet can't leave until four when we close. David would not be impressed.'

'I'll have a word with him.'

'He's not here.'

'Ah. So, who's in charge?'

Reluctantly, Delia had to confess. 'Me.'

'In that case . . .' Johnny spotted Harriet as she appeared from the back office. 'Harriet, get your bag, we're going.'

Harriet looked worriedly at Delia, then back to Johnny. 'But—'

'The boss says it's fine.' Johnny smiled at Delia. 'Don't you?'

'No, but . . . as it's snowing, off you go.'

It only took a few minutes for Harriet to collect her bags, warm coat, and boots. She hugged Delia goodbye. 'Thank you.' She kissed her cheek. 'Happy Christmas, and don't worry about Johnny. I'll look after him. We'll miss you terribly.'

'I really will, darling.' Johnny collected Delia in his arms and held her tight. 'I love you so much. Have a good time with Rose and Sammi, and see you on Boxing Day at Wilder Hoo. You will miss me, won't you?'

'Yes, very much. Happy Christmas, and all my love to Vivienne and Harvey. Please drive carefully. Let me know if the snow gets worse, won't you?'

Johnny was already at the door. 'It'll be fine. Bye!'

She watched as Johnny and Harriet ran through the light and fluffy flakes that were settling on the car roofs and ugly wheelie bins and the shoulders of Harriet's coat.

She sighed. Just another hour until closing time, and then Sammi would be here.

Sure enough, he arrived at Gilson's bang on time as the last of the clients were being helped into their coats.

'Taxi for Miss Jago?' He called across the salon, making Delia and a couple of the junior stylists giggle.

'Give me five minutes and I'll be out of here.'

'No problem. I'll bring the van round.' He blew the junior stylists each a mischievous kiss. 'Have a good one, girls. Won't be as good as the one I'm having with your boss though.'

Bags collected, alarm switched on and door locked tight, Delia finally made it out to the pavement, where Sammi was watching the drifting snowflakes.

'What are you doing getting cold?' she tutted. 'It's freezing. Why aren't you in the van?'

'I like the way the snow has given the King's Road a frosted yuletide air. Almost Dickensian.' He took a deep breath. 'There's a lot of life to enjoy, isn't there?'

'Are you going soppy over a bit of snow?'

He turned to look at her. 'Me? Soppy? Puh-lease! Not at all – I was just reminding myself that the world is full of beauty.'

Delia looked up into the dark Chelsea sky and felt the snow as it feathered her face. 'You're right. We don't give ourselves enough time to appreciate the small things, do we?'

He put his arm around her shoulder. 'We are going to have a lovely Christmas.'

'I hope so.'

'Come on, give me your case.'

He opened up the back of the van and Delia glimpsed rolls of fabric and two armchairs clearly due for reupholstering.

'Just picked up a consignment of kelims,' Sammi told her. 'They'll cover those chairs beautifully. Ah, and I have a something for you.' He reached into a large black bin liner, pulling out a coral throw edged with soft lilac. 'Cashmere, from my mum. Happy Christmas.'

Delia touched the softness. 'How kind of her. I love it.'

'No time for tears and thank yous.' Sammi put the throw back in the bag and closed the doors. 'I promised Auntie Rose I'd have you home before midnight. We don't want to bump into Father Christmas, do we?'

They arrived at Jago Fields with ten minutes to spare. The snow had petered out by the time they got to Bristol, and Cornwall was free of it. From the lane, Delia could see the Christmas tree in the window of the small sitting room, where it always stood. A beacon for Father Christmas.

As they climbed out of the van, the back door opened, throwing a rectangle of golden light into the darkness, with Auntie Rose's outline silhouetted against it.

The nagging worry about seeing her aunt again slipped away the moment Delia saw her bright smile.

'You're here! You made it! Let me take a bag. How was the traffic? I hear you had snow up country? Have you eaten? You must need the loo. What can I get you?'

Delia laughed. 'We're fine.'

'Hello, Auntie Rose.' Sammi allowed himself to be squashed into her strong hug.

'You've grown!' Rose let go of him. 'Or have I shrunk?'

'I've definitely grown. Very rude of me,' Sammi said apologetically.

'Come in, come in.' Rose rounded them up, got them into the kitchen, and locked the door on the cold night. 'So, what shall we do first? Why not put your bags upstairs and come down when you're ready. Delia, you're in your old room, Sammi in the spare room.'

As Delia came back downstairs, she could hear Rose and Sammi talking in the kitchen. Rose was asking, 'How is she really?'

'In . . . what way?' Sammi replied.

'The Johnny way. I've never met the man! If I ring and he answers, he can't wait to hand me over to Delia. Why isn't he here with her? What's going on? And don't give me any old excuse. Something isn't right. They've only been married a year. Are they happy, do you think? Or—'

Delia didn't want to hear any more. She hurried on down the stairs, making sure her footsteps sounded loudly this time, and pushed open the door to the kitchen.

'So lovely to be home again,' she declared, as brightly as she could. 'All cosy and warm, and look at those bacon sarnies. Yum.'

Rose smiled. 'Let's eat these in the other room.'

The sitting room, lit only by the fire and the tree lights, looked magical. It reminded Delia of all the Christmases of her childhood, and she felt tears build in her eyes. Her mum ought to be here.

She pushed sad thoughts away and looked around the room again, focusing on the happy memories.

'The perfect Christmas Eve,' she said, climbing onto her mother's old armchair and tucking her feet beneath her. 'It's so good to be home.'

'It's good to have you. With or without Johnny,' Rose added with a little laugh.

Delia ignored it. 'Johnny will be in his element, showing Wilder Hoo off to Hattie. It's looking a lot better since we've been working on it, but once hypothermia sets in, you don't really care.' Delia made herself laugh. 'I'm being mean. But really, I'd rather be here.'

Auntie Rose agreed and raised her glass of mulled wine. 'To us and those who love us. Happy Christmas.'

'Happy Christmas.'

They lapsed into silence, enjoying the fire. Delia was glad that Auntie Rose hadn't brought up the wedding and her disappointment at not being there. Delia wouldn't have had an answer anyway.

Sammi pulled himself out of his chair and stretched.

'Are you off to bed?' asked Delia.

'No no. I've just noticed, there is something missing by the tree.'

Auntie Rose looked at it, trying to see. 'What's missing?'

Sammi cocked his head, listening. 'Excuse me for a moment, but I believe I heard sleigh bells coming from my bedroom. A delivery perhaps?'

He came back with two small boxes. 'Here we are. The tree is missing presents underneath it.'

'Oh, no no no!' Delia said. 'You said we weren't doing presents this year.'

'Shush,' he told her, and handed one to each of them.

'This is very naughty of you, Sammi,' Auntie Rose protested.

'Stop complaining, the pair of you. Anyway, they're not real presents. They're just a little something from me to you. Open them now. Both together, please.'

In tandem, Rose and Delia undid their ribboned boxes and delved into layers of golden tissue paper before bringing out perfect silver bangles. One each.

'Sammi, you shouldn't have!' Delia slipped it over her wrist and twirled it around. 'It's beautiful.'

'Do they fit?' he asked anxiously.

'Perfectly,' said Rose, showing him hers. 'Thank you, Sammi. You really shouldn't have.'

'I know. I'm so lovely – everybody says so.'

Auntie Rose held out her empty mug. 'Are you lovely enough to get the last of the mulled wine and top us up?'

When the wine was drunk, they trooped up the stairs, saying their goodnights on the landing.

'Merry Christmas.' Rose gave them each a kiss. 'And thank you for coming all this way together.'

'Honestly, there's nowhere else I'd rather be,' Delia said.

Sammi smiled. 'Me too.'

Delia slept better than she had for a long time.

The grinding routine of early starts and late finishes at Gilson's, plus the tension between her and Johnny over the Christmas plans, had affected her more than she had admitted. Waking up in her childhood bed, she felt secure and at peace.

She reached out and checked her phone. Almost nine o'clock: a proper lie in.

She wondered what was happening at Wilder Hoo now? Johnny hadn't messaged her last night, but that didn't worry her. The mobile signal at Wilder Hoo was atrocious.

She got out of bed and made her way down to the kitchen, where she found Sammi at the sink, sleeves rolled up, peeling potatoes while the radio played Christmas carols.

The kitchen looked as it always had, busy with pots and pans and ornaments Delia had known since childhood. Looking around the place, she couldn't quite believe that this would be her last Christmas at Jago Fields.

Determined not to let such thoughts spoil her mood, she came up behind Sammi and slid her arms around his waist, putting her cheek to his back. 'Happy Christmas.'

'Aha!' Sammi grinned, turning round. 'She's alive!'

'Very much so. Where's Auntie Rose?'

'Collecting some eggs from the hens.'

'Of course she is. That used to be my job. What can I do to help?'

'Not much. Rose has been up since sparrow's fart.' Sammi finished the last of the potatoes and popped them into a saucepan with their mates. 'I think we're ahead of the game. We put the turkey in the bottom of the Aga, so that should be falling off the bone by early evening. All veg prepped. You can make a pot of tea.'

The tradition at Jago Fields was to eat late, giving the day an easy feel.

Breakfast was scrambled eggs and coffee, over which the three of them decided how the rest of the day would pan out.

The westerlies were scooting the clouds across a bright, watery sky, but there was no sign of rain.

'Who fancies a walk?' asked Rose.

'I'd love one,' Sammi said.

Delia agreed. 'Where shall we go?'

'What about Nanjizal?' asked Sammi. 'All those summers you, me, and Harriet spent down there, swimming in the little lagoon by the Song of the Sea Cave. I'm definitely up for that.'

'We could park at Land's End. It's about a thirty-minute walk from there.' Rose stood up, heading to the pantry. 'I made some pasties. I can warm them up and take them with us if you'd like.'

They did all very much like.

It didn't take long to get down to Land's End in the old Landy. When they pulled into the carpark, there were only four cars, including theirs, and a mini coach from which a gang of about eight women were alighting.

'Look at them,' Rose commented. 'Not a raincoat or proper boots between them.'

As Sammi got out, a sharp gust almost blew him off his feet, and as he steadied himself, an umbrella flew past him and got itself jammed under the Landy.

A shout came on the wind. 'Sorry!'

Delia climbed out of the Land Rover to see one of the women from the mini coach running towards them. 'I'm so sorry. Did it hit you? We totally underestimated the Cornish weather.'

While Sammi bent down to retrieve the umbrella, the woman turned to look at Delia.

'Oh my God. It's you, isn't it?' She turned and waved at her friends, who were huddling out of the wind. 'You'll never guess who this is!' Then she turned back to Delia. 'I'm so sorry. I know it's your private time and you don't want to be disturbed, but I'm a hairdresser and so are my mates. We absolutely love your work. We always watch your demo masterclasses online.

I remember that magazine spread where you talked about growing up down here. Oh, it was lovely. We just love you.'

Delia blushed. 'That's so kind.'

'As far as I'm concerned, you should have won Hairdresser of the Year last time. The guy who won is an absolute tosser.'

All members of her party had now gathered round, phones at the ready. 'Do you mind? Can we have a picture with you, Delia? It'd make our Christmas, honest to God.'

Sammi stepped in. 'Let me take the pics, ladies.' He was immediately laden with phones. 'Right. Smile! Everyone say SCISSORS!'

'Does that happen a lot?' Rose asked Delia as the fans retreated, leaving them free to head out to the coast path.

'Sometimes,' Delia said modestly 'It's bit embarrassing. Johnny doesn't like it.'

'Doesn't like his wife getting attention?' Rose looked horrified. 'He should be damn proud of you.'

'No, it's not that,' said Delia, quick to defend him. 'It's just it can get a bit intrusive, that's all. It makes me feel uncomfortable, and he tries to protect me from it.'

'Come, on you two.' Sammi was striding past them. 'I want to have my pasty at Nanjizal before they go cold.'

The path to Nanjizal was not an easy one. They clambered over rocks and steps and a bridge, with the sea always there to lure them on.

At last, they got down onto the wobbly boulders of Nanjizal and plodded their way to the lagoon, where they could sit on a stout rock and eat their pasties.

'This is living, Auntie Rose.' Sammi smiled with a mouthful of pasty inside his cheek. 'No one makes a better pasty.'

Delia was looking out at the natural crack in the rock called The Song of the Sea and the way it teased the glimpse of the

Atlantic beyond. She looked back at her aunt and Sammi and smiled. She was so glad she was spending Christmas with them.

Rose put her hand on her niece's knee. 'I had no idea that you are now a recognized face. Famous! How proud Chris would be.'

Back home, as they divested themselves of their many layers of coats and jumpers, Delia's phone pinged with a message from Johnny:

> *Happy Christmas. We're still at The Vare. Lunch excellent. Harriet having a ball. Getting on v well with Ma and Pa. They think she's hilarious. Hope your day is good. Love to you all. J x PS Phone signal awful as per.*

CHAPTER TWENTY

'Morning, my love.' Auntie Rose was mashing yesterday's veg for a bubble and squeak breakfast when Delia crept downstairs on Boxing Day morning. 'How's your head?'

Delia smiled lopsidedly. 'It's better than I think I deserve.'

Last night had been wonderful: a perfect dinner, lots of red wine, and several games of Canasta. Delia had won every time.

'Breakfast will sort you out. Would you get the bacon from the fridge for me? Do you fancy a fried egg on top of the bubble and squeak?'

'Yes, please.' Having handed over the eggs and bacon, Delia settled at the table, propping her sore head on her hand. 'Is Sammi up?'

'He's gone for milk. Have you heard from Johnny yet?'

'A text last night.'

'Is he OK?'

'Yeah,' said Delia, who then added a small white lie. 'Sends his love.'

'Ah, that's nice. Harriet enjoying herself?'

'Yeah.'

Delia knew that Rose was digging for more information but she wasn't going to get it because Delia didn't have any more.

Rose carried on. 'And they're still expecting you for lunch today?'

'Erm.' Delia swallowed, remembering Johnny's casual text about how much fun Vivienne and Harvey were having with Harriet. 'Change of plan; would it be be okay with you if Sammi and I stayed here another day?'

Rose's heart leapt with happiness. 'By all means. There's still an awful lot of turkey to be eaten. Why the change of mind?'

'Your cooking's better than Vivienne's.'

After feeding her hangover, Delia felt better. Rose and Sammi were surprised and delighted that she wanted to stay another day and began to make plans.

'I think we should all go for a swim,' Rose said

Sammi looked horrified. 'Rose, have you lost your mind? It's Boxing Day. Midwinter. And anyway, I don't have my costume.'

'We can buy one. The surf shop on the beach will be open today.' She held her hand up to stop Sammi's protest. 'No arguments! This will be fun.'

The beach was busy because the sun had come out and the wind had dropped, giving a welcome warmth to the day.

The surf dude shop assistant persuaded Sammi into a well-cut pair of swim shorts.

'How do I look?' Sammi asked, as he came out of the changing room.

'Cool.' Delia smiled. 'But I suggest you also get a pair of wetsuit boots, gloves, and a bobble hat, because it's going to be pretty chilly in the water.'

'I won't need all that.' Sammi scoffed. 'I'll be in and out like the SAS.'

Surf Dude nodded sagely. 'I'd listen to them if I were you.'

Sammi raised an eyebrow, and asked, man to man, 'Would you go swimming in a bobble hat?'

'Too right, I would. Game changer, mate. I don't like the feeling of my balls jumping up to my tonsils.'

'Oh well. In that case, bobble hat it is.'

As they walked down to the beach, Delia was still chuckling. 'You were flirting with that young man.'

'No, I wasn't.'

'You so were, and to be fair, I think he liked you.'

'I think he did, too.' Rose stopped and began to peel off her warm clothes before revealing her old swimsuit beneath.

'I'm sure I don't know what you mean, and if you say another word, I'm walking back to the car,' Sammi said huffily.

'We won't say another word,' Delia meekly replied, but she was still smiling.

It was wonderful to be here, with Sammi and Rose, in the bright cold air. She never felt this close to nature in London – and she could never imagine Johnny wanting to go for a Boxing Day swim.

She pushed the thought away, focused on the moment as all three of them, booted, gloved, and bobble-hatted, walked down to the water's edge.

'Take it slowly, Sammi,' Rose advised. 'Your body needs to accept the temperature bit by bit. We won't be in for long.'

A small wave washed over Sammi's knees. 'Arrgh.'

Delia giggled. 'Deep breaths. Don't freak out.'

'I have swum in the Cornish Atlantic before you know . . . Aaarrgggh.' Another wave crashed over his thighs.

'Come on, you can do it.' Rose was striding ahead, and after splashing some water on her arms and chest to acclimatize, she was in and swimming.

'There,' Delia said. 'You're not going to be beaten by Auntie Rose, are you?' And she, too, fully immersed herself and began swimming.

When Delia reached the bigger waves and turned, she saw Sammi watching, knee deep and helpless, looking cold and cross. She was about to swim back to him when she saw the figure of Surf Dude approaching. Smiling, she kept back, but she could just hear their conversation over the sounds of splashing swimmers.

'Hey. How's it going?' Surf Dude said.

Sammi turned his back on the sea and tried to look cool. 'Fine.'

'Hey, look out, big wave coming.'

It hit Sammi before he had a chance to see it. Delia giggled at the sight of her old friend knocked off his feet,and tumbling under the water. A moment later, Surf Dude caught him with a strong arm and pulled him up. 'Watch yourself.'

'Thank you.' Sammi was gasping, pushing his dark fringe out of his eyes.

'No excuse not to swim now you're truly dunked. By the way, I'm Isaac. How do you do?'

'Doing better now I can breathe. Sammi.'

They shook hands as if they had just met in a gentlemen's club.

'Right, well, I'm going to catch some waves. Happy Christmas.'

'Happy Christmas.' Sammi gave Isaac a little wave, and as he turned back, Delia caught his eye and grinned.

'They call this "Cold Water Swimming" now,' said Rose once they were out, rubbing a scratchy towel briskly over her limbs. 'Ridiculous. In my day, this was simply swimming in the sea. Feels good though, doesn't it?'

Sammi had his eyes on Isaac leaping onto his surf board. 'It does.'

Delia, feeling a warm glow as blood pumped around her body, energizing her, followed his gaze. 'Isn't that the guy from the shop?'

'Is it?' Sammi feigned nonchalance. 'Could be.'

Delia gave him the side eye. 'Very handsome.'

He shot her a warning glance. 'Shut it.'

The kitchen at Jago Fields was smelling good.

Sammi dipped a spoon into the turkey curry as it slowly bubbled. 'Try this. Open wide. Careful, it's hot.'

Delia blew on the proffered spoon and tasted. 'Oh my goodness. That is delicious.'

Rose had a bottle opener in her hand. 'As soon as I knew you were coming, Sammi, I got hold of a dozen bottles of Cobra beer. Sainsbury's are very good nowadays.' She stooped into the fridge and pulled out three bottles. 'From the glass or the bottle?'

'Bottle,' Sammi and Delia chorused.

'A toast.' Rose passed the bottles round. 'To every Christmas we have ever had in this little house.'

As they drank, Delia felt her eyes begin to well up. She thought back to all the happy Christmases she had known here, all the time she, her mum, and Auntie Rose had spent together. She raised her bottle. 'And here's happiness to the new owners of Jago Fields.'

'Hear hear!' Rose said.

They drank again. Then Sammi raised his bottle. 'To the future, whatever it may bring. May we face adversity with courage, happiness, and gratitude.'

'Ring me when you get to Wilder Hoo, won't you, darling?' Rose neatened the woolly scarf tied around Delia's neck, and Delia felt the warmth of the gesture. It was the kind of thing her mum would have done.

She sighed and hugged her aunt. The three nights they had been under Rose's roof had gone too fast.

'I will, but remember the signal up there is pretty poor and they don't have a landline.'

'So you keep telling me. Oh, Delia, this has been so lovely. And to have Sammi here, too.'

'I wouldn't want to be anywhere else.' Sammi smiled and submitted to Rose's strong embrace.

'When I move into the new place, you will come down, won't you Sammi?'

'Try keeping me away.'

'Johnny and I will come as soon as we can,' Delia added.

'That would be lovely. Now, off you both go, and thank you, Sammi dear, for looking after Delia. You have my number if you want to call me. Anytime.'

They climbed into Sammi's van to begin the journey up to Wilder Hoo.

'Bye,' Delia shouted over the noisy diesel engine. She looked back and stuck her arm out of the window, waving until they had turned the corner and Rose was out of sight.

When the van drew up at the gates of Wilder Hoo, Johnny and Harriet were sitting waiting for them in Johnny's, or rather Delia's, car.

Johnny jumped out and opened Delia's passenger door. 'Hi. Thought we'd meet you up here so that you don't have to drive all the way down to the house, Sammi mate. You can just drop Delia's bags here and get back on the road to London. Thanks for looking after her. We've missed you, haven't we, Hattie?'

'We have! It's been so much fun – honestly, I could barely breathe for laughing last night. Hi Sammi! Harvey was hopeless at charades, and Viv just brilliant! She should have been an actress.'

Delia watched speechlessly as Johnny put her bags into the smaller car and dismissed Sammi with a handshake and, 'Good to see you, and happy New Year!'

Delia blushed. Johnny couldn't realize how rude he was being. 'Sammi?' she said, turning to him. 'Come in for a cup of tea? Or a pee?'

He shook his head. 'I'd better get going.'

Delia gave him huge hug and whispering into his ear said, 'Thank you for making the last Jago Fields Christmas so happy and memorable. I'll be back in London next week. My New Year's resolution is to spend more time with you, having fun. I love you so much.'

'Love you, too – ouch!'

Harriet had jumped onto his back. 'I'm not letting you go without a hug,' she squealed.

'Well, you're strangling me at the moment.'

'Oops.' She jumped down to face him. 'Was Christmas good at Jago Fields?'

'It was great. You should have been there. Seriously. Like the old days.'

Harriet had let go and was snatching at Delia. 'We have had an amazing time here, Dee. Vare Hotel, incredible. Food, wine, service. Harvey and Viv are such nice people. They've invited me down anytime I like, including *next* Christmas.'

Sammi climbed into the van. 'OK. Well, I'm off.'

He tried to catch Delia's eye but Johnny was holding her attention with a prolonged kiss.

'See you next year,' Sammi muttered as he drove away.

CHAPTER TWENTY-ONE

Delia felt the change the minute she stepped into Wilder Hoo's great hall.

Nothing visible. But something atmospheric.

It wasn't the installation of a great, twinkling tree standing by the stairs and stretching its branches high enough to tickle the dusty chandelier, nor the crackling log fire in the usually stone-cold, cavernous fireplace

No, it was something else.

'You're just in time for sherry elevenses.' Harriet grinned as Johnny closed the great doors. 'Vivvi's new thing. I love it.'

'Do you want your bag upstairs?' Johnny asked.

'Of course she does.' Harriet nudged Delia. 'Dee and I need a drink. We'll be in the saloon.' Harriet lowered her voice as Johnny headed upstairs. 'Midmorning sherry gets me through the day. Your in-laws are batshit.'

Delia laughed. 'Not just me then?'

'Definitely not.' Harriet glanced up the stairs. 'They're still in bed, so we have the saloon to ourselves. Seriously, Dee, Johnny has massive issues with both of them – desperate to get their approval at all times. And that bloody great tree in the hall? Vivienne found out that, in the old days, there was always a tree in the hall, so naturally she had to have one, too, as though a massive tree makes up for the rips in the curtains and holes in the floor. If I ever meet that bloody housekeeper, I'll have words with her.'

'Mrs Joy?' Delia asked. 'You haven't met her either?'

'No. She's good at doing the necessaries invisibly, isn't she? Well, the saloon tree was already chopped, in situ, and Vivienne had told me that it was waiting to be decorated. She was talking about her heirloom baubles as if they were made by Fabergé. Hardly! My gran had the same ones. Woolworths 1962. I didn't show them the respect that Viv told me to give them, but I did my best. And *then* Johnny starts shouting that he's cut down another bloody tree for the hall. Daddy furious, Mummy thrilled, Harriet pissed off. We had no more decorations, so what were we going to do? Make snowflakes out of newspaper?'

They entered the saloon, and Harriet closed the door firmly. 'Chuck a log on that miserable fire, sit down, and I'll pour the sherry.'

Sherry poured, Harriet passed Delia a glass, and then sat in the opposite armchair. 'To cut a very long story short . . . that afternoon, what should turn up in the hall but a huge bundle of fairy lights with a note from Mrs Joy? She'd found a few boxes at the garden centre.'

'Bless her.'

'Curse her more like. Another outing for me up the rickety stepladder, this time Johnny giving me orders while Viv had a cocktail.' Harriet sighed. 'Now all we need is a dozen Dickensian orphans to entertain us singing jolly carols around it.'

'Have there been any visitors?'

'Nope. And that's a funny thing. I'm not sure Viv and H have any friends down here. If they are going to make a success of Wilder Hoo PLC, they'd better get some. Are you hungry?'

Delia patted her tum. 'I had an Auntie Rose breakfast special.'

Harriet rested her head on the chair back and looked at the ceiling. 'Bless that woman. How was she? Was she OK about – you know, her not being at the wedding and all of that?'

Delia hesitated. She was about to answer when the door crashed open and Vivienne tottered in, wearing her dressing gown and last night's make-up.

'Hattie, darling. Would you be a love and get some coffee on. I hear that Celia – Johnny's wife, do you know her? – is arriving today, and I shall need my wits about me.' She advanced towards the fire. 'Darling, did you light this? You are wonderful.'

Harriet jumped out of her chair, all smiles. 'Delia is right here.'

'Happy Christmas, Vivienne.'

'Oh good God.' Vivienne clutched her dressing gown to her throat. 'You're early, darling. What time is it?'

'Just after twelve.'

Vivienne closed her eyes and lay back in the chair, seemingly exhausted.

Delia and Harriet exchanged glances. 'I'll be back with the coffee,' Harriet whispered, leaving Delia with a silent, possibly sleeping Vivienne.

She decided the best course of action was to close her eyes, too, and relax.

Within moments, the peace was broken with the arrival of Johnny, who dropped a kiss on Delia's head. 'Have you missed me?' he asked.

His deep navy eyes were searching hers, and she felt the familiar pull of attraction between them. 'I have. Very much.'

'We have over an hour before we are due at The Vare for lunch. Fancy a cuddle? Upstairs?'

'I do.'

'Come on then.' His hand clasped hers, and together they crept from the saloon into the great hall and up the stairs.

'The tree looks lovely,' she said, putting her hand out to brush the branches as they pushed through the carved spindles of the banister. 'With the fireplace lit, it looks as it must have done centuries ago.'

'Harriet's idea. She's been an angel. She painted Ma and Pa's room, too. They adore her.'

Delia was taken aback. 'Harriet painted it?'

'Yes. Why? What's the matter?'

'No, nothing, it's fine. It's just . . . I promised Vivienne I'd come down and do it when you were away filming. She chose the paint, and I've bought it already.'

They were at the top of the stairs now and approaching their bedroom. 'You're not upset, are you?'

'Not at all. It's just . . . very kind of Harriet.'

Johnny lifted her hand to his lips. 'Hattie is sweet, but she's not you.'

CHAPTER TWENTY-TWO

In the New Year, Johnny's filming schedule ramped up. Delia helped him learn his lines each night for the next day and soothed his nervous excitement as best she could.

The jitters lent him a short temper and an inability to sleep, the culmination of which meant that Delia was the recipient of his insecurities and mood swings, for months as filming dragged on.

But, come March, he promised to cook a special dinner for her thirty-seventh birthday, and invited Harriet and Sammi, too. But when they arrived they found that Johnny hadn't even started cooking. He was accusing Delia of taking him for granted and walked out.

Sammi and Harriet were shocked, but Delia quickly covered for him. He was simply exhausted with all the filming, and she tried to reassure them – and herself – that everything was fine. 'Poor man. So many scripts to learn and the director is constantly adding changes. His brain gets overloaded. Let's go to the pub instead.'

A couple of weeks later, when he was in a better frame of mind, she tackled him about it.

'Why did you walk out on my birthday, Johnny? I was so looking forward to your lovely dinner and being with Harriet and Sammi. What happened?'

His reply was sulky. 'You were late because you went to the pub with Sammi and Harriet first.'

'We weren't late.'

'I don't want to talk about it.'

'Why not?' She was treading carefully. 'Is it the job? I know that this job is huge for you, but I'm here to support you. Just *talk* to me.'

'I don't want to talk about it now.'

'When will you?'

He leapt to his feet and shouted, 'STOP NAGGING, WOMAN,' then left the room, slamming the door behind him.

She was grateful when he started night filming and had to stay in hotels close to the location. Sometimes, she didn't see him for ten days together, which gave her space to reframe their problems. She told herself that she must be more understanding and supportive. He was nervous, tired. This was his big break. He deserved some leeway for that.

She decided to book a holiday for them both when the job ended – somewhere sunny and relaxing, where he would recover and the old, loving Johnny would return to her. She hung on to the thought, and in the meantime, went to Wilder Hoo once a month as usual, doing what she could to help Vivienne and Harvey.

Things were a little better there. The new boiler she'd organized was still producing hot water. The hole in the roof had been plugged, and a rudimentary but safe source of electricity had been added to the most used rooms.

She was glad to do these things for Wilder Hoo, despite Harvey and Vivienne's lack of gratitude or any sign of the restoration work beginning.

Loath to spend any more of her own money, she cooked and cleaned for them instead. At least she didn't have to shop: Mrs Joy always left the fridge and larder well stocked, with a little note thanking Delia for spending her weekends there scrubbing down the old pantry or tackling a dusty bedroom. She'd lost track of how often she'd taken down unrepairable silk curtains, chucked out the moth-eaten carpets, or scared mice and spiders with the vacuum cleaner.

'Do you have a window cleaner?' she asked Vivienne once, but her mother-in-law simply shook her head, as if she had been asked to explain Einstein's theory of relativity.

'Window cleaner? Can't you do that, Celia dear?'

One night, over Mrs Joy's fish pie kitchen supper, Delia found herself alone with Harvey. Instinctively, she felt that her father-in-law might be more forthcoming about Wilder Hoo's regeneration in Vivienne's absence.

So she asked, 'How is the Spanish deal going? Any positive news about the arrival of funds for Wilder Hoo?'

He held her gaze longer than necessary before answering. 'Interesting question.'

'Oh?'

'I've been thinking about speaking to you on that very subject.'

'Really?'

'I wouldn't ask if I didn't think you weren't going to get a huge return on this.' Harvey sat back in his chair, relaxed. 'The thing is, the Spanish project has been held up by a small shortfall in funds. We need just enough to get it over the line – small amount for big gains. It's a rock-solid investment opportunity for anybody, but it has to be the right person. There are a lot of people who want to be in on this but . . .' He paused. 'I'm offering you, or Johnny, or both of you, first dibs. What goes into the pot will, I guarantee, be worth double in the next six months.'

Delia sipped her wine, thinking hard. 'Have you mentioned this to Johnny?'

'Not yet. He's so wrapped up in this marvellous new job, and I don't want to bother him, take his eye off the ball, but I'm certain he'd agree with me on this one.'

'How much are we talking about?'

Harvey mentioned a figure – not big enough to take all Delia's savings but apparently big enough to help the deal go through. She rubbed her chin, thinking. 'I see.'

'What do you say?' he asked. 'In six months, you'll have twice that back in your account. Easy. Maybe more. And I know Johnny would be pleased that you made the right decision. A little extra cash is always welcome, isn't it?'

'And this is all you need to finish the Spanish project and get Wilder Hoo started?'

'Exactly that. Once the Spanish project is up, running, and sold, the money will cascade into Wilder Hoo. Trust me.'

'Can you send me the paperwork to look at? I'd like to show it to David, my boss, who understands this sort of stuff. He's a good sounding board.'

'Sure. Absolutely.' Harvey paused, then frowned. 'Only problem is, getting the paperwork over from my Spanish lawyer will take a week or so, and if you *are* going to invest, you have to act quickly or you'll miss the opportunity. I need the money tomorrow.'

Delia hesitated, thinking quickly. It was a lot of money, but this was *Harvey* – her husband's dad. He wouldn't turn his own daughter-in-law over. And Johnny would be disappointed if she didn't take this opportunity to back his family. She wasn't sure she could handle Johnny being disappointed in her again.

She swallowed, then she said, 'Yes, OK.'

'Thank you, Delia. You won't regret it.' She heard the relief in Harvey's voice. 'No need to tell Johnny about this just yet. Let it be a fabulous surprise for him. He's always wanted to go on a safari – you could take him now.' He stood up and came to her side of the table, holding out his hand. 'Shake on it? Carlisle-Hart to Carlisle-Hart?'

Alone upstairs in the bedroom, Delia pulled on her cardigan. The room was damp again, cold and draughty. She thought about how nice a proper shower would be, a modern loo, and warm central heating. This house had so much potential.

She'd be lying if she said she didn't feel a certain anxiety over the money she was prepared to hand over, but overall, she felt glad to be able to offer Harvey and Vivienne some real help – more useful to them by far than all her cleaning and painting. At last, poor old Wilder Hoo would have the treatment it needed – to be saved from dereliction and made handsome again. The money from Spain would fund the plans they had for Wilder Hoo, giving it the future that it deserved. And as Harvey had assured her, in six months he'd pay her back double what she had lent him.

CHAPTER TWENTY-THREE

'When do we get to see this on screen?' Sammi asked, after Johnny had entertained them with off-colour, gossipy revelations about his co-stars.

'Looking like the New Year,' Johnny answered. 'Depends on the edit, but the channel is really keen for it to kick off the January season. Give the viewers something to watch for free at home after all the Christmas bills start coming in.'

'Is that how they really think?' Harriet asked. 'How clever of them.'

'How to manipulate the masses.' Sammi sighed. 'None of us are the free-thinking beings we imagine ourselves to be.'

'Talking of which . . .' Delia wriggled with pleasure. 'I have a surprise for Johnny.'

He shone his most handsome smile on her. 'Have you?'

'How do you fancy spending your birthday in Saint-Tropez?'

Johnny's mouth opened wide in shock and delight. 'What? When? Where are we staying?'

'Hotel Byblos.'

He reached for his phone and googled it. 'Bloody hell, Delia! It looks incredible and' – he was scrolling – 'delightfully expensive!'

'You deserve it. Think of it as a late honeymoon.' She laughed, but a small tweak of anxiety hooked at her insides. She had never spent so much on a holiday before, but the Spanish deal should cover the credit card bill easily. Johnny deserved this – *they* deserved this. A relaxing break was all they needed to get back on the right footing.

Returning from work a few weeks later, Delia was exhausted. The salon had been non-stop, everyone wanting beach-ready hair for the long summer holidays.

Now, she was looking forward to the promise Johnny had made that morning. 'I've got an audition at four this afternoon, but it shouldn't take long, so I'll pick up takeaway on the way home. What do you want? Indian?'

'Yes please.'

But when she turned the key in the front door, the flat was in darkness and there was no enticing aroma of curry coming from the kitchen.

Some of the old feelings crept into her mind. What if the only reliable thing about Johnny was his unreliability? Where was he? He'd had the audition at four. It was now after eight.

She switched on the small table lamp that illuminated the tiny hall and the emptiness of the peg where Johnny's jacket should be hanging.

Maybe he was setting dinner out in the garden? 'Johnny?' she called into the empty flat.

The voicemail on the phone was blinking. They were the only people in her age bracket who still had a landline, let alone a voicemail on it. It was for his parents' sake, because Wilder Hoo had no internet or WiFi. Maybe Johnny had left a message; he was always losing his phone, leaving it in taxis or restaurants. Miraculously, it always reappeared. She'd probably find it in a minute on the edge of the bath or in the kitchen or between the cushions of the sofa.

She pressed the button to play. 'Hey, my darling boy.' Vivienne's voice. 'I tried your mobile. Where are you? Just a quick one. I've ordered a tin of caviar from Harrods Food Hall. You could pick it up tomorrow before you drive down? After all, it is your birthday, and I think *I* deserve to celebrate. Do I look old enough to have a thirty-seven-year-old son? Don't answer that!' Her horribly tinkly laugh infuriated Delia and she blew a long raspberry at the machine message before holding two fingers up and roundly delivering, 'Up yours, Vivienne.'

So, Vivienne thought they were going to Wilder Hoo, did she? This weekend? The very weekend that they were going to Saint-Tropez? Well, she had news for her.

It was past midnight before Johnny rolled in, smelling of the pub.

Delia had fallen asleep on the sofa, waiting for him. The slam of the door woke her in an instant.

'Hi,' she called out.

He stood in the doorway between the hall and the lounge and looked at her impassively.

She flashed him a quick smile, desperately gauging his mood and not wanting to ignite any unnecessary aggression. 'I've been worried.'

'What for?'

'Well, you.' She tried another smile. 'I thought you might be home earlier.'

He threw his eyes heavenwards and sighed. 'For fuck's sake, Delia. It's not right –*you're* not right. Can't you see what you are doing? Your jealousy and neediness mean I can't even have a pint with a mate?'

Delia shrank a little inside. She had to head this off at the pass. 'Can I get you anything?'

'No.' He had turned his back on her and was taking his jacket off. He let it drop to the floor. 'If it's all right with you, I'm going for a waz.'

The bathroom lay just off the hall, next to their bedroom. He never closed the door, no matter who might be there. Johnny gloried in his human functions. Farts. Burps. Shits.

Delia left the sofa, went to the kitchen and stood in front of the sink, staring back at her reflection in the dark window.

He was standing behind her now. Too close. 'When did you turn into such a miserable, boring old woman?'

Delia felt the fear but picked up the kettle and began to fill it.

'Do you know how hard it is for me living with you?' He stepped closer to her, and she felt his breath on her neck.

'I could ask the same of you,' she answered.

'Really? You think? I'm not mad though, am I?' he went on. 'I don't have a mental illness like you do.'

Delia flinched. 'I don't have a mental illness.'

'Then why has the doctor given you pills?'

Heat rose in her cheeks. Over the past few months, while Johnny was regularly away filming and she'd had to keep up her own work and the monthly visits to Wilder Hoo, she had found herself not looking forward to things the way she used to, and crying, alone, too often. A couple of weeks ago, she had seen her doctor, who advised a course of antidepressants.

'I got a bit low.' Her voice was tight. 'I'm not *mad*.'

'Doctors don't give pills out unless you're ill.'

'I'm depressed, Johnny – not mad.'

'So *I'm* the mad one? Is that what you are saying?' He laughed. 'I'm the sane one in this relationship.'

'Don't be unkind.'

'It's not being unkind. It's speaking the truth. You have depression because you never had a dad.'

'Lots of people don't have dads, but it doesn't mean there's anything wrong with them.' Delia turned to face him. 'I'd rather an absent father than a cruel one.'

He rubbed a hand over his face wearily. 'My dad worked his arse off for Mum and me. Money was tight but we had love.'

Delia couldn't stomach yet another row. 'I think I'll go to bed.'

'Yes. You do that. Oh, and by the way, thank you for asking, the audition went very well. Now bore off to bed.'

CHAPTER TWENTY-FOUR

Delia clung tightly to their plans for Saint-Tropez. All they needed was a break, a chance to reset. A birthday away would bring back the Johnny she had fallen in love with.

But the next morning, when she started to talk to him about packing, Johnny scowled.

'What are you talking about? We're going to Wilder Hoo this weekend.'

Delia couldn't help her exasperation. 'But this is the weekend I've booked Saint-Tropez. I told you the dates.'

'No, you didn't. Seriously, Delia, we can't just let my parents down like this.'

She stared at him. 'Can't we just put it back a week – go to Wilder Hoo next weekend?'

'No way. It's my birthday, and my parents like to spoil me. They're not getting any younger, and I don't know how many birthdays I might have left with them.'

In a sudden flash of anger, Delia wondered how many more birthdays she and Johnny might have left together. She swallowed hard, trying to stop the furious tears rising to her throat. 'Johnny, I've booked the flights and the hotel – everything's already paid for. This was meant to be a wonderful birthday treat, and—'

'Yeah, I didn't want to say anything when you first mentioned it, because Sammi and Harriet were there, but it's not OK to just organize things like that behind my back, especially if it's costing a lot of money. We're married – we have to make these kinds of decisions together.'

Delia felt her heart sink. She couldn't believe he had managed to turn her birthday present for him into some kind of betrayal.

'Just call the insurance people and tell them we had a family emergency, that we can't go.'

'You want me to *lie*?' she asked, horrified at the thought. 'Absolutely not. Johnny, I've been really looking forward to this trip, and I've spent a lot of money, and I'm not just going to let it all fall through. So it's either Saint-Tropez with me or Wilder Hoo with your parents, without me.'

Johnny shrugged his shoulders. 'I told you: I'm going to Wilder Hoo. You do what you want,' he snarled. 'You always do.'

Delia found it strange to be in Saint-Tropez on her own, but in some ways, it was a relief. With a view of the sparkling sea, she was able to reflect. As she wandered the streets, weaving between pastel-coloured houses, she began to see patterns in Johnny's behaviour.

There were four distinct parts. Part one was the best: he was loving and calm, the man she had first fallen for. That would last a few weeks until part two: he'd start to get moody. She'd be treading on eggshells, trying hard not to provoke him, but inevitably that lead to part three: Johnny would instigate a huge fight, blaming Delia for making him angry, for taking him for granted. In the aftermath of the row, she'd be punished with The Silent Treatment. Then, part four: Delia generally caved in and apologized. Johnny would forgive her, and they were straight back to part one. All loved up.

Was it her fault? That was the question Delia kept coming back to. The one she just couldn't answer.

She tried to talk to Johnny about it when she got home, to discuss everything that had happened between them, all the problems that wouldn't go away, but he just shook his head.

'Stop trying to analyse everything. Let it go, Dee. We're rubbing along OK together, aren't we?'

Delia turned away so he wouldn't see her cry.

When Auntie Rose next phoned, no doubt to ask about their holiday, Delia rejected the call. When Sammi texted her with the same questions, she didn't reply.

The next few months were surreal. Johnny moved into the spare room, and there were fewer rows. He was neither horrible nor nice. They shared the shopping and cooking and household chores, and still went to Wilder Hoo once a month to see his parents. At home, they talked around safe topics. There was no further discussion of the trip to Saint-Tropez, no mention of the state of their marriage. In a way, that suited Delia; it seemed the easiest path to tread.

If they talked too much, if she let herself really think about the future, about what she wanted, there might be no going back. She didn't want to think of a life after Johnny. She was holding on to how good they could be together, how happy they had once been.

If she just held on a little longer, perhaps they could have their happy ending.

*

One November evening, they were at Wilder Hoo for their regular monthly visit. They'd just tucked into one of Mrs Joy's macaroni cheeses from the fridge, with a sherry trifle waiting for pudding. Johnny and his parents were abandoning the kitchen to return to the saloon.

'Celia, dear,' said Vivienne, 'would you bring the coffee and trifle upstairs? Much warmer up there.'

The weather had lately turned wintry. The evening dark had descended, as had a strong wind, bringing flurries of heavy rain.

'No problem.' Delia got the trifle from the fridge and put it on the kitchen table. She didn't want to forget it.

Washing up on her own was a welcome respite from the strain of pretending she and Johnny were happy. She put in her AirPods and continued with an audiobook she was enjoying.

She didn't hear Harvey return. When she saw his reflection in the dark of the kitchen window, it made her jump.

'Hi.' She smiled, taking out her AirPods.

'Glad to catch you on your own,' he said, lowering his voice, 'I have news.'

'I hope it's good?'

His smile framed his horribly yellow teeth. 'Not exactly as I had hoped.'

She whispered, 'Is it the Spanish money?'

'Yes.'

'There's a hold-up?'

'No. It's, erm . . .' He lifted his head and scratched the stubble under his chin. 'It's been lost.'

'Lost?' Delia repeated, confused.

'Gone. I'm so sorry. The project hit a few problems, and there is no money. That sometimes happens in business.'

'But . . .' Delia was staring at him. You told me the land deal had gone through and the apartments were going up? And other assets . . .?'

'Unfortunately not. The whole lot has been sold off. The backers had to recoup their losses.'

Delia felt unbelievably foolish. '*I'm* a backer.'

'But not one of the big boys, I'm afraid.'

'Dad?' Johnny's voice came echoing along the kitchen passage. 'Ma needs another G&T . . .' He stopped in the doorway, looking between their guilty faces. 'What are you two talking about?' He shot Delia a warning glance. 'What's she been telling you, Dad?'

'We were just having a little chat, weren't we, Dee?' Harvey smiled as he walked to the pantry to collect the drinks.

Delia's shock had turned to anger. She heard her voice ring clear. 'I lent your father some money to help him with the Spanish project. He said it was a good investment, but it's gone bust.'

Johnny blinked. 'How much?'

Harvey reappeared with a bottle of gin and two large bottles of tonic under his arm. 'Let's get these to your mother.'

But Johnny barred his way. 'How's the Spanish project going, Dad?' he said, his voice clipped.

Harvey turned to look at Delia. His expression was one of pure disdain. 'She's told you, has she? You need to keep that wife of yours under control, son. Tell her to keep her mouth shut.'

Keeping his eyes on his father, Johnny told Delia, 'Dad's right. Best not to discuss this with anyone outside the family. What happened, Dad?'

Harvey turned his palms up to the ceiling, raising his shoulders to his ears. 'Brexit? Spiralling costs? Unskilled labour?'

'And you didn't see it coming?' Delia was furious. 'Why on earth did you ask me to invest? Why tell me a cock and bull story about what a sound investment I was making?'

Johnny turned to her, eyes narrowed. 'Why didn't I know about this?'

'Harvey told me not to tell you.'

'Is that true, Dad?'

Harvey shrugged. 'It was hardly big bucks, son.'

Johnny glared at Delia. 'How much, Delia? Tell me. Now.'

When she told him, he turned on his father. 'How could you, Dad? How could you!'

'Don't speak to me like that.'

'Fuck you!'

Harvey's eyes blazed. 'How dare you speak to your father like that!' He took a step towards Johnny, squaring up to him. 'You apologize now.'

Delia watched, thinking she might have to separate them. Johnny was shaking – with fury, she thought.

Harvey took another step towards him. 'Well? I'm waiting.' A fleck of spittle arced out of Harvey's mouth and landed on Johnny's lip.

He put a finger to it and dropped his gaze to the floor. 'Sorry, Dad.'

Delia was seething. 'No, Johnny. Can't you see? Your dad is bullying you like he always has and, after this, always will.'

'Delia, it's fine. Leave it. Dad's right.' He dipped his head and blinked. 'Don't make it worse.'

Delia didn't know quite what happened next or how she got to Mrs Joy's trifle bowl so quickly. The next thing she was aware of was the cool of the trifle in the palm of her hand as she scooped out a fistful and flung it into Harvey's face. 'You're a bully and a cheat and a liar.'

He turned his face to her, leering through the custard and tinned peaches and colourful strands of sugar dripping from his cheeks. He lifted his right hand and slapped her.

Taken off balance in the surprise, Delia stumbled and fell hard, her head, kicking back, banged onto the unforgiving flagstones.

The room fell still.

Johnny, unmoving and silent.

Harvey rubbed a tea towel over his face, removing the trifle remnants.

'I told you, Johnny. Keep. Her. Under. Control.' He collected the gin bottle and the tonics and headed out. 'And bring some ice up for your mother.'

Delia watched as Johnny walked to the freezer, filled a bowl with ice cubes, and headed upstairs without a backwards glance.

Delia lay on the floor, her heart pumping so hard she was breathless. She waited for minutes that felt like hours, hoping Johnny would come back, ask if she was OK, but the room remained silent.

Eventually, she pulled herself up and sat on one of the kitchen chairs, letting the dizziness settle, before going to the sink and running her burning cheek and the large bump on the side of her head under the cold tap.

She didn't want to stay another minute in Wilder Hoo. Instinct told her to run, and she did.

Out of the back door, across the lawns, through the woods, and down the cliff path, past the dunes and down to the sea, where she all but collapsed onto the cold wet sand. The rain had stopped, and the wind had subsided, but her teeth chattered, not just with the cold but with the shock of what had happened.

Everything had been a lie. She could see that now. Not just Harvey's investment, but her and Johnny's relationship, too.

The warning signs were all there. That first day they met, when he'd asked her to come to Cornwall with him out of the blue. Their first date, how instantly loving he had been to her. How easily he had beguiled her. Was all that fake? None of it real?

Then she thought back to all the horrible episodes of The Silent Treatment. Johnny's constant need for attention. The dramatic walk-outs. She had opened her life up to him so willingly.

How could she have been so stupid? Not only had she happily given him her trust, but she'd given a huge chunk of her savings to his father.

What kind of foolish, gullible, stupid person does that?

She began to cry – great fat tears and wracking sobs that hurt her throat and ribs.

What was she going to do? What could she do?

The sea calmly lapped the dark shore and began to soothe her. Her mind fell to ease, and a seed of comprehension was sown.

She was alone.

No one had come to find her.

No one was looking for her.

She must go back to the house, return to London with Johnny and talk calmly and sensibly about what had happened and why it must never happen again. They would also have to look at their finances. There would be some belt-tightening to be done. Maybe Johnny and she should have some couple's counselling. It wouldn't do any harm. Both of them had had difficulties where fathers were concerned. Maybe, in some crooked and unfathomable way, they had been attracted to each other because of their fathers.

Johnny had been damaged by his parents, but if they worked together, she might still be able to fix him. This determined focus quietened her mind. She stood up and flexed her limbs, willing some warmth into them. Harvey had done her a favour in a way. He'd lost the Spanish deal, which meant he'd lost his dreams for Wilder Hoo. And she would never have to come down here again. That would be a weight off poor Johnny's shoulders, too. Yes, life was going to be much happier without Harvey and Vivienne in it.

She turned her back to the sea and began her return to the hated house.

When she reached it, everything was in darkness. Not a light at any window.

She didn't know what time it was or how long she'd been away because she'd left her phone in the kitchen with her AirPods.

The back door was locked.

She went round to the front doors, but they were locked, too.

A cold sensation began to crawl from the pit of her stomach. Johnny must be in bed, so . . . had he deliberately locked her out?

She picked up a handful of gravel and threw it at the bedroom window, hurling more and more handfuls until it was clear to her, to anybody, that no one was coming.

In one of the barns, she found Harvey's tractor wrapped in a large sheet of tarpaulin. Next to it, backed into a draught-free, dry corner was an old trailer piled with sacking. Delia shaped a mattress and headrest from it. She lay down and wept again, dispirited, disbelieving, and broken-hearted.

She closed her eyes and prayed for sleep, trying to disassociate herself from the awful reality she found herself in.

*

She didn't know how long she had slept for. It didn't feel very long, but a bird up in the rafters was singing, which meant it must be close to dawn.

Her head was aching, and the lump on her head was tender. She desperately needed a hot cup of tea and an aspirin. She stretched her cold muscles and squinted up at the patch of sky, framed by a hole in the roof. A streak of daybreak was growing. Maybe Johnny was awake?

She left the protection of the barn and walked stiffly towards the house, then stopped. Were there headlights flickering through the trees lining the drive?

She took a moment to listen. Yes, a car was definitely approaching.

Picking up speed and hope, she moved as quickly as her wobbly legs could carry her. When she reached the front of the house, she stood on the top step, watching as, thank God, Johnny's car came steadily towards her. Now she and Johnny could get away from here together, just the two of them, and work on their future.

She lifted both arms and waved as he drove the last few metres to the circle of gravel and parked.

'Johnny.' She ran to open his door. 'Where have you been?'

He said nothing, but Vivienne, sitting in the passenger seat, did. 'I'll tell you where we've been. Harvey collapsed last night. An ambulance came and took him straight to A&E.'

'Oh no. How awful. What happened? How is he?'

'He had a massive stroke,' Vivienne snapped. 'How do you think he is?'

'Is he being looked after well? What do the doctors say?'

Johnny spoke, his voice tight. 'I had to sit with my mother and watch her husband, *my father*, breathe his last.'

Delia shook her head, uncomprehending. 'What?'

He turned his furious eyes upon her. 'Are you fucking deaf as well as stupid? Dad is *dead*.'

'And *you killed him*!' Vivienne spat.

'But how did I . . . ? He hit me, and—'

Vivienne began screaming hysterically. 'Get her out of my sight, Johnny! Get this bitch away from my house!'

CHAPTER TWENTY-FIVE

London, two months ago

The divorce was quick and brutal. Delia felt as though she were in a dream, reeling from everything that had happened, how abruptly her life had fallen apart. She ate, slept, went to work, lived alone in the flat that had been theirs, her whole life now surreal.

The grounds for divorce were for Delia's unreasonable behaviour. She didn't contest them. What was the point?

Johnny's assets were few: a small amount of savings, an irregular income, and half of their London flat. Delia had put up most of the deposit with money from her mum's life insurance, but she couldn't summon the energy to protest when Johnny's solicitors pressed for fifty per cent of the flat.

There was Wilder Hoo, too. Johnny owned it now – Harvey had left it to him rather than Vivienne, presumably due to some old-fashioned ideas about male heirs. Delia didn't care why, and nor did she ask her solicitors to press for a share in it. She wanted nothing to do with the place.

With her hefty mortgage doubled overnight, Delia considered selling the flat, meaning that finding a good estate agent was now on her endless to-do list. The trouble was, when she wasn't at work, she found it almost impossible to get off the sofa. Instead, she would lie there for hours, staining the cushions with tears.

She couldn't bear to tell anyone the whole story of what had happened. She didn't tell Auntie Rose anything about the money or why the divorce was so hurried. She had written in her Christmas card that after Harvey had died so suddenly, she and Johnny realized they weren't right for each other after all.

When Auntie Rose phoned her in response, she refused to answer.

On the day that the divorce came through, Delia took a day's holiday from work. She sat on the sofa in her pyjamas, willing herself to move, but even the smallest things felt too hard.

When her phone rang, she was relieved to see Harriet's name on the screen. It was so kind of her to call and check she was OK, especially when she was on holiday in Majorca this week.

'Hi Delia.'

'Hi Hattie.' She was glad to hear her cheery voice. 'How are you? How's Majorca? Is it sunny?'

'Yes, very. Umm. I have a bit of news for you. I hope you'll be OK with it.'

Delia smiled. 'Don't tell me, you've fallen for some snake-hipped waiter who's actually a millionaire and wants to whisk you away to a life of endless pleasure?'

'Gosh no, but . . . sort of . . .' Hattie sounded uncomfortable. 'OK, I'll just say this very quickly. Johnny and I have been seeing each other for a few weeks.'

Delia felt sick. Her hands began to shake. 'What? This is a joke, right?'

'No, it isn't. I'm sorry, Delia, but you were never right for each other. When he told me what you did to Harvey—'

'I did *nothing* to Harvey.' Delia's voice was steel.

'Well, that's not quite true, is it? I'm sure that somewhere in the middle lies the truth . . . Look, Dee, I don't want this to come between us—'

Delia had heard enough. She ended the call before Harriet could say another word.

All week, at work, Delia pretended to be fine. She said nothing to anyone as she dreaded Harriet's return. How was she going to be able to work with her, look at her, speak to her again? If there ever had been a girl code, it had now been smashed to a zillion tiny, pointy shards.

She kept the news to herself, not even telling Sammi. She was afraid that if she began to tell anyone, her anger would be white hot and dangerous – embarrassing. No, she had to keep it to herself until the pain and humiliation had time to work its way out of her system.

Not that she could imagine when that would ever be.

That Friday, when she arrived at work, she found David ashen, standing at the reception desk as if he was waiting for her.

'David? Are you OK?' He motioned for her to follow him to his office, where he flopped onto his chair.

'Shut the door, darling. I don't want anyone to hear this.'

'What?' Delia was worried. 'Are you ill? Is it your mum?'

'No. It's . . . I got a call from Harriet this morning. Something dreadful has happened.'

Delia swallowed. 'If it's what I think it is, I know.'

'She told you?'

'Yes.'

'Oh God.' He began to weep. 'So young. I know you two had gone your separate ways, but I just can't believe it.'

Delia frowned, surprised by David's reaction. 'I'm glad you know. I found out a few days ago, but—'

'What do you mean she told you a few days ago?' asked David. 'She's only just left the hospital.'

'Hospital?'

'It's Johnny. They rented scooters – there was a collision. You didn't know, did you?'

Delia's heart tripped. 'Are they OK?'

'Harriet's fine, but Johnny . . . he was killed instantly.'

The earth under Delia's feet dropped away, and she sank down into the nearest chair.

David came to crouch beside her, taking her hand in his. 'She wanted me to tell you . . . perhaps you should take the next week or two off . . .'

Being by herself in the flat was a double-edged sword. It did mean that she could stay in her pyjamas all day, barely washing or cleaning her teeth and living off tinned beans, but it also meant being alone with her thoughts.

She kept replaying the events of her marriage with Johnny, forever sticking on that bitter Christmas when he'd invited Harriet to Wilder Hoo. Had they really just been seeing each other for a few weeks? What if it had been longer, if he'd been seeing one of her closest friends behind her back all that time?

And what did it really matter now?

She had loved him once, and now he was dead, and in the tumult of her emotions, it was hard to separate her grief for Johnny from her grief for the end of their marriage, the end of the happy ending she had longed for.

She dreaded working at the salon alongside Harriet, but when she returned to work, she found David had accepted Harriet's resignation.

Delia had been living inside a vigorously shaken snowglobe for a while, but she was beginning to feel that the blizzard was clearing.

Returning home from work one evening, she found a letter waiting for her on the doormat. It had a sense of importance about it, so she carried it with her to the kitchen, where she collected a bottle of wine and a glass. She took them to the sitting room, opened the thick envelope and extracted the single sheet of paper inside.

Dear Mrs Carlisle-Hart,

Re: The Last Will and Testament of Mr John Harvey Carlisle-Hart (deceased)

I trust you are well.

I write to inform you that your late ex-husband Mr John Harvey Carlisle-Hart has left a bequest in your name.

He leaves you the entire estate of Wilder Hoo, Vare Castle, Cornwall.

Would you be free Tuesday next at 2.30 p.m. to visit my office where we can go through the particulars?

With condolences,
Mr Thomas Whilley LLB (Hons)

The next day at Gilson's, with a thick head and a short fuse, Delia's head finally burst. She threw a client out of her chair and on to the street with her wet hair. She was signed off work for six months.

Part Two

CHAPTER TWENTY-SIX

Kernow Autumn, April, present day

It was well into the afternoon by the time Delia finished telling Auntie Rose everything. She had gone through it all, from start to finish, just as she had resolved the night before. She knew the pieces of the complicated jigsaw formed an unpleasant picture.

They sat together in a silence that shimmered with emotions, but which was now settling into clarity and relief.

A log shifted in the grate, scattering red sparks to the bed of hot ash.

Auntie Rose ran her fingers backwards and forwards over the linen cover of her armchair and sighed. 'And that's the real reason you and Sammi came to Cornwall this weekend? To put Wilder Hoo on the market.'

'Yes.'

'I'm sorry I wasn't more understanding last night,' said Rose slowly. 'Cordelia . . . you have had a very bad time, haven't you?'

Delia looked into her lap and sniffed. 'It's not been great.'

Auntie Rose got out of her chair and knelt by Delia. 'You won't believe me now, but I promise, you will get through this.'

'Maybe one day.' Delia wiped away another tear. 'It's all such a mess. Even if I kept Wilder Hoo, I'd never be able to make anything of it.'

'I know, but you have me, and you have Sammi, and you have dear David in London, who is very definitely in your corner.'

'I can't expect you to mop up after me.'

'That's exactly what I'm here for.' Auntie Rose squeezed her hand. 'Oh, my love. I wish you'd told me all this before.'

Delia shrugged her shoulders. 'I know. Looking back, I wish I'd just called you, talked to you, but . . . During the end of my marriage, I suppose I was embarrassed. I knew you and Johnny didn't really get on and it was easier for me to just . . . I don't know. I see now that I was manipulated, that I lost myself. He said things that I believed . . . went along with. Maybe he was right. I *was* mad.'

'No, darling, no. I was taken in by him at first, when I saw how happy he made you, but . . . he came between us.'

Delia nodded. 'I'm ashamed I let that happen, but I didn't realize it, really. I split myself off from everything but Johnny – that's the only way to describe it. Work was my salvation. I could be good at that. And when I got home, I simply didn't have the energy to answer your or anybody's messages. Johnny swept me off my feet, totally love-bombed me and then . . . It was all so clever, so insidious, but I loved to be loved, and he knew that.'

'What an arse,' Rose said. 'What an absolute tit.'

Delia wiped her eyes and, in spite of herself, began to giggle.

'That's better.' Rose smiled. 'Laughter and tears. Get it all out.'

Delia nodded, but her laughter was fading. 'I can't really believe he's dead. It makes it all so much more complicated . . . I suppose it makes it harder to hate him.'

'I can see,' said Auntie Rose. She got to her feet with one final press of Delia's hand. 'Right, let me make you some lunch.'

The April sunshine fell through the kitchen window and lit the small table as Delia took a seat. Rose's new kitchen was modern and compact.

'I know what you're thinking.' Rose put a plate of sandwiches in front of her.

'Oh really? What?'

'That this kitchen is a far cry from the one we had at Jago Fields.'

'Well, don't you miss it?'

Rose poured tea from a teapot Delia didn't recognize. 'Yes . . . and no,' she said. 'I still have all the happy memories.'

'You didn't bring much with you. What happened to the old brown teapot?'

'There are some things that are too sad to hold onto, and anyway, it was old and too big for just me. It's good to let things go – including the past.' She tapped the side of her head. 'It's all in here and in my heart. No one can take that away.'

'No, they can't.' Delia took a bite out of her sandwich. She could feel a change between them, a return to something closer to their old warmth. 'But . . .'

'What?'

'That old kitchen was the centre of our lives, wasn't it? Birthdays, Christmas, summer holidays. Mum and you always baking.'

'Yes, and your grandmother loved that kitchen before us. She must have baked hundreds of cakes and loaves and pasties in her time. But to be honest, I was glad to say goodbye to that old Aga. Say one bad word to it and it would sulk for the rest of the week.'

Delia smiled. 'The kitchen at Wilder Hoo would have been like that once.' She dropped her head into her hands and sighed.

'With the right person, it could be again?' Rose ventured.

'It'll have to be someone who can afford it. The place is a money pit. Bloody Harvey. Bloody Johnny.'

'Why *did* he leave it to you?' Rose asked.

Delia shook her head. 'I don't know.'

Rose folded her arms across her chest, suddenly all businesslike – the expression that she'd once used when bartering a good price for lambs at market. 'You and I are going to pay Wilder Hoo a visit.'

'Why?' Delia whined. 'There's no point.'

'There's every point and please drop that tone of voice.'

'But—'

Rose stopped her. 'No buts. With you or without you, I'm going to take a look at the old place. Once I have seen it, I'll give you an honest opinion. If it is the white elephant you describe, then sell it. But if I think there's a chance it can be saved, we'll save it.'

Delia blinked and looked at her aunt as if she were mad. 'So you're the expert now, are you? The avenging angel who can fix all wrongs and make them right? No, I'm washing my hands of it. It's my house. I own it, and I can do what I bloody well like with it.'

Rose only shook her head. 'I shall be ready to leave at ten-thirty tomorrow morning. With or without you.'

'I can't go.'

'Why?'

'My ankle is too sore.'

'No, it isn't. I saw the way you came into the kitchen. You're walking much better.'

The thought was making Delia's hands tremble. 'I just . . . I don't want to go.'

'Oh, for heaven's sake. You're a grown woman. Yes, you have made some foolish decisions in your life, but since you have decided to sell up, where's the harm in me taking a look before it's sold? Hmm? To satisfy your old aunt?'

The next day was a glorious one for the drive. The spring sky was the sharpest of blues against the trees, whose leaves were in bright-green bud. Auntie Rose had insisted on taking the top down on her new car, her excuse being, 'You need some fresh air. Want the radio on?'

Whether Delia wanted it on or not was immaterial. Rose twiddled from Radio 4 to a Seventies music station, and as they drove along, the voices of both women singing at the tops of their voices trailed on the breeze.

'Take the next right,' Delia shouted above the rushing wind in her ears.

'Here?' Rose shouted back. 'Oh yes, I see the sign. That *has* to change. It looks like a hangman's gibbet.'

Delia laughed. 'I always said that.'

The potholes on the long drive seemed to have somehow increased since Saturday, but Rose guided the low-slung car expertly. 'Don't want to take the sump out.'

As they passed the unkempt parkland, Delia's mood took a dip. It was all too much – the whole situation. The memories this place held. She didn't want the responsibility of any of it.

Auntie Rose took her hand off the gear stick and patted Delia's knee. 'It's going to be all right, you know. One way or another.'

Delia studied her aunt's expression as they pulled up onto the drive and Rose took a good long look at Wilder Hoo's facade.

'Beautiful,' she said eventually. 'Not overdone. Grand in its simplicity.'

'Thank you, Kevin McCloud,' Delia huffed as she limped out of the car. 'That's exactly what he'd say.'

'Well, why don't we ask him and the *Grand Designs* team to come and help?'

Delia managed a smile. 'Why don't you shut up?'

Unexpectedly, they were startled by the front door creaking open. A moment later, Mrs Joy was walking down the steps to meet them. 'You're here at last. I'm so glad to see you again, Miss Jago.'

Delia blinked, surprised. 'How did you know I was coming?'

'Oh bless you. I've been hoping. Now here you are.' She offered her hand to Rose. 'Pleased to meet you. I'm Mrs Joy, the housekeeper.'

'Good to meet you, too. I'm Rose, Delia's aunt. I hear you are an incredible cook.'

'Oh, just a home cook. Nothing special.' Mrs Joy turned to Delia. 'I've lit a fire in the saloon, just in case you need to put that leg up.' Then she turned to Rose. 'It's the only chimney breast that doesn't smoke now, thanks to Miss Jago's help. The old house really appreciates the warmth. Come on in. I'm just finishing off in the kitchen. Oh, and see that big stone by the front door? That's to keep it open. It has a habit of slamming shut, and on a lovely day like today, it's good to let the fresh air in.'

Delia felt a glow of gratitude. She hated the noise when the doors slammed.

Mrs Joy went inside, but by the time Delia had hobbled up the steps, helped by Rose, there was no sign of her.

Rose stood in the middle of the great hall, turning a full circle to appreciate every bit of it. 'Just as I hoped. It's gorgeous.'

Rose used her foot to push the heavy stone into place. 'I like that. Lovely bit of polished granite.'

Delia shivered. 'I honestly don't care. Let's get the tour over and get out of here.'

Rose pursed her lips. 'Hold your horses. I haven't come all this way not to see it all properly. Delia, I'm doing this for you.'

'I know,' said Delia, looking across at her aunt. 'I'm sorry.'

'Good. Now where do we start?'

Delia led the way.

Rose was clearly on a mission, testing the wooden frames of the sash windows, inspecting each room for damp. She seemed genuinely thrilled at the size of the old 'below stairs' kitchen and its maze of rooms.

'Same sort of larder with the marble shelves we had at Jago Fields, isn't it? Who needs a fridge with this? Oh dear. Mouse droppings on the floor? You'll have to get a cat.'

Delia rolled her eyes at every comment, compliment, and suggestion, saying each time, 'The new owner can do what they like.'

'The things we could do with this garden!' Rose almost swooned as they explored the outside. 'I think lavender with pink Mrs Sinkins – such a heavenly perfume – and perhaps some sprawling rosemary. What do you say?'

'Vivienne asked me to make up a planting plan once.' Delia sighed at the memory. 'Took me ages. She never even read it.'

Rose was still looking around in wonder. 'Poor Vivienne. Losing her husband and son must have been awful for her. Where is she now?'

'Last I heard, she was back in Spain. They had a villa. I suppose it wasn't swallowed by Harvey's debts.'

'I wonder what she thinks of Wilder Hoo coming to you. Have you been in contact?'

'No. Sleeping dogs and all that.'

'Probably for the best.' Rose turned her gaze to the rooftops peeking out above a copse of trees. 'What's over there?'

'Farmhouse. Outbuildings. Harvey was going to do them up as holiday lets.'

'Let's go see.'

'I'd rather not.' Delia swallowed hard. 'The barn where I slept that last night . . .'

'It's up there, is it?'

'Yes.'

'Another day then. Shall we take a look at the beach?'

On the drive back to Kernow Autumn, Rose couldn't stop talking about Wilder Hoo and what she would do if it were hers.

'All you need is a good team of builders to fix the roof and work their way down through the house. Get it dry, replumbed, rewired, replastered. New kitchen. New floorboards. Refurbish the old windows. Then concentrate on the farmhouse and the cottages. As soon as they're done, you'd have rental money coming in. That would help enormously in funding the interior of Wilder Hoo. And while all that's being done, make the land work for you. Farmers would be thrilled to have the grazing, and you wouldn't need to worry about mowing – the cattle and sheep would do that for you . . . Oh, and what about weddings! In the fields and overlooking the sea; who wouldn't want to get married against that backdrop? Put up some yurts, add a shepherd's hut as the honeymoon suite, and . . .'

Delia had tuned out. There was no way she was going to keep Wilder Hoo. As soon as she had the valuations from the estate agents, she was going to get it sold. Once it was off her hands, she could get back to rebuilding her life: return to work, figure out a way to have a civil relationship with Harriet, and reset herself, her life and her future.

That was all.

Easy.

Her phone rang. 'Hi, Sammi.'

'Hi. I'm outside Auntie Rose's. Where are you both?'

Her heart lifted. 'You're back in Cornwall? I thought you weren't coming until Friday?'

'My demanding client backed off in the end. Plus, I have orders from Auntie Rose.'

'What?' Delia turned accusing eyes on her aunt. 'Really? She has said nothing to me.'

'I can explain,' Rose said, taking the turning into Kernow Autumn. She raised her voice so that Sammi would hear her clearly. 'We'll be with you in just a minute!' She gave Delia a liar's grin. 'Bless him. We had a lovely chat on the phone last night about Wilder Hoo.'

'Whoa, whoa, whoa!' Delia was clambering out of the car. 'What is this – an intervention? Did you order Sammi to come back from London to bully me into keeping Wilder Hoo?'

Auntie Rose refused to say anything more until she had closed her front door and ushered Sammi and Delia into her sitting room.

At last, she turned to Delia. 'Yes. Yes, this is what you'd call an intervention. Sammi and I both think you might be best resigning from your job, leaving London altogether and taking on Wilder Hoo.'

'What . . . ?' Delia held her hands to the heavens. 'You're asking me to give up a career I love to take on a house I hate?'

Sammi answered, 'It depends on what the estate agents come up with, but if it's good news, then yes, I think you need to get out of London, out of the salon, and—'

'And what? I *need* the security of Gilson's. Don't you see that? Right now, the ground is shifting under my feet like an earthquake and you two want me to throw away the one thing I have in my life that pleases me, that I'm good at, and that pays a wage? And for what? To take on a flipping huge money pit? No, no, no. Are you two out of your minds?'

'Do you really think it's good for you to be at the salon, the place you met Johnny, the place where Harriet worked?' asked Sammi.

Delia fell silent for a moment. 'Wilder Hoo has far more memories of Johnny. Look, I know you're trying to help, but this is my life. The difficult things I have come through—'

'You are coming through,' Rose contradicted. 'You're not through them yet.'

'Aaarrrggghhhh.' Delia had had enough. She picked up her phone. 'I am going to call a taxi and get a train to London now. Today.'

'Let me drive you,' Sammi offered.

'No thank you.' Delia's voice was low and polite. 'First Johnny, then Harriet, now you two – all of you thinking you can control me. Well, you can't. I am going to live my life the way I want to, starting now, this minute.'

CHAPTER TWENTY-SEVEN

The next morning, Delia woke in her London flat with a pounding headache.

On the train home, she had managed her confusion and upset over Rose and Sammi's apparent betrayal by ordering two miniatures of gin and tonic every time the trolley went by.

She didn't remember arriving into Paddington station or the taxi home back to the flat, but she did know that the moment the door closed behind her, she'd burst into tears and thrown herself at the wine in the fridge.

Now, fit for nothing, she squinted at her phone and saw three emails waiting for her. Each from one of the estate agents.

With her head banging and her eyes swollen, her priority was not to open them but to get to the bathroom and throw up.

Being sick was horrible and left her with a wobbly feeling in her stomach and a need for some Coca-Cola and some more sleep.

She woke four hours later, well into the afternoon, and remembered the emails.

She took a glass of water, two paracetamol, and a packet of ready salted crisps into the lounge, where she climbed onto the sofa and opened her laptop.

Each email was more dispiriting than the one before. She wrapped a coat over her pyjamas and ran to the local supermarket to buy another bottle of wine. All the while, her internal dialogue was screaming vengeance on Johnny.

Back in the flat, calmed by wine and feeling teary, she knew she had to speak to a person who was at least alive. It had to be dear, forgiving, turncoat Sammi.

Crashed on the sofa, she looked about for her phone. Unable to spot it by merely moving her eyes and head, she reached for the next best thing, her laptop, which was right next to her.

Subject: Sorry for myself

Hey.

Are you back in London?

Sorry about leaving Cornwall like that.

But you and Auntie Rose ganging up on me like that wasn't fair. We need to talk about it.

Anyway, I've now heard from all the estate agents. Bolitho's, the least negative report of the three, is pasted below. You'll see from it your and Auntie Rose's master plan is a non-starter and I'm right to want to sell up.

Dear Miss Jago,

Thank you for your invitation to view Wilder Hoo. I understand that you received the property on the death of your ex-husband, Mr John Carlisle-Hart, and are now the sole owner. I gather you wanted a guide valuation of the freehold property and land, with a view to selling as one lot.

Initially, I based my report on what I knew at the time – that is to say that Wilder Hoo is an attractive property with important local history attached to it. It also offers an exciting array of options, including the sale of the house itself and/or parcels of land as building plots or pasture.

However, after a short search my assistant found that your late husband's parents, Mr and Mrs Harvey Carlisle-Hart, made several unauthorized changes during their tenure, including but by no means limited to:

A) the removal of the bell from the tower of the fourteenth-century chapel
B) the addition of unsuitable roof tiles to patch areas of water ingress on the roof of the main house
C) The cutting down of five ancient oaks from the parkland

There is no record to suggest that Mr and Mrs Carlisle-Hart sought approval of these changes. It would appear they simply took it upon themselves. These changes must be reversed/rectified immediately. I'm afraid that no retrospective planning permissions can be granted.

As I am sure you are aware, Wilder Hoo is a listed building and as such is liable to very stringent guidelines on repair and maintenance or any changes which may not comply with planning rules. Unfortunately, any dispute of these guidelines can prove very expensive. The cost of reversing the unsuitable alterations to the church and replacement of the bell, as one example, could be very substantial.

While we would be very happy to market the house and its estate, we would have to make any potential buyer aware of the inherent financial burden their purchase would bring.

I may also mention that a small but vociferous local group are keen to bring the above to public attention and could make things a little more difficult in the future.

Rather than put it on the open market, you may have better results putting it up for auction.

It is with regret that I cannot bring you better news.

We shall await your further instructions.

Yours sincerely,

Juliet Garnet

So, there you are, Sammi.

The house and its acres are a worthless pile of crap with a load of people lining up ready to make my life more hellish than it already is.

I miss you.

D xxx

PS Can you come over for dinner one night this week?

His email came back almost immediately:

Hey, you!

I'm going to Pakistan day after tomorrow. Seeing my grandparents and also looking for some interesting bits of furniture to bring back for my clients, who are really into the whole Pakistan/Indian vibe. Fabrics, too.

Are you around the week after?

S x

Delia noted that he made no apology for the intervention, and she started typing a huffy reply which he didn't deserve. Eventually, she deleted it and started again.

Choose your day the week after. I'm off work until the doc says I'm good to go, so I'm free whenever. Thank God for darling David and his continuing pay cheques.

D x

PS How about the day you get back?

Delia had been counting the days, but at last Sammi was back from his trip and coming over that evening. She made an effort to tidy the flat and open up the little garden with its table and chairs and fairy lanterns hung in the branches of the single tree.

He was due at 7.45 p.m. but now it was 8, and he hadn't arrived. Where *was* he? She tried his mobile, but it went straight to voicemail.

He was meant to be collecting their takeaway on the way. Should she ring the restaurant? Ask if he had come in yet?

He'd never let her down, would he? *Oh God, please don't let him have been in an accident.*

She went to the kitchen and opened the wine she'd managed to avoid. Just a glass. To steady her nerves.

She gulped it down and poured another.

She began to feel a little less anxious.

She checked the clock again. Ten past eight. *Come on, Sammi.*

The doorbell rang, and there he was: handsome in his jeans and pale-blue silk shirt, carrying the takeaway and a larger bag with the name of a business in Islamabad.

She flung herself at him. 'Oh, thank God. I thought something had happened to you.'

'A slight delay on the food order. That's all.'

She reluctantly let him go. 'I thought we'd eat in the garden?'

'Lead on.'

They stepped out into the last of the sun, which was spreading pink and golden streaks across the surrounding roof tops.'

'I'm so happy to see you.' She took his hand and squeezed it. 'I've missed you.'

'It's only been a couple of weeks.' He placed the takeaway bag on the unlaid garden table. 'Shall I get some plates?'

'Did I forget? Sorry. I was too busy worrying about you. Fancy a glass of wine? The bottle's open.'

'I think I'll have just water to start with.'

Over dinner, Sammi kept the conversation uncontentious. Delia had finished the bottle of wine and gone to fetch another, while Sammi had barely started his food. He knew that anything remotely relating to Wilder Hoo and her future could spark another row.

He adored Delia and always would, but right then, jet-lagged and longing for his own bed, his deep well of sympathy and empathy was dangerously low.

Delia topped up her glass. 'Want some?'

'No, thanks.' He checked his watch. 'Can I make you a coffee?'

'Are you leaving?'

'No, no. Not yet. But I will have to go soon.'

'Oh Sammi.' She pulled a sad face. 'Don't.'

'Don't what?'

'Leave me. I have been so lonely while you were away. I missed you, and I miss work and . . .'

Her voice wobbled. Sammi braced himself for the self-pitying tsunami that was about to drown him.

'Darling Dee, of course you miss work, but . . .'

Her face crumpled and she began to sob. 'My life is a mess. What am I going to do, Sammi? What am I going to do?' She reached for her wine glass, but her grip was uncertain and it slipped from her fingers, falling sideways, cracking itself against her plate. As if in slow motion, it rolled off the table edge and down onto a terracotta plant pot, sending a million sparkling shards into the grass.

For Sammi, it was the last straw, and in frustration he shouted at her. 'For fuck's sake, Cordelia!'

Like a helpless, frightened little girl, she was immediately apologetic. 'I'm sorry. I'll clear it up. I'm sorry, Sammi.'

She was on her knees now, amongst the broken pieces of glass, drunk and hopeless. He pulled her up. There was blood on her legs and the palms of her hands.

'Don't touch anything. You're too pissed. For God's sake, just stand still. I'll sweep up and then deal with the glass in your knees and hands. Just don't touch anything.'

'You're angry with me,' she whined.

'No. I just want you to keep still.'

'I wanted another glass of wine.'

'*No*, Delia.' His voice rose again.

'But my knees hurt, and ow . . . my hands hurt. I'm so tired.'

The pent-up frustration erupted from Sammi. '*You're* tired? I'm fucking exhausted. I'm jet-lagged, but I came tonight because you asked me, you begged me. Dee, do you know how difficult you are to deal with right now? I know things have been tough, but you have so many good things in your life. You have a job, you have Auntie Rose, you have this flat, you have Wilder Hoo.'

'I hate that house!' she wailed, mouth open, eyes a mascaraed mess. 'Don't ever say its name again.'

'OR,' Sammi roared, 'you could pull your finger out and start using your brain and turn your disastrous life into an Olympic-size win. Show bloody Johnny and everyone else the incredible woman you are!'

'I'm not though, am I? I have nothing left in me.'

'That's bullshit, and you know it! For God's sake, you'll never get past this if you don't *try*!' He shook his head as her sobs turned to whimpers. 'Go to bed, Delia.'

Obediently, her head hanging, she went back inside.

Sammi left her to it.

He swept the grass as best he could, collected up the takeaway cartons, plates and cutlery, and dumped them in the kitchen.

Lastly, he poured himself a fresh glass of wine and went to find Delia. She was lying on her bed, still dressed and sniffing.

'Do you have a first aid kit?' he asked gently.

'Yes. Over there.' She pointed without lifting her head at a small pile of toiletries and make-up.

He sat on the edge of her bed and gently cleaned her cuts, pulling out fragments of glass, and applying small dots of antiseptic cream.

'I'm sorry, Sammi,' she muttered. 'Do you hate me? Go home and get some sleep. Don't worry. I'll be OK.'

'Let me get you into bed.' He helped her undress down to her underwear, then fetched a large glass of water and a couple of pain killers. 'There's a sick bowl on the floor in case.'

'Thank you, Sammi. I'm so sorry. I didn't mean to—'

'Yeah, I know. Get some sleep. We'll talk in the morning.'

Alone in her front room, Sammi sighed. He hated confrontation, hated being angry with Delia. But how on earth was he going to get her back on track? He couldn't leave her alone in the flat, so he emptied the bag from Islamabad and took out one of the three exquisite Kantha blankets within.

He had bought two of them for clients; the third was a gift for Delia, but right now his need was greater than hers.

He slept fitfully, the jetlag not helping, and spent a lot of the dark hours trying to think of a way to help Delia back. He was her best and – with Harriet having disappointed them both – perhaps her only friend.

As dawn broke, he gave up, got up, and went out to get some coffee and almond croissants.

Back at the flat, he sat himself down in the kitchen with his breakfast, opened his laptop and did some work as he waited for Delia to rise from her pit.

'Hey.' Delia appeared an hour later, eyes swollen but with an apologetic half smile. 'Thank you for putting me to bed.'

'What are friends for?' He turned back to the screen and continued to type.

'Can I make you a coffee?' she asked.

'I got you one. Just needs a minute in the microwave.'

'OK.' She looked down at the counter. 'Did you buy this croissant for me?'

'Yeah.'

'My favourite. Thank you.'

He kept his concentration on his work, aware that she was fidgety and watching him.

'Are you very cross with me?' she asked hesitantly.

Sammi sighed and pushed the laptop away. 'Yes, actually.'

'I'm sorry.' Delia bit her lip. 'Everything you said to me last night was right.'

'I'm surprised you remember.'

'I remember breaking a glass, and you swore at me, and I was drunk . . . I'm so sorry.'

Sammi sighed. 'Yeah, well, you need to stop acting like a victim. You have to get Johnny out of your head. It will take time to process, but the human brain is very good if you just let it mend. No wine. No crying. No mad emails. Just good food, proper sleep, a sensible routine, and most important of all, *time*.'

Delia sat down at the table beside him. 'Where do I start?'

'Start going out again. Meeting people. Find a nice boyfriend.'

She gave him a shy smile. '*You* need to a find a nice boyfriend.'

'Oh, that's nice. Thanks. You know why I can't do that.'

Delia put on a baby voice. 'Because your mummy and daddy wouldn't like it.'

Sammi took a deep steadying breath. 'That's not a nice thing to say.'

'It's the truth,' she snapped, 'and it wasn't exactly nice when you said I was being a victim!'

'*That* is one of the main things you have to process.'

'And one of the main things *you* have to process is that you like men.'

'Wow. Nice. Really nice. And yes, I like men as much as I like women, but I'm single by choice.' He rubbed his forehead. 'And right now, I'm focused on looking after you, as well as trying to grow my business – two full time jobs right there. There's no room in my head or in my bed for anything or anyone else.'

Delia inhaled deeply. 'Right. Sorry. It's time for me to move on, isn't it?'

Sammi sighed. 'Do I smell the whiff of burning martyr?'

She gave in and smiled. 'I do know I need to get my life going again. Yesterday I started to write a plan.'

'Show me.'

She grinned. 'Let me get my laptop.' She was back in less than minute. 'OK, here we go. Number one: go to the bank and ask for a loan.'

'What for?'

'Repairs to Wilder Hoo.'

He raised his eyebrows in surprise. 'Delia, are you saying that maybe – just maybe – Rose and I had a point?'

'Maybe,' she replied. She swept her hair back and exhaled. 'OK, I'm going to make a brilliant pitch to the bank – all about Wilder Hoo and how it will be worth millions once I've sorted out all the problems. I'm going to ask them for seed money and then work on crowd-funding – enough to begin work on the immediate problems of the house and the chapel. Then, I'm going to ring round people who might give me a grant or be willing to invest in the rebirth of Wilder Hoo, a lost gem of an estate which, when it rises like a phoenix from the ashes, will be one of the greatest visitor attractions, hotels, wedding venues, and eco systems in the country.' She bit her lip anxiously, but continued, 'And . . . it'll be a bloody gold mine. Better than the Lost Gardens of Heligan and the Eden Project and . . . and Truro Cathedral put together.'

'Delia, this sounds wonderful. I'm thrilled you want to take on Wilder Hoo, but . . . Well, from that email you forwarded to me, it sounds like you'll have your work cut out for you.'

'Do you think it can be done? This is *me* asking. Not my bloody in-laws.'

'All I'm saying, darling, is that you should manage your expectations.'

She stood up decisively. 'You know what you've just done?'

Sammi laughed. 'Sounded like a chauvinistic pig?'

'Well, yes, but also . . . you've just put fire in my belly. Neither you, nor Johnny, nor Johnny's horrible parents, nor that bitch Harriet can stop me. This is my life, and I'm taking control of it.'

Sammi grinned. 'That's the Delia I love. You're magnificent! This is a moment to remember – a red-flag day with a huge exclamation mark in the middle of it.'

'I really mean it, Sammi.'

'Where will you live?'

'Wilder Hoo.'

'And what sort of time scale are we talking?'

'For what?'

'To have it operating as a money-making concern and be giving you a profit?'

She stared at him defiantly. 'A year from today.'

'A bit ambitious.'

'I mean it. You watch me.'

'Well, today is the twenty-seventh of April.'

'Shake on it?' She held out her hand.

'If you're sure.' He took her hand and shook it.

'Right. Let's celebrate,' she said.

He laughed. 'You drank all the wine last night, so it'll have to be glass of water each.' He filled the glasses, passed one to Delia before raising his own. 'A toast to the return of the lost Delia Jago and the rising of Wilder Hoo!'

That afternoon, after Delia had showered and was feeling a lot better, she got on the phone and booked a meeting with the bank, made an appointment with a local estate agent, and rang Auntie Rose to tell her the plan.

Later, she and Sammi lay on the floor and shared a bag of Percy Pigs while going over all the points the estate agents had made in their appraisals.

Sammi seemed more upbeat. 'The good news is that they're all pretty much in agreement: the house is amazing but needs a ton spending on it. The location is incredible. The park and farmland, gardens and beach are all exploitable . . . They've all said they'd need to have the land properly measured and surveyed or whatever, with a search to see if there are any odd covenants or mine shafts or flocks of pixies . . . you know the sort of thing.'

Delia smiled. 'Do pixies come in flocks? And are they protected? Like bats?'

Sammi laughed. 'One of the estate agents I showed around knew a lot about the history of the place because a relative of his had worked there after the last war.'

'Interesting.'

'Yeah, he said it had been an amazing estate once, making a decent living and employing lots of locals. During the First World War, the Big House, as he called it, was a hospital for injured soldiers, then in the Twenties it became a girls' boarding school.'

'I didn't know that.'

He also said something about the Americans using it as a secret base for D-Day planning. It's possible that Churchill, De Gaulle, Field Marshal Montgomery, and Dwight Eisenhower met there to discuss various strategies.'

'Wow. I'm surprised Harvey didn't know about that. He loved that stuff.'

'Proof, if proof were needed, that Harvey was an idiot.'

Delia nodded. 'He really was.'

'Anyway,' Sammi went on, 'in the Sixties, it looks like a new family bought it and turned it back into a home with a working farm. You can imagine a tenant farmer in the farmhouse, the barns full of hay and calves, can't you?'

'Wouldn't it be wonderful to bring all that back? What happened to that family?'

'They ran out of money in the recession in the Seventies. They just locked up and walked away. It was empty for ages after that, I think, and that was when the rot literally set in.'

Delia sighed. 'It's all rather sad.'

'Yeah.' He passed her the last Percy Pig. 'Also, this man remembered when Johnny's parents bought it.'

'Really?' Delia's interest was caught. 'What did the locals make of them?'

'At first, everyone thought they were the best thing to happen to the old place. Vivienne and Harvey must have had the gift of the gab. But as the years went on and nothing changed, the locals lost their patience . . .'

'Oh, they were full of themselves. But so believable. I fell for it as easily as I fell for Johnny.'

Sammi opened a bag of Haribo. 'Want one?'

'Yes please.'

'Why do you think he left you Wilder Hoo?'

Delia sighed deeply. 'Out of spite. To hurt me.'

'Really? Not as atonement for his horrible behaviour?'

Delia's hollow laugh was her answer. 'No.' She felt the familiar sting behind her eyes. 'Let's stop talking about it,' she said flatly.

'Sure. Absolutely.' Sammi pulled his phone from his pocket. 'I made a playlist for you. All the good stuff. All the naff stuff.'

'Aw. For me? Why?'

'You're driving down to Cornwall,' said Sammi, wagging a finger at her. 'And you'll need to go soon. Remember the twenty-seventh of April next year!'

CHAPTER TWENTY-EIGHT

Wilder Hoo, June

Delia woke at sunrise, the brightness easily pouring through the tall, un-curtained window. She checked the time and groaned. It wasn't even six.

She lay back on her makeshift camp bed and pulled the duvet over her shoulders. The first night in the empty saloon had been cold.

What had she done?

Yesterday, her flat had been packed up, and all her belongings were now in a removals van, hopefully heading down the M4, M5, and A30, due to arrive mid-afternoon.

A wave of lonely, angry tears washed over her, and she had to sit up and gulp for air, just hanging on to her sanity.

She grabbed her phone to ring Sammi, then shrieked with frustration, remembering there was no WiFi in Wilder Hoo yet. She'd have to get in the car and drive up to the main gate to have any hope of catching the fragile signal.

At least, the removals crew were cheerful. When she'd chatted to Del the team boss and the others as they packed up the van yesterday, they'd been excited to be heading to Cornwall: two days on the road and a night in a Newquay hotel with a bar, not to mention the possibility of having a surf, was a holiday for them.

And here she was, having spent a cold night in a large mansion, with tall ceilings and a window which a Queen had once looked from to admire the formal gardens, woodland, and the sea sparkling in the distance.

Sitting on the edge of her makeshift bed, Delia rested her elbows on her knees and her head on her hands. She still couldn't quite believe she'd packed up the life she had lovingly built, and all for this old place.

On the china-blue carpet in front of her, amongst the tattered newspaper pages in which she had wrapped it so carefully, was a photo of her aged nine, sitting in between her mum and Auntie Rose on a boat trip. She was wearing her pink tracksuit bottoms, her favourite T-shirt, and a wide grin.

Her mum was in her 'holiday dress': white with sploshes of printed golden daffodils and cinched at the waist, while Auntie Rose was wearing jeans and a green T-shirt printed with the words *Me? Sarcastic? Never.*

They had gone to the Isle of Wight, one of the few holidays her mum and Rose had been able to afford. It was Delia's first trip on a boat, first visit to an amusement arcade, first stay in a guest house.

Mum and Auntie Rose must have saved for a long time. Looking back, Delia remembered that nothing had been refused her. Fish and chips, the cinema, a new swimming costume, crazy golf, candy floss. All lavished on her.

Unannounced, her throat again constricted with unshed tears. If only her mum was with her now.

'Oh, Mum. There's so much to do, and I don't know where to start. What would you do?'

She pictured Mum shaking her head, sighing deeply, and putting the kettle on before getting out pencil and paper and making a list.

'Yeah. You're right.' Delia kissed the captured faces of those much-loved women and stood up. Sitting feeling sorry for herself was a pointless exercise. 'You two are going up on the mantelpiece so that we can all keep an eye on each other.' She wiped the dirty shelf with the sleeve of her jumper and placed the precious photo centre front, then wiped her tearful eyes with the cuff of her other sleeve.

If only she could speak to Mum now, or send some kind of heavenly email?

'I miss you so much.' Delia ran a hand over her tousled hair. 'I'm in such a pickle, and I'm so tired. I need a boot up the backside.'

She wiped her nose and imagined her mum's voice:

Get yourself organized, Cordelia. Make your bed. Unpack the bits you brought down with you and make that list.

'You're right.' She sniffed. 'I know.'

Since Delia's ridiculous pronouncement that she could achieve for Wilder Hoo all that the previous owners over the past fifty odd years hadn't been able to, some things had gone irritatingly well.

The bank had not laughed her out of town; in fact, they had agreed to a small but helpful loan against the cash sale on the London flat, which had sold satisfyingly quickly. The estate agent had five viewings quickly confirmed during the first week of it coming on the market and two offers the following week. The bidding war that commenced became ridiculously exciting and was eventually won by a third candidate, a young woman who came in at the eleventh hour and blew all the other offers out of the water.

Delia felt wobbly with the speed of it all.

Next, she had to ask David – by phone, because she was too scared to meet him face to face – if she could have a twelve-month sabbatical to get Wilder Hoo up and running.

'And will you come back after the twelve months are up? And the old house is sorted?' he questioned.

'I honestly don't know, but that's my plan.' He deserved honesty, after all.

His anger was terrible. His voice became strangulated to such a degree that it made him cough. She held the phone to her ear, listening to him choking and gasping for breath.

'David. David? Breathe. Are you sitting down? Call one of the girls into the office . . . David? I'm panicking here!'

Suddenly, the choking and gasping stopped.

'David? Are you there? Can you hear me? . . . Right, I'm calling an ambulance.'

Then she heard a chuckle.

'David? Are you all right?'

'Of course I am. I was kidding. Thought I'd put the willies up you for fun.'

'Well, it wasn't very funny – I thought you were dying!'

'Did you want me to die because you were leaving? Darling, I've been around the block once or twice, and I'm not going to expire because you have other fish to fry.'

'Oh.' Delia was glad he couldn't see her blushing.

'Anyway, I have a little adventure of my own in mind, too.'

'Do you?'

'Yes. My dear mum is not doing so well. I need to spend more time with her so . . . I'm selling up!'

Delia blinked rapidly. 'Selling what up?'

'The business, darling. Forty years is plenty, and all good things, etc. I've done my research and I like the look of St Mawes.'

Delia brightened. 'You've moving to Cornwall, too? St Mawes is lovely. Very posh and very yachty.'

'Exactly. Mum used to sail down in St Mawes when she was young, and she's all for it. We're going to rent for a while to see if we like it and then possibly buy something adorable. I could do with a lot less stress in my life, so there we are. Good night, London, hello Cornwall. Are you horrified or pleased?'

'I'm taken aback! I never imagined you leaving Gilson's.'

'Thought I'd die in the saddle? No, darling. Not for me. I'm ready to stroll around in deep-red linen trousers, a blue blazer, and a little captain's hat – you know the sort. Cocktails every night at six, and fish and chips on Friday.'

Delia began to laugh. 'Oh, David. What are we doing! Are we mad?'

'Quite bonkers, dear, but it gets the blood flowing, doesn't it!'

Now, in the saloon at Wilder Hoo, Delia walked over to the windows to get a better view of the terrace. It was in a state. There were great holes in the balustrade where mortar was missing, and weeds were growing between the flagstones.

'Come on, Jago,' she said aloud. She had begun to enjoy speaking to herself. It gave her a sense of company. 'This won't get the baby bathed, will it, Mum? I must be mad. Don't you think? I just hope it's going to be worth it.'

She looked around for her slippers and socks, then realized the socks were already on her feet. She must have slept in them. 'Good thinking, Jago. Now where are my slippers?'

She found them under her dressing gown and put them both on, before collecting up the empty log basket and making her way out of the room, along the corridor, across the great hall, and down to the chilly kitchen.

She stopped for a moment and closed her eyes, trying to picture it as the working kitchen it had been and could be again.

'Positive thoughts, Jago!'

The back door was stiff on its hinge, but she got it open and trudged outside to the old bunker. There were enough logs to fill the basket for another few days, plus a half-empty bag of kindling, and an unopened box of firelighters – all enough to keep her warm before she got the electricity turned back on. Another thing to do quickly. She'd need to get the water sorted, too. It hadn't really crossed her mind before she left London that none of the services would be switched on.

Returning to the saloon, she laid the fire and briefly wondered if the chimney was clear or blocked by a jackdaw's nest. She took a chance and lit it. A small billow of smoke leaked into the room but just as quickly was sucked back up the chimney as the flames began to do their job.

'Phew.' She addressed the photo on the mantelpiece. 'Was that you making the fire draw so well?'

She imagined a sense of positivity in the room, and for the first time since she had arrived, she smiled. 'Mum, you wouldn't happen to have a pot of tea and a bacon sandwich for me, would you?' She waited. 'No? I'll drive down to the local Tesco, then. I think it opens at seven. I could get one of those small barbecues on wheels, set it up on the terrace. Would it boil a kettle?' A thought popped into her head. 'Good idea. Yes. There's a hardware shop in Penvare, and it might have a little camping gas stove. Thank you, Mum.'

She sat down to write a shopping list on her phone. If there was a signal, she could have ordered a luxury shop online, but . . . she stopped typing and looked around her. 'Wilder Hoo? Are you listening? I hope you are, because I'm bringing you into the twenty-first century, whether you like it or not. Do you hear me?'

'Hellooo?' A voice that was definitely human was calling her. Delia froze.

Footsteps sounded outside the saloon door. The handle turned, and Delia's heart leapt into her mouth.

'Hello.' The smiling face of Mrs Joy appeared, and Delia instantly relaxed. 'I saw the smoke from the chimney and thought it must be you. I hope you don't mind, but I thought you might like a thermos of tea and a bacon sandwich.'

Delia could have cried. 'Mrs Joy! Why would I mind? I was just thinking about exactly that! Thank you. Thank you so much.'

'Oh, it's nothing, Miss Jago.'

'Please call me Delia.'

'If you're sure?'

'I'm sure.'

'Good.' She held out the flask and tinfoil wrapped sandwich, and then her eyes fell to the camp bed and wrapping paper littering the floor. 'Now then, I'm here to help. Where do we start?'

'I was just writing a shopping list.'

'Oh, I love a list.' Mrs Joy pulled a pen and a small red notebook from her old-fashioned but smart fake croc handbag, then snapped it shut with a satisfying clunk. It reminded Delia of the late queen, who always carried a similar handbag, either for a state occasion or a walk with her corgis. 'While you are out shopping, what would you like me to do here?'

'The removals van is due mid-afternoon – I came ahead of them last night. Would you be able to show them where to put my bed, sofa and table if I'm not back in time?'

'In this room? Making the saloon a sort of temporary bedsit?'

'Yes, I suppose.'

'Of course. And I'll tidy up a bit to make some space before they get here.'

'That would be amazing. Are you sure you don't mind, though?' Delia added, with a sudden thought. 'You can't have been paid since . . . Well, I don't have much money to—'

'Oh, don't worry about all that. There's more to life than money, my dear. I'm more than happy to help until you know how you're fixed. Shall we set up a little kitchen in here, too? Somewhere to plug the kettle and the microwave you bought a while ago now?'

'Oh yes! That would be great . . . wait, there isn't any—'

'Electricity. Ah yes. I'll tell you what I'll do: I'll ring the electricity company and the water company. They'll remember me from when I had to have them stopped after Mr Carlisle-Hart died . . .' She put her hand to her mouth. 'Oh! I don't mean to upset you.'

'That doesn't upset me. It was sad and all, but . . .'

Mrs Joy nodded. 'He wasn't the right person for Wilder Hoo, was he? Not like you.'

'You think I am?'

'Oh yes. I can feel it. The house likes you. You've got the drive to bring it all back.'

Delia pulled an anxious face, teeth gritted. 'Have I?'

Mrs Joy smiled. 'Of course you have.' She patted Delia's shoulder. 'We're a team now. Oh, that reminds me. You'll need satellite TV, internet, and WiFi put in. I don't know about you, but I love to catch up with a bit of daytime telly when I'm on tea break.'

Delia laughed. 'Are you an actual fairy godmother?'

'If I had a penny for every time I've heard that.' Mrs Joy chuckled. 'Now, you get that tea and sandwich down you, then get yourself washed and dressed – I brought a packet of wet wipes with me. I thought they'd do you before the water gets turned back on. I'll go and get my pinny. See you later.'

Delia ate and drank her breakfast like a ravening wolf, then gave herself a quick wipe down with the wet wipes, got dressed, and set off for the shops.

CHAPTER TWENTY-NINE

She was back three hours later, with a car loaded with small appliances, equipment, and food. She knew Mrs Joy would be as excited as she was to unpack them.

As she turned the last bend in the drive, looking forward to seeing the broad steps running up to the now-familiar porch, she found the removals lorry blocking it instead, and a further three Transit vans cluttering the gravel: one from the electricity board, another from the water board, and a third from a satellite TV company.

'What on earth . . .?' She climbed out of her car, rather irritated that her access to the front door was blocked so completely.

'Mrs Joy?' she called from the great hall. 'I'm back!'

'In the saloon,' Mrs Joy shouted.

When Delia reached the saloon, her mouth gaped.

Mrs Joy was directing proceedings from the comfort of Delia's old sofa.

Del and Joe, the removals men, were hanging curtains, while their colleague Sally was drilling what looked like a television bracket into a wall. Another woman was out on the terrace, holding a satellite dish and talking to yet another man, who was feeding wire through a hole in the skirting.

'Here she is.' Mrs Joy was beaming. 'What do you think, Delia? They've been working so hard.'

As the workers turned and waved, Delia took it all in.

Her bed was now reassembled and ready made with fresh sheets and plumped pillows. It was positioned almost in the centre of the room.

'Are you happy with it here?' Mrs Joy asked. 'We thought you could see the fire, the television, and the garden while you snuggled down.'

'Yes, it's . . . perfect.'

'And the sofa – pretty little thing, isn't it? – we thought in front of the fire but at an angle. Is that all right for you? Oh and before you ask about the curtains, I remembered last night that they were still in storage. They were made for this room but were never put up.'

Delia felt a small tingle in her spine. 'Last night? But you didn't know I was coming down last night . . . ?'

'The estate agents let me know.' Mrs Joy didn't miss a beat. 'Now then, where would you like your table and chairs? I was thinking along the back wall there. Perfect place to set up a small kitchen. What do you think?'

Before Delia could answer, yet another man walked in, wearing plumbers' overalls and wielding a spanner. 'All done, Mrs Joy. Water's back on and the boiler's working nicely. Just call me if you need me . . . oh, and the oil truck has arrived. He's topping the tank up now.'

'Thank you, Kevin.' Mrs Joy patted his hand. 'You're a good boy.'

'Anything for you, Mrs Joy. You know that. Remember, any problems give me a bell. Bye.'

Delia couldn't take it all in. She sank into her bed, staring stupidly and watching all that was going on.

When Mrs Joy returned from seeing the last of the workers off, she was smiling. 'That's what I call a good day's work.'

'I don't know how to thank you,' Delia said quietly. 'How did you make all that happen?'

'Old friends are good friends,' said Mrs Joy, removing her pinny and folding it neatly away. 'Did you get all the shopping you needed?'

'Yes. It's still in the car.'

'I can help you bring it in?'

'You've done enough!'

'Well, if you're sure, I'll see you tomorrow. We can set up the little fridge.

Delia frowned, 'How do you know I bought one?'

'I saw your list this morning. I'm terrible for looking at other people's lists. Right, I'll be off. Sleep well.'

'I will. Thank you again.'

'My pleasure. I'll let myself out – you stay there. Bye.'

When Mrs Joy had departed, Delia shook her head in wonder. Her television was mounted on the wall. The beautiful curtains, heavy linen chintz, hung perfectly.

She walked around the room, counting the new plug sockets that had been fitted: six double plugs and two extension cables with USB ports, which reminded her to charge her phone and laptop.

She plugged her phone in to charge, and it immediately pinged. She frowned. It couldn't be an email – there was still no WiFi. Maybe a stray text had managed to grab on to her phone while she was out shopping?

She checked it just in case. It was a welcome email from the satellite company.

Her phone actually worked! She was back in the twenty-first century. She grabbed the television remote and pressed the on button.

'Bloody hell!' she said to no one and plonked herself on her sofa. The screen burst into life showing all the channels.

Laughing, she muted it, then tapped a number into her phone, which connected in seconds.

'Auntie Rose? It's me!'

The next morning, Delia woke refreshed and calm. She was looking forward to making herself a cup of tea, but first she had to empty the car. She was reluctant to climb out of bed, but the need for a cuppa was stronger.

Once again, she had woken with the dawn, and outside, she found the early sun starting to warm Wilder Hoo's front face, softening it with a golden glow.

The stillness of the air gave her pause, and in that moment, she saw the beauty surrounding her.

The mist rising over the parkland.

The sky above, of softest blue, with puffs of pearly clouds dancing across it.

The squadron of early house martins wheeling in breathtaking formation, chasing down insects on the wing.

A skylark somewhere singing.

The trees in the drive, standing as erect as soldiers, guarding her, guarding Wilder Hoo, shaking the night from their leaves.

The air was sweet, and Delia drank it down.

Standing on the steps in her pyjamas and slippers, she felt the house wrapping her in a blissful embrace.

'Oh bloody hell,' she gasped. 'Sammi and Rose were right all along. I've fallen in love with the place.'

It was all hers now. Every blade of grass, slate paving stone, fence post, mouse nest, and rotten beam. All hers.

Something shifted in her. It all felt, in that moment, like everything that had come before was all right.

This was where she belonged.

When Mrs Joy arrived, she seemed delighted to find Delia and her saloon kitchen all set up.

'Doesn't that look homely!' she exclaimed, glancing down at the appliances set out on a trestle table – another purchase that Delia had made the day before. 'I like it.'

'May I offer you a cup of tea and some toast?' Delia said, in the voice of an aristocratic butler.

'I'll take a tea but no toast, thank you.' Mrs Joy settled herself on the sofa and watched as Delia proudly poured out the tea and popped the toaster. 'And I like your larder bookcase. Very clever.'

'You are sweet. Necessity is the mother of all inventions,' Delia said, stirring the tea bags in the teapot.

'Indeed it is.' Mrs Joy laughed. 'No sugar for me, thank you. I can't believe how happy the room looks.'

Delia ran her eyes around the place. 'Does it look happy?'

'Can't you feel it? I bet your Auntie Rose will see the difference when she gets here.'

'Yes, she will.' Delia handed Mrs Joy her mug, then stopped. 'How did you know Auntie Rose is coming today?'

'You mentioned it yesterday.'

'Did I?'

'Well, I thought you did. Maybe it's my memory playing tricks.' Mrs Joy calmly sipped her tea. 'You make a very good cup of tea.'

After breakfast, Delia went upstairs to take a very welcome – and now wonderfully hot – shower in the old bathroom which she and Johnny had always used. That felt like centuries ago now.

The shower was the type that hung over the bath and was antediluvian in age. She would give it all a good scrub later; it might come up as good as new if she put her back into it. A lick of paint on the walls, a pretty bathmat, and some new towels – all jobs to add to her lengthening list.

She had left Mrs Joy downstairs, unwrapping the last couple of boxes, which held Delia's more sentimental trinkets and treasures. She'd brought them down in the car rather than leave them to the jolting of the removal truck.

When Delia came downstairs, clean and fresh with a towel wound over her wet hair, she found Mrs Joy watching a bit of *Lorraine* on the television and holding her mum's old Clarice Cliff milk jug decorated with the 'Crocus' pattern.

'Isn't this a lovely piece?' Mrs Joy said, twisting the jug expertly in her hands. 'Not a crack or a chip. Clarice was a lovely girl, wasn't she? So talented.'

'Did you know her?' Delia asked in surprise, rubbing her hair dry.

'Bless you, no. But I knew of her, of course. Such a talent. Now, where would you like it?'

'On the mantelpiece, I think – next to the photo of me and Mum and Auntie Rose, please.'

Mrs Joy carried it carefully and placed it next to the picture, before studying the likenesses. 'I can tell you're all related. The same eyes and smile.'

'You think so?'

'Oh yes.' She stood back and admired them, then turned to face Delia. 'The other bits I unpacked are on the table.'

Delia's face softened as she spotted the two packs of well-handled playing cards. 'We used to play Canasta. Mum was a whizz at it – hard to beat her. Those cards were my grandmother's. I could never get rid of them.'

Mrs Joy nodded. 'Of course not. They've been touched by the hands of women you love.'

'That's a lovely way to think of them. Or am I just being too sentimental?'

'I don't think anyone can be too sentimental, Delia.'

She looked round at her new friend, feeling warmth and gratitude flooding through her. 'Thank you, Mrs Joy.'

'What for?'

'Everything. For understanding. For yesterday's bacon sandwich and tea. For the water, electricity, phone, WiFi, television . . . and for not laughing at that ancient pack of cards. Honestly, since you arrived, things have started to feel so much better.'

Mrs Joy smiled. 'It's what I'm here for.'

At last, Delia has returned. I'm embarrassed by my poor reception. She is camping in my charming saloon, where Her Majesty Queen Victoria once took tea. A fire was ablaze in the grate then. The scent of the wisteria, which shaded the terrace, drew Her Majesty's eye to the knot gardens below. I had plenty of house staff looking after me then. Cleaning, polishing, sweeping – nothing left undone.

Who is there now to attend to the damp, the cracked windows, the rotting wainscots?

I watched as Delia pulled her woollen jumper closer last night. Even a lit fire cannot defeat the night air from creeping through the loose panes. She cries and talks to herself when dear Mrs Joy is not present.

I wish I could have put on a better welcome for her. At least the saloon is the part of me most free from damp, and it does have the carpet to cover my stained and slightly wormy floorboards.

I wish I could show her how excited I am to see her. My saviour! A reluctant and unhappy saviour, but one who will do her best by me, I feel sure.

I may be very old, but I have always been a good host. I will try to help her as much as I can. Poor girl.

I need her. I have been alone and unloved for too long.

Empty.

Fretting.

Anxious.

Falling apart.

Pigeons are roosting in my attic. Mice scamper in my kitchen cellars. My once great garden has been reduced to misshapen hummocks of unidentifiable fauna, sprinkled with rabbit droppings. Great swathes of damp have settled in my plaster cornices and the treads of my once glorious staircase.

I was very beautiful in my day, you know.

Women treated me as their protector and their child, dressed me with fine silks and beautiful furniture built by craftsman, ceramics from Italy, framed grandmasters. When the winter storms prevailed and the cannon balls of the Parliamentarians threatened to breach my walls, I stood firm and strong, guardian of all within.

My gentlemen owners brought their London cronies down to flaunt me. Their blithesome shouts ringing on the breeze. Riding out across my acres and down to the sea to bathe or catch fish. How my masters delighted in the covetous glances of their friends, the jealousy and resentment that they could own something as richly handsome as me.

And now, it is I whose heart aches.

May I confide in you?

I have hopes and dreams.

I feel things are changing.

It is June, my favourite month, and the sun is warm. The breeze is soft.

The woodland above the beach is rustling gently, while the choughs are kiting and chatting, riding on the thermals above the cliffs.

The life of early summer is warming my flagstones.

And she, Delia, has returned.

At last, I have a guardian again.

I always knew she was the best of the bunch. The poor dear didn't get off to a good start; she was never happy here. Those people were not my sort of people. She didn't like them, and they didn't like her. I heard the rows, saw them bickering.

Has time softened her feelings towards me, I wonder?

How I have longed for company.

There is no one left, other than the jackdaws, gulls, mice, and pigeons, and not one of them known as a conversationalist.

The sea however – the sea is always talkative.

The great Atlantic Ocean. Capricious in her moods. Easily seducing the human creatures who play in her gentle waves, but as quickly dragging them down with a hidden rip. Down to the shingle, seaweed, and sand. Lungs bursting, eyes blinded. Where is the sky and the air? Then innocent. Swelling, dimpling, wrinkling. Throwing the victim up above the white horses, their tips cresting the waves and whipping their manes behind them.

The sound of the tide is the percussion of the sea. I have a word for it: merdrum. Mer for the sea. Drum for the percussion.

Listen attentively, and you will understand. Timpani, base, snare. The shimmer of a splash. The purr. The rumble. The roar. I have listened to it since the beginning of time.

Have I mentioned I am noted in the Domesday book? Something to be very proud of, I think you will agree. It shows my pedigree:

Wilder Hoo. There demesne for 26 ploughs and 32 villeins and 21 slaves. It is worth 5 shillings since 10 years. Now possession of land worth 40 shillings. The manor house has taken away 3 estates with 17 acres of pasture. 2 hides, which have never paid gelt, worth 2 shillings. To the west, pasture 7 leagues long and 10 acres of woodland worth 10 shillings.

Things have changed a lot since then, of course. At the very beginning, I wasn't more than a piece of land covered in trees. Then came an ancient settlement, followed by the first manor house – the seed that grew me into what I am now, one of the finest Great Houses of Cornwall. Well, not as fine as I was, but nothing that can't be improved with a little spit and polish.

Replace the roof.

Treat the damp.

Repair the windows and frames.

Kill the woodworm.

Some carpet, curtains, furniture . . . and mousetraps.

I must find Mrs Joy; she will help. And my faith is with Delia. If only I still had the servants to abolish the cobwebs, light the fires, clean the windows.

Ah well, no point in dwelling in the past.

CHAPTER THIRTY

Before they left, the removals crew had stacked inside the library all of Delia's stuff that wasn't needed immediately. Mrs Joy and Delia now stood in the doorway, surveying it all.

'It doesn't look much, does it?' Delia walked over to a stack of boxes. 'I wonder which of these has the crockery and cutlery.'

'I suppose your flat wasn't as big as Wilder Hoo,' Mrs Joy said soothingly. 'I like that wardrobe though. Edwardian, would you say?'

'Maybe. It was my mum's, and before that it was her gran's. Auntie Rose let me take it when I moved to London. There's a matching chest-of-drawers somewhere here too. I always thought it was rather dark and gloomy, but it'll suit Wilder Hoo.'

Mrs Joy nodded. 'Just imagine how this house was when it was at its peak. Every room the epitome of its time. Sumptuous drapes. Specially commissioned furniture inlaid with mother-of-pearl. The fires lit through every season. The wall sconces and chandeliers burning bright with candlelight. Those were the days. The parties here were the best in the county.'

'How do you know all this?' Delia asked, smiling.

'I've always enjoyed history – listening to the old folk reminiscing. The great hall would always be turned into the ballroom, with a small orchestra seated next to the stairs. Everybody danced so beautifully then.'

Delia could see the faraway look in Mrs Joy's eyes. 'It's as if you were there, Mrs Joy.'

Mrs Joy snapped back to the present. 'I wish. *Strictly Come Dancing* is the closest I get to such things.'

'If only these walls could speak, eh?' Delia looked at her watch. 'Right. Let's see if we can't sort these boxes out. I'm looking for cutlery, crockery, and my clothes – especially warm jumpers.'

Auntie Rose arrived a couple of hours later, with an overly large suitcase. She greeted them both with real warmth.

'How lovely to see you again, Mrs Joy. Oh, you have been busy, Delia. Is everything unpacked yet?'

'Not quite. Just three more boxes to go.' Delia was on the floor amongst a pile of shoes and boots. 'I think the boxes over there are books. They can stay put for now.'

Auntie Rose looked at the empty floor-to-ceiling shelves, 'You could just put them up in here? Start your collection?'

'Not yet.' Delia got up and kissed her aunt. 'Thanks for coming.'

'I'm excited to be here at the start of it all.'

Delia pointed at Rose's suitcase and laughed. 'Is that why you have packed enough for the month?'

'You don't mind me staying for a couple of nights, do you?'

Delia gave her a hug. 'Stay as long as you like. We'll have to share the bed, though. At least it's big enough.'

'I couldn't think of anything nicer.'

*

Later, as they ate their sandwich lunch on laps in the saloon, Rose congratulated Mrs Joy and Delia on the inroads they had already made.

'It's all so cosy in here. The bed, sofa, and television. How did you manage to get everything sorted out with the electrics and WiFi and hot water so quickly? I had to wait for five weeks before I got my WiFi fixed at Kernow Autumn.'

'It's the village. I've been here that long I know almost everybody.' Mrs Joy told them. 'I've known most of them since they were children.'

Rose mulled that over. 'I suppose if it was me in Bozinjal, it would be the same.'

Delia got up and took their plates to the trestle table. 'Cup of tea? Now we've found all the kitchenware, I can offer you decent mugs.'

'Yes please,' both Rose and Mrs Joy replied.

Delia filled the kettle from the tap of a large plastic water container sitting on top of her larder shelves. It saved her having to walk all the way down to the kitchen each time she needed to make tea or clean her teeth.

Rose smiled across at her, impressed. 'You're making this room an absolute home! So comfy.'

'All down to Mrs Joy.' Delia handed out the mugs and settled herself on the floor, facing the two women on the sofa. 'Cheers.' She raised her mug. 'To Wilder Hoo and its future.'

'I'll drink to that,' said Mrs Joy.

'To Wilder Hoo,' said Auntie Rose.

Mrs Joy took a sip of tea, then put her cup down to rummage in her pocket for her red notebook and pencil. 'Now then, I think we need to make a list of all that needs doing and put it into order of urgency. I have been thinking very hard about it, and we don't want to make any early or expensive mistakes.'

'I actually have a plan of my own,' Delia said.

Auntie Rose turned to her, eyebrows slightly raised. 'Oh?'

'Yes,' Delia began. 'It's not easy to explain but . . .'

'Go on,' Mrs Joy said encouragingly.

'Well, I've hated this house all the time I've known it. I resented the attention it was receiving from Harvey and Johnny, the huge plans they talked about. The money they needed, the money they'd make. Johnny saw it as his inheritance – he'd be a man of means at last. The penniless unknown actor would have wealth and bragging rights. He used to talk about holding open-air productions of Shakespeare in the grounds – with him starring, of course. As a family, they would have loved that. The thought of money, position and power.And I don't blame them for having those.' Delia frowned. 'But it was all driven by greed. Not love. This morning – and this may sound a bit woo woo, but anyway – This morning I stood on the front porch watching the sun come up, listening to the birds, and from nowhere I felt – and this is the weird bit – I felt such a rush of love from the house itself that I knew my job was to love it back.'

Mrs Joy and Auntie Rose sat in silence, never taking their eyes from Delia, and she laughed, blushing. 'You're looking at me as if I'm insane.'

Mrs Joy shook her head. 'But I feel it, too. Exactly that. Always have. But you have put it into words. Bravo.'

Rose shook her head. 'That's all very interesting, and romantic but how will this *love* be manifested? I mean, there is a lot to do and, let's face it, there isn't the money to squander.'

'I really don't know,' Delia answered. 'But I feel that if we listen to the house, or at least open our minds to it, we'll find a way. We have until the twenty-seventh of April next year.'

Auntie Rose shook her head. 'It will be a stretch, my love. Think of the expense of it all! To have every room furnished, painted, the kitchen done, not to mention the leaky roof and the golf course and all that nonsense . . .'

'But that's what I'm saying, Auntie Rose. We don't have to turn the clock back for the house. We can push it forward. Sammi bet me that I'd have it going as a money-making concern, be making a profit. He said nothing about the house being fully refurbished, or the farm and barns and chapel rebuilt.'

Mrs Joy clapped her hands. 'There we are then! Forget turning it into a hotel or a wedding venue or a golf course.'

Auntie Rose frowned, but a moment later, a smile crept across her lips. 'Yes. I see what you are getting at. As long as the building is safe for something like public tours and cream teas . . .'

'Exactly,' Mrs Joy agreed.

'But you'll have to sell a hell of a lot of cream teas. And we would definitely have to hire in loos and whatnot. We'll need insurance, too . . .'

Delia began to chuckle. 'This house is beginning to get inside your head, too, now, isn't it?'

'No. I'm just trying to think logically – something that your mother never did. You two are like peas in a pod in that regard.'

'We think with our hearts, not our heads?'

'Yes. Off in fairy bloody land half the time.'

Mrs Joy was smiling. 'Look at you two – both of you wanting to reach for the moon while arguing about who will build the rocket.'

Rose and Delia began to laugh. 'What?'

'Oh, you know what I mean.'

Which made them all laugh even more. Their laughter filled the room and slid through the draughty window panes, out onto the terrace, on through the garden and the woods, until it reached the glinting waves of the sea.

The house breathed a sigh of contentment.

The campaign to restore Wilder Hoo had begun.

CHAPTER THIRTY-ONE

The following morning, Delia woke next to her aunt, who was sitting up and noisily tapping into her mobile phone.

'Could you be little more loud?' Delia asked, her voice croaky with sleep and last night's celebratory wine.

'Cordelia. Did you sleep well?'

'I could do with a bit more.'

'We did get a lot done last night, didn't we?'

Delia ran a hand over her face, rubbing some life back into it. 'I'll check the budget again today – make sure we've thought of everything. We have very little room for error.'

'You wrote it all down. We should have enough to make the building watertight by the autumn . . .' Rose continued to tap away at her phone. 'I'm just sending an SOS on my socials.'

Delia struggled to pull herself upright, then squinted over her aunt's shoulder to see her screen. 'It's called posting, Auntie Rose. What are you posting about?'

Auntie Rose gave an innocent smile. 'Nothing.'

'You're not on a dating website, are you?' Delia asked in disgust.

'I wouldn't tell you if I was. You're so judgmental.'

'So you *are* on one then?'

'There are some very nice people out there.'

'And some sleazebags,' yawned Delia.

Auntie Rose tutted. 'Just because you are scared to death of meeting anyone. I, as it happens, am not.'

Delia felt her smile slip away. 'I'm not scared to death.'

'Yes, you are, and I understand why.' She pulled back the duvet and got out of bed. 'Fancy a cuppa, or is it too early?'

'What time is it?'

'Almost six.'

Delia slumped back onto her pillow. 'Why are you awake so early?'

'Because the early bird catches the worm.' Rose padded over to the kettle and filled it from the plastic jerry can of water. 'Right, what we need is a couple of rounds of Marmite toast, and a pint of tea. Mrs Joy will be here at nine.'

'Can I have another hour's sleep then?'

'Oh no. You and I have a marketing strategy to work on.'

'I am not going on your dating site, if that's what you mean – advertised like something out of Exchange and Mart.'

Rose laughed. 'Exchange and Mart! Where have you been, 1972? Anyway, they're online now. And no, I wasn't looking at dating sites – this is Instagram. You agreed to this last night. We have to let people know about Wilder Hoo and the twenty-seventh of April challenge.'

Delia was horrified. 'Did I agree to that?'

'Yes. Remember, I told you that I took a social media course at Kernow Autumn. Hugh says I'm one of his best pupils.'

'Hugh? The man from Bridge Night?'

'That's him.'

Delia frowned, sitting up straighter in bed. 'Well, I'm unagreeing to it now. I don't want everyone knowing our business.'

'That is a shame,' said Rose. 'Because I've already put it out there.' She handed a stunned Delia a mug of tea, then began buttering the toast. 'Don't you remember *anything* about last night? You gave me the job of marketing manager, so that's what I'm doing: marketing Wilder Hoo. I took some lovely pictures of the front of the house yesterday, so I've just posted them along with the date of the Grand Opening next year. How much Marmite would you like?'

Delia blinked, sipping her tea and trying to take it all in. 'I don't like Marmite.'

'Well, you're having some. Lots of vitamin B12. Good for your nerves.'

'My nerves are fine!'

'They'll have to be when you see the number of followers we're going to get. Here's your toast.'

Delia took the toast. 'Eugh.'

'My pleasure,' said Auntie Rose, ignoring her. 'Look, you have a huge year ahead. Not just Wilder Hoo and all that will entail, but also you have to get yourself a social life. Find some new friends. Ah ah ah!' She wagged her index finger. 'Don't look at me like that. You need a man in your life.'

'Like I need a hole in my head?' replied Delia sharply.

'Listen to me and eat your toast. Cordelia Jago, you are a beautiful woman. Very talented, but very stubborn. You need to get yourself out there.'

Delia slowly chewed a piece of the toast and swallowed it down with her tea. 'No.'

'Why not? Because you're scared?'

'I'm not *scared*.' Delia swallowed another bite of toast. 'I'm just busy with the enormous job of sorting out this house!'

'You have to face your own feelings,' Auntie Rose said gently. 'Johnny hurt you, and you're frightened to date in case you get hurt again.'

Delia wiped a crumb of Marmite toast from the corner of her mouth and lay back down. 'I need more sleep.'

Rose settled down to her phone and began chuckling. 'You're going to like this.'

From under the duvet, Delia murmured, 'I'm not.'

Rose ignored her. 'We've got several likes already and a few comments. Shall I read them to you?'

'No.'

'There's one from Hugh. Bless him. His comment is: "Remarkable house and remarkable women embark on challenging restoration project." Isn't that sweet?'

'I suppose.' Delia gave up trying to sleep and sat up again. 'So, do you *like* this Hugh, Auntie Rose?'

'Really, Delia. He's just a friend.'

'Is he married? Does he have any money of his own?'

'We do not discuss anything as vulgar as money, and he is widowed.'

'Children?'

'A son in Hong Kong whom he rarely sees and a much-loved grandson.'

Delia scoffed. 'Some spotty little IT nerd?'

'There you go. SO judgmental!' Auntie Rose sniffed judgmentally.

'But I am right?' Delia asked.

'He is not spotty. In fact, he shares his grandfather's good looks, but he does work in IT, yes.'

'How old?'

'Early twenties.'

'Much too young for me.'

'Whoever said he was meant for you?'

'As long as he's not, then that's fine.' She snuggled down again. 'What's his name?'

'Alfie.'

'It would be.'

'There you go again, Judge Delia.'

Mrs Joy arrived on the dot of nine, bringing with her the plumber from the other day.

'I hope you don't think I'm getting ahead of ourselves, but Kevin and I have been thinking. It's all very well you and Rose camping in the saloon, but what you really need is a proper bedroom or two and a working bathroom upstairs – like a little apartment. Then the saloon can be the office HQ. That was Kevin's idea.'

Delia and Rose looked at Kevin, who blushed from his boots up.

'Me and Mrs Joy were talking,' he mumbled. 'You don't have to say yes.'

'What an excellent idea,' said Auntie Rose. 'Don't you think, Delia?'

Delia shook her head. 'Lovely as that sounds, I'm afraid I'll have to say no. There's no money in the budget.'

'But—' Rose began.

'No.' Delia was firm. 'I need the roof sorted before we can even think about any niceties.'

'Well . . .' Mrs Joy raised a hand like a schoolgirl desperate to give the right answer. 'Kevin and his brother Kenny are roofers.'

Delia frowned. 'I thought you were a plumber?'

'I am, but Ken's a roofer, and I help out sometimes,' Kevin said, looking at his steel-toe-capped boots.

'Oh. I see.' Delia found herself smiling. 'In that case, would you be kind enough to give me a quote for the roof?'

CHAPTER THIRTY-TWO

Wilder Hoo, July

Good weather settled itself over Cornwall like a warm blanket. The days were long, soft and dry, while at night, a bright moon threw its beam across the sea and land.

Later, in the early hours when all people were abed, a benign rain fell, just enough to water the fields and flowers.

It became Delia's routine to get up soon after five and, without disturbing Rose, take her morning tea out onto the terrace. The scent of damp earth and fresh grass reminded her of early Cornish mornings walking with her mum to check on the livestock and collect the fresh eggs. In the coop, she and her mum would stroke the sleepy hens and then watch as they strutted, beady-eyed, into the sunshine, clucking, stretching, and squabbling over the dust baths.

Wilder Hoo's terrace was a good place to stand and think.

Now that Kevin and Kenny had clothed Wilder Hoo in scaffolding, the house was less of a worry to Delia. The scaffolding gave it the character of a fortress. Impenetrable. Unassailable. Comforting.

Kevin and Kenny were putting in all the hours, and had even taken Delia up on the roof to show her precisely what needed doing and why. She began to become very familiar with pediments and gullies, chimney stacks and guttering, flashing and shrinkage, pests and storm damage.

But worrying though it might all sound to her, the boys were very reassuring. 'Nothing to fret about, Miss Jago. It's been up 'ere for a hundred years or more. By the time we've finished, it'll stand for another hundred years at least.'

Imperceptibly, she began to relax. The twenty-seventh of April seemed a long way away now. Nine whole months away. She could have baby in that time – not that she wanted to. That past dream she'd had with Johnny was long gone and, if she let it, left her feeling unsettled and sad, so she tried hard never to think about it.

The fact that things were at last happening to the house made her feel better, more optimistic. The bank was taking a close interest in all she was doing and was impressed with how she was running the budget. This was a true fresh start for her and Wilder Hoo. She wanted things to be kept simple. She didn't have to worry about the past, only the future. She had the freedom to do what she wanted.

She was less irritated by the small things now. Washing up left undone, no milk in the fridge, the constant noise of drilling and hammering, she found herself unbothered by.

Only the other night, as she had stepped over a pile of ironing in order to get to the sofa and crash out, Auntie Rose had commented, 'You're getting back to your Cornish roots, Cordelia.'

Delia looked at her, puzzled. 'Why do you say that?'

'Not so long ago, you would have been fretting about that ironing and getting the ironing board out.'

'I'll do it dreckly,' yawned Delia, using the Cornish pronunciation of the word *directly*, meaning: *it'll be done tomorrow, next week, next month . . . or next year . . .*

Rose chuckled. 'Spoken like a true Cornish woman.'

Auntie Rose, when she wasn't FaceTiming Hugh, was happy taking snapshots of the garden, the great hall, the abandoned outbuildings, and the beach, and getting them out on Wilder Hoo's social media.

Mrs Joy, when she wasn't making sandwiches and pasties, snacks and cakes for everyone and anyone, had started the epic task of going through every room in the house, from the attic to the cellars. She removed the dust, debris, and damp from every crevice. Moth-eaten curtains were taken down and either saved if possible or used as rags. Windowpanes were polished until they gleamed, rugs and carpets steamed and vacuumed, old furniture dragged out to the outhouses or given a lick of paint.

In her pocketbook, she made notes for each room, recording damp patches, wordworm, and radiators that needed draining.

Although Delia had refused the idea of a proposed apartment within the house, Mrs Joy and the boys had privately decided that it was to go ahead, which is why Mrs Joy gave the Carlisle-Harts' bedroom, dressing room, and walk-in wardrobe extra special attention.

Their old suite of rooms had the best view over the terrace, all the way down to the ocean. It also had its own beautiful, west-facing balcony – a mid-Victorian addition with an attractive glass and copper roof, now green with verdigris.

Mrs Joy and Kevin agreed that the rotting floorboards needed replacing, but other than that, it was perfect. Mrs Joy diligently recorded that in her book, too.

With everyone else engaged in fruitful work, Delia felt free to get on with some outdoor jobs.

Each morning after breakfast, she would walk a different part of the estate, familiarizing herself with the boundaries, making notes or taking photos on her iPad.

In the parkland, there were countless trees that needed intrusive ivy cut from them, and in the woods, two or three beech trees were leaning at alarming angles after the Atlantic storms that battered this part of the coast.

The fields were thigh-high in grass now, and if Delia knew how, she would have got the old tractor out from the barns and cut the hay herself. Instead, she made a note to ask around for anyone who had cattle or horses and needed the grazing, then, on second thoughts, wrote another note reminding her to google long grass and its suitability for cattle or horses.

By the end of July, she had a good idea of how hard it was to keep up with the many acres of land that she had no idea how to manage.

Time at Wilder Hoo was slow – and delicious. Delia marvelled that she didn't miss her previous life and wondered who that person had been. She'd been so happy when she'd first left Cornwall for London. A big fish in the small Bozinjal pool of talented hairdressers, she hadn't had a clue what life in the capital would be like.

Looking back, she wondered how she had survived. She'd trusted David and Jean, who believed in her talent and had simply cracked on with it. Fearless? Courageous? Naive? She couldn't remember. How had hairdressing taken up so much of her life and her thinking? Whether she was in the salon or jumping on and off the London buses, it had been her everything. Now, she rarely thought of it. How had she survived the city for all those years? The rain and cold of winter. The humidity and pollution of summer.

And then there was Johnny.

Without him, she wouldn't be where she was now.

She rarely dreamt about him anymore, but he was still in her mind. Fragments of memories, not all bad, but even the happy times still hurt.

How much time she had wasted on a relationship that had never been right for her.

And now here she was, thirty-eight years old. She'd be forty before she knew it.

She no longer saw him sitting in the kitchen or pouring drinks on the terrace.

A complicated man. Capable of love but also capable of cold cruelty.

Poor Harriet. Or maybe lucky Harriet? She hadn't had time to be on the receiving end of his anger or sadism.

Delia hadn't been in contact with her since Johnny's death, but then neither had Harriet made contact with her. She knew Harriet had messaged Sammi, wondering if he'd like to go for a coffee and 'talk things over', but he had decided not to reply. 'That's a whole can of worms that doesn't need opening,' he'd told Delia in their last video call.

Delia had pretended she wouldn't mind, pointing out that her relationship with Harriet was different to his relationship with her, but she was secretly relieved and grateful.

Maybe one day they would connect again and be able to talk carefully and without feeling about Johnny. But then again, maybe not.

And as for Vivienne and Harvey? Delia felt not a jot of emotion. The two of them were self-obsessed and unpleasant. No wonder Johnny had been as he was.

And now, Wilder Hoo, the house she had hated, was her home, her project and . . . obsession? She couldn't imagine what the future held, but living anywhere else seemed impossible. These days, this summer, she and the house shared a rhythm. She was free to make her plans and do the things she needed to or wanted to, and the house supported her.

All these things went through her mind as she acquainted herself with the land that was now hers.

At the end of most working days, it became her habit to walk to the beach to swim.

The dipping sun glinting off the water closed her mind off from the real world and lifted her spirit to a more dreamlike place.

The beach and the ocean were where the start and end of her love for Johnny had been rooted and uprooted. If she thought too much about either of those times, the internal scaffolding she had built around her heart grew weak and shaky. But gradually, those memories stopped haunting her every hour of every day. They were fading with the shifting sands of each tide.

'I can't believe this weather!' she said one afternoon as she joined Mrs Joy for their regular four o'clock cup of tea on the terrace. Mrs Joy liked routine and provided the punctuation of a day with regular tea and snacks.

'Enjoy it while you can.' She patted Delia's hand. 'It's good to see you looking so well. Fresh air suits you.'

Rose came out to join them, holding an envelope. 'Look what I have found.' She handed it to Delia. 'Recognize it?'

Delia didn't need to open it. 'It's the planting plan for the knot garden that I did for Vivienne, isn't it? Where did you find it?'

'I was taking some photos of one of the barns, the sun coming through the rafters – *very* Instagrammable. Darling Sammi puts little hearts next to every picture I take. We've got almost two and a half thousand followers now.'

'Oh well done, Rose. That's wonderful,' said Mrs Joy.

Rose beamed. 'Thank you.'

'But the envelope?' interrupted Delia, 'Where did you find it?'

'Oh, there were some lovely old wooden crates and hessian seed bags that I thought would look great if they were rearranged a bit, and I was moving them, I saw the envelope poking out from under.'

'Did you read it?' asked Delia.

Rose looked affronted. 'Of course not!'

'But you did, didn't you?' Delia raised an eyebrow.

'Well, yes, I *skimmed* it,' Rose admitted, 'but only to make sure it wasn't something upsetting.'

Delia took the folded sheet of paper from the envelope. 'Would you like me to read it aloud?'

'Yes please,' said Mrs Joy, intrigued.

Dear Vivienne,

Thank you for asking me to work on a plan for your knot garden. I appreciate how busy you are.

Rose snorted. 'Busy? Busy doing what exactly?'

'She had her charities and whatever,' Delia answered. 'Now shush. Let me finish.'

I hope you like it. I wanted it to be timeless, elegant, feminine, and sweet smelling. Reflecting the woman you are.

Rose laughed heartily. 'Goodness me, Cordelia! Such outrageous sucking up. I never had you down as a toady.'

'I was trying hard to build a relationship,' said Delia. 'Do you want me to finish or not?'

'I'm sorry.' Rose held her hands up. 'I won't say another word.'

Delia gave her a steely look. Then returned to the letter, 'Right, where was I?'

I've enjoyed researching the sort of planting popular in Victorian gardens, and I think the shortlist below offers authenticity. I've chosen as many scented flowers and herbs as possible.

Dianthus

Daphne

Heliotrope (wonderfully old-fashioned and smells divine)

Pelargoniums

Salvia

Verbena

Lavender

Rosemary

Of course, we can add or take away anything you'd prefer.

I think a well-clipped lavender hedge would make the perfect frame.

Excuse my poor drawing skills, but the little pencilled plan gives you an idea.

We could get the existing beds dug over in September, get rid of the weeds and add a good mulch, then we can underplant daffodils and tulips for the spring. What say you?

All love,

Delia

Rose was disdainful. 'What was her reply?'

Delia refolded the letter and put it back in its envelope. 'I didn't get one,'

Mrs Joy looked furious. 'That silly woman was jealous of you. I hope you know that. You were everything she wasn't: young, beautiful, successful, and clever. You sent her this lovely garden design – she could never have done that.'

Rose nodded. 'I didn't have to meet her to know she was the kind of woman who gives women a bad name.'

'Don't be too hard on her,' said Delia, with a stab of misplaced loyalty. 'We are sitting on her chairs on her terrace . . .'

'*Your* terrace,' Rose said angrily. 'Harvey left it to Johnny, and Johnny left it to you. Don't feel sorry for her, Delia. She never showed you any compassion, did she? I'm sure she's perfectly happy in Spain, drinking her liver away with some other appalling women. Finding that letter of yours today, carelessly chucked in with a lot of other mess she'd left, just goes to prove what sort of person she is. You could have made that garden for her, and you wouldn't have to be worrying about it now.'

Mrs Joy folded her arms in agreement. 'And now, you *are* going to plant that garden. You're going to do it this summer. In fact, there's no time like the present. Go today. Right now! Before you lose the spark.'

Delia wondered several times whether her satnav was to be trusted as it took her down quiet lanes that grew more narrow with every corner she rounded. Eventually, at the end of a rutted, bumpy track, she arrived at an open gate, where a wonky, handpainted sign leaning on a wheelbarrow welcomed her to Penvare Plant Nursery.

Several polytunnels stood in rows and a large rooster, wobbling his wattle, gave her a warning crow before rounding up his hens.

Of humans, there was no sign.

Once out of the car, Delia walked tentatively to the first polytunnel and peered into it. Immediately, she was transported back to her mum's old greenhouse at Jago Fields. Great trusses of tomatoes were staked up, drenching the air with their distinctive smell, and next to them were rows of aubergines, chard, basil, and possibly padrón peppers.

'Hello?' she called, but no answer came.

Outside again, she mooched past the other tunnels, popping her head in, just in case there was any sign of life. She carried on until she came to a gate leading into another field, where rows of fruit trees, dahlias, roses, and all manner of flowers, some ready potted, were basking in the sunshine.

She was crouching to look at the label on a large lavender when a voice behind her said, 'Phenomenal.'

She looked up quickly to find a man in a checked shirt standing behind her, sleeves rolled up over tanned arms.

'Sorry. Didn't mean to startle you.' His voice was gruff. 'The lavender. It's called Phenomenal. Makes for a very good hedge. Compact. Good strong stems and a haven for the bees. Smells good, too.'

Delia stood up. 'Hi, sorry. I was just looking. I couldn't see anybody, so I . . .'

'Don't let me stop you. Are you looking for anything in particular?'

'Well, actually . . . I'm hoping to recreate a knot garden.'

'Are you?' He smiled. 'Lovely. Victorian or further back?'

'I believe there was originally a Tudor garden there but . . . I'm not sure.'

He turned his head away and scratched his chin, thinking.

It gave Delia a chance to look at him. A nice face – round but not plump, tanned, without beard or moustache. His dark hair was cut short with a fringe that he was now raking to one side. His eyes looked dark, too, but in the sunlight, she couldn't tell, and anyway he wasn't looking directly at her.

She looked at the rest of him: only a couple of inches taller than her, with a slight roundness to his stomach but a broad chest and shoulders.

'Do you have anything in mind?' he asked.

'Oh, err, yes. I was thinking colourful, scented, and perhaps with some herbs.'

'What sort of soil have you got?'

'Oh. I don't know.'

'Well, tell me a bit about where you are, and I can show you some plants that you might like.'

'Thank you.'

He set off down a long dry soil path, which led to the back of the field, where a brick wall stood about two metres high. Halfway along it was a wooden, studded door, silvered with age. It reminded Delia of Wilder Hoo's front door.

He turned the rusty latch and pushed the door open. 'After you.'

'Oh my goodness!' Delia's eyes feasted on the jewelled flowerbeds beyond. 'A walled garden!'

'Gorgeous, isn't it?'

'How old is it?' she asked, fascinated.

'Possibly eighteenth century but could be earlier.'

'Who did it belong to?'

'We think it might have belonged to a community of nuns who lived in alms houses here. Long gone now. It's possible the villagers and local farmers helped to build the garden and the nuns gave them what they grew in return. Only an educated guess, though.'

'Who looks after it now?'

'Me mostly.' He glanced at her, and she saw that his eyes had a glint of green and hazel. 'I can give you a tour if you have the time?'

'I'd love that.'

'Good. I'm Ray, by the way.'

'Delia.'

'Nice to meet you, Delia. I must warn you that I'm a bit of a geek when it comes to talking about plants. My kids are very unimpressed.'

'I was the same growing up,' Delia replied with a smile. 'My mother and aunt had a smallholding. My mum was in charge of the greenhouse, but my aunt did the garden.'

'Where was that then?'

'Bozinjal.'

'Oh, I know. Right down west? Mining country?'

'That's right, but my family preferred being above ground to being below.'

'Don't blame them.'

Delia easily fell into step with him and, side by side, they walked the brick path, with Ray pointing out plants he thought she might like as they went.

When she got home, Mrs Joy and the boys had already left, and Auntie Rose was sitting in the evening sun on the terrace.

'There you are! Had a good time?'

'I did,' Delia replied, sitting down at her side. 'I met a lovely man called Ray at Penvare Plant Nursery. A proper gardener. Very knowledgeable. He showed me the most incredible walled garden. Made me *very* jealous. When I told him about the knot garden here, he was really excited. He's coming over day after tomorrow to take a look at it and give me some ideas.'

Rose raised an eyebrow. 'Maybe you have given him ideas?'

'Stop it. He's got a family. He's just a nice man – that's all.'

On the day of Ray's arrival, Mrs Joy and Rose were skittering about like show ponies on a tight rein, all restless and head tossing.

'I've made a Victoria sponge – no man can resist a slice of that,' Mrs Joy breathed. 'We'll have it on the terrace.'

'And I'll bring the tea tray,' added Rose. 'Just to give you a hand.'

'Arrgghhh. Stop it, the pair of you!' Delia shook her head at them both. 'He's just a nice man who's coming to look at my garden.'

'There's a joke in there somewhere, but I'm too much of a lady to tell it,' Rose sniggered.

Delia's expression was pure ice. 'I swear to God, if you say or do anything embarrassing, I'll never speak to you again.'

Ray was due at ten, but his well-used Transit van rattled onto the drive five minutes early.

Delia walked down the front steps to greet him. 'You found us.'

She was happy to see that apart from wearing a different shirt, he had made no other alterations to his appearance. He looked as he had the other day – a nice, normal gardener.

'Wow. This is quite a house you've got here.' He cupped a hand over his eyes, the better to see it all. 'You're having the roof done, are you?'

'Not before time. We've been lucky that it's been so dry.'

'Hi Ray!' Kevin's voice called down from the scaffolding.

Ray grinned, looking upwards. 'Is that you, Kevin?'

'Aye. Kenny's with me, too. Been fishing?'

'Went the other night. Got some bass. What about you?'

'Too busy with work, boy.'

'I hope you're doing a good job for Delia here?'

'Always. You know us.'

Delia laughed. 'Everyone seems to know everybody round here.'

'Those boys are good 'uns.' Ray raised his face and voice to the roof once more. 'Catch you later, lads.'

Delia took Ray straight round to the back of the house and the lumpy, weedy area that was the knot garden.

'Nice,' he said. 'Good size. There's a lot we can do with this.'

We? Delia wondered, then quickly dismissed the thought.

'Yoo hoo!' came Rose's voice from the terrace above. 'Anyone for tea and cake?'

'No!' Delia shouted back. 'Ray and I are busy.'

'Never too busy for tea and cake,' Ray called up to Rose. 'Thanks very much.'

Delia sighed. 'You don't have to be polite. It's my aunt, Rose, and Mrs Joy – she used to be the housekeeper here and still helps out. But they're a couple of time-wasters.'

Ray smiled. 'I've got plenty of time.'

Rose and Mrs Joy welcomed Ray up to the terrace, shooing him onto the comfiest of the old chairs. After they had provided him with tea, no sugar, and a large slice of Victoria sponge, they began their ruthless cross-examination.

Delia was left to listen like a mortified teenager.

Where did he live?

A small cottage.

Was he married?

Divorced.

Children?

Two daughters who shared their time between him and his ex-wife.

Ages?

Eleven and fourteen.

Was Penvare Plant Nursery his own business?

Sadly not. He just worked there.

Would he like to come round for dinner one evening, perhaps with his partner?

Ray smiled and shrugged. 'I don't have a partner.'

Delia stood up too quickly and knocked the table with her foot, almost depositing Ray's tea into his lap.

'Delia, you're not usually this clumsy. Are you feeling quite well?' Rose asked mischievously.

'I don't want to waste Ray's time that's all. He's here to give me ideas for planting, not sit chatting to you two.'

Ray stood up too. 'Thank you for the tea and cake and maybe I'll see you again.'

Mrs Joy and Rose smiled beguilingly. 'Oh yes. We do hope so.'

'This way Ray.' Delia pointed him towards the steps and as he turned his back she flicked a furious glance at her aunt. 'I'll see you two later.'

CHAPTER THIRTY-THREE

Wilder Hoo, August

The weeding, digging, and mulching of the garden became Delia's therapy. Her skin turned from golden to nut-brown. Her hair reached down to her waist these days, and she tied it back with whatever was to hand – usually a piece of garden twine or an elastic band dropped by the postman. She had never been one for make-up or scrutinizing herself in a mirror, even when she had worked in the salon: the only image of importance to her was that of her clients. Fashion was something she had never followed either. Her work clothes were practical and black. Black jeans. Black T-shirt. Albeit very cool ones.

For someone who worked in a visual industry, she had been a rarity, simply wanting her work to shine while she faded into the background. David had once or twice encouraged her to do magazine shoots where she was the model, not the client, and she had never felt less comfortable.

Now, her once funky black jeans and T-shirts were cut down to shorts and tank-tops and marred by soil and sweat.

A couple of times a week, at the end of his working day, Ray would drop round to deliver new plants, offer encouragement, and accept the tea, sandwich, or biscuit that Mrs Joy 'just happened to have made'.

Delia enjoyed those days, and together, she and Ray would sit on the terrace parapet with their mugs of tea, dangling their legs over the side and saying little as they watched the sun lowering to the horizon.

'I've been thinking about the hay you could take off those fields,' Ray said. 'If I had a tractor, I could do it for you.'

'I have a tractor,' Delia said.

'Do you? What sort is it?'

'John Deere.'

'John Deere? Nice.'

Delia nodded. 'I'd rather have a Massey Ferguson. My grandad had one, but Johnny—' She hesitated. She hadn't discussed anything about her past with Ray, but now, here it was. She swallowed and made herself continue. 'Johnny, my ex-husband, and his father bought the John Deere at a farm sale. It's still in one of the barns. It's old, though. I've never seen it actually working.'

'Mind if I take a look?'

In the shade of the barn, the tractor's silhouette was unmistakeable.

'There she is. Let's have a look.' Ray lifted the tarpaulin. 'Have you got the key?'

Delia thought for a second, then said, 'Hang on.' She went to a row of six-inch nails hammered into the door frame. 'Could be one of these?' She held her arm out, displaying the many keys hanging there as if they were prizes in a game show.

It took a while, but eventually they found the right one.

'It's highly unlikely it'll start,' Delia said.

'Let's just give it a try.' Ray jumped up into the seat and gently slotted the key into the ignition. 'Hang on to your hat.'

Delia closed her eyes, expecting a huge bang with a cloud of exhaust fumes, but Ray managed to coax a short but definite turnover of the engine. 'Promising.'

'A bloody miracle!' Delia laughed.

Ray removed the key and jumped down, tapping the huge back wheel fondly. 'I reckon I can get it going. Needs a bit of TLC, but that's the joy of the old combustion engine. Quite simple really – not like the modern computer-driven ones. I wouldn't know where to start with those, but this, if you'll allow me, I could do something with.'

'It's yours.' Delia was happy to give it away. 'Do what you want.'

They both agreed that Ray would come and go as he pleased to work on the old thing, and he promised to try to get it going in time to cut the fields before the weather turned.

Elated by this unexpected possibility of good news, they almost skipped back to the house.

'There you are!' Auntie Rose called from the terrace above them. 'I have people I want you to meet.'

Delia jogged up the steps ahead of Ray, to find Rose clutching a large jug of Pimm's in the company of two men.

The first, she recognized as Hugh, Auntie Rose's handsome bridge partner from Kernow Autumn.

'Hello, Hugh,' said Delia. She held out her hand for him to shake, but he leant in to plant a warm kiss on her cheek.

'Delighted to you see you again.'

'Likewise.' Delia glanced at her aunt with wide, approving eyes.

Hugh turned to the man next to him. 'And this is my old friend, Martin.'

'How do you do?' Martin shook Delia's hand firmly. 'I hope you don't mind me gatecrashing like this.'

'You are very welcome.' Delia found her gaze fixed on his extraordinarily handsome face.

'And this is Ray,' Rose explained to Hugh and Martin. 'He's helping to transform the formal garden you can see down there.' She directed them to the digging below. 'This time next year, it will be in full bloom, won't it, Delia?'

Delia found it hard to tear her eyes away from Martin's wide smile and very good teeth. An actual silver fox. 'Hmm?'

'Next year the knot garden will be in full bloom,' Rose repeated.

Delia gave herself a shake. 'That's the plan. Isn't it, Ray?'

'Sure is.'

Rose raised the jug of Pimm's. 'One for you, Ray?'

He pulled his van keys from one of the many pockets of his long khaki shorts. 'I'd love to, but I'd better get off. Promised my daughters I'd bring fish and chips for supper.'

Delia turned her attention to Ray. 'Thanks for today and for looking at the tractor.'

'My pleasure,' he said, with a small smile. 'Have a good evening, everybody.'

After Ray had left, Delia excused herself and went to take a shower. When she returned, with freshly washed hair and wearing a pretty linen shift dress, she found the terrace table laid and Hugh and Martin placing on it large platters of cold chicken, and steaming new potatoes gleaming with butter and sprigs of mint.

'Here she is,' Martin said.

'There you are, Delia.' Rose appeared with a bottle of wine in each hand. 'I haven't seen that dress before. Don't you look nice. Now then, Hugh, Martin you take the seats facing the ocean.'

Hugh tucked his napkin into the second buttonhole of his shirt. 'Your photos don't do justice to that view, Rose. It looks like the French Riviera from here.'

'It's a good evening to see it,' Rose agreed. 'What you can't quite see from here is the beach beyond the woods. Delia swims there almost every evening, don't you?'

'I do.'

'What's the temperature at this time of year?' Hugh asked.

'Pretty warm at the moment. It should stay that way through September, then start cooling end of October. The last hurrah for the half term.'

'Interesting,' Martin said. 'Is it open to the public?'

'Not yet, but one day maybe,' replied Delia.

'So you have plans for all of this? The house and grounds?'

Delia suddenly knew she wanted to tell him all about it. 'It's a bit of a long story.'

Martin inclined his head, his expression both empathetic and filled with sincere interest. 'I'd like to hear it.'

'So would I,' added Hugh. 'Rose has told me a little, but I'd love to know more.'

'OK, erm. Right.' Delia took a deep breath. 'Several years ago, I met and married a man whose parents owned all this . . .'

Martin and Hugh listened quietly, only occasionally adding a 'What?' or a 'good gracious me!' As Delia told the story, keeping her tone measured and the facts simple, she found it all easier to talk about than she had expected. A few months ago, she'd never have been able to speak of her marriage so calmly.

Rose reached out and stroked Delia's arm when the story reached its conclusion.

'So now, whether I want it or not, it's mine. With all its problems.' Delia took a good mouthful of wine. 'All I have to do is get to the twenty-seventh of April next year and prove to my friend Sammi that it can make money. '

Martin sat back in his chair, not taking his eyes from her. 'And if you lose?'

'Really. I honestly have no idea. To lose it now would break my heart. I've grown to love it. I feel like . . . it's where I belong.'

'And believe me,' Rose told Hugh and Martin, 'it's taken a long time for her to believe that.'

Martin leant his elbows on the table. 'How would you feel about having a few children come and camp out in the grounds? I work for a small children's charity in Truro – very underprivileged children who don't get the chance to have holidays, and coming to camp here would be such a treat for them. Wilder Hoo and you could give them something they have never had.'

Delia shook her head. 'That's not something I can even consider right now. The place just isn't safe for children.'

'It's absolutely impossible,' Rose agreed. 'They'd need toilets and running water, and we'd need insurance. Imagine them climbing about in the barns and falling off the roof. Or getting swept out to sea? No.'

Hugh picked up his glass of wine. 'Martin quite understands all that, don't you Martin?'

'Of course, of course.'

'He gets very excited when he thinks he's found something the children would like. However,' Hugh said, looking at his friend, 'I think tonight your timing is a little out, Martin.'

'My apologies,' Martin said graciously. 'Please forgive me.'

'Don't be silly,' Delia replied. 'Maybe one day, but not now.'

Rose stood up. 'Who is for pudding? Mrs Joy has made a gooseberry crumble big enough for ten, so I hope you all have room. Hugh, would you help me take the plates down to the kitchen and bring the crumble up.'

'Of course, darling.'

Delia couldn't help smiling at the word *darling*.

Their footsteps faded away into the house, and Delia and Martin were left alone.

The dark was settling over the house and garden, and the black shadows of bats on the wing flew above them.

Delia broke the silence. 'So, how do you and Hugh know each other?' she asked.

'I sold him a car. Years ago now.'

'What sort of car?'

He laughed. 'Typical Hugh at the time. Remember, this was the early Nineties. It was a 1970 Aston Martin DB6. Dark blue with cream seats. More than twenty years old by the time he had it, but such a beautiful machine. The King has one – given it as a twenty-first birthday present, I think. But now he's converted the petrol engine to one that runs on wine or whey or some such.'

'Really?'

'Yes. You can look it up. Anyway, I was a spotty young car salesman in a garage that specialized in the sale of classic cars. Hugh was a successful slightly older businessman. We built our friendship on that car. It was always in the workshop for niggling things. Maintaining a classic car isn't the most economical of hobbies. I felt rather bad for him after one very expensive bill, so I offered to take him for a pint and the rest is history. I got to be a family friend.'

'Oh?' Delia leant forward and lowered her voice. 'What was his wife like?'

'Very nice. When she died, Hugh and his son were absolutely floored.'

'What are you two gossiping about?' Rose asked, as she and Hugh reappeared with the crumble and a tray of coffee.

'Martin was telling me how Hugh and he met.'

'That bloody Aston.' Hugh laughed. 'Cost me a fortune and sold it for a pittance. But by God, she was a looker.'

Rose tapped his arm. 'That's enough of that. Coffee?'

After the men had left and Rose and Delia were washing up, Rose asked, 'What do you think of Martin?'

'He seems very nice.'

'And extremely handsome?'

Delia blushed. 'Yeah. I suppose.'

'Oh come off it. I haven't seen you wear a dress once since you've been here and yet here you are.' Rose laughed.

Delia admitted her attraction. 'OK he's nice. How old is he?'

'Fifty-five. I know that because he's the youngest resident in Kernow Autumn. He's known as the Toy Boy.' Rose laughed. 'And he has no baggage. No wives, no children. If you don't snap him up, someone else will.'

Delia laughed. 'Maybe he doesn't want to be married. Maybe he's gay.'

'He isn't gay. Hugh told me he had a long relationship with an older woman whom he adored, and she broke his heart.'

'Well, there you go. I'm definitely not the one to console him.'

Rose pulled the plug on the dirty dishwater and snapped off her rubber gloves. 'Look, you're almost forty, skint, single, and childless. He's comfortably off, single, and childless. You could do a lot worse.'

'I did do a lot worse.'

'That's old history. You have to move on.'

Rose immediately sensed she had said the wrong thing as Delia's mouth had drawn itself into a thin line.

After a short silence, Rose picked up a tea towel and began helping Delia with the last of the drying up. 'What did you make of Hugh?'

'He's also very handsome and for some unfathomable reason seems to like you. Quite a lot. What do you feel about him?'

'Oh, you know. He's very nice. Kind. Generous. We enjoy each other's company. He's rather good in bed.'

'Eugh! I really don't want to know.'

'Stop pretending you're shocked. Yes, I have sex, and I'm glad of it . . . but, the one thing that bothers me is, what if he starts hinting about sharing our lives together? I'd have to say no. I like my freedom. I like my independence.'

'Me too, Auntie Rose. Me too.'

CHAPTER THIRTY-FOUR

Wilder Hoo, September

'Sugar is on the table, boys.' Delia poured the boiling water into the teapot. 'Grab the milk from the fridge.'

Kevin and Kenny were dripping wet. 'Bleddy rain. Good job we got the roof finished before the weather broke,' said Kenny.

Delia passed them a mug of tea each as a sudden heavy fall of rain clattered against the kitchen window. 'I'm so glad Ray got the hay in when he did. If you two hadn't fixed the barn roof, and if Ray'd left it another week, we wouldn't have all those bales stacked in the dry. Thank you for helping with that.'

'No worries.' Kevin stirred two sugars into his tea. 'We'm happy to help. Best job we've taken for a long time, innit, Ken.'

''Tis true. You've been a pleasure to work for, Miss Jago.'

'How many times do I have to tell you, boys? Please call me Delia. Seriously, you've been such a help. I'm going to miss you next week when you're off elsewhere.'

The two brothers exchanged furtive looks, which Delia saw clearly.

'What?' she asked.

'Well, truth is,' Kenny began, 'we really like working on this house. We'd be happy to stay on and fix as much of it up as we can.'

'I thought you had work lined up elsewhere,' Delia said. 'What happened to that?'

'Nothing. We'd just rather be here.'

'Oh.' Delia frowned, not quite understanding. 'I barely pay you what you're worth as it is. You could earn proper money on a big new build or—'

'Maybe we could, but we want to stay here. There's the plumbing to finish off, and remember the idea of your apartment upstairs? Mrs Joy and your aunt want us to get that done.'

Delia laughed. 'Oh, do they!'

'Your aunt loves you and that, but I think she's had enough of living in the saloon.'

'Has she?' Delia knew when she was being stitched up.

Just then, there was a knock on the back door. 'That'll be the post.'

Mike, their local postman, was a sweet man with a cheery personality, but right now he was looking very soggy.

'Morning. Roads are terrible. There's a river flowing down Penvare High Street.'

'Do you want to come in?'

'No, no.' He handed her a couple of fliers and an envelope. 'Hope they're not damp. You all dry in here?'

'Yes, we are, thank you.'

'Right, I'll be off. See you tomorrow.'

Delia closed the door and sat down, putting the fliers to one side before looking at the envelope. 'I wonder who this is from,' she said to the boys. 'I don't recognize the handwriting.'

She opened the letter, read the first few lines, and her heart skipped a beat.

'Oh my God . . .'

'You all right, Miss Jago – Delia?' asked Kenny. 'You've gone a bit pale.'

'Yes. No . . . I mean, I'm fine,' Delia murmured, her eyes skimming over the rest of the letter. 'Just a bit of a shock . . . a surprise.' She stood up abruptly. 'I need to find my aunt.'

She found Auntie Rose in the saloon, scrolling through Instagram.

'Have you seen this!' She pushed her phone towards Delia's eyes. 'I posted that photo of the library and its yards of empty bookshelves, asking for books to fill them – any books, children's, gardening, science, racy novels . . .'

Delia pushed the phone away. 'Great, but . . . something unbelievable has just happened. This letter . . .'

She held it out to her aunt, but Rose was still in full flow. ' BBC *Spotlight* have messaged me. They want to come and film here—'

'What?' exclaimed Delia.

'I've just told you,' Rose huffed. She began to speak slowly and clearly, enunciating every syllable: 'The BBC want to send a film crew to see Wilder Hoo's library . . . What's that letter you're holding?'

Delia dropped to the sofa. 'I'm going to have to sit down to read it to you.'

She cleared her throat and began:

Dear Miss Jago,

My name is Margaret Jackson. I met you once, a very long time ago, on your first day at Just Jean, the hairdresser's on Cosy Corner in Bozinjal. You may remember spilling coffee over a client? Well, that was me. You were so upset that I felt very sorry for you and gave you a small tip.

And now I see that you are back in Cornwall. I have wanted to contact you for almost a year but didn't know how until my daughter-in-law showed me pictures of Wilder Hoo on her Instagram.

I have to tell you something that you may find difficult and shocking. It's about my late husband, Gary Jackson. Your father.

Rose shifted slightly in her chair. She was staring at one spot on the carpet, avoiding Delia's eyes.

Delia inhaled deeply. 'Is this true?'

'Oh, Delia . . .'

When Rose said nothing else, Delia continued:

I didn't know for a long time that, when I met Gary, he was also seeing someone else. He was a bit older than your mother, and he should have known better, should have behaved better. But what happened happened. She was pregnant, and he left her, and he married me instead.

After your mother's funeral he was really upset, but he wouldn't tell me why. Eventually, after a long time, months later, the story came out. He wasn't a man who talked about his feelings, but that day he broke his heart. He made me promise not to tell anyone, especially our boys, and I kept that promise until we read his will.

Rose sighed. 'Oh shit.'

Delia read the rest:

It was only at the reading of Gary's will that my sons found out they had a half-sister who was entitled to her share in our farm. That was Gary's final wish. I hope you will accept the enclosed cheque as full and final settlement.

What is past is past, but I want you to know that he deeply regretted walking away from you and your mother. The man he was then was not the man he became. In his own way, he loved your mother and felt such guilt that he could not have known and loved you, too.

I would rather you didn't contact me, either to thank me or rail at me. My boys and I would prefer to close the chapter here.

Good luck and best wishes,

Mrs Gary Jackson

Delia slid the letter back into its envelope and wiped her eyes.

Rose sat motionless, her fists balled in her lap, her anger plain on her face.

'Did you know he was dead?' Delia asked.

Rose shook her head.

'But you knew he was nearby?'

Rose nodded, and Delia stood up. She walked to the long windows and the view to the sea.

'Is there anything you want to ask me?' Rose said. 'We haven't spoken about your father since you were seventeen.'

'Where would I start? I made the decision never to go looking for him a long time ago. In a way, I'm glad I never knew him. I had you and Mum, and that was always enough.'

Delia took a deep breath. As she held up the cheque, she felt a rush of excitement run through her. This money could change everything.

'He's paid his dues,' she said. 'I'm going to ask Kevin and Kenny, right now, to make Wilder Hoo's kitchen great again.'

CHAPTER THIRTY-FIVE

Wilder Hoo, October

A few days later, while Delia was on her way to the bank, Sammi called her.

'Hi, Cornish Girl. How's it going?'

'Surprisingly well.' She laughed. 'How about you?'

'Fed up with London. It's done nothing but rain. The trees that should be cheering us up with their autumnal colours are just bare branches, their leaves squished and clogging all the drains.'

'How's business?'

'It was absolutely mad until the last few weeks. Bloody clients have fled to find the winter sun; then they'll go skiing, maybe a brief return to London for Christmas, then New Year in Sydney or Buenos Aires. They won't be making any enquiries about their interior decor until Easter.'

'Poor loves.' Delia laughed. 'Why don't you come down here for a few days? The house is now watertight. The plumbing and heating works. I have a barn full of hay bales and the knot garden is planted.'

'I'd love to see all that,' Sammi replied, 'and maybe I can help a bit? But don't worry about making a bed up for me. No offence, but I'll stay at The Vare Castle. I like my rooms furnished.'

Sammi's van, a new black one with his business name, HASHMI INTERIORS, written on its back and sides, purred up the drive just as dusk was settling. Mrs Joy and Rose had set lighted candles in all the front windows to greet him.

'What a fabulous welcome!' he exclaimed as he stamped into the great hall, the cold air clinging to his coat.

Mrs Joy fussed around him, while Rose and Delia showered him with hugs and kisses.

'At last, you are here!' Delia's eyes shone. 'We've missed you.'

Sammi stepped back. 'Let me look at you, Delia.' He surveyed her from top to toe. 'You're looking good. Relaxed. Happy.' Then his eyes narrowed. 'Who is he?'

Delia laughed. 'Oh do shut up.' She took him by the arm and headed for the saloon. 'Auntie Rose and I have a little job for you to do tomorrow.'

'Anything – just ask.'

'Our local BBC news programme, *Spotlight*, is coming to film in the library tomorrow afternoon, but it's not looking very inspiring. We wondered if you could work a bit of magic in there?'

Sammi grinned. He remembered his first visit to Wilder Hoo, when he had sensed the house was trying to speak with him. All these months later, he wondered if he would feel it again. 'I'll do my best.'

'But first,' said Mrs Joy, 'dinner is ready. I hope you're hungry.'

Sammi slept well at The Vare Castle and arrived at Wilder Hoo early the next morning, breakfasted and ready, only to find the great hall empty.

'Hello!' he called.

'I'm in the library,' Delia shouted back.

Pushing the door open, he found Delia sitting on the floor, surrounded by half-opened cardboard boxes.

'What's all this?' he asked.

'Stuff from the old flat. It's all rubbish.'

'One person's rubbish is another person's treasure – hey, isn't that vase one I bought you?'

'Well, *that's* not rubbish obviously. That's staying.'

Sammi raised his eyebrows. 'Curious, because it looks as if it's on the charity shop pile?'

'If you're going to question everything, we're going to get nowhere.'

'Where's Auntie Rose? Getting her war paint on for the BBC?'

'No. She's left me to it. Hugh was missing her.'

'Hugh?'

'Her handsome new boyfriend.'

Sammi smiled. 'Good for her.'

'Yeah, he's nice, but I'm not pleased she's left me to sort out the whole BBC thing that she set up. I never wanted a bloody film crew here.' Delia looked around the library with a sigh. 'I should have sorted the room out days ago, but there's always so much to do here.'

'When are they due?'

'One o'clock.'

An hour later, all the boxes were emptied. 'See. Rubbish.' Delia waved a hand at the piles of shoes, gym clothes, assorted glass vases, a collection of mismatched cups and saucers, a tennis racket, a hula hoop, a box of Christmas lights, and an array of dusty silk flowers.

'Hmm.' Sammi was flicking his gaze over everything, evaluating what was workable. 'So, the BBC are coming here to see a library that has no books and to ask anyone with a spare book to bring it over and start filling the shelves?'

'That's it.'

'Hmm,' he said again. 'Is Mrs Joy here?'

'She has weekends off.'

There was a knock at the library door.

'Only me.' Mrs Joy put her head round the corner. 'I was passing and thought you might need some help.'

Sammi smiled. 'Mrs Joy! Just the woman. Does Wilder Hoo own any pretty tablecloths?Or curtains? Preferably vintage?'

'I expect I can find something. What do you want them for?'

'This big and very empty room needs an intimate, cosy reading spot. Don't you think?'

Within a quarter of an hour, Mrs Joy had delivered half a dozen embroidered linen tablecloths and a pair of very long, burgundy velvet curtains.

'You're an angel.' Sammi kissed Mrs Joy's cheek and made her blush. 'Delia, go to my van and get my tool kit and stepladders please? The magic starts now.'

Mrs Joy and Delia stood back and watched as a totally focused Sammi began. The shelves on either side of the fireplace, he lined and draped from ceiling to floor, his fingers nimble as they created soft folds stapled into submission. The strings of Christmas lights were added, and when he was satisfied, he called for Mrs Joy and Delia to begin arranging the harlequin sets of mismatched china and glass.

'That's it, yes – the green and the violet together . . . to the right a bit more, and tilted towards the window . . . yes, perfect. Mrs Joy, would you happen to have a large something to put the silk flowers in? A milk churn, perhaps?'

While she went off to find something suitable, he directed Delia to lay the tablecloths, overlapping each other, to create a rug effect in front of the hearth. 'Nice, yes.'

Mrs Joy returned. 'Will this do?' She was carrying a gallon-sized copper jug.

'Where do you find all these things ?' Delia asked, mystified. 'I thought I'd looked through every cupboard and attic room, and I never found anything like that.'

'No time to chat!' Sammi decreed. 'The crew will be here in twenty minutes. Mrs Joy, you get on with creating a spectacular flower arrangement for the jug – maybe pick some foliage from outside – and Delia, you help me with the chair I have in the back of the van.'

The crew arrived just as Sammi gave his creation the final nod of approval.

Whatever the film crew had imagined they were coming to, it wasn't what met them.

Sammi had created a small oasis, a book readers' heaven in the vast empty space that was the library.

Silk hydrangeas and beech-tree twigs tumbled from the giant copper jug in the hearth. Glass and china twinkled within their velvet shelves. The carpet of embroidered linen was an inviting path to Sammi's huge, leather-scuffed armchair, which was nestled amongst it all. The only things missing were actual books.

Delia looked at Sammi and mouthed silently, 'Thank you,' putting her hand to her heart.

Mrs Joy was in her element. 'I expect you could all do with some refreshment. I'll make some sandwiches, and I've got some scones, too.' And she bustled off, happy.

Meanwhile, the camera crew were running lighting cables and reflectors across the floor, checking on angles for the best shots.

The reporter, a tall young woman called Syd, approached Delia at the edge of the library. 'Miss Jago?'

Delia smiled. 'Delia, please.'

'Thank you. Is your aunt about?'

'She couldn't be here today. Didn't she tell you?'

'I was expecting her to give me the interview, but interviewing you, the actual owner will be even better.'

'Interview?' Delia gulped. 'Well, I—'

'It'll be very straightforward: how Wilder Hoo came to be yours, a brief history of the building, and then it's all about the books you want people to donate. How many you need, the subjects you'd prefer, all very easy. Does that sound OK?'

Sammi was leaning against the far wall, listening. He gave Delia a reassuring thumbs up.

The sound man approached her. 'Mind if I put this mic on?'

Within moments, Delia was mic'ed up and sitting on the old leather chair in front of Syd, who was perched on a large camera case.

'Ready?'

Delia's mouth had gone very dry, and her lips were sticking to her teeth. 'Yes.' Her voice suddenly sounded high pitched.

'Everybody rolling?' Syd asked the crew, who affirmed all was ready. 'Here we go then . . .'

Dusk was gathering as the crew put the last of their equipment into their people carrier.

'Thank you so much for a great interview, Delia.' Syd shook her hand. 'You're going to get a lot of books sent in! And Mrs Joy, we won't need to eat tonight. Your cream tea was amazing.'

'My pleasure. When will it be on the TV?'

'Scheduled for Monday,' Syd told her. 'I hope you like it. Goodbye, and thank you again.'

Delia, Sammi, and Mrs Joy waved them off from the top of the steps until the red tail-lights disappeared.

'I'll be off, too,' Mrs Joy said. 'That was fun.'

'It was. And thank you for helping as always,' Delia hugged her.

Sammi smiled. 'Don't know what we'd have done without you, Mrs J.'

When Delia and Sammi were settled back in the saloon, Sammi said, 'Mrs Joy is a bit of an enigma, don't you think?'

'In what way?'

'Just turning up like that, even though it was her day off.'

'She's always doing that.'

'And you've never wondered?'

Delia frowned, confused. 'Wondered what?'

'If she isn't some kind of phantom?'

She laughed. 'Are you mad? Sammi, I'm paying her these days. What would a ghost want with money?'

'Depends on the ghost . . . How about the house? Have you heard it speaking to you yet?'

Delia was about to give him a flat *no*, but remembered the time when she was standing outside Wilder Hoo and looking at the land around it, the moment she suddenly fell in love with it all. ' I don't know what you mean.'

'I must be mad then.' Sammi put his arm over her shoulder. 'It's been a long day. Fancy dinner with me at The Vare?'

Sitting in the once-familiar dining room of The Vare Castle, Delia felt relaxed and at ease. Not a single thought of Johnny, Vivienne, or Harvey sprang up to discomfort her.

'We'll have a bottle of the Camel Valley Rosé Brut, please,' Sammi ordered.

'Of course, sir.'

When the waiter had gone, Delia raised an eyebrow. 'Business must be going well to afford wine as good as that.'

Sammi lowered his voice. 'I've been shortlisted to do a range of wallpapers, paints, and accessories for a very famous interiors company.'

'No!' Delia's face lit up with happiness. 'When? What? How?'

'I should find out in January if it's going ahead. Things inspired by the colours and designs of Pakistan. I'd design and then work closely with their manufacturers to get it absolutely right.'

'That skinny boy from the newsagent's done good!'

'That moody girl from the hairdresser's didn't do too bad either.'

The waiter arrived with the sparkling rosé and poured them a glass each.

'To us,' Sammi said.

'To you.' Delia smiled. 'I'm so proud of you, Sammi. You'll be so busy, I may never see you again.'

'Ah.' Sammi dropped his gaze to the tablecloth. 'That's something I want to talk to you about. You see, while my clients are flying off to the southern hemisphere or to the Alps, I find myself with very little in my diary.'

'Good. You can use that time to work on your pitch for the new product range.'

'Yes, exactly, but I need to be somewhere quieter than London. Where the air is fresh and full of inspiration.'

'Good thinking. But where?'

'Where do you think?' he replied, smiling.

'I don't know. How about France, or maybe Italy?'

Sammi sighed. 'No, you idiot. Here. In Cornwall. To be more precise, at Wilder Hoo. With you.'

CHAPTER THIRTY-SIX

Wilder Hoo, November

Two days after the BBC *Spotlight* Wilder Hoo library appeal, postman Mike stood sweating at the front door, two knee-high stacks of parcels at his feet.

'I saw the programme. I was thinking there might be a few more bits and pieces than usual for me to deliver here, but this isn't all of them – I've got more in the van.'

Within a week, fifty per cent of the library's floor space was covered with boxes that reached almost to the ceiling.

Every day, they came in ever greater numbers, until, after almost three weeks, just when they were running out of room, the flow thankfully slowed.

Auntie Rose phoned Syd at the BBC with an update. 'We've had a marvellous response, but I think we need to close the appeal for a while.'

Syd came back with her crew to film the giant columns of boxes with a heartfelt thank you from Delia and Auntie Rose, and a plea for 'No more!', which naturally provoked another influx.

'It's like when my wife put bubble bath in the Jacuzzi,' postman Mike told them. 'They wouldn't bleddy stop.'

Sammi had been staying at The Vare Castle all this time, as there was nowhere suitable for him to comfortably sleep yet.

She didn't mind sleeping alone at Wilder Hoo. She enjoyed her own company. The chance to slope off, cupping a hot drink, and think about how far she had come in the last few months. Occasionally she would also sit quietly and reread the letter from Mrs Jackson. Her father's widow. Processing the shock and all the information it contained was going to take a long time. Her immediate reaction had been to grab the money and put it to work. Perhaps that had made her look hardhearted and then she remembered her mum, left to bring her up singlehandedly, and didn't feel so bad. This particular morning she was escaping the noise and dust of Kev and Ken's drills as they installed the new kitchen.

'Ah, there you are.' Sammi appeared beside her, making her jump.' Her peace broken.

He rubbed his hands together. 'Nippy this morning. What are you doing out here?'

'Nothing. What are you doing here? Has the Vare lost its lustre?'

'The Vare is very lovely but I get a bit lonely and I don't have enough space for all the designs I'm working on.'

She knew what he was angling for. 'I know we talked about turning one of the barns into a studio for you, but I can't take Kevin and Kenny off the jobs that need to be done before that.'

Sammi sighed. 'I know. If I was any kind of handyman I'd do it myself but that's not my forte.'

A solution flashed into Delia's brain. 'Of course. Why hadn't I thought of this before?'

'What?'

'All those books that were donated to our library are still sitting in their boxes. Auntie Rose was supposed to be in charge of that, but she and Hugh are making the most of their romance together. Currently they are up in the Highlands staying in a Scottish castle. So, what I'm really looking for is a man with exquisite style who would transform the magnificent Wilder Hoo Library into the sumptuous space it deserves. Now if only I could think of someone.' She turned her wide innocent eyes to Sammi.

'Well, I suppose I could always give it a go.'

Delia threw her arms around his neck. 'Would you Sammi?'

'For you my love, anything.'

Neither of them saw Ray, standing on the lawn below, holding a bucket of autumn-bronze chrysanthemums, the last from his polytunnel. He felt awkward, like a Peeping Tom, but he couldn't stop himself from watching, motionless, as Delia melted into the arms of a brown-skinned, handsome stranger.

Ray's mind was thrown into uncomfortable confusion. Who the hell was this guy? He and Delia had been friends for months, and she'd never mentioned a boyfriend. He'd thought—

He told himself that it didn't matter what he'd thought. Delia was just a client. Who he liked. He was allowed to like someone without it being made into a big thing.

If this was a new boyfriend then, sure, he wished her well.

He certainly didn't want her to see him carrying a bucket of chrysanths and looking like a fool. Swiftly, he made his way round to the back kitchen door and left the bucket outside on the step, hoping that Kevin and Kenny, working away in there, wouldn't spot him.

'All right, Ray?' Kenny knocked at him through the glass. 'What are you doing out there?'

'All good. Just dropping off a bucket of chrysanths. Didn't want them to go to waste.'

'I'll let the boss know,' Ken replied with a thumbs up. 'She'll like that.'

'Ha!' Ray forced a smile and made his way to his battered Transit van as swiftly as possible.

That night he had an email from Delia.

Hi. Thank you for the beautiful flowers. I love the colours. Why didn't you come and say hello? I could have introduced you to my friend Sammi. He's staying for a while, though, so plenty of time for you to meet. How are things? Girls all OK?

Speak soon. Delia.

He waited until the next day to reply.

Hi, glad you liked the flowers. Girls all good. Busy couple of weeks ahead as long as the weather holds.

R

As November came to a close, Wilder Hoo was taking shape at last. The new kitchen was a dream; the boys had done a wonderful job. Cupboards, drawers, cabinets, and a very large kitchen table they had salvaged from a farm sale, brought the room back to being the heart of the house.

The flagstones were now polished and shining. An enormous, second-hand, shiny black Aga, now hunkered in the nook of the original range, filling the rooms below stairs with warmth and the aromas of Mrs Joy's cooking.

Gary Jackson's 'guilt' cheque had paid for everything Delia had imagined for it.

She still couldn't think of him as her father. He was a man she'd never known, who had never been a parent to her – except perhaps in this final gift. She was grateful, of course, but whenever she thought of how he'd treated her mum, her heart hardened.

Delia and Mrs Joy became decorators now, painting the warren of passages and rooms that had been the throbbing heart of the house back in the day: the laundry, the butler's room, the still room, and the housekeeper's room.

'Imagine all the staff buzzing about down here,' Delia said. 'Like *Downton Abbey*.'

'Not quite like *Downton*,' Mrs Joy replied. 'At lot less of us then.'

'Less servants?'

'Yes.'

'I hope you were never made to feel like a servant?'

Mrs Joy laughed. 'There were points in time when I might've, yes.'

Delia couldn't comprehend how things must have been. 'All these rooms. What do you think we should do with them?'

'The butler's room would make a wonderful office for you. And the others . . . Well, they'll let you know in time.'

'Sammi is always chatting with the house. I'll get him to ask.'

Mrs Joy smiled. 'I know just what he means.'

One of the upstairs bathrooms had now been restored and repainted – Harriet's choice of paint from when she'd spent Christmas with Johnny and his parents had been satisfyingly killed off.

Tired of his Vare hotel isolation, Sammi moved into the butler's bedroom – it was a little sparse, but he created a homely space with a comfy mattress piled high with exotically mirrored, embroidered cushions.

The boiler was serviced, new radiators were working, and Wilder Hoo felt almost impossibly warm.

Delia kept a close eye on the thermostat, preferring it not to go over 19°C, horribly conscious of the fuel bill and her shrinking finances. Consequently, they spent most of their time in the kitchen, at the newly sanded second-hand table.

'Fancy a glass of wine, Cordelia?' Rose was reaching for glasses in one of the new kitchen cabinets.

Delia looked up from her laptop. 'Yes, please. And there are some M&S crisps in the pantry.'

'How very civilized. Haven't you done enough work for today?'

'I'm checking off all the jobs we've done and making a list of what still needs sorting.'

Rose poured the wine and sat down opposite her. 'Read the "jobs done" list first. We can be rather smug about what we have achieved.'

'OK . . . The library – Sammi has done a great job. Enid Blyton, Jilly Cooper, Dostoyevsky, Rushdie, and Shakespeare nestled together in fiction. Then, in the hobbies and pastimes section, we have many *Haynes* car manuals – handy if you have a Hillman Imp, Triumph Vitesse, or Rover P4 100 – *Crochet for Beginners*, *How to Care for Your Tortoise*, and *So You Want to Be an Astronaut*. The cookery section is vast, as is the gardening one and, on the top shelves, out of reach, we have many, many editions of the *Kama Sutra*, *The Joy of Sex*, *Tantric Sex*, and *The Encyclopaedia of Unusual Sexual Practices*.'

Rose laughed. 'Marvellous. Can I borrow one for Hugh?'

'Eugh! Stop it.' Delia took a sip of her wine. 'Although, that's a point – I have been thinking that we should open the library up to anyone and everyone now. It needs to be useful as well as admired. We could ask visitors to bring a book they don't want and swap it for one they do. Free of charge, but with a little collecting tin for charity.'

'Lovely idea . . . OK, What other jobs have been done?'

'The great hall is gleaming. I don't know what polish Mrs Joy used on the stairs, but the smell is amazing. Everything down here in the kitchen is done, and Sammi's very happy in the butler's bedroom for now. Next, all we have to do is fix the rotten floorboards in the drawing room, decorate the old dining room, and the saloon. That'll get us to the twenty-seventh of April and our grand opening day. Upstairs can wait. It's clean and dry and that's the best we can do for the time being.'

Rose raised her glass. 'Well, here's to the twenty-seventh of April!'

Both women sipped their drinks.

'I almost forgot,' Rose said, 'Martin is back.'

Delia looked up sharply. 'Hugh's friend?'

Rose nodded. 'Hugh saw him last night. He asked after you.'

'Did he?' Delia had been rather disappointed not to see him again after the time he'd come to supper with Hugh. 'I thought he was still in Australia.'

'He was but now he's back. I think he'd like to get to know you better.'

'Because he wants Wilder Hoo to host a charity camp out?'

'Now who's being cynical? I seem to recall that you were rather taken by him.'

'I might have been if he'd stuck around long enough to find out.'

'Well, he's back and asking after you so where's the harm? Just a dinner? It might be nice. Something to dress up for. To enjoy.'

Delia took another sip of her wine. Recently, she had been thinking about how much she enjoyed Ray's company as they shared the gardening. He had woken her up to the possibility that not all men were like Johnny. Ray never boasted about anything or challenged her ideas. He was just nice, gentle Ray. 'I'll think about it.'

CHAPTER THIRTY-SEVEN

Wilder Hoo, December

December in Cornwall was slow and quiet. The cliffs and wild beaches were free from the crowds and reclaimed as the personal domain of locals and their dogs.

At Wilder Hoo, Delia found herself with not much to do. With the weather cold and brisk, and the days growing ever shorter, the garden had been put to bed weeks ago. Meanwhile, Delia's funds were running low, so any work still not done in the house would have to wait.

She was weary, mentally and physically, and she was glad that the house was quiet for the first time in months.

Rose had gone home to Kernow Autumn, desperate to put up her Christmas decorations and invite friends and neighbours to her pre-season cocktail party, and Hugh had plans to take her to Truro to see the lights and enjoy the Christmas Market.

Kevin and Kenny had taken off to the Big Apple to watch their ice hockey team, the New York Rangers, play at Madison Square Gardens.

And Sammi? Well, he was back in London, visiting the trade shows to test interest for his new collection of wallpaper, fabrics, and paints.

Mrs Joy was now the only person who popped in and out, usually with a quiche or chicken casserole, so to all intents and purposes, Delia was alone.

She persuaded herself that she needed the solitary space and empty peace of Wilder Hoo. To sleep there on her own. To roam its empty rooms, imagining how they would look furnished and decorated.

Then later, with too many glasses of wine in her, cursing Harvey, Vivienne, and Johnny for not having done even the smallest repairs to the house. All their ridiculously grandiose plans, and the sweet FA they had actually achieved. For all the money she'd spent, she could see so many more things crying out to be mended.

On those nights, she'd fall into bed pissed and furious – then wake the next morning to dehydration, a banging head, and loneliness.

'Come on, Cordelia Jago,' she told her reflection in her small make-up mirror one morning. 'What is it that you want that you haven't already got? Hmm?' She touched her fingers to her face and then to the wrinkles between her eyebrows. 'Shall I get some Botox? What would be the point? Let me think . . . no, no point at all. I could just go back to bed? That would be nice, and no one to judge me. I could hibernate – wake up in the spring. Watch the bulbs that Ray and I planted come up. Haven't heard from him for ages. Hope he's OK.'

She felt the warmth of a shaft of sunlight falling through the saloon window, lighting up her unmade bed. She looked around the room, her home for the last however many months.

Hadn't there been a plan once to move upstairs, into her own little home within a home?

She sighed. 'So much to do and no inclination or money to do it. Perhaps a walk would do me good. Just down to the beach and back, then I shall return to bed . . . with Netflix.'

She decided to stay in her pyjamas but cover them with her warm, windproof coat. No one would see her after all.

Outside lay a cold but beautiful day. The sky a deep gentian blue with woolly white clouds speeding across it.

'Well, this is nice,' she told herself. 'You should do this more often, Cordelia.'

Out onto the terrace, down the steps, and a short pause to check the knot garden, which looked exactly as she and Ray had left it a few weeks ago, plain soil hiding the plants and bulbs sleeping below. Next, across the lawn, which was boggy but green, and into the shelter of the woods, where the top canopy began to rustle loudly as a blustery wind picked up.

'Hello trees. Anyone want a hug?' She leant against the nearest beech tree, put her ear to its bark and closed her eyes. 'Give me all the gossip. I'm ready for it.'

Ray had once told her that if you really concentrated, you could hear the living sap rising in the trunk. She tried it for a couple of minutes, then gave up and patted the tree. 'Next time maybe.'

Walking out of the woods and onto the cliffs, she could hear the sea over the tall dunes. The onshore breeze pushed her back, so strong that she could lean herself against it and trust it would hold her up. It was hard to breathe in a wind like this, but she gave all her senses up to it, seduced by its buffeting and the sight of the restless sea.

On the beach, she watched the waves as they pulled themselves to the point where they became opaque, then curled and fell foaming onto the strandline.

'Hey!'

Was that a voice behind her? She turned to see who it was, but the wind whipped her hair into her eyes, obstructing her vision.

'Hey Delia!'

When she pushed the hair from her eyes, she saw Ray standing above her on the dunes. Her breath caught, and she found herself smiling.

'Hi.' The wind snatched the word from her lips.

Ray cupped his hands around his mouth. 'I'll come down.'

'Don't you love this wild weather?' Delia said when he reached her. 'It takes me back to when I was growing up at Jago Fields. Mum and I would go up to Chapel Carn Brea just to watch the swell. Mum always packed a pasty just in case.'

'You can't beat a pasty,' Ray said.

They stood watching the sea for a while, before Delia asked, 'What brings you down here?'

'I was passing and thought I'd see how the garden, and you, are.'

'We're both hibernating. How did you know I was down here?'

'Mrs Joy. She was delivering a basket of hot food that smelt amazing.'

'Is it Thursday?'

Ray smiled. 'All day.'

'On Thursdays, she always brings me something for the weekend. She worries.'

'That's nice. To have someone worry about you.'

'Yes.' Delia shivered. 'It's freezing out here. Have you had any lunch?'

'Not yet.'

'Come up and share whatever Mrs Joy delivered. I'm not taking no for an answer.'

The kitchen was warm and welcoming when they got back. Delia took her coat and boots off, forgetting she only had her pyjamas beneath. She remembered as soon as Ray looked at her.

'No wonder you were feeling the cold, maid.'

She flushed bright red. 'I wasn't expecting to see anyone, and . . .'

Ray began to laugh. 'Delia, you've cheered me right up. Off you go and get some warmer clothes on. I'll put the kettle on.'

When she returned, there was a pot of tea on the new table, which Ray was running his hand over in appreciation. 'The boys have done a good job on this, haven't they?'

'They really have.' Delia was looking in the fridge. 'Lunch is either Mrs Joy's mulligatawny soup with homemade tiger bread or her sausage plait. Which do you fancy?'

'Mulligatawny please,' he answered. 'Beautiful kitchen. Must have cost you a fortune.'

'Not exactly. It was a sort of gift from someone I never knew.'

'How come?'

Over lunch Delia told him her story.

When she'd finished, he leant back in his chair and blew through his lips. 'How did you feel about your mum and aunt not telling you the truth all those years?'

'Full of anger. I was only seventeen and didn't have the emotional maturity or vocabulary to explain it to myself, let alone anyone else, so I took it out on Auntie Rose. I couldn't get over the lies she and my mum had told, the fake cards and letters, the important job he was doing for other people around the world . . . to be fair, I think it was my mum who insisted on all that. Auntie Rose wanted me to know the truth early on, but Mum overruled her.' Delia sighed, remembering the tumultuous emotions that had overwhelmed her all those years ago. 'Now that I'm older, I do sort of get it. Mum wanted to protect me from all the hurt she'd felt. But at the time . . .'

'You lost a mother and a father in one fell swoop?'

'Now you put it like that, yeah.'

'How did you feel when you got the letter with the cheque?' Ray asked. 'Could you . . . forgive him? I mean, he hadn't forgotten you after all?'

'I felt . . . nothing. If he had really wanted to know me, nothing was stopping him. He could have talked to Mum and Auntie Rose. We could have had a really good relationship, if he'd made the effort. But he didn't. He didn't want my existence to poison his wife or his sons against him. He wanted to be Daddy Perfect – but not to me.' Delia sighed. 'He was a coward. What a terrible truth to reveal to your family after you're dead and buried.'

Ray nodded slowly, then glanced around the kitchen. 'Still, if he bought you this . . .'

'Yes, I am grateful for his money,' Delia said quietly. 'Every day I look around this kitchen and tell my mum it's for her. It's everything that she would have loved and deserved.'

Ray paused, his brow furrowed in thought. 'What about your two half-brothers? Have you thought about reaching out to them?'

'Their mother made it very clear in her letter that none of them wanted that.'

'I'm so sorry all that happened, Delia.'

'Yeah. Well. That's life.' She wiped her nose on her kitchen towel napkin, then stood up to fill the dishwasher.

Ray got up too. 'Well, thank you for a lovely lunch, Delia. Call me if you ever need anything.'

*

Christmas was drawing near, and while Delia managed to keep up the appearance of being as excited as everyone else, inside, she was dreading it. She didn't want to be at Wilder Hoo with all its painful yuletide memories. But what was the alternative?

Her phone rang. It was Auntie Rose.

'Hello, Cordelia. Tell me, do you have a Christmas wreath for Wilder Hoo's door? Because Martin, Hugh, and I have had a fabulous lunch, and now we're at Truro's Christmas Market, and there's a lady here with a wonderful stall chock full of wreaths. What do you like? Trad or contemporary . . .'

'No thanks.'

'Don't be silly – you must have one. What's the matter with you?'

'Can I spend Christmas with you at Kernow Autumn?'

'Of course you can?' Auntie Rose's voice grew softer. 'Are you OK?'

'Not . . . Not really . . .'

'Right. I've been away too long. You've got yourself spooked being all alone there. We're coming over right now. Don't move.'

On arrival, Rose took one look at Delia's unhappy face and immediately took charge. 'Hugh, go and make some tea. Martin, the log store is outside by the back door. There's a basket waiting to be filled. Delia and I will be in the saloon. Come along, Delia.'

Ensconced on the sofa, Rose began to gently question her. 'What's happened?'

'Nothing, really. I just . . . don't want to spend Christmas here.'

'Why exactly?'

Delia looked at the ceiling, willing tears not to fall. 'I do love Wilder Hoo, now anyway, but I can't get out of my head all the horrible memories . . . I want to have a Christmas like we used to have at Jago Fields.' Her voice caught as her throat tightened.

Rose nodded. 'I understand. If you want Christmas at Kernow Autumn, then that's what we should have, but . . . what will you do next year? And the year after? The memories will always be here until you make some fresh ones.'

Delia sniffed. 'I'm not ready to do that just now.'

'Oh yes you are. You are a Jago, and Jago women are warriors. We have had to be. So, this Christmas, you and I are going to exorcise the past and welcome in the here and now.'

Hugh nudged the door open with his foot, his hands full of the tea tray. 'Found some fruit cake. Mrs Joy, I suppose?'

Martin followed with the log basket. 'I'll get the fire going.'

Rose smiled at both of them. 'Delia and I have decided that we are having Christmas here this year. Nothing over the top – just the two of us. Nice and relaxed.'

'Just the two of us?' Delia shook her head. 'If we're to make memories, I think it should be more than the two of us. Hugh, you'll come, won't you?'

Hugh looked up from pouring the tea. 'I'd absolutely love to. Yes please. If you're sure?'

'Auntie Rose would be miserable without you.'

Rose raised an eyebrow but didn't protest.

Martin, putting a match to the newly laid kindling, said over his shoulder, 'It would be an honour to spend Christmas here.'

CHAPTER THIRTY-EIGHT

Against all the odds, when Rose took control, things always worked out well. She and Mrs Joy, while enjoying each other's company, had also discovered the pleasure of the unspoken game of one upmanship. Rose accepted Mrs Joy's unrivalled knowledge of the Wilder Hoo Way of Doing Things, but she also enjoyed challenging them.

'This year, there will be no tree in the great hall.'

Mrs Joy gave a small cough. 'But—'

'No buts, Mrs Joy. Remember, we are doing this for Delia. Fresh and different. Nothing to remind her of the past.'

'I suppose you're right.'

'I am, and instead of the tree, we shall decorate the great hall's chimney breast. Give it the drama it deserves. Swags of fir and pine, holly berries and mistletoe. Twinkling lights and glistening baubles. Father Christmas will have a beautifully decorated chimney to bring his parcels down. And in the grate, a fire roaring twenty-four seven. Remind me to get some more logs, would you?'

Mrs Joy, pen and notebook in hand, gave a small, satisfied smile. 'I called them yesterday. Being delivered tomorrow.'

Rose nodded in admiration. 'Well done, number one. The great hall needs to be the welcoming heart of Christmas. Scented oranges, cloves, patchouli, carols playing . . .'

Mrs Joy looked up from her notepad. 'How do you spell patchouli?'

'Goodness only knows.' Rose was too busy visualizing her design concepts. 'The great hall will be great again – impressive in its grandeur and second only to the library, which hasn't had its proper opening yet. The library will be the *pièce de résistance*, the focus of all fun. Somewhere to gather and play cards, sing carols, read or do a jigsaw . . . maybe even dance! And that is where we shall put the tree.'

'In the library?' Mrs Joy was staring at her, open-mouthed. 'There has never been a tree in the library.'

'Well, there will be now,' Auntie Rose said very clearly, ignoring Mrs Joy's sigh of exasperation. 'And we'll decorate the fireplace in there, too, only bigger and better than the hall.'

Mrs Joy wrote all this down, her brow furrowed in thought. 'I see. So, the library is to become the sitting room?'

'Yes.'

'But where will we sit? We don't have enough chairs?'

Rose caught a flash of gleeful triumph in Mrs Joy's eyes and delighted in picking up the challenge. 'Well, we can, err . . . bring the sofa from the saloon, and then . . .'

Mrs Joy played her trump card. 'Mr Sammi is coming, isn't he? Supposing I phone him and see if he has any spare furniture in London that might be suitable? He always seems to have something. And his van is nice and big.'

Rose acceded graciously. 'Well done, Mrs Joy. And ask if he has any decent rugs while you're at it.'

Mrs Joy wrote that down, then asked, 'Would you like to sign off on the food shop next?'

'Don't worry about that. I like to go to my butcher in Bozinjal and choose for myself what's best. He and the local farm shop have everything we need. Family tradition.'

'Perhaps I could make some mince pies?' Mrs Joy offered. 'And maybe I can help you prep on Christmas Eve?'

Rose thought for a moment, then answered. 'That is an excellent idea. In fact, if you have no better plans, Delia and I would be delighted if you joined us for Christmas and Boxing Day too.'

Rose saw sudden watery tears forming in Mrs Joy's eyes.

'That is so kind of you. I would love to come. And I can't wait to give that new kitchen a real go. It deserves to be used to capacity.'

'That's that sorted then. And remember, don't tell Delia any of this. Sammi's visit will be a surprise, and the only decoration she thinks she's doing is a small tree in the kitchen. She knows nothing about the plans we have up our sleeve.'

Mrs Joy tapped the side of her nose and whispered, 'Mum's the word.'

Delia was meeting up with Ray for a walk. They'd met in the carpark at Carnewas and were now bent against the stiff breeze roaring over the cliffs.

After their last meeting, she had emailed him and apologized for spilling her life story to him over the mulligatawny soup:

What must you think of me?

His reply came immediately:

Hi. We all need to let off steam from time to time. I'm coming over your way in a couple of days. Fancy a walk and a coffee?

Now, here they were, shoulder to shoulder and stomping along the coast path.

'All ready for Christmas, are you?' he shouted over the wind.

She shook her head. 'I'm not, but Auntie Rose is. To be honest, it's not my favourite time of year. Not like when I was small. My mum made everything magical.'

'Mums do that, don't they?'

'They do! How about you? Where are you spending Christmas?'

'At home.'

They reached a stile. Delia climbed over first then waited for Ray to join her before asking, 'With the girls?'

Ray stared straight ahead. 'No. They'll be with their mum.'

'Ah.'

'Mm.'

'You won't be on your own though?'

'The wind must have caught her words because he didn't answer.

Delia fought to stop herself asking any more, but her brain was too quick for her. 'You're always welcome to come to Christmas with us.' Immediately she knew she shouldn't have asked.

Ray kept his eyes on the path.

'That's a very kind offer, but . . .'

He kept walking, turning his head to look at the sea, then back down to his boots.

A slippery incline gave both of them a chance to concentrate and not have to speak for a few seconds.

'Sorry. That sounded rude,' Ray mumbled.

'Not at all. I didn't mean to put you on the spot.'

'You didn't. It's just that . . . I haven't decided yet.'

'No. Of course.'

The path grew narrow, and Ray took the lead. Behind him, Delia's mind was in overdrive. Why didn't he know what he was doing at Christmas? It was only next week. Was there a girlfriend he hadn't mentioned? And if he hadn't mentioned her, then why not? Or did he just not want to spend Christmas with Delia? She stared at the back of his neck with his slightly curly overlong hair being buffeted by the wind.

The sun came out and was suddenly so bright it made her squint, but building on the horizon was a black cloud. Within minutes, a sharp wind picked up again, and a piece of grit flew into Delia's eye.

'Ow.' Delia stopped and turned her back to the wind.

'You OK?'

'Sand in my eye.'

'Let me see.'

'Don't worry. I'll get it.'

Ray ignored her and removed his gloves. With one hand holding her chin and the other lifting her eyelid, he examined her. 'I see it. Do you have a tissue?'

She found one in her pocket.

He took it and in moments had gently removed the piece of grit. 'Is that better?'

'Much. Thank you.' She blinked and rolled her eyes a couple of times to make sure they were pain free.

When she looked back at Ray, she saw that his eyes had not left her face. His expression was unreadable.

'What?' she said.

'Just making sure you're OK.'

'Thank you, I'm fine.'

He broke eye contact, checking his watch. 'Ready to head back? It'll be dark in half an hour. We might just catch the coffee shop before it closes.'

The cafe's windows were streaming with condensation when they arrived, and Ray insisted that Delia sat at a table while he ordered from the tired woman behind the counter

'I'm just closing,' she told him pointedly. 'Only takeaway.'

Delia watched as Ray gave the woman a warm smile. 'Two cappuccinos to take away then, please.'

Back outside in the gloomy carpark, with rain threatening, Delia thanked him for her coffee and said goodbye. 'I'll drink it on the drive home.'

Ray turned the collar of his Barbour jacket up. 'I'll do the same. It's not a night to be looking at the stars, is it?'

Delia looked up and shivered. 'No, it isn't.'

'Well then, if I don't see you before, Merry Christmas, Delia.'

It seemed he had decided, then, not to spend Christmas at Wilder Hoo.

Delia pushed away the faint sting of disappointment. 'Merry Christmas, Ray.'

She expected to exchange an innocent, festive peck on the cheek, but he was already turning towards his van.

'Thank you for everything you've done at Wilder Hoo this year,' she said. 'I don't know what I would have done without you.'

'I should be thanking you for the work.' Unlocking the van door, he climbed into the driver's seat. 'Drive carefully, won't you? There'll be a frost tonight.'

'And you.' Delia got into her car and shut the door, before opening the window enough to answer anything else he might say, just in case – but with a brief wave of his hand, he put the old van in gear and was off.

Delia set off home very confused.

Was she so starved of men's company and affection that she imagined he would suddenly ask her out on a date, that he'd want to spend Christmas with her when he'd never shown the slightest romantic interest in her?

Or she in him.

And why her unhealthy fascination about his private life? Which was none of her business.

I should be thanking you for the work, he'd said. That was what she was to him – a gardening client.

She didn't fancy him. Didn't want him as a boyfriend.

She liked him as a gardener, and yes, as a friend.

And she was grateful to him, for not being the sort of man who would ever make an inappropriate move.

They were equals.

She laughed at her idiocy.

He clearly didn't fancy her.

And that meant there could be no misunderstanding.

Just friends.

Phew.

And yet, being with him reminded her of how nice it was to share affection with another human.

Just not with Ray.

In fact, definitely not with Ray.

The narrowness of the dark lanes, the inefficiency of the wipers on the icy drizzle, sharpened her concentration and pushed Ray to the outer reaches of her mind.

When she finally pulled up outside Wilder Hoo, she was glad to find Rose and Mrs Joy in the warmth of the kitchen, sipping sherry.

'It's not even Christmas and you two are already three sheets to the wind,' she teased, shaking the rain from her coat.

'You're just in time,' Auntie Rose said. 'Pass me a glass and join us.'

Rose pulled the cork from the Harvey's Bristol Cream bottle and poured Delia a healthy slug. 'Cheers.'

'Cheers to Christmas,' Delia said. 'So, what have you two been up to?'

'Just chatting,' Rose said.

'Yes. Just chatting,' Mrs Joy added, while shutting her notebook and pen and placing them firmly inside her handbag.

Delia narrowed her eyes. 'What's going on?'

Rose sighed theatrically. 'Oh, you always spoil a surprise.'

'What surprise?'

'If you must know, I'm having a little pre-Christmas cocktail party tomorrow night at Kernow Autumn, and I want you to come with me. A chance to forget all your responsibilities and have some fun.'

Delia tipped her chair back to reach for a large bag of crisps that was sitting on the countertop behind her. 'It's a long drive there and back for just a drink.'

'You're right, it would be, which is why we're going to stay in my little apartment for two nights for a couple of reasons. One, you need a change of scenery, and two, you can help me with the Christmas food shop.'

Delia shook the crisps out into a bowl and pushed them to the middle of the table. 'The old butcher and the farm shop, like you and Mum always went to?'

'It's tradition.'

'It is, but do we need to be away for two nights?'

'Emphatically, yes! I've been neglecting Hugh.' She pulled a sad face. 'Darling, please say yes.'

CHAPTER THIRTY-NINE

They set off for Bozinjal after breakfast the next morning, Rose behind the wheel and Delia next to her, balancing a tin of Mrs Joy's mince pies on her lap.

'I'm actually looking forward to meeting your fellow Kernow Autumn inmates,' Delia said.

'They're very sweet and will be desperate to interrogate you, especially when they've had a drink or six. And please don't be outraged if one of the boys pinches your bottom. They're old and from another time.'

'I'm not tolerating that old excuse!' Delia folded her arms. 'If any old goat touches me inappropriately, I'll give them a slap.'

'For heaven's sake, don't do that – they'll think you're flirting with them. A slap on the cheek is tantamount to foreplay.'

Delia laughed. 'Oh, Auntie Rose, you have changed. What happened to my cosy aunt who cooked and cleaned and ran Jago Fields single-handedly?'

'I was never *cosy*. But I found my liberty, time to be me and explore what I was missing.'

Delia frowned a little. 'Did looking after me hold you back?'

'Truthfully? No. It was Christine dying that knocked the stuffing out of me. You were always our joint focus. We wanted you to have the freedom of choice that we hadn't had. We often talked about what your future might look like and forgot to look at our own. And when she died . . . well, the only thing I knew was to simply keep going.'

Delia took this in solemnly. 'I'm so sorry.'

'What for?'

'All the Christmases and birthdays and visits I should have turned up for, but . . .'

'But you were doing exactly what your Mum and I wanted for you.'

Delia spent a few minutes blindly staring out of the window, recalling how life had been in London: the salon, the long hours, the success, meeting Johnny . . . it should have been so much fun, but there was precious little fun that she could remember.

She pulled her focus back to the here and now.

'What was your turning point, Auntie Rose? The moment that changed things for you?'

'I met a man.'

'I'm guessing not Hugh?'

'No, Hugh came much later.'

'So, who was he?'

Rose sighed. 'Oh, he was wonderful. Funny. Kind. Gentle. Loving. Thoughtful. He made me feel like I was the only woman in the world. Unfortunately, I met him when he was at the start of his cancer diagnosis.'

'Oh, Auntie Rose.'

'Mmm.' Rose took a deep breath. 'It's an old cliché I know, but his zest for life spilt out of him and affected everyone around him. You couldn't be sad when you were with him. Even when he was in the hospice. Even when I went to visit him and found his wife – the wife he hadn't bothered to tell me about – sitting by his bed as he told her how much he loved her.'

'*What?*' cried Delia, appalled. 'What did you do?'

'I said I must have got the wrong room and bid them both goodbye.'

'What an arse!'

Rose chuckled. 'Yes. But a very charming one. I couldn't be cross for my sake, but I was cross for hers. He died not long after. He was only fifty-five. After that I made a pact with myself to live life to the full. Try everything. Deny myself nothing. Have some bloody good fun. I have him to thank for that. He was the catalyst that helped me decide to leave Jago Fields. And look what I have now: a maintenance-free home, no cows to feed, no eggs to collect, and luckiest of all, Hugh.'

'To Hugh!' Delia cheered.

Rose smiled. 'Indeed. To Hugh!'

While Rose and Delia were heading to Bozinjal, Mrs Joy was welcoming Kevin and Kenny at Wilder Hoo. 'Come on in. The coast is clear. I'll get the kettle on, and I want to hear all about New York and your hockey team.'

Two hours after that, she ushered in Sammi, who had arrived with his new long wheelbase van sagging with the weight of its contents.

Mrs Joy hugged him. 'You made it! And at such short notice.'

'Anything for you, Mrs Joy. You know that. How much time have we got?'

'They're planning to get back the day after tomorrow, but Rose reckons she'll be able to keep them down there a bit longer if we need her to.'

'Excellent! Right, you get the kettle on, and I'll go upstairs and see if I can give Kenny and Kev any help.'

At Kernow Autumn, Rose's small sitting room was pulsing with laughter and the chink of cocktail glasses. The heat from so many bodies necessitated the opening of the doors onto her small patio garden, and many were out there now, admiring the strings of twinkling lights hung around her summer gazebo and the stunning Christmas tree that dwarfed almost everyone.

'You like it?' Hugh growled flirtatiously.

'You know I love everything you do, Hugh darling.'

'Stop it, the pair of you,' Delia said. 'Or I'll have to get one of those swimming pool notices: *no dive bombing and no heavy petting*.'

Martin arrived with two glasses of mulled wine and handed one to Delia. 'Here, get one of these inside you. It'll warm you up.'

'As the actress said to the bishop,' giggled Auntie Rose.

Delia sighed. 'If you don't stop right now, I'm going to ground you for the rest of the holidays.'

Martin smiled. 'They're always like this.'

'Sorry, sorry.' Rose wiped her eyes. 'We don't mean to embarrass you, do we, Hugh?'

'Goodness, no. Very bad form. Please accept our apologies.' He cleared his throat. 'Martin, has Delia seen your eight-footer yet?'

Cue more screeching laughter, Rose and Hugh clutching each other for support.

Martin, straight-faced, looked at Delia and explained, 'He means the tree.'

'Is that what you call it?' cackled Rose.

Delia flashed her a warning look. 'No more mulled wine for you two.' She returned her attention to Martin. 'It's beautifully decorated.'

'All my own work. Come and take a closer look.'

If the tree had looked magical from a distance, close up it became a work of art.

Tiny silver unicorns and angels hung on every branch, twisting and turning in the air, reflecting the light of the thousands of bulbs. Amongst them a string of sleighs carrying Father Christmas, drawn by his reindeer, chasing each other over and around the branches. Satsumas, studded with cloves and hanging from ribbons of Cornish tartan, scented the night air.

And at the top of the tree was an angel with an expression of such sweetness that Delia almost wept.

'This is beautiful, Martin. I could never do anything as stylish. Must have taken you ages.'

'Not really. I love doing this kind of thing. Do you have your tree yet?'

She shook her head. 'Not yet.'

'Christmas isn't Christmas without a tree and carols.' He bent down to an extension cable and flicked a switch. 'Can you hear?'

Delia listened. 'What is that?'

'Prokofiev. "Troika". I always hide a speaker under the tree. Music makes the mood.'

'I love it.'

'Good.' He grinned and took her empty glass. 'Want a top up?'

CHAPTER FORTY

'Good morning.' Delia eased open the door to Rose's bedroom, took a quick look around to check if Hugh might be in there too. 'What a party that was!'

Under the duvet, Rose's shape shifted. 'You enjoyed yourself?'

'I did. I've brought you a cuppa.'

'Oh, you angel.' Rose sat up and turned her bedside light on. 'Want to jump in next to me?'

'Where's Hugh?' Delia said, climbing in next to her aunt.

'We both like our own space. I have my boundaries, and he has his.'

Delia nodded as she sipped her tea. 'I can understand that.'

'What about you and Martin?' Rose enquired rather mischievously.

Delia rolled her eyes. 'What about me and Martin?'

'You seemed to be getting on awfully well.'

'Yeah. It was nice. He chatted about Australia and his friends over there. He's very excited to spend Christmas with us at Wilder Hoo.'

'And?'

'That was it.'

'Oh.' Rose was disappointed. ' I thought he was keener than that.'

'Oh he is . . . he's taking me out to lunch today.'

When Martin arrived to collect Delia, Rose gave him the once-over and nodded. 'You look very smart. Come on. Delia? Cary Grant has arrived.'

Delia hadn't packed anything suitable to wear for a lunch outing, so Rose had insisted on adding one of her bright pashminas to her all black ensemble of jeans and roll-neck jumper.

'Hi, Martin.'

'Hello, Delia. I love that scarf. Have you got a warm coat? I've got the top of the car down. The sun is out, and I thought you might like to feel the wind in your hair, even if it is almost Christmas.'

'Martin has a vintage sports car. Red,' Rose added helpfully.

'A 1982 Porsche 911 actually,' Martin said.

Delia knew little about cars but was impressed anyway. 'How lovely. I only have my old walking coat – not very posh but it does the job.'

'As long as you're warm.' Martin held his hand out to her in a courtly gesture. 'Ready?'

Whizzing through the lanes with Martin was, Delia had to admit, the most exciting thing she had done for . . . well, years. There was no forced conversation – difficult above the noise of the wind and engine in any case – so she relaxed into the pleasure of not having to worry about small talk.

Occasionally he would mouth, 'You OK? Warm enough?'

She'd grin and nod, then continue to absorb the beauty of the rugged countryside flashing past.

She didn't know where they were heading and didn't care. All she knew for certain was that she felt totally carefree.

Their route took them along the coast road with spectacular views of the rolling Atlantic and cliffs. After almost an hour, the little car slowed, wending its way down a valley into the picture-perfect cove of Portloe and its harbour.

Martin parked up and killed the engine. A blissful silence engulfed them.

'I haven't been here since I was a child,' Delia told him, looking around her. 'Mum and Auntie Rose used to bring me. We'd eat pasties on the slipway there and fish for crabs.'

'Happy memories.' Martin stretched his long legs as he got out of the car, then skirted the bonnet to open the door for Delia. 'I hope you're hungry. I've heard wonderful things about the food here.'

The Lugger Hotel lay right on the water's edge and had a sunny terrace overlooking the harbour.

They were welcomed at reception by a smiling woman, who offered to take their coats.

'Can we eat out on the terrace?' Delia asked.

The waitress laughed. 'Of course. Make the most of the winter sun. We offer blankets if you get too cold. Or you can always come inside.'

Delia and Martin settled themselves and smiled at each other across the table.

'Well, this is an adventure,' said Martin.

'Are we mad?'

'Very probably.

The menu was simple and good. Martin went for ribeye steak, while Delia plumped for roast cod and a bowl of chips to share.

'Last night was fun, wasn't it?' Martin said. 'I do love Hugh and Rose. They're so good together.'

'They certainly do seem happy,' Delia replied. 'Do you think they're in it for the long haul?'

'Would you mind if they were?'

'Hmm . . . As long as Rose is happy . . .'

'Hugh is a good man.'

'I hope so.'

Martin's eyes connected with hers. 'There are good men out there, you know,' he said, sounding serious. 'You were unlucky.'

'Oh God, I blabbed my story to you, didn't I? In the summer, at Wilder Hoo, the first time we met. I hoped you might have forgotten. How embarrassing.' Delia smiled apologetically. 'Anyway, I'm not looking for a man of any kind.'

'That's a shame.'

'Not at all. I'm perfectly happy.' She picked up a chip with her fingers and bit into it. 'So, now you owe me your story. Here you are, a well-spoken, well-educated, handsome, sports car driver . . . all of which point to past success and financial security. Why aren't you happily married with 2.5 kids, a house in the Cotswolds, a flat in town and three yellow labradors?'

Martin sat back and laughed. 'That was never on the cards for me. And anyway, what about you? You must have hundreds of men beating their way to your door.'

'Oh goodness no! That's not me at all. And anyway, I need to get Wilder Hoo up and running first.' She swiftly changed the subject. 'Tell me more about the children's charity you work with. In Truro, I think you said?'

As they ate, they traded stories of their past and shared a plate of Christmas pudding and custard. When the sun began to dip, Delia shivered.

Martin insisted on paying the bill and Delia let him, on the strict understanding that the next lunch would be on her.

Back in the Porsche, this time with the roof firmly on, Martin drove the shorter route back to Bozinjal.

The Christmas pudding had made Delia drowsy, and she closed her eyes and relaxed back into the bucket seat.

'Warm enough?' Martin asked.

She smiled. 'Perfect.'

She was almost asleep when Martin slowed the car. 'Look. Christmas trees for sale. You don't have one yet, do you?'

Delia roused herself. 'No, not yet. I was planning on a little one for the kitchen. Nothing too big. Can we fit a small one into this tiny car?'

'We can do anything we like!' he replied.

'I've sold the best of them,' the man told them once they'd parked and got out to look. 'Got no big ones left, but there's a couple of nice three-footers, pot grown, if you're interested.'

Martin took the choosing very seriously, and after a lot of close examination, picked one that was neither too fat nor too thin, with well-distributed branches. They managed to squish it onto the jump seat behind them, with its pointy end resting between the front seats.

'How much do I owe you?' Delia asked as she got in.

'Nothing. It's my Christmas present to you.'

'But—'

'No buts. It's also my thank you for inviting me to spend Christmas at Wilder Hoo.'

'My pleasure, Martin,' she said, and really meant it. 'My absolute pleasure.'

Rose was very impressed when Martin dropped Delia and her smart little tree off.

'He bought you a tree as a Christmas present? How romantic is that!'

'Not romantic,' Delia objected. 'Just . . . thoughtful.'

Rose raised her eyebrows. 'Thoughtful, romantic . . . two sides of the same coin?'

'It's just a tree, for goodness' sake!'

Rose pretended to zip her lips. 'I'm saying nothing.'

CHAPTER FORTY-ONE

The next day, Mrs Joy and Sammi were overly excited, awaiting the arrival of Rose and Delia. The great hall's fireplace was burning bright. A huge log was gently roasting and filling the air with the scent of woodsmoke.

'Oh, Sammi.' Mrs Joy was bouncing like a child. 'You did it. Wait until Delia sees all this!'

Sammi rubbed his stubbled chin and surveyed his work. The vast garlands of beech, holly, ivy, and conifer, glittering with red and green baubles, were draped now across the chimney breast and staircase.

'It took us a while, Mrs Joy, but we did it.'

'We did! With half an hour to spare.'

Meanwhile, with Delia on the road back to Wilder Hoo, Rose was chattering a river of nonsense to her.

'Hugh and I aren't giving extravagant gifts to each other. Instead, we've decided to have an "experience day", like an escape room or tea on the Orient Express – something to look forward to. I can't believe it's Christmas Eve tomorrow. Where does the time go? Mind you, I am looking forward to preparing the veg and stuff with Mrs Joy. I might even roast the potatoes tomorrow and then roast them again for Christmas Day. Twice roast potatoes are very trendy now. It's a recipe I saw in *Woman & Home* magazine. Hugh is bringing Martin up tomorrow night . . .'

Delia tuned back in. 'Oh yes, Martin told me. Hugh and he are staying at The Vare Castle, aren't they?'

'Yes. So sweet of them, because of course we don't have anywhere decent for them to sleep, do we? Shame really, but there we are. They'll have a lovely time at The Vare though. All that comfort and luxury. Not to mention warmth. Not that Wilder Hoo doesn't have warmth, not now the kitchen has the Aga and . . .'

On and on she prattled, until they turned off the main road and onto the long drive to Wilder Hoo.

'Oh look!' Delia pointed to clumps of fresh, white snowdrops growing through the grass. 'I'd forgotten they were there. They're early this year. Vivienne always wanted me to pick them for her dressing table, but I hated doing it. Same with the primroses. There'll be carpets of them in the woods soon.'

Rose smiled. 'I'll look forward to seeing them. New memories and a new year. The bad times are over, my darling.'

They rattled over the cattle grid and drew up at the wide steps.

Rose tooted the horn in a jolly little melody.

'What's that for?' Delia asked, getting out of the car.

'Just being silly,' Rose said.

Delia heard the creak of iron hinges on the front door as it opened. When she looked up, she gasped. 'Sammi!'

'Surprise!' He ran down the steps and threw his arms around her. 'Happy Christmas!'

'You're back! Are you staying? When did you get here? Did you know about this, Auntie Rose?'

'Yes, and it's been jolly difficult not to tell you.'

Mrs Joy appeared. 'Lovely to have you back, Delia.'

'Did you know he was coming, too, Mrs Joy?'

'Guilty as charged.'

Delia laughed brightly. 'I'm never going to trust any of you ever again.'

Mrs Joy started to shepherd everyone up the steps. 'Come on into the warm.'

Delia sniffed the air. 'I thought I could smell woodsmoke.' Crossing the threshold, her eyes took in the transformation. 'Oh my . . .' Her hands went to her face as she saw the crackling fire, smelt the pine and fruity citrus of the fresh branches and leaves, and was spellbound by the splendour of Sammi's decorations. 'What? Who? *How?*'

Slowly turning three-hundred-and-sixty degrees, she took in all that was new. An oak table, round and highly polished, stood on a jewel-coloured rug in the centre of the great hall, a jigsaw box ready to be opened upon it. Two high-backed chairs with tapestry seats sat either side of the fire, and a large rocking horse, outlined in fairy lights, was waiting for its rider in the corner by the front door.

Sammi came up behind her and slid his arm around her waist. 'Do you like it?'

'I love it,' she breathed, tears building in her eyes.

'Then you might like to see the library?'

The library fireplace was also alight and the chimney breast was decorated even more intricately, with extra sparkle and glitter. The long room was divided into three separate spaces: a gathering of comfortable chairs and side tables around the fire, two pairs of inviting sofas at either end of the room, sitting on a medley of gorgeous rugs; and, upstaging all that, an enormous Christmas tree standing to attention by the windows leading to the terrace.

Delia's mouth literally gaped. 'How have you done all this? Whose furniture is this?'

'Oh, you know . . .' Sammi said airily. 'I have a friend in the furniture rental trade . . .'

'Oh, so it's not staying?'

'Who can say?' Sammi looked at her with a twinkle. 'Ask no more.'

Rose cleared her throat. 'Sammi dear, is upstairs available?'

'What's happening upstairs?' Delia asked with suspicion.

Sammi grinned. 'Follow me, and I'll show you.'

He took Delia by the hand, led her to the top of the stairs, and stopped outside the old master bedroom.

'Ready?' he asked.

Delia took a steadying breath, then nodded.

'In you go.'

She slowly pushed the door open and stepped in.

The horrible old bed, rickety side tables, and Vivienne's dressing table were gone. Nothing remained of the old occupants.

Not the curtains.

Not the stained carpet.

Not the least vestige of Vivienne's trademark Issey Miyake perfume.

All gone.

Instead, everything was soft, clean, white, and simple. Even the floorboards.

The low winter sun shone through the spotless glass of the windows, lighting up a pristine king-size four-poster bed, immaculately made with crisp bed linen, standing in the centre of the space.

Delia could not speak.

Sammi said, 'Kevin and Kenny did it all. They've replaced the rotten floorboards on the balcony, too. See those two Lloyd Loom chairs and the table out there?'

'Yes?'

'They found them in one of the barns. Painted them up and now you can sit out there and watch every sunrise and sunset.'

'Oh gosh.' She was shaking. 'I don't know what to say?'
'It's your apartment,' Rose added. 'Remember we talked about it, but it never happened?'

'Yes but I never expected . . . it's wonderful.'

Sammi laughed. 'You like it?'

A sudden lump in Delia's throat blocked any words. She nodded.

Sammi stepped over to the door to the old bathroom. 'The boys have given the en suite the same treatment. Take a look.'

He opened the door, Delia stepped in, automatically clamping her mouth shut to avoid breathing in the old grim aroma.

'Oh!' She let the breath go. 'The smell has gone! How did they get all those old stains off?'

Sammi laughed. 'It took a while. But it's better, yes?'

'I never thought I'd like to use that bath or the loo, but now . . . it looks like something out of a magazine.'

'Good! Kevin and Kenny were pleased with it. And over there' – Sammi pointed at the door on the opposite side of the bedroom – 'the boys have revamped Harvey's grim and frankly creepy dressing room, giving you a walk-in wardrobe.'

Delia peeked inside. 'I'm going to have to buy some decent clothes to fill it.'

'If you wouldn't mind,' said Rose. 'And preferably not the usual black. I'll come with you.'

Mrs Joy appeared at the door with a bright smile. 'Welcome home, Delia.'

CHAPTER FORTY-TWO

Wilder Hoo, Christmas Eve

Mrs Joy and Rose had been sequestered in Wilder Hoo's kitchen since early light.

Sprouts, carrots, red cabbage, peas, and broccoli were prepped and resting in the pantry on the cooling shelf. Pigs in blankets were cooked and in the fridge, ready to reheat for tomorrow, as were the roast potatoes.

Mrs Joy was stirring a pan of cheese sauce. 'How's that cauliflower?' she asked.

Rose shook the colander where the cauliflower was draining. 'Ready to go.' She pointed to a blue and white china bowl. 'In here?'

'That's the one.'

Rose tipped the cooked cauliflower into the bowl, and Mrs Joy poured the cheese sauce over it.

'You make a mean cauliflower cheese, Mrs J.'

'I've been doing it a long time, Rose. How's your cottage pie for tonight?'

'Oven ready.' Rose picked up the checklist they'd been working from. 'Turkey stuffed?'

'Yes.'

'Brandy butter?'

'Done.'

'Trifle?'

'I'll do it tomorrow morning.'

'Fruit salad for pudding tonight?'

'Could you do that?'

'Certainly,' replied Rose. 'I'll do the cheese board at the same time.'

'Bless you.'

'I must say, we are a very good team.' Rose patted Mrs Joy's shoulder.

'Aren't we just?'

They both turned at the sound of a knock at the back door.

Ray stood on the back step, shifting nervously from one foot to the other. 'Hi,' he said, when Rose answered the door. 'I hope I'm not disturbing you?'

'Ray. This is a lovely surprise. Come on in. Mrs Joy has got a batch of mince pies about to come out of the oven. You can test them for us.'

'I've come at the right time then,' he said, smiling.

'You have. What brings you here?'

'I've managed to get hold of twenty bags of top-quality compost from a farmer friend of mine who mixes it with horse manure. He calls it Brown Gold. Couldn't get hold of any last year. It's always in demand. I thought Delia might like it as a Christmas present. Ready for the knot garden.'

Rose laughed. 'An unusual present, but I'm sure she'll appreciate it. I think she's still asleep.'

Ray's heart sank a little. 'Oh well, don't disturb her on my account.'

'I'll give her a shout. It's about time they both got up.'

'Both?' Ray wasn't quite sure if he'd said the word aloud.

Rose nodded. 'Yes. Sammi's here for Christmas.'

'Sammi?' Ray repeated. That was the guy he'd seen Delia with on the terrace a few weeks ago. Things must be serious between them if he was here for Christmas.

'Yes, they stayed up until the wee hours. They have a lot to catch up on.'

Ray's eyebrows did a weird little jump. 'Oh right. . .'

'They're so sweet together.'

'Good. I hadn't . . .' He looked at his watch. 'Oh goodness. Look at the time. I'm so sorry, but I must dash.'

'No, you don't.' Mrs Joy was carrying a plate of golden mince pies towards him. 'Sit yourself down and have one of these first.'

Ray had never been more eager to leave. 'No, I really must—'

'Sit down,' Mrs Joy ordered. 'Help yourself.'

He sat down, and Rose pulled up a chair next to him. 'So where will you be spending Christmas, Ray?'

'At home.'

'That's nice.' She smiled. 'Just you and your girls?'

'Erm . . . no, not this year. They're with their mum and her, erm, partner. I've just dropped them off actually.'

The look of unbearable sympathy Mrs Joy and Rose exchanged forced him to smile. He made his voice bright and cheerful. 'It's great actually. They're happy, and I'm happy that they're happy so . . . it's all good.'

Mrs Joy was clearly not to be fobbed off. 'Where are you having your Christmas dinner?'

'I've got a fridge full of stuff at home, so it'll be rather nice actually. Probably have a pint in the morning at the pub, then the rest of the day is my own.'

It was clear by their head shakes that Rose and Mrs Joy were not having that.

'You are coming here,' Rose declared.

Ray winced. He was still processing the news that Delia was upstairs in bed with someone called Sammi. There was no way he wanted to spend Christmas with Delia and her new boyfriend. 'No, really, I—'

'And for supper tonight. Seven o'clock.'

Ray floundered. 'I couldn't impose.'

'It's no imposition. The more the merrier. Now, eat your mince pie – should be a bit cooler now.'

Mrs Joy settled down opposite him, 'You can meet Sammi. You'll love him.'

Ray didn't think he would.

'Can you keep a secret?' Rose dropped her voice. 'Delia doesn't know, but Mrs Joy and I have organized a Christmas house party for her. Starting tonight, ending on Boxing Day. Tonight is mulled wine, and cottage pie. Kevin and Kenny are coming.'

Mrs Joy winked. 'So it's not as if you won't know anyone.'

Ray felt his heart sink. For weeks now he'd been struggling with confused feelings towards Delia.

Not that he was bothered by Delia's romantic life. She was a free agent, but he had got to know her pretty well while working together in the garden.

She was a good person, and when she sketched the story of her unhappy marriage as they'd pruned and planted, weeded and watered, he realized that he had developed a desire to protect her. He didn't want her to get hurt again.

Nor did he want to watch her spend Christmas with another man.

'As much as I love cottage pie, I—'

'You've already told us you're not doing anything else. Please come.' Rose's voice softened. 'I know Delia would love you to.'

Ray pictured himself sitting in his house, alone with a Marks & Spencer chicken pie and a couple of pints of Doom Bar, watching the *Gardeners' World* Christmas special, which, to be fair, he was looking forward to.

Then he recalled the faces of his daughters when he'd dropped them off at their mum's earlier. They had lit up at the sight of the Christmas tree their mum had put up in the sitting room.

'Dad's so mean,' his daughter Meghan told her. 'He said it wasn't worth us having a tree at his house.'

'Did he?' His ex-wife had given him a shrivelling glance. 'Christmas wouldn't be Christmas without a tree to put the presents under . . . would it?' The last two words she aimed squarely at him.

'Well, I'll be off.' He'd smiled. 'Bye, girls.'

'Bye, Dad.'

They hadn't even turned round. They hadn't even asked what he'd be doing without them.

A spark lit something in him now, and he made his decision. 'You know, Mrs Joy, Miss Jago,I would love to spend Christmas with you. Thank you. Can I bring anything?'

'Just the bits you might need for a two-night stay. A toothbrush, a sleeping bag and a change of undies.You men will be camping on the sofas in the library.'

'Like a dormitory?'

Mrs Joy laughed. 'Exactly. You'll all have such a fun time: Sammi, Kevin and Kenny, Martin . . .'

'Sammi, too?' Ray queried, surprised.

'Oh yes.'

Ray grinned. 'Marvellous. Well, see you tonight.'

The rest of the day at Wilder Hoo was filled with pleasurable busyness.

Sammi's two tasks were to stack the fresh load of logs into the log store and to find a quiet spot to wrap his presents.

With the cooking sorted, Mrs Joy and Rose were sitting in the saloon, feet up, reading magazines and chatting while Delia worked around them, happily taking all her clothes, toiletries, and other bits from the saloon up to her new room.

Having put everything away just where she wanted, she stepped out onto the landing and called over the banisters, 'Sammi?'

'Yes?' His voice came from the library.

'Would you bring up the little Christmas tree that Martin gave me? Have you got any picture hooks and a hammer?'

'Sure. Give me a minute.'

He arrived breathless, having run up the stairs two at a time.

Delia was on the bed unwrapping a photo in a frame. 'Would you put this up for me?'

He took the frame. 'Look at you! How old were you there?'

'About nine, I think. It was our first proper holiday. We went to the Isle of Wight. Mum looks so pretty in that summer dress.'

'She does. Good legs, too.'

Delia smiled. 'And look at Auntie Rose. Hair all short and spiky.'

'Very cool. Where shall we put it?'

'The bathroom. I can say hello every morning and goodnight every evening.'

Sammi banged in the nail and hung the picture. 'Happy?'

'Very.' She yawned. 'I'm tired. I might have a bath and a little nap before Auntie Rose's cottage pie. Why did she make such a big one? We'll be eating it for days.'

Sammi laughed. 'Christmas is all about leftovers. See you later.'

Mrs Joy and Rose were already in the library, sitting either side of the fire, when Delia finally came downstairs. Sammi was pouring the sherry.

'Here she is!' His face lit up. 'Just in time for the selfies round the tree.'

'Hugh and Martin will be here any minute,' Rose added. 'They'll want to be in the photos, too.'

As if on cue, two bright beams shone through the curtainless windows overlooking the front of the house. Forming a welcome party, they trooped out onto the front steps, Delia ahead of the rest.

'Hugh. Martin.' She welcomed them both with a kiss on the cheek. 'Don't you both look good. How's the hotel?' She spotted more headlights coming through the trees. 'Now, who's this?' She frowned. 'Looks like a delivery van. They're working late, whoever they are . . .' She squinted as the van came into view and its lights hit her face. 'It's Kevin! Kenny!' She ran down the steps to meet them.

They climbed out the van, both grinning. 'Surprise!'

'I didn't expect to see you! My bedroom is a dream – I can't thank you enough! What are you doing here?'

But before she could welcome them properly, another set of lights was coming into view and rumbling over the cattle grid.

'Now who's this?' She glanced at Auntie Rose, who acted as if baffled.

The engine stopped, the headlights turned off, and Delia waited to see the occupant. Her heart thudded when she saw who it was.

'Ray!'

She walked over to him and almost hugged him, but instinct stopped her. She didn't want him to get the wrong impression.

Not after the last time they met. And anyway, why would she want to hug Ray?

'Hello.' He smiled. 'Hello everyone.' He gave them a small wave.

They waved back in return.

Delia was struck by how good he looked, sort of confident and wearing clothes that she hadn't seen him in before. Even his hair, usually rather windblown, was combed neatly. 'I wasn't expecting to see you,' she said.

'Rose invited me this morning.'

'Hi, I'm Sammi.' Sammi stuck his hand over Delia's shoulder. 'You've done wonderful things in the garden, I hear?'

'Er. Yeah.' Ray took his hand and shook it.

Kevin and Kenny ambled over and greeted him.

'Hi lads.' Ray gave them each an affectionate punch on the arm. He lowered his voice as he spoke. 'Would you two boys mind helping me with some bags of compost? I don't want Delia to see them yet though.'

Fifteen minutes later, hands washed and smelling fresh, Ray headed for the library. He was grateful to Kenny and Kevin for helping him carry the Brown Gold round to Delia's log store. Hugh's friend Martin had lent a hand, too, although he'd seemed to regret offering once he realized what they were carrying.

Soon, the entire party of nine was assembled in the library enjoying a pre dinner glass of sherry and conversation.

Ray had been cornered by Rose and Hugh, who were telling him all about a castle they'd stayed at recently in the Highlands, and as they chatted he noticed that Delia was in the company of Martin who was leaning into her and making her laugh. He felt sick with jealousy. Rose was still talking, 'And we went to the most beautiful gardens. You wouldn't believe what they can grow up there. Apparently it's the gulf stream that helps.' Ray was confused for a moment but managed to pull his attention back to Rose. 'Amazing', he said, hoping he'd hit on the right response.

Luckily Rose was being distracted by Mrs Joy, who was standing by the door and giving her a thumbs up. 'Ah dinner is ready.' She raised her voice for the room to hear. 'Ladies and gentlemen, dinner is served in the kitchen. Do follow me.'

The kitchen looked spectacular. Fairy lights were strung around the ceiling, while candles flickered in glass vases. The table was laid simply, with a slender rope of berried holly and mistletoe running its length. Rose's ginormous dish of cottage pie was steaming in the centre, with tureens of vegetables either side.

'When did you do all this decorating?' Delia asked in surprise.

'When you had your nap,' Rose said. 'Sammi gave us the heads up.'

'Clever.'

Martin, holding his hands out in front of him like a surgeon preparing for an operation, was shouldering his way towards the sink. 'I wish I'd known we'd be lifting bags of horse manure this evening. I mean, who gives manure as a Christmas present?'

'I do, and it was supposed to be a surprise,' Ray said quietly.

'Ray!' Delia turned to him, beaming. 'You got me some Brown Gold?'

Martin switched the tap off and picked up a tea towel. 'No, dear, it's horse shit.'

Delia laughed. 'It's legendary in these parts. You can grow anything using it – isn't that right, Ray?'

But he didn't get the opportunity to explain.

'Right everybody. Sit down,' Rose commanded, plonking a jug of gravy and bottle of tomato ketchup on the table. 'Delia, you are the head of the table, because without you, none of us would have even heard about this fabulous house. Sammi and Martin, you're either side of her. Hugh, next to me. Kevin and Kenny, you have Mrs Joy between you . . . who have I missed out? Oh, Ray! You're on the end there, opposite Kenny and next to Hugh.'

'Great.' He smiled, feeling anything but great.

He looked up the table to see if Delia had noticed, but she was giggling with Sammi and hadn't seen any of his humiliation.

Hugh tapped his shoulder. 'Jolly glad to be sitting next to you. I need to hear all about your Brown Gold. Rose and I are starting a compost club at Kernow Autumn. Perhaps you could give us some tips?'

It was going to be a long night.

When every last spoon of the cottage pie was gone, Kevin and Kenny having three helpings, more bottles of wine were opened and sent around the table.

Ray, who knew he should probably slow down, kept his eye on Delia, who was looking more lovely as the evening wore on. He couldn't remember ever having seen her with her hair down. He hadn't known how long it was, what with it always being screwed up in a hair clamp or under a beanie . . . and now he saw it covered her shoulder blades and had such a lustre he wanted to stroke it.

She caught his eye, smiled at him, and mouthed, 'Come and join us up this end.'

He began to get to his feet, but as he did so, Sammi took Delia's hand and was pulling her up into a tight dance hold, spinning her around.

'Sammi, stop!' She was laughing helplessly. 'You're going to make me sick.'

He stopped but didn't let her go. 'We need music. Where's the music?' He was clearly quite drunk.

Ray wished he had the courage to rescue her, but even as the thought entered his mind, Delia said, 'Come on everybody. We can dance in the great hall.'

Rose grabbed Hugh.

Mrs Joy was collected up by Kevin and Kenny.

Only Martin and Ray were left staring at each other. Ray felt as if he'd just received a heavy blow to his head, his senses suddenly unreliable.

'Do you dance?' Martin asked.

It took Ray a moment to understand the question. 'No. Not for a long time.' He pointed at the table covered in the wreckage of their supper. 'Why don't we get all this lot into the dishwasher and tidy up a bit?'

'Good shout. I love clearing up.' Martin began turning up the immaculate cuffs of his shirt. 'There's something very satisfying about making order out of chaos, isn't there?'

Half an hour later, rubbish and recycling sorted, dishwasher purring, the kitchen was immaculate.

'I suppose we'd better go and join the party.' Ray sighed.

Martin removed his rubber gloves. 'I think we deserve another glass of something first.'

'No, no. I've had enough.'

'Just a small one. I know where Hugh put the brandy. Sit yourself down.'

Ray gave in. Upstairs, the party was clearly in full swing, and neither he nor Martin seemed to be missed.

Martin came back with a bottle of brandy and a bottle of tequila.

One small brandy was all it took for Ray let his guard done. 'Delia's a remarkable woman, isn't she?'

'She certainly is,' Martin replied. 'Of course, she won't be able to keep the place going.'

Ray bridled. 'Why not?'

'She has no experience.'

'She's done pretty well so far.'

'Granted, but this house is a long-haul project. She'll need help – a good team, financial backers, strong leadership.'

'Are you saying she needs a man to be a success?'

'No, no,' said Martin, taking a sip of his brandy. 'I'm saying that while she should be the "face" of Wilder Hoo, she needs someone sweeping up behind her.'

'Sweeping up behind her.' Ray stood up, absolutely incensed. 'You do know she ran a very successful hair salon in London, don't you?'

'Technically she was the style director and "face" of Gilson's. Not the business brain,' Martin replied calmly. 'If anyone could help her it would be somone like Sammi who runs his own business, and I could always offer advice as a consultant . . . but I can't think of anyone else. Can you?'

The brandy and Martin's smooth assumption that Ray would never be in the running sucked every ounce of confidence out of him. Why had he dared to think that maybe he and Delia could have a future.

She was way out of his league.

She'd been a success in London.

She owned this incredible house and garden. She needed professional business men not a skint gardener and divorced father of two.

Ray wanted to go home right that minute, and he would've done if he hadn't had too much to drink. The only answer was to drink some more.

Martin drained his glass, pushed his chair back, and stood up. 'I think it's about time we joined the party.'

Ray took the tequila with him.

CHAPTER FORTY-THREE

Wilder Hoo, Christmas Day

Delia was dreaming. Climbing one of the apple trees at Jago Fields. The apples were as big as melons and shining red and green, but no matter how high she climbed, they were always just out of her reach. She laughed as she climbed, completely unafraid, even though the branches were now brushing the thick fluffy clouds that bounced on her head and tickled her knees.

She needed to get to her mum. She could hear her calling. 'Cordelia . . . Cordelia . . . It's Christmas, my love . . .'

'Is it?'

'It is.'

'I love you, Mum . . .'

'I love you, too.'

Delia opened one eye to find Auntie Rose by her bed, holding a mug of tea.

'Oh it's you.' Her lips were dry. 'I was dreaming about Mum.'

'How was she?'

'I didn't see her, but she was there . . . up in the clouds.'

Rose smiled and sat on the edge of the bed. 'She would have loved last night's party.'

'Wouldn't she! All that dancing.'

Reaching across the white duvet, they squeezed each other's hands. 'She's here,' Rose said.

Delia smiled. 'I know.'

They sat in silent memory for a moment before Rose stood up. 'Mrs Joy is cooking an enormous breakfast for everyone. Ready in about half an hour.'

Fortified by the tea and a shower, Delia got dressed and went downstairs. She really wanted to see if Ray was OK. She'd not had a chance to talk to him over dinner, and the last she'd seen of him, he was organizing some kind of drinking game with the men – rather out of character, she'd thought.

She had made her excuses and gone to bed.

Descending now into the great hall, she could hear low conversation coming from the library. The designated boys' dormitory, Mrs Joy was calling it. Hugh was the only male exempt, as he and Rose had slept in the saloon.

Delia quietly stepped over to the closed door and threw it open. 'Happy Christmas everyone!'

The room was in chaos: bedding and sleeping bags on sofas and the floor, and five men in varying states of undress.

Sammi shrieked. 'Don't you ever knock before you come into a gentleman's room?' He hastily grabbed a T-shirt and was holding it over his nether regions.

'Sorry!' Delia turned her eyes from Sammi, only to get a full frontal of the naked, gym-honed physiques of Kevin and Kenny. 'Hi Delia,' they said, completely unabashed.

'Oh.' Delia blushed and looked away. 'Hi guys.'

Sudden movement caught her peripheral vision, and she turned to see Ray's bare bottom disappearing behind one of the sofas.

'Sorry. Sorry, guys!' she said. 'I didn't mean to . . . embarrass . . .'

'You haven't embarrassed me.' Martin, showered, shaved, and fully dressed, was coming towards her. I'm just on my way to breakfast.' He offered her his arm. 'Shall we?'

Sitting at Mrs Joy's Christmas breakfast spread was, as Hugh said, 'Like a medieval banquet!'

'Eat up,' she told them, 'There's nothing more until the turkey tonight.'

Rose was mixing an enormous jug of Bloody Mary and insisting everybody had a glass. 'A cure all for those of you who played last night's tequila musical chairs. Whose idea was that again?' she asked pointedly, staring at Ray.

Ray shut his eyes in mortification. 'It was me.'

'Legend,' Kenny said through a mouthful of black pudding.

'Absolute legend,' his brother agreed

Ray had rather hoped that none of the chaos he had facilitated last night would be remembered in any detail.

He'd woken up with a cracking tequila headache, followed by a hazy recall of his stupid game. He hardly knew these people and was dying a thousand deaths of hot shame – not helped this morning by Delia having seen his bare bum diving behind a sofa.

Delia was sitting opposite him now, tucking into a plate of bacon and eggs, making him feel even more queasy.

He couldn't look at her as he said to everyone, 'I want to apologize to all of you for last night. It was stupid, and I hope I haven't upset anyone.'

'No way.' Kevin waved his fork.

'Best game ever,' Kenny agreed.

Delia laughed. 'It's a Christmas Eve that will go down in history. I can't believe I went to bed and missed it all.'

'I loved it,' Martin said, reaching across the table for some more hash browns.

'Only because you kept winning!' Kevin told him. 'You didn't have to do the tequila forfeits.'

'That, my lad, is called skill.' Martin lifted his Bloody Mary. 'To Ray, our Christmas Head of Games.'

Delia could see that Ray was suffering – partly due to his hangover, but there was clearly something else discomforting him, too. She had wanted to talk to him more last night, but he was at the far end of the table, and Martin and Sammi had taken all her attention.

Martin was very good company – fun to talk to, perfect manners, and handsome. He even smelt good, but she just didn't feel the spark.

She must ask Sammi what he thought of him. Was the fact that Martin had never married or had children a red flag?

She laughed at herself. Here she was, in her late thirties, divorced, and no children. Hardly a catch herself.

After breakfast, a plan was made to either go for a walk or relax in front of a film.

Delia opted for the walk. 'You'll come, won't you, Sammi?'

'Sure.'

'Me too,' said Martin.

This rather scuppered Delia's plan to talk to Sammi alone.

'Ray? Would you come, too?' she asked. He was looking very grey around the gills and clearly a walk was the last thing on his mind, but maybe it would help. 'Just down to the beach and back?'

Ray tried a smile. 'Great. I'll get my coat.'

*

'What a beautiful day.' Delia stepped out onto the terrace. 'Nippy but not a cloud in the sky.' She began to walk down the steps, Martin on her left, Sammi on her right, Ray trailing behind.

She stopped at the bare earth of the knot garden, waiting for Ray to catch up. 'I can't wait for the spring. These beds are going to look amazing, aren't they?'

'Yuh. Hopefully.'

Martin and Sammi were now walking a little ahead of them, so Delia took the opportunity to lace her arm through Ray's. 'Is your head very sore?'

He winced. 'A bit.'

'I'm sorry I missed the tequila musical chairs. Sounds like fun. Maybe we can play that tonight?'

'No, it's very much a game not to be played more than once in a lifetime.'

Delia laughed. 'Did you just make it up?'

'Yes. Seemed a good idea at the time.'

They carried on walking slowly, the distance between them and the two ahead, lengthening. 'Have you spoken to your girls this morning?'

'I tried, but they're not answering. I'll try again later.'

'You must miss them.'

'Yeah. Yeah, I do, but, you know . . . it is what it is.'

'And what is it?'

He shook his head. 'I wish I knew.'

'I think I do,' she said.

Ray looked utterly wretched. 'Do you?

She squeezed his arm with hers. 'Yes. You're a bit hungover and you haven't spoken to your girls yet. But you'll feel better when you speak to them.'

'Yeah, you're right.'

She laughed. 'Of course I'm right.'

*

A walk under a winter Cornish sky and the light of a pale primrose sun seemed to be what everyone needed. When they got to the beach, they joined in a ferociously competitive game of stone skimming. Delia was good and looking to be the winner with a twenty-four hop skim, but Martin pulled off an unbeatable twenty-seven.

Delia shook his hand in gracious defeat, then wandered up to the top of the beach where the sand was dry enough to lie down and watch the seagulls riding the breeze above her. She closed her eyes and drifted.

'Hey. Am I disturbing you?'

She opened an eye. Sammi was flopping down next to her. 'Yes, but I don't mind. What are the other two doing?'

'They're looking for Lego pieces. Apparently the holy grail is a black octopus. One was found on Marazion beach last year.'

'The ones that fell off a container a few years ago?'

'Yep.'

Delia propped herself on one elbow and saw the two men bent over the strandline of shells and seaweed.

'What do you think of Martin?'

'He's all right. Bit of a show off, having to win everything. Not my type. Why?'

'He's been very nice to me. A while ago I felt some chemistry but now not so much . . . what do you think?'

Sammi's eyes widened mischievously. 'Oh, the ice queen is melting?'

'Not melting exactly, but . . . I don't know. Auntie Rose seems to think we'd make a good couple.'

'My darling Dee.' Sammi took her hand. 'Martin is a very nice man, but he is not the one for you.'

'What makes you say that?'

'Let's look at the evidence. He's never been married. No children. He's stylish and handsome and . . .'

'You think he's a heart-breaker? Commitment-phobe?'

'Possibly, but not where women are concerned.'

Delia made a face. 'He's not gay, Sammi. Auntie Rose told me he'd been in a long-term relationship with a woman.'

Sammi raised his eyebrows. 'Well, he would tell her that because he's deep deep in the closet.'

'Has he actually told you?'

'He doesn't need to.'

Delia thought for a moment. 'So . . . you and him? Do you like him?'

Sammi shook his head and smiled. 'Suppose I asked you if you fancied every straight man you met? It doesn't work like that, does it?'

'Sorry. No.'

'Forgiven.'

They watched as Martin and Ray sifted through a mound of bladderwrack.

'I have a game for you,' Sammi said.

'OK.'

'Of the three remaining single, straight men in the house, Kevin, Kenny, and Ray . . . '

She arched an eyebrow with suspicion. 'Stop it – Kevin and Kenny are *way* too young for me.'

'Just play the game. In order, tell me, who would you snog, marry, or avoid?'

Delia's laughter was loud enough for Martin and Ray to abandon the Lego hunt and join them.

'You sound like you're having fun.' Martin sat down next to Delia before Ray had a chance. 'I've got something for you. Hold your hand out.'

She did so, and he placed within it a tiny, perfectly formed yellow shell. 'A souvenir of this Christmas Day.'

Returning to Wilder Hoo, they found the rest of the house party lolling in the library, which had been tidied back into its magical Christmas order. Kevin and Kenny were being given a bridge lesson by Rose and Hugh, while Mrs Joy was by the fire, reading a classic Barbara Taylor Bradford.

She looked up when the beach party arrived. 'Did you have a good walk?'

'Glorious, thank you, Mrs Joy,' Martin said. 'You're looking at the Wilder Hoo skimming champion.'

Hugh, without taking his eyes off the cards said, 'For goodness' sake, don't let him play bridge with us. He'd beat us hands down.'

'Anyone for a hot chocolate?' Delia asked. 'I'm taking orders. Ray, you'll help me, won't you.'

As they walked down to the kitchen, Ray's phone buzzed. He checked the screen. 'It's the girls. Can I join you in a minute.'

'Take as long as you need.'

Under the dimmed lights, the smell of the turkey slowly cooking in the bottom of the Aga filled the air and made Delia's tummy rumble.

Waiting for the milk to warm, Delia thought about Sammi's question. Snog, marry, or avoid. The idea of marrying anyone was much too scary a proposition, so she concentrated on the snog or avoid choices. She liked Kevin and Kenny and wouldn't want to avoid them. They were uncomplicated, decent young men. She might have snogged them when she was younger, but now, she was much too old for either of them.

Which only left Ray, who she would never want to avoid. Kind, gentle, complicated Ray. Complicated because he was rather hard to read. He could be very warm, and they'd be getting along fine, but then something would change and he'd become hard to reach again.

Could she kiss him? If the timing was right, maybe. But would he want her to kiss him?

She shook her head. It was all too confusing to think about. Bloody Sammi and his games.

Oh, and Martin . . . gay? Was Sammi right? If so, it would be one less thing to think about.

Ray came back just as she was taking the milk pan off the hob.

'Girls OK?' she asked, pouring the milk into a large flask.

He didn't answer, so she turned to look at him. He was looking a bit unsteady, dazed.

'Ray, what's happened?'

'It's erm . . .' He drew a deep, shuddering breath.

She left the milk. 'Sit down. Is it the girls? Are they all right?'

'Yes . . . They're fine . . . very well, actually . . . excited . . . their mum and . . .' He cleared his throat. 'Their mum and Craig, her boyfriend . . . are taking them to live in Singapore.'

'What?' cried Delia.

'He's got a job out there for two years, starting in the spring. With a nice duplex.' Ray rubbed his head. 'Whatever a duplex is . . . and it has a shared swimming pool, and there's a good English school for the girls to go to, and they'll go on holidays to Australia and New Zealand and surf in Bali, and . . . They both sounded so excited.'

'Oh Ray.' Delia put her arms around him.

A moment later, Sammi's footsteps rang in the passage.

'Hi. Can I help with the hot chocolate, only everybody upstairs is . . .' Delia put a finger to her lips, and he stopped. 'What's happened? Are you all right?'

'Ray's had some difficult news.'

Ray went over it all again, and when he finished, Sammi gave his opinion. 'Your ex-wife is a piece of work, isn't she? How long has she known? Why tell you today of all days?'

Ray smiled thinly. 'Would you mind not telling anyone else just now?'

'It's nobody's business but your own,' Delia said, getting up. 'Sammi, would you finish making the hot chocolate and take it up?' She turned to Ray. 'Mrs Joy and Auntie Rose will be down soon to get the dinner ready. We could talk outside, if you like? Just a quick walk and a chat.'

Ray nodded gratefully. 'Sounds good.'

Wrapped up once again, against the late afternoon chill, Delia and Ray walked past the knot garden without saying a word. The last streaks of sunset hovered over the tree line as the darkening sky grew heavy above them.

A pair of jackdaws took off in the gloom and headed for their roost in the woods.

Ray took a deep breath and blew it out hard. 'Thanks for looking out for me. You're a wonderful woman.'

'I'm really not.'

'Well, I think you are. You've been very kind. Thank you.'

She looked at him. 'You'd do the same for me.'

'I would.'

'How are you feeling now?'

'Better.'

Good. That's what friends are for.' They walked a little further, to the edge of the woods, but it was getting dark, and they turned back.

Wilder Hoo stood in silhouette, light from within blazing from the windows. The house Delia had once wanted to run away from was opening its arms to her.

Ray said, 'If anyone had told me last year that I'd be invited to a Christmas house party at Wilder Hoo, I would never have believed them,' Ray said. 'And yet here I am.' He nudged her gently with his elbow. 'With its owner.'

Delia shook her head. 'I'm only the latest custodian who hasn't a clue what's going to happen next.'

Ray took her hand. 'If you need anything, anything at all, ask me and I'll do it. That's what this friend is for.'

When they got back to the kitchen, they found the table laid, Rose and Mrs Joy cooking and Martin carrying a small, lidded cardboard box. 'There you are. What have you two been up to?'

'Went to inspect the knot garden,' Delia replied. 'What's in the box?'

'My special crackers. Homemade. Look.' He opened the box and showed them the nine golden crackers, decorated with rhinestones, real holly, and tiny little robins sitting on fat green velvet bows.

'You made these yourself?' Delia was incredulous.

'Absolutely. They'll be the finishing touch to this gorgeous table. Oh, and I put a couple of bottles of Champagne in the fridge earlier. Anyone object to a glass?'

It was a silly question.

The bubbles were opened and poured, and Martin proclaimed a toast. 'Here's to them that love us and damn the ones who don't. Cheers!'

The seating plan was very different to the previous night. For a start, Rose placed Mrs Joy at the head of the table, saying, 'Ladies and Gentlemen, I give you not just the greatest cook in Cornwall, but tonight she is the Turkey Queen!'

Kevin and Kenny lifted the enormous bird, plump and golden on its platter, and placed it in front of Hugh, to carve.

Martin, the self-appointed sommelier, ensured that wine, red, white or bubbly, flowed without cease.

Delia made sure that Ray was safely seated between her and Sammi to protect him from any awkward questions, but she had no need to worry. The group had gelled nicely over the last twenty-four hours, and chat between them had grown easy with teasing and shared jokes. She had wondered if Ray might drink too much again to ease his internal disarray, but he hardly touched his wine, opting instead for water.

Glistening sprouts, roasted potatoes, Yorkshire puddings, red cabbage, jugs of gravy, dishes of cranberry, and bowls of bread sauce kept everyone busy and happy until each of them gradually leant back and patted their tums, agreeing it was the best Christmas dinner they'd ever had . . . apart from Martin, who had told them how he had once eaten a fish he'd speared and cooked over a small fire on a Tahitian beach.

'I was very young,' he added. 'I wouldn't do it now.'

The pudding was doused in warmed brandy and flared blue when it was lit, while brandy butter, clotted cream, custard, and ice cream were liberally spooned as required. It was then that Rose noticed that no one was wearing a paper hat.

'Hang on a minute – we haven't opened the crackers yet.'

'No, no, no!' Martin roared above the noise, stopping everyone in their tracks. 'Do not pull the crackers. They are not made to *pull*. There is no snap or hat or motto inside. These are unique works of art and in themselves are my gift to each of you.'

An unmistakeable sense of disappointment settled around the table.

'But . . .' He stared them all down. 'Be not dismayed – I do happen to have these.' From under his chair, he pulled out a gaudy box of supermarket crackers. 'These have everything you could wish for, including the classic, Wind-Up, Gold Cup, Racing Penguins.'

Quickly, the centre of the table was cleared for a racetrack.

Martin bellowed instructions. 'The penguin must be wound to capacity, but not over wound. That is most important. When wound sufficiently, hold your penguin tight, and place it on the start line but DO NOT let go. Hugh, what did I just say? . . . OK, yes, you can pick it up, but if there's a next time, you will be disqualified. That goes for the rest of you, too. The last penguin to finish this first race will be eliminated, and then we race again until we have only one penguin left. Is that clear?'

They all nodded.

'Good. Penguins ready? . . . GO!'

CHAPTER FORTY-FOUR

Wilder Hoo, Boxing Day

Delia woke slowly, stretching herself, arms above her head. She opened her eyes, then quickly shut them again. The sun was very bright and poured itself over the balcony and into her bedroom. Should she get up and meet this glorious day head on? Or should she wrap herself into her warm duvet and go back to sleep?

She reached for her phone. If it was before eight o'clock, she'd stay in bed. If it was after, she'd get up.

It was eight twenty-five.

'Now or never,' she told herself and got out of bed.

The floorboards were warm beneath her feet where the sun was heating them, bouncing its light off the glass baubles on Martin's little Christmas tree.

The day was promising to be a good one.

She pulled her dressing gown on and went to the balcony windows to look at the view below. The garden, the woods, and the Atlantic Ocean were all laid out like a drawing in a children's book.

Her phone pinged.

Hi. I'm making tea. Want one? Sx

She replied:

You absolute beauty! We could drink it on my balcony? Bring coat. 😰

Sammi settled himself on one of the two Lloyd Loom chairs and took in the view. 'This is glorious.'

'I've never been out here before.' An image of Vivienne swam into her mind. 'Johnny's mother was frightened of falling through the rotten planks and landing on the terrace.'

'So she wasn't entirely mad then.'

'Not *entirely*.'

'Darling.' Sammi's expression was serious.

'What?'

'You do know that Ray has the hots for you, don't you?'

Delia laughed. 'No, he hasn't.'

'He has. Seriously. It wouldn't take much.'

'To what?' Delia asked sharply, with a frown.

'For you to let him know you're interested.'

She sipped her tea, ignoring the colour flooding to her cheeks. 'I'm not interested in Ray or anyone else.'

'Oh, but you wanted my opinion on *Martin*.'

'Shows how appalling my intuition is, doesn't it? Maybe I thought I liked him because I sensed he was unobtainable, safe.'

'And by the same token, you're not interested in Ray because he's obtainable and therefore frightening?'

Delia pursed her lips. 'I'm happy on my own.'

'Yeah, right.' Sammi smiled an irritating little know-it-all smile and changed tack. 'In other news, Martin is cooking bubble and squeak for breakfast, and he is trying to drum up a swimming party.'

'Swimming? Today?'

'Why not? We could make it a tradition. Remember two years ago when we swam down at Sennen?'

'Ha!' Delia scoffed. 'Rose and I swam – you were an absolute wuss.'

'It was very cold.'

'Until the guy from the surf shop got in, too . . . what was his name?'

'I don't know who you're talking about.'

'Oh yes you do. Now what was his name . . . Ivan? Isaiah? Isaac! Yes, that's it. The handsome Isaac. You flirted with him.'

'I did not flirt with him . . . if anything, he flirted with me.'

'So, are you going to swim today?'

Sammi grinned. 'Of course, it's tradition.'

The swimming party met in the great hall.

Kevin and Kenny were each carrying a surf board.

Martin, in his dressing gown, exhibited his vividly patterned swim shorts. 'Vilebrequin. Got them down in St Tropez. Ray's wearing my spare pair.'

Ray merely nodded, apparently too reserved to display them under his track pants and fleece.

Sammi was in Bermudas and sweatshirt, Delia in her usual racer-back onepiece covered with her dry robe.

Auntie Rose doled out the towels.

'Sure you won't come, Auntie Rose?' Delia asked.

'Another time. Mrs Joy and I are making turkey curry for supper.'

*

Outside, the morning sky was bright and wispy clouds lingered in their transparency, no movement in them, just a thinning as they dispersed.

Delia had decided not to engage too deeply with Ray today. It would feel inappropriate after yesterday's upset. He probably wouldn't want it brought up again, and her own feelings towards him were muddled, to say the least. The conversation with Sammi had only confused her more. Maybe, in other times, they might have explored an innocent romance, but both of them had been hurt, and both of them were vulnerable. The perfect recipe for a big mistake.

It was a relief to see him pair up with Martin on the walk down to the beach.

Ray had been having a long conversation with himself, too. It had kept him awake until the small hours, until he finally decided on a strategy which was: *If you don't know what to do, do nothing. Keep your powder dry and stay cool.*

In any case, his head was all over the place. He'd known Delia for less than a year, and he liked her – was it a crush or something more?

Yesterday, when his ex had dropped the Singapore bomb . . . Delia had been so kind, and now, she was walking with Sammi and clearly avoiding him. He couldn't work out exactly what the situation was with Sammi. If they were dating, why was Sammi sleeping in the library with the rest of them? And if they weren't . . .

He was on a precipice: in danger of making a fool of himself.

'. . . honestly, you'd love it.' Martin finished whatever he had been saying that Ray had not heard a word of.

'You must come. I insist.'

Ray inwardly winced, wondering what he'd committed himself to. 'When is it again?'

'April. Providing it doesn't snow.'

Ray hoped fervently that whatever Martin's invitation was about, he'd forget all about it by April.

Kevin and Kenny ran through the dunes and straight into the sea, sending great arcs of water droplets to shine like crystals in the sunlight. As quick as seals, they were swimming out to the deeper water and the rising waves.

Martin carefully folded his dressing gown, before gently jogging down to the water's edge and dipping his feet in. 'Come on, Ray. It's not as cold as you'd think.'

Ray was a Cornishman brought up on the cold waters of the North Coast Atlantic. It held no fear for him. He stripped down to his borrowed shorts and felt the sun on his skin. He took a deep, long breath of Cornish air and held it for a few seconds, feeling his mind fall quiet. This was what he needed.

He smiled at Martin. 'Come on then.'

He looked back at Delia one last time, unable to help admiring her slender figure and lean limbs.

Delia watched as Ray calmly dived under the waves without hesitation, popping up the other side a moment later, then heading out towards Kevin and Kenny.

'He's in good shape,' Sammi said.

'Yeah,' she said, 'he is.'

She walked quickly into the water and began to swim, not as far out as the boys. She had no interest in body surfing with them, so she began a nicely paced crawl crossing the length of the beach and back. It was as she made a turn, her eyes secretly searching for Ray, when something crashed into her. Pushing her under the water. Disorientating her. She couldn't work out which way was up. Sand and seaweed swirled about her, making it impossible for her to see anything that might offer direction.

As her lungs began to burst, a strong arm wrapped itself around her and pulled her up into clean air. 'I'm so sorry. I wasn't looking. Are you OK?' Ray's concerned eyes were staring into hers. Droplets of sea water on his lashes. His board was floating nearby. 'I had to swerve to avoid Kevin, and I didn't see you . . . I'm so sorry. Are you OK?' he asked again.

'I'm fine.' She coughed and rubbed the back of her head. 'Just a bump.'

'Are you sure?'

'Yeah.' She felt his arm loosen around her.

'You're cold. Let's get you back to the beach.'

On the beach, Sammi and Martin were waiting with Delia's clothes and towel like anguished parents.

'Oh Dee, we saw it all!' cried Sammi. 'Are you OK? You look frozen. Come on, let's get you dry and warmed up.'

When Martin had rubbed the circulation back into her arms and legs, Sammi helped her into her dry clothes.

Ray stood back, helpless, but when she was dressed and shivering less, he examined the lump on her head. 'How does it feel?'

'A bit sore, but nothing serious.'

'Are you feeling dizzy? Sick?'

'A bit sick, but I swallowed some sea water.'

'Do you want to rest here a bit longer or get back to Wilder Hoo?'

Delia looked around as the beach seemed to sway. 'I'd like to go back.'

The small party gathered up their bits and began the walk back to the house.

When Auntie Rose heard what had happened, the colour drained from her face. 'I'm taking you to A&E.'

'I'm fine, honestly,' said Delia. 'I just need a cup of tea and a sit-down.'

Rose was having none of it. 'You can have a sit-down in A&E.'

Delia sighed. 'I know you're thinking of what happened to Mum, but—'

Rose was reaching for her car keys. 'Christine didn't think it was serious either. Let's leave that to the hospital to decide. Sammi, fetch a blanket, would you? We're going now.'

Sammi was on it. 'I'm coming with you.'

After they left, the atmosphere in the kitchen became palpably tense. No one knew quite what to say.

Ray was at the table, drinking the tea Mrs Joy had pressed on him. He was feeling awful.

Kevin and Kenny had tried to reassure him, but it was clear they were out of their comfort zone and, after giving all they could, eventually gave in to the siren call of the new video game that they'd rigged up in the library.

Their departure left Ray with Mrs Joy and Hugh, who explained to Ray why any head injury put Rose into panic mode.

'So that's how Delia's mum died?' Ray asked miserably.

Hugh nodded. 'I don't think Rose will ever really recover from her sister's death. And with Delia being her last surviving relative . . . well, if anything happened to her.'

Ray nodded. 'Makes me feel even worse.'

'It was an accident,' Mrs Joy said. 'Could have happened to any of you.'

Hugh patted Ray on the shoulder and left him to Mrs Joy's gentle care.

'I'm getting you a large brandy and lovage,' she told him. 'That'll settle you. You're still in shock, love.'

'No thank you, Mrs Joy. I think I'll just find a quiet space to be on my own for a bit. You will tell me if you hear anything?'

'Of course I will.'

He found himself in the quiet dark of the great hall and sat on the stairs, his head in his hands. It was good to be alone and unseen with his thoughts. If anything bad happened to Delia he'd never be able to look himself in the eye again.

After a few minutes he heard footsteps coming down the stairs behind him and a gentle hand on his shoulder.

'Ray? What are you doing sitting in the dark?' It was Martin.

'Just thinking.'

'About Delia?'

'Yeah.'

'Any news?'

'Not yet.'

Martin sat down next to him. 'How are you?'

'Feeling pretty shit actually.'

Martin put an arm over Ray's shoulder. 'She'll be OK.'

'How can you be sure?'

'Because Sammi and Rose are with her and they'll make sure she's OK.'

Ray lifted his head and turned to look into Martin's face. 'I thought you'd be a bit more worried about her.'

'Of course I'm worried about her. But she has the two people who love her most by her side.'

Ray frowned. 'But you've been all over her these last couple of days.'

'Ah,' Martin said. 'This is awkward. If you think I have romantic designs on Delia, you cannot be further from the truth.'

'Doesn't look like it from where I'm standing. If you're leading her on—'

'I am most definitely not leading her on. Rest assured.' Martin sighed, stretching his legs out in front of him and pulling at the knee of his trousers before tucking his legs back beneath him. 'The fact is . . .' He whispered something into Ray's ear.

Ray was flabbergasted. 'You mean you're . . .'

Martin nodded. 'Indeed I am.'

Ray looked at Martin with respect. 'Thank you and I'm sorry I seem to have pushed you into sharing something so personal.'

'Doesn't bother me, but it can bother others, which is why I decide who I tell.' Martin smiled. 'Do I detect a fondness on your behalf for Delia?'

Ray decided to be honest. 'Yes. I think she's amazing.'

'I think you should tell her; after all, there is no one standing in your way now, is there?'

Ray rubbed his chin. 'There is actually. Sammi.'

Martin almost choked on his sudden laughter. 'My dear Ray, I say again. There is no one standing in your way.'

It was late when Delia returned home with a clean bill of health and relief all round.

'The doctor couldn't have been sweeter,' Rose told everyone. 'No blood, no bruising, just lots of rest.'

After an exhausted Delia was tucked up in her bed, the others sat quietly around the kitchen table, eating bowls of Mrs Joy's turkey curry and remembering all the funny things that had happened over the past few days. And when the last dish was dried and the last light turned off, no one slept better than Ray.

CHAPTER FORTY-FIVE

Wilder Hoo, late December

Two days later, Delia was sprawled on the sofa in the saloon next to Sammi as she read Rose's latest email. The two of them were rattling around a bit after everyone had left. Even Mrs Joy had gone, and Wilder Hoo felt empty.

> *Hello.*
>
> *It's so good to be home! I am completely exhausted. Darling Hugh told me that I deserved a little break so he only went and booked two weeks in Jamaica for us! Wonderful surprise. Our room will be one of those over-the-water bungalows. V posh for a simple Cornish girl.*
>
> *Martin wanted me to tell you how much he enjoyed Christmas at Wilder Hoo and meeting you both. He would have told you himself, but he had an invitation to ski in Aspen with someone called Brad and dropped everything.*
>
> *What are you two up to? Any news from Ray?*

Happy New Year and all my love,
Rose Xxx

'I think we should get some fresh air today,' Delia said, reaching for another mince pie

'Hmm . . .' Sammi was looking at his phone, not really listening. 'Oh my God!'

'What?'

'It's happened!'

'What's happened?'

'You know I told you about the interiors company who had shortlisted me to work with them?'

Delia's eyes lit up. 'They've come back?'

'Yep. Final offer. Two years' collaboration with a range to include paints, fabric, rugs, soft furnishings . . .' He was grinning. '. . . and they want to call it . . . *Sammi Hashmi Designs* in big letters, terrible font choice, but I can sort that, with *Colours of Pakistan* underneath.' He looked at her, totally astounded. 'It's happened. My dream has actually become a reality.' He leapt up, and the two of them began pogoing around the room, squealing and hugging until they ran out of puff.

'I am so proud of you, Sammi!'

'Me too! I'd better ring Mum. She's going to go berserk.'

Next day, the kitchen table was covered in objects that Sammi had collected that morning from a walk around the estate. Shells, stones, feathers, a rabbit skull, and a string of iridescent tinsel.

Delia was in the library, updating a list of things that needed to be done before the twenty-seventh of April, talking to herself out loud. 'If we open just the gardens, the priority is to spend time and money outside. We can leave the more expensive indoor jobs to another time. I wonder how much public insurance is?

And Portaloos? How about a pasty stall? Teas, coffees, chips? But then who'll take all the rubbish away?' Frowning, she wrote a note in her little book, a Christmas present from Mrs Joy.

She glanced up as Sammi came into the room. 'Do you think I should get a lifeguard for the beach? How much do you think a family of four would be prepared to pay for an entrance fee? How much would you pay, Sam?'

Sammi clearly wasn't listening. He was holding a delicate little shell up to the light. 'Isn't this the most beautiful colour you've ever seen? It would make a great paint colour. I'd call it . . . CornLight.'

Delia stared hard at Sammi, then her eyes fell to his muddy boots. 'This is the library, not a pig pen.'

'But I wanted to show you these!' In his other hand, he held up a stick covered in lichen and a piece of bladderwrack attached to a limpet shell, like they were priceless trophies. 'These absolutely meet the brief for the entire concept of Sammi Hashmi Designs.'

'Do you have to wear your boots in the house though?'

'It's my vision. I want to share it with you.'

'Which is all very lovely, but to me it looks like stuff we had at school on our nature table in year one.'

Sammi raised his eyebrows.

'Oh, for heaven's sake. I don't expect to hear from him. He is spending as much time as he can with his girls before they leave for Singapore.' She waved a hand to her notebook. 'I'm busy. He's busy. The twenty-seventh of April and your stupid bet is getting very real now.'

Sammi merely smiled. 'So, you haven't heard from him then.'

At that moment, over at Penvare Plant Nursery, Ray was in the polytunnel, checking on the lavender and geranium cuttings. There was no sign of rot, which pleased him – and also gave him a reason to phone Delia. Last summer, she had asked him to put a dozen of each aside for the knot garden and the terrace. She particularly liked the deep black/red geranium Tommy and the lavender Melissa Lilac, which would make a very good hedge. He wanted to phone her this afternoon, but the girls were coming to stay until after New Year, and he'd promised to take them to the cinema tonight.

For a brief moment, he imagined taking the girls and Delia out to the pictures together. They'd get along so well, ganging up on him with silly jokes.

He put the thought from his mind and counted twelve lavenders and twelve geraniums, then put them to one end of the growing bench. They would have to wait and so would he.

The girls loved the film, and he enjoyed the ninety-minute snooze it gave him, even though it was punctuated by regular digs in the ribs from eleven-year-old Lexi, who giggled, 'Dad, you're snoring,' while fourteen-year-old Meghan on his other side curled her lip-glossed lips and whispered furiously, 'Dad. Stop it. You are so disgusting.'

By the next afternoon, Delia had had enough of Sammi and his 'curation of molecules from the universe.'

'What the hell are you talking about? Where is the old sarcastic Sammi? Hmm? Listen to yourself. CornLight? MoonWall? You're just inventing a sort of grey colour – that's all. What's happened to the colour-loving man I used to know? This just isn't you.'

His face sagged. 'I'm scared.'

'Scared of colour?'

'Scared of *failure*.' He flopped into a chair. 'There's this awful pressure to create a collection of new, unthought of, never-seen-before designs, and I don't know how to do that.'

'Oh, Sammi. You don't need to do anything more than you already do. They have given you this chance because they love your vitality and the vividness of your work. The colours you use and the way you use them are already different from anyone else's. People find so much joy when they walk into a room you've designed.'

'Really?'

'Yes! Look at the way you brought the library back to life. It's a showstopper.'

He twiddled with a thread on the sleeve of his sweater. 'Delia, what would you say if I told you I didn't want to work in London again? Everybody wants things done yesterday. It kills creativity. I'd much rather find a studio down here.'

Delia had a feeling what was to come next. 'What are you asking?'

'Those small barns you have. They need some work doing, but Ken and Kev think it's nothing they couldn't fix.'

'You absolute worm. When did the three of you go sniffing round them?'

'It wasn't my idea. The boys are really keen on taking one or two of them as their own workshops. Would make sense to have them on site – there are still so many repairs to be done to Wilder Hoo . . . and if you don't charge them any rent, they'll do you a good deal . . .'

Delia's eyes narrowed. Her first instinct was to be absolutely furious. The three of them in cahoots, thinking they could decide what she should do with those barns! On the other hand, she didn't actually have any plans for them as yet, and it would be handy to have builders on tap, and a resident designer who could furnish the house in all his new wallpapers, paints, and fabrics. Not to mention how lovely it would be to have Sammi close by. The house could be his shop window. Magazines would do shoots. Instant, classy marketing.

'Get your coat,' she told him. 'I want to have another look at those barns.'

CHAPTER FORTY-SIX

North Cornwall, New Year's Eve

It wasn't even 9 a.m. but Ray's ex was on the phone. 'Craig is being awarded his kick-boxing masters black belt tonight, and it would mean a lot to him to have the girls there.'

Ray felt a hard knot of anger forming in his gullet. 'Well, I'm very sorry, but Lexi, Meghan, and I have plans for tonight.'

She sniggered. 'What, fish and chips on your old sofa and *The Holiday* on the television? That's just a usual night when they stay with you. You can pick them up from ours tomorrow and do all that then.'

'I'll ask them what they want to do and call you back.' He ended the call.

'Girls,' he said outside their bedroom door. 'Can I come in?'

'Just a minute!' He heard hurried movements before, 'OK. You can come in now.'

He glanced around the room, looking for anything suspicious, but whatever it was was now out of sight. The girls were sitting primly in their pyjamas, phones in hands.

'I was thinking about what we might do today,' Ray said. 'We could drive up to Plymouth? The sales have started. Have a spot of lunch down on the Barbican then come down with me to the nursery, help me sow the broad beans.'

Meghan looked at Lexi, then back to her dad. 'Mum's taking us to Plymouth next week. To look for things for Singapore.'

'Ah.'

'Yeah. And to be honest, Dad, gardening is not something I want to do.'

'But you used to love coming down and helping me? Rides in the wheelbarrow. The sparrows you trained to eat from your hand.'

Meghan sniggered in the same way her mum did. 'We were kids then.'

'You still are.'

'Lexi is, but I'm not.'

'And I'm nearly not,' Lexi said.

'Right, well, we still have the fish and chips to look forward to later.'

Meghan slid a sly glance to Lexi, who said, 'You know Craig does kick-boxing?'

Ray felt his heart sink. 'No.'

'Well, he does and he's really, really good at it, isn't he, Meg?'

'Yeah. Like, really good. He's getting the highest thing you can ever get given to him tonight.'

'Is he?'

'Can we go?' Lexi asked. 'Please?'

Ray sighed. 'What about our fish and chips and staying up until midnight, eh? That's going to be fun. Saying goodbye to the old year and welcoming the new one in.' He sounded desperate, even to his own ears.

'Can't we do a pretend one another time?' Lexi asked hopefully.

'No. It only happens once every three-hundred-and-sixty-five days.'

'But not on leap years,' Meghan jumped in, as if she was telling Ray something he didn't know. 'That's three-hundred-and-sixty-six days.'

'Yes, I know what a leap year is, Meggy.'

'I don't like being called Meggy anymore. That was my baby name. I'm Meghan or Meg now.'

Ray tried to ignore how much that stung. 'Right,' he said, to change the subject, 'what do you fancy for breakfast?'

'What is there?'

'I got a variety pack of cereals. You like those.'

'Craig says they're the worst things you could feed a child,' Lexi said sadly. 'I used to like Coco Pops.'

'He needn't know if you had some.' Ray grinned mischievously.

'He would know, because he always asks us what we eat when we've been here.'

Ray briefly entertained the idea of punching Craig's lights out. What a prick. Two years, his ex had been seeing Craig behind his back. Two years! There had been a lot of water under the bridge since then and Ray, although tested to the limits, had achieved a place of peace, enjoying his quiet, uneventful, safe, and secure life. Still, he treasured the time he spent with his daughters.

'Have you got any kefir?' Meghan asked.

'No. But I've got bacon, eggs, toast, some frozen waffles, and hash browns.'

He could see the desire in their eyes. Now he'd got them. He took their order for bacon and egg sandwiches, with a waffle on the side.

Over breakfast, the girls tucked into their plates of unapproved food, telling Ray all about the Christmas they'd had.

'It was really lush,' Lexi told him. 'What did you do, Dad?'

He told them about Wilder Hoo and mentioned Delia, but not in too much detail.

'Were there any young people there or was it all just old people?' Meg asked.

He smiled. 'Just us oldies.'

'Good,' Lexi said. 'Old people need to have friends.'

Ray nodded. 'You are so right, Lex.'

He wondered what Delia was doing and how she was going to see in the New Year.

'You could go and see them tonight when we're not here?' Lexi suggested. 'So that you're not on your own?'

Lexi had always had a softness of heart. He wanted to scoop her up and hug her tight, then tickle and make her laugh like he did when she was little, but he didn't do that. They were older now.

His heart ached as he looked across at them. In a few months, they would be in Singapore, and by the time they got back, Lexi would be firmly a teenager and Meghan almost an adult. Sometimes, he felt they were already almost strangers, always ready to highlight his shortcomings. How much worse that could grow over the next two years.

He would miss them so very much.

'I'll be fine,' Ray said. 'I'll ring your mum and find out what time she wants me to drop you.'

At Wilder Hoo, Delia and Sammi were exploring the barns. 'What's that . . . leaning against the wall at the back?' Delia pointed to a glint of something shiny sticking out from a sheet of blue plastic.

Sammi clambered over a pile of tin buckets and pulled at the plastic. 'It's brass and . . .' He pulled more of the plastic away. 'It's a bedstead. I wonder if it's got all the bits though.'

They dug about and found it was not one bed but two. 'These are really nice. Victorian?' Delia suggested.

'I'd say so.' Sammi was lifting another sheet of plastic. 'Hang on, I think there's another . . .'

'Have you got everything packed and ready to go back to Mum's?' Ray asked the girls later that afternoon.

'Nearly.'

'I'll go and de-ice the car then. Meet you downstairs.'

Ten minutes later, as they set off towards his ex's, Meghan suddenly told him, 'Someone rang while you were doing the car.'

'Who was it?'

'I don't know. She just asked if you were there, and I said no.'

Ray's heart missed a beat. 'A woman?'

'Yeah. I think so.'

'Young? Old?'

Meghan shrugged. 'I don't know.'

'And she didn't leave a message?'

Meghan looked at him as if he were a moron. 'I told you. No.'

The barns had been very cold, so Delia was warming up in a very hot bath.

She had made a mistake in calling Ray. It had been a spur-of-the-moment thing, just wanting to . . . to . . . talk to him. It must have been one of his daughters who'd answered. Her telephone manner needed some work. She probably, hopefully, hadn't told him that she'd called. But if she had, would he suspect it was Delia?

*

Driving back home, Ray was pondering over the missed phone call. If it was someone he knew, they'd have rung his mobile, but the call had been to his home phone. It wasn't unusual for Cornish homes to have landlines as mobile signal was so patchy, so . . . who could it be?

He tried to push away the hope that it might have been Delia.

Wait a minute . . . if he dialled 1471 on the home phone, a recorded message would give him the last number that called.

He drove a little faster.

In his haste, he fumbled the key in the front door lock, before getting it open and almost running to the phone. He found a broken biro and an old envelope in the hall drawer, then dialled 1471.

You were called today at 16.52 hours. The number was . . .

Please press 3 to return the call.

He pressed 3.

Delia was out of the bath and wrapping a towel around herself when she heard her phone ringing in the bedroom.

Probably Auntie Rose. 'Hi.'

Silence.

'Hello? Is that you, Auntie Rose?'

'Oh, Delia. Hi, it's Ray.'

Delia froze. 'Oh. Hello. How are you?'

'Good. I'm good. I think I . . . missed a call from you earlier?'

Delia winced. 'Yes, I . . . just thought I'd wish you happy New Year.'

'Thank you . . . and you.' Ray paused. 'Are you doing anything special tonight?'

'Oh no. Early night, I expect.'

'Me too,' Ray replied. 'You're not on your own, are you?'

'Sammi's here.'

'Oh good, good. He's OK, is he?'

'Yes. Actually, we had a most amazing day . . .'

She told him everything about the new plan for the barns and the treasure trove of furniture they'd found, all the fun they'd had. 'I think you'd love it.'

'Sounds right up my street.'

Delia threw caution to the wind. 'What are you doing tomorrow?'

CHAPTER FORTY-SEVEN

Wilder Hoo, January

'How long do you reckon all this has been here?'

Ray and Delia were in the barns, looking at a mouse-nibbled chaise-longue.

'I know the house was requisitioned during the First World War to use as a hospital for those injured in France,' Delia told him. 'So maybe the owners stored their stuff in here to keep it safe?'

'But that's over a hundred years ago.'

'Yeah. Mad, isn't it? And there's a gorgeous leather chesterfield next door. Come and have a look.'

Sammi was in the roof space above and called down to them through the ladder-hole. 'You won't believe what's up here!'

Later, back in the warmth of Wilder Hoo's kitchen, the three of them sifted through the photos of everything they'd found: tea sets, a dinner service, wine glasses, decanters, vases, candlesticks, a set of mahogany dining chairs . . . the list was endless.

'I don't understand it,' Delia said. 'How come none of us had found all this ages ago?'

'Sometimes things hide in plain sight?' Sammi suggested.

'Who cares,' said Ray. 'You've found it now, and there may still be more to come.' He grinned. 'You'll be able to do some amazing things with all of this.'

Mrs Joy returned, unannounced, three days later. Delia came down for toast one morning, and there she was, apron on, preparing a chicken.

'Oh.' Delia put a hand to her heart. 'You gave me a fright.'

'I got an early train. Happy New Year.'

'And happy New Year to you, too. We've missed you.'

'What have you been up to while I was away?'

Delia had a lot to tell her. She started with Sammi's design contract, followed by the findings in the barn.

Mrs Joy listened attentively, asking few questions but supplying some answers.

'I know you call them barns now, but they were actually stables for the horses of the house. When the war came, the young men signed up to go to France and took their horses with them. Then, when the house became a hospital, all the stalls in the stables were removed to create space to store the best bits of furniture.'

'Oh. I see!'

'And the spaces above were where the stable lad lived. I'm glad that at least one roof is still watertight. Those bits of furniture and the portraits would have been ruined.'

'Did I tell you about the portraits?'

'You didn't have to. It's common sense. The family must have had lots of pictures, and they had to be stored somewhere. When you're ready, Ken and Kevin will put them on the staircase wall – where they should be.'

Delia laughed. 'As long as they're not too creepy.'

January slid into February with ease. Kevin and Kenny were going great guns in the barns. They had struck a deal with Delia not only to do all the repair work she needed, and to create Sammi's studio, but also to convert one into a workshop and a flat that they would rent for a peppercorn amount.

'I must be the luckiest woman in Cornwall,' she kept saying. 'To have resident builders and my oldest friend all under one roof! I really am living the dream.'

March came with a little snow and then bright sunshine. Swathes of daffodils lit the margins of the drive and swooped over the open parkland. Auntie Rose made sure to come up and photograph it all for Instagram.

And there was Ray. He might not be living at Wilder Hoo, but he was there as much as he could be.

Delia had made contact with Cornwall Council about her plan to open the grounds to the public on the twenty-seventh of April.

After giving her a rap on the knuckles for asking at such short notice, the woman dealing with her case was actually very helpful. The reams of paperwork and red tape, however, were not.

Delia would have become entirely desk-bound if it hadn't been for Ray. He was now working three days a week at Wilder Hoo and insisted on winkling Delia out of the saloon HQ and into the garden on at least two of those days.

'You need sunlight and fresh air.' He rarely took no for an answer.

And she was a good pupil.

Over the weeks, any awkwardness there might have been between them was gone.

When Lexi and Meghan flew off to Singapore, he drove up to Heathrow at the crack of dawn to hug them and wish them luck and give them each an envelope with two hundred Singapore dollars inside. He held back his tears as he watched them go through departures. Afterwards, sitting alone in his car, he didn't want to go home. He couldn't face it at the moment. The only place he wanted to go was Wilder Hoo, so he did.

Delia had known that this would be a difficult day for him and had told him that he was not to come to work, but when he popped his head round the door of the saloon, she shut her laptop and hugged him. 'You OK?'

'Yeah.'

'Fancy a cuppa?'

'Yes please.'

'I'm glad you're here, because that clematis we planted needs tying up.'

Nothing else was said. Nothing needed to be.

Delia's permissions for the opening on the twenty-seventh of April came through on the first of April, so of course she thought it was a joke and took some convincing by the nice lady at the council that it wasn't.

'I've even got you approval for the wedding licence, so you can host weddings at the house, but it won't be validated until the autumn.'

'Thank you. Thank you so much. I can't believe it.'

'Good luck. I might even come up myself. My husband loves looking around other people's gardens.'

Delia leapt to her feet, a grin spreading over her face, and ran down towards the kitchen.

Three o'clock every afternoon had become the time when everyone who was at Wilder Hoo gathered for a cup of tea and a slice of whatever cake Mrs Joy had baked that day. It was a chance to exchange anything important or unimportant. Delia virtually skipped through the doorway, bursting to tell everyone that Wilder Hoo's first public event was actually happening.

Sammi almost choked on his slice of Victoria sponge. 'That's wonderful! Incredible! Well done, Dee. Now all you have to do is prove to me that you can make a profit.'

'Oh, I will,' she said, grinning like the Cheshire Cat. 'Not only do I have a fish, chip, and pasty van, I have teas, coffees, Mrs Joy's cake stall, face-painting by Auntie Rose, and a sand castle competition on the beach. I'm also thinking of approaching an up-and-coming designer to take a stall advertising his latest design range and selling silk shawls sent by an Islamabad factory who, as we speak, are loading them onto a freight airplane.'

Sammi looked worried. 'You rang my uncle in Islamabad.'

'I did.'

'And he's given you his best price?'

'I think so.'

'What colours did you ask for?'

'I didn't have to. He is duplicating your last order, so you'll know it's good.'

At last, a grin spread over Sammi's face. 'You little beauty!'

The last thing to do was to message Auntie Rose and tell her to go large on the Instagram posts to spread the good news and add a link to tickets. Delia also asked her to ask around for any lifeguards who would be happy to look after the beach that day, for all the pasties he/she could eat.

Auntie Rose replied with a thumbs up emoji and: *AATK.*

Delia typed: *What?*

Always at the keyboard! Get with it, Delia.

Auntie Rose never failed to amaze her.

Delia's to-do list was almost complete. She just had to send a deposit to Willy's Best Bogs for the Portaloos and she was done, which meant more time working in the garden, with Ray.

*

'The tulips should be just perfect come the twenty-seventh.' Ray shook off his gardening gloves and wiped his forehead. They were sitting together on the lawn. 'As long as it doesn't get too hot for them.'

'I can't thank you enough, Ray. Without you, the fields wouldn't be harrowed, the wildflower meadow wouldn't have been sown . . . nothing would be as good as it is.'

Ray was watching a bumble bee settle on a patch of daisies. 'You don't need to thank me. I'd do anything for you, Delia.' He turned and looked into her eyes. 'That's what friends are for.'

Delia felt the shift between them. Was she reading it right? She didn't want to make a mistake. And yet, his eyes were still looking into hers. She broke the moment and looked down at the trowel she was gripping tightly. His gloves lay between them and he picked them up. His shirt sleeves were rolled to his elbows and for the first time she noticed how strong and well-muscled his forearms were. Capable. The kind of arms that would hold a person with such security that you'd never want them to stop.

'Ray—' she started, but he held up his hand.

'Please. I've wanted to tell you something for a long time. Looking for the right moment, you know? And maybe this is it.'

'Ray . . .' Delia tried to respond.

'Please let me say this before I lose the courage.' He took a deep breath. 'Delia, I see you in a way I have never seen any other woman. You don't hide yourself. You have no guile or artifice. You don't play games. You don't flirt or need constant attention. You're just you. And just you is wonderful. You never give up or give in. You never make me feel stupid or uncomfortable.' He gave her a crooked smile. 'I have fallen hopelessly in love with you.'

Delia's response was pathetic. 'Oh?'

'Oh God.' Ray's face was stricken. He ran a mud-crusted hand through his hair. 'I've really messed this up, haven't I?'

She reached out and touched his beautiful arm. 'No, you haven't. I'm just rather . . . surprised and . . . scared,' she said simply.

'Of being hurt again?' Ray asked.

She nodded.

'Me too.' He smiled.

'Yes. But, I am a grown woman and when a grown man says the things you have said, I should want to kiss you and I don't want kiss you . . . because that would feel like there is no going back.'

'Is this your gentle way of telling me that I've made a complete tit of myself and ruined everything?'

She shook her head. 'No. I'm not saying that—'

Sammi appeared from nowhere. 'You two OK? You're both looking very serious. What's happened?'

'Nothing.' Delia smiled at him, but what she wanted to say was, 'Everything.'

'Good. Your Auntie Rose is on the phone in the saloon. She says it's important.'

Ray stood up and held his hand out to help her get up. It felt familiar. The right fit.

Together they walked across the lawn and up the terrace steps. At the top, Ray let her hand go. 'You go and talk to your aunt.'

'Where will I find you?'

'In the kitchen, I have a hot date with Mrs J and her teapot.'

Walking into her office was like walking on air.

She picked up the phone. 'Hi Auntie Rose.'

'I'm sending you an email right now. Read it and then delete. It's totally confidential. Do it now and ring me back.'

The email appeared instantly, and she opened it. 'Oh my God. Oh, for goodness' sake. Whoa. This can't be true.' She read it through again, deleted it, and rang Auntie Rose.

'Are you certain it's genuine?'

'Yes. I rang their office as soon as I got it, and it's deffo legit.'

'Blimey.'

'My thoughts exactly.'

'So, what do we do next?'

'We write back and formally let them know it is our pleasure and honour to welcome them to Wilder Hoo on twenty-seventh April.'

'What do we do about security?'

'They'll have that all in hand.'

'I can't believe it! What a day this is turning into!'

Auntie Rose sensed a certain fresh energy in Delia's voice. 'Oh yes? What else has been happening?'

Delia glanced over her shoulder to make sure no one was listening in. 'Promise you won't say anything?'

'Of course not. What is it?'

'It's Ray. He says he's fallen in love with me.'

Auntie Rose gasped. 'At last! And what did you say?'

'I haven't yet . . . and now this . . . oh, Auntie Rose! Isn't it wonderful!'

'Yes the email is fantastic.' Auntie Rose dismissed it. 'But let's talk more about Ray. How do you feel about him?'

'He has lovely arms . . .'

'Aha! And you can see him as more than a friend?'

'I think, maybe . . .'

'Oh, for goodness' sake,' Auntie Rose said irritably. 'Could you use his toothbrush if you had to? Yes or no?'

'What's that supposed to mean?'

'If you love him the answer would be a definite yes.'

Delia didn't have a chance to answer because Sammi burst in carrying a huge bunch of flowers. 'Got to go Auntie Rose. Let's speak tomorrow.'

She put the phone down and pointed at the flowers. 'Are they for you?'

'No. They are for you.' Sammi glowed with excitement as he pulled off the small, sealed envelope from the wrapping. 'So, who are they from? Go on. Open it. I need to know.'

Delia was grinning from ear to ear. Ray was a man of surprises. She pushed her hair behind her ears. 'Let me look at the flowers first. I want to know what he's chosen.'

'Oh, so you know who they are from, do you?'

'Perhaps,' she teased him.

'Ok. Whoever it is, they are they are very pretty.'

She examined the exquisite blooms and exhaled with a knowing sense of satisfaction. 'Camellias and white cherry blossom. Only he could have thought of them.'

'Who? Who?' Sammi was getting over excited.

'It has to be Ray. Let me read the card.' She cleared her throat. 'Darling Delia, good luck with the grand opening of Wilder Hoo. Sending you heaps of love and success from snowy Aspen! Martin.'

'Martin?' Said Sammi.

Ray's head popped round the door and spotted the flamboyant bouquet. 'Nice flowers. Who are they from? Great choice.'

'Yes, aren't they lovely?' Delia agreed. 'Obviously, they're from Martin. They're so chic.'

'Wouldn't it be lovely to date someone like him, just for the flowers.' Sammi was wistful.

'I would need more than flowers,' Delia added.

Sammi laughed, 'Well, *you* wouldn't get anything else, but Ray might.'

Delia began to laugh but Ray looked horrified.

Sammi felt the need to explain gently, 'Ray dear, Martin is gay.'

Ray said awkwardly, 'Well, yes. I know. He told me. At Christmas. But I thought it was between us.'

'He told you?' Delia asked.

'Um yes, because I got a bit . . . um . . . well, I was worried that he was leading you on and when I confronted him about it, he told me . . . did you know?'

Delia nodded, 'Yep, I knew.'

'No, you didn't know until I told you,' Sammi laughed. 'You thought he fancied you.'

'That doesn't matter now.' She flapped her hands trying to move the confusion on.

Sammi refused to let it go. 'Here's the thing Ray, she thought those flowers were from you.'

Ray shot Delia a panicked look. Delia bit her lip.

Sammi could see that he'd touched a nerve. 'Ah. I'm going to get out of here and see you later. Bye.'

On their own neither knew quite what to say.

'I wish I had sent those flowers to you.' Ray leant towards her.

She smiled, 'Me too.'

His kiss was gentle and warm and Delia melted into him. After a while she broke away. 'Can you keep a secret?'

'Yes.'

'Auntie Rose rang to tell me that The Duke and Duchess of Cornwall want to come to our Grand Opening! Informally and with the children.'

'Really?'

'Yep.' Delia's eyes shone. 'And I am happy because I have you to share the secret with.'

CHAPTER FORTY-EIGHT

Wilder Hoo, 27th April

Delia was rushing around, checking things off in her notebook.

The parkland and gardens were dressed in full party rig. The bunting was up. St John's Ambulance were here. Handmade arrows were on posts with directions to Willy's Best Bogs, the sandcastle competition, Daffodil Walk, etc. Ray was nervously inspecting the tulips in the knot garden. They were at their peak, but it would only take a sharp spike in heat for them to be spoiled.

Sammi's stall was the most stylish, but Mrs Joy's cake stall smelt best.

'The woman is a machine!' Hugh said to Rose, sotto voce. 'How the hell did she churn out fifty pots of preserves overnight?'

'I have no idea, but once the gates are opened, I want you to buy three pots of her lemon curd . . . and get the recipe if you can.' Her eye was suddenly caught by a young man walking down the drive. He looked familiar. 'Wait here, Hugh, and keep an eye on the pasties.'

Rose followed the young stranger as he tentatively climbed the steps to the front door and knocked.

'Hello. Can I help you?' She was right behind him and made him jump.

'Hi.' He held his hand out. 'I'm Isaac? I've come about the lifeguarding job?'

'Well, well.' Rose knew him now. 'You work at Sennen, don't you?'

'I did. But I'm just back from a year in Thailand and saw your advert thing on Instagram. Have we met before?'

'Yes. Two and a half years ago, I came down on Boxing Day with my niece and her friend, Sammi?'

Isaac's grey eyes gleamed. 'I remember.'

'Do you? See that colourful stall over there, with the silk shaws, etc.? That's Sammi's. He's a highly-regarded interior designer, you know . . .'

'Go and say hello to him,' Rose said. 'You'll make his day. But, more importantly, I want you on the beach ready for lifeguarding duty half an hour before we open, understand?'

'Yes, I'll be there. Thank you.'

Returning to Hugh, Rose said, 'I have a feeling you and I might be needed to look after Sammi's stall later.'

'Righto, number one. Whatever you say.'

'Now, wait here while I find Delia.'

Delia was by the tombola, watching as a police dog with her handler was quietly sniffing around. 'She looks so sweet, but I wouldn't want to cross her,' Delia said seriously. 'Her full title is PD Magpie, but at home she's just Maggie.'

Rose glanced around. 'Have you seen any security yet?'

'No. But they're supposed to be unspottable, aren't they?'

'Oh yes. Good point.'

Delia's walkie-talkie crackled into life. 'This is main gate. Light traffic on road. Gates open to the public in ninety minutes.'

Delia's adrenaline levels spiked. 'I can't believe we've kept this secret for so long.'

'I know! Hugh will be furious when he finds out.'

'Ray, too.'

Rose gave Delia the side eye. 'You told him, didn't you?'

'Yes. And you told Hugh, didn't you?'

'Yeah. And Sammi'

'So did I! Oh, we are hopeless!'

'By the way, see the handsome young man Sammi is laughing with over by his stall? That's your lifeguard for today. The same one from Sennen. You remember?'

'Oh yes,' said Delia, grinning. 'I remember.'

A woman in a black suit walked over to Delia. 'Miss Jago, the principals are eight minutes away. Would you like to take your position on the steps as rehearsed, please? Their Royal Highnesses the Duke and Duchess of Cornwall will get out of the vehicle first, followed by the children. You will take them inside the house, where you will have the informal meet and greet. On first meeting, you say Your Royal Highness and curtsey. After that, you can call them sir and ma'am to rhyme with jam.'

'Yes, I remember the briefing.'

'Good. Because this is a private visit, they will not be doing a walkabout, but I understand that the children are keen to try the sandcastle competition.'

Delia felt her heart sing. She could still hardly believe that this was happening. 'Oh, that's great.'

'They will then return to the house, where you will give them a short tour before departure. All clear?'

Delia nodded.

'OK. Standby.'

Two police outrider motorcycles came first, blue lights flashing. Behind them was a Range Rover, then a people carrier, another Range Rover, and two more bikes.

The doors of the people carrier slid open, and there they were: William and Catherine, George, Charlotte, and Louis.

'Hello, and thank you so much for having us,' Catherine said. She looked serene and beautiful, with the three children grouped politely around her. 'This is so good of you. George is desperate to look around. He's learning about the Domesday Book and so wanted to see what an actual old manor house looked like.'

Louis tugged at Delia's arm. 'Where can we make the sandcastles?'

Charlotte pulled him back. 'Shush.'

Later, when Delia looked back on the hour she was with them, it felt as if time had stood still and yet raced ahead at the same time. After that, opening day was hectic, with Delia rushing from stall to stall, checking that everyone was enjoying themselves. Far more people had arrived than she'd expected, and the grounds were swarming with excited visitors, peering up at the grand house and examining the gardens.

It was all such a maelstrom that Delia didn't have a chance to catch up with Ray or Sammi. She was caught by the local press, who wanted to know every detail.

'How did you keep the visit secret?'

'Why did they come to Wilder Hoo?'

'Did you get a good look at the famous sapphire engagement ring? How big is it up close?'

When the sun dipped beneath the horizon and Wilder Hoo closed for the day, Delia escaped to saloon HQ, where Auntie Rose, Hugh, Sammi and Ray were waiting to congratulate her.

'Bravo.' Hugh led the applause. 'A brilliant day was had by all and it's all down to the remarkable grit of two marvellous women. Delia and Rose Jago.'

'How do William and Kate deal with that level of attention?' Delia said, collapsing onto the sofa next to Ray. 'How do you teach your kids to deal with it?'

Auntie Rose was at the desk, checking her newsfeed. 'Nothing but positive feedback from the BBC. Let's face it, the world loves the British Royal Family. They've put Wilder Hoo on the map today, and we are grateful.' She beamed. 'Right, I want everybody except Delia and I out of the room while we tot up the takings. There's a bet at stake here. Will Wilder Hoo have proved itself a commercially viable venture or not? Go on, shoo, all of you. Mrs Joy has made another mountain of sandwiches to keep you busy.'

As soon as they were on their own, Delia and Rose let out a whoops of relief and hugged each other. 'We did it. We bloody did it.' Delia shook her head in wonder.

'If you mean we actually got the event off the ground then yes we did. But have we made a profit?'

Together, they went through the slow process of collating their takings from the gates and the stalls, Delia counting and Rose double-checking.

'So,' Delia asked, 'if we minus all that we spent, from how much we earnt, where do we stand . . . ?'

Auntie Rose double-checked and tapped it into her calculator. The result came up and she passed it to Delia.

'Oh. Well, I suppose we'd better go down and tell them.'

*

Sitting around the kitchen table, Mrs Joy, Ray, Sammi, Isaac, Kevin, Kenny and Hugh waited for Delia and Rose, chatting over the day.

'Did you see that sandcastle Prince Louis made?' Kevin asked. 'Ken and I were well impressed with the way he built the buttresses.'

'Catherine bought two jars of my Lemon Curd,' Mrs Joy said. 'She wants me to send her my recipe.'

'William had nothing but praise for your tulips, Ray,' Hugh told him. 'He said the king would be envious.'

'What about George and Charlotte wrapping themselves in your beautiful shawls, Sammi?' Isaac smiled. 'They loved them.'

'Shh,' Mrs Joy quieted them. 'I can hear footsteps.'

Delia and Rose arrived in the kitchen looking absolutely exhausted.

Mrs Joy offered them tea but they declined.

Sammi couldn't look at Delia's face.

Hugh tried to sound upbeat. 'Come on then, girls. Tell us how we did.'

Rose gestured to Delia, 'Go on. You tell them.'

Delia began. 'Taking all our expenditure into account, and the takings, we end up with a figure of thirty-seven pounds and forty-two pence!'

'Ah well,' Sammi said sadly. 'We tried.'

Rose stopped him. 'Not so fast, Sammi. We didn't lose thirty-seven pounds and forty-two pence, we made thirty-seven pounds and forty-two pence.'

EPILOGUE

Who would think that the small amount of thirty-seven pounds and forty-two pence could change the lives of so many?

The next day, the papers were full of the Royal Visit. Wilder Hoo now firmly back on the map, featured in magazines, TV programmes and on social media. It stood out as the latest desirable destination. The history of the house and the incredible story behind its rebirth fascinated everybody who read about it. Delia refused all interviews, but Rose and Hugh were very happy to become the public faces of the old house.

Delia and Ray now had the time to explore their feelings towards each other and declare themselves a couple – 'About time, too,' Auntie Rose had snorted – and under their guardianship Wilder Hoo began to thrive.

They hosted summer camps for Martin's charity for children. There were book clubs in the library and Cornish cookery courses and house tours with Rose. There were garden tours with Ray. And Sammi, whose reputation was growing in the

United States, held design workshops in his newly converted barn. Isaac built a small team of lifeguards to help run the beach and opened a coffee shop and a surf school. Kenny and Kevin continued work on the house but also taught family woodwork classes in their barn.

Life was good and got even better when Delia discovered she was pregnant. Ray cried when she told him the good news and immediately proposed, but Delia refused. 'We don't need to. I like it just the way we are.'

'I do too,' he admitted. 'It feels better that we are together because we love each other, not because we have a contract.'

It didn't stop him asking again when their second child, Genevieve, a sister to Jory, was born – but again, they agreed it was something that wasn't for them.

Unlike Sammi and Isaac, who definitely wanted to get married and did so in a glamorous, colourful, joyful ceremony on the famous Wilder Hoo terrace. Mrs Joy made the wedding cake and watched as Sammi and his husband cut into it as Champagne corks popped and guests cheered. She wiped a tear from her eye as she stole away, leaving a note on the kitchen table.

Dear All,

I have never liked goodbyes, so forgive me for leaving quietly on this, the happiest of days. My work here is done and I am needed elsewhere – but if you ever need me, just call and I shall come.

I wish you all the very best for the future, and thank you for bringing Wilder Hoo back to life.

Yours most sincerely,

Mrs Constance Joy.

Where once you reached me via three miles of mud and potholes, you can now take the smooth drive from the highway through parkland dotted with red deer, well-tended pasture full of sheep, and a sweeping landscape of mighty oaks, dusky magnolia trees, and red camellias.

If the eyes grow full of all that beauty, they still gasp at the sight of the house, me, Wilder Hoo, as I appear in all my majesty before you. The sun may be burning in my ranks of glassed windows. Or maybe the stone of my frontispiece glows warm against the granite walls.

And still, and still, there is more for the glutton within you. Knock on the thick oak doors that tower above you, enter my halls, and walk through me to the pièce de résistance: *the vast balcony terrace. Wide and deep, with a sweeping, seductive staircase to lead you to the sweet-smelling parterre filled with roses, lavender, heliotrope, and jasmine, and then on, and on, to the beech woods, the cliff top, and the tangled rocky path down to the beach and the ocean.*

ACKNOWLEDGEMENTS

I want to thank Kim Young and Lynne Drew (my editors past and present) who gave me the time and encouragement to write this book.

My thanks to everyone at HarperCollins for their patience and care in getting it over the line. If it takes a village to bring up a child, it takes a huge publishing house to produce a book!

Thanks, too, to my daughters Grace and Winnie who gave me great some great ideas. Anything that is funny is theirs!

Thank you to my wonderful literary agents Luigi Bonomi and John Rush who both keep me on track.

With love to you all,

Fern x